"HOW A ... ... Gord blurted
out. Then, remembering that he spoke to an illusion,
he sighed and hung his head.

"The nine black sapphires in the necklace you
hold," said the phantasm, "are your means of returning to your world. This, then, is my . . ."

Gord was dumbfounded. Had the illusion actually
heard his plea?

". . . final gift to you. Free the ebon stars from
their prisoning metal. Place eight circling one, think
of your own place, and there you shall be.

"Your choice is this: Keep the stones and stay here
in Shadowrealm as a prince. You will be free to journey to many places, but no more will you be human.
If you use the power of the gems, then as a mortal
man you will be subject to the hazards of whatever
fate lies in store, but you will be flesh and blood
again, in your own world."

The illusion vanished, and the young adventurer
was left terribly alone. What was his decision to be? If
he stayed, he would be a lord of this place, a walker
of planes. To counter that, however, was the longing
he had for the solid world, the sunlight and vivid
colors of Oerth. He deliberated for only a moment.

"Now I do what I must do," he said, using his
dagger point to prize the sapphires from the necklace.
"I am who I am, and will remain a mortal man."

The circle of eight gems began to glow as the ninth
was placed in the center of their midst. . . .

CITY OF HAWKS

by Gary Gygax

**The story of Gord's early years —
his growth from a helpless infant
to a formidable enemy of Evil**

Cover art by Ray Rubin

Edited by Kim Mohan

GORD THE ROGUE™ Books
CITY OF HAWKS

First Printing, November 1987
Printed in the United States of America

Distributed by the Berkley Publishing Group, 200 Madison Avenue, New York NY 10016

9 8 7 6 5 4 3 2 1

I S B N : 0-441-10636-6

New Infinities Productions, Inc.
P.O. Box 127
Lake Geneva WI 53147

Dedication

With many thanks and unaccustomed gratitude, I dedicate this novel to my Thoughtful Editors, Kim Mohan and Pamela O'Neill. They manage a task which is painful to any author in ways which are so subtle I can only shake my head in admiration.

Greyhawk City

The map on the facing page depicts the city in which Gord grew up and shows the areas into which the city is subdivided. Old City is the oval-shaped section of the city in the northeast quadrant of the map. The wall around the city and the wall separating Old City from New Town are shown as double lines. Another wall separates the Foreign Quarter from the northern two-thirds of Old City.

The Selintan River lies to the west, and the tributary known as the Grey Run flows around the south and east sides of the city. Direction of water flow is shown by arrows. The Bastion is located on the island (appropriately named Bastion Isle) directly to the east of the city. Two bridges connect The Bastion with the city proper, and another bridge crosses the Grey Run at the southern end of the city.

Boundaries between the various quarters and areas are not always firm (except, of course, where a wall serves as the separator) and may change as one faction or another becomes larger or stronger than its neighbor(s). Gates in the walls are indicated by circles and identified by numbers. Other locations in and around the city are identified by a one- or two-letter code. A key to the letters and numbers is given below and at the bottom of the facing page.

B: Beggars Quarter
BR: Brewers Quarter
C: The Citadel
CB: Clerksburg
CR: Craftsmen's Ward
F: Foreign Quarter
G: Garden Quarter
H: The Halls
HI: High Quarter
HU: Hutsham
L: Labor Quarter

LO: Low Quarter
P: Public parks
PL: Plaza D'Haut
R: River Quarter
S: Slums
SH: The Shacks
ST: The Strip
T: Thieves Quarter
TR: Trade areas
U: University area
X: Prison workhouse

Scale: 1 inch = 3 miles

1: Southgate
2: Longgate
3: Hillgate
4: Midgate
5: Oldgate
6: Lordsgate
7: Fairgate
8: Highgate

9: Guarding Gate
10: Lowgate
11: Rivergate
12: Markgate
13: Waghalter Gate
14: Safelock Portal
15: Craftgate
16: Beggars Gate

Other books by Gary Gygax

Saga of Old City

Artifact of Evil

Sea of Death

Night Arrant

Chapter 1

THE DUN-WALLED METROPOLIS loomed along the east bank of the river. Even this broad watercourse showed but a faint glimmering of reflected light, so dark was the night. Sputtering cressets limning the massive lines and curves of the city wall seemed oppressed by the near-palpable gloom.

The crackling torches, oil lamps, and candle lanterns that burned along the city's thoroughfares cast scarcely a glow against the underside of the vaporous strata suspended above the oppressive place, a glow that was absorbed by the thick, dark atmosphere before it could spread any higher. The night sky of the Free City of Greyhawk, usually a warm, golden red, was now a pallid rust color. On this, the Night of Valpurgis, the city's many, massive gates were shut fast. Huts and hovels scattered around the outside of the walls were dark although they were, presumably, occupied. Shutters were locked, doors bolted fast.

Sentries paced in pairs along the broad battlements, nervously alert. All others were safe within their own places, charms and amulets prominently displayed, probably muttering prayers and pleadings to ward off evil. Not even thieves, and most assassins, dared to roam about on this night, while those who served demons or devils sought to commune with such malign beings, busily chanting and gesturing in the unhallowed interiors of vile temples and cursed shrines.

Fog rolled and slid in chilled masses that crept from above the dark river and its marshy verges. The slight breeze that swept up the Selintan was all that kept the fog from completely wrapping the city and its environs in a blinding shroud. In this murky mist, a small boat upon the surface of the river was all but invisible. The thick, vapor-laden air muffled the sounds of its creaking oars, so that from just a short distance away the noise was as soft as the passage of a mouse through tall grass.

"Hard on your right oar, boatman!" The command, uttered in a voice just above a whisper, came from a dark-cloaked man standing in the bow of the skiff. The riverman grunted and strained against the rapidly flowing river that seemed determined to sweep them past the destination they sought.

"So soon. . . ." Although they were softly said, the woman's words came clearly to the man who directed the progress of the little vessel.

"I hope it is soon enough," he replied. The bundle that lay in the stern stirred slightly, but nothing further was said. The standing man gave additional directions to the rower, then spoke again to his companion. "Have courage, wife. Our fate must not be tied with his!"

The mighty stones of the city wall thrust into the Selintan as if they were the prow of a titanic ship of granite. The towering blocks formed The Citadel, the strongest and most heavily fortified portion of Greyhawk City. The Citadel was the heart of authority in the city, its fortress and palace, administrative center and garrison. Few people, citizens or travelers, sought out this place, yet the little boat was headed precisely there. With no small amount of effort, the riverman managed to steer the skiff into the shadow-black finger of water that curled around the southern face of the bastion.

Again the standing man gave orders. "Quietly now," he hissed. "Keep straight on." The rower softened his stroke and sent the boat ahead slowly. Then . . . . "Cease rowing," the black-cloaked passenger commanded.

The boatman made an imperceptible gesture, a sign to ward off evil, as his skiff thumped against granite. Although the fog didn't allow the oar-handler to see more than a few feet away, the man he carried had known about . . . seen . . . the stones jutting out of the water around the hidden landing. "Demonsight," the boatman muttered under his breath.

"Call it cat's eyes," the cloaked man countered. The rower started, for he had barely whispered his thought. After surreptitiously making the sign against evil again, the fellow reached out and grabbed a rusted iron ring and pulled the skiff against the stones. The boat came to rest, held in place by the rower, against a small stone ledge into which was cut a narrow flight of steps leading upward to an ironbound door — a postern gate of sorts that was evidently the destination of the passengers.

As if the contents of the bundle had become aware of the group's arrival at this place, a tiny wail issued from inside the swaddling clothes still resting on the floor in the stern of the boat. The woman crooned in a soft, soothing tone as she bent and carefully cradled her arms to pick up the tightly wrapped, squirming bundle.

"Help her stand, boatman," the other passenger said, taking a rope and stepping from his place in the bow onto the landing to hold the boat in place. The riverman hastened to comply, fearful of provoking the wrath of a man who had demon powers. In a minute both woman and infant were standing beside the dark-garbed man, and the skiff was being propelled from sight by the frightened rower.

"Now we cannot turn back," the woman whispered.

"We never could," the man said tonelessly, taking her arm and helping her up the narrow steps with her precious burden.

The small door groaned inward, rust-bound hinges making an eerie sound, before either man or woman touched the portal. Neither of them spoke, and the infant was again quiet and still. No light showed where the old oaken portal gave into the stonework; only a deeper darkness was revealed. Still guiding the woman but now walking slightly ahead of her, the man stepped boldly into the blackness. Perhaps he did have demon-sight, or cat's eyes. As the two of them moved fully into the low passage, the hinges groaned again and the thick door closed fast, moved by no human hand. Man, woman, and child were swallowed up by the granite fortress.

* * *

"You were wise to come to me." As he spoke, the tall mage kept the gaze of his deep-set, colorless eyes riveted upon the dark-clad man he addressed.

The man had flung back his cloak. Beneath the voluminous garment he wore rich attire — velvet and silk of the same midnight hue, but showing signs of wear and stains of travel. The face could seem young at first glance, but close inspection would make apparent lines and creases in the visage, and a pair of eyes that revealed the worry and fatigue that lay behind them.

"Your aid is most appreciated," the man said in reply after a few seconds. His voice was still toneless.

There was a silence as the frail spell-worker sent

12

his gaze from man to woman, and then to the tiny bundle she clutched closely to her breast. The mage made several odd gestures, magical passes, while his deeply sunken eyes seemed to become lightless pools gazing into some nether world. "You seem un- scathed," the man intoned at last. "No sending touch- es you, nothing ill lingers near the babe. . . ."

"I am not just anyone, Wanno," the other man re- marked dryly. "Do you suggest I would come to you bearing signs for the enemy?"

"Of course not. Still . . . those who have aligned themselves 'gainst you and your lady are far from av- erage, shall we say?"

"It is him — our son! They resent such a rare occurrence and have made alliances unnatural," the woman interjected. Her voice, although still low in volume, bore a steely tone of anger and determina- tion. Her once-beautiful face was as hard as her voice now, a sharp relief depicting resolve and something akin to hatred. The softening of expression when she looked down at her child, then at her husband, and finally stared at the mage, showed that her feelings of hate were only for those who threatened. "Can you really give him safety, Wanno?" she asked the mage, hope and doubt plainly written upon her counte- nance as the two emotions struggled with each other inside her.

"Look about you," the robed spell-binder said with no small amount of pride. His gesture swept the little room, a place draped with strange tapestries and cluttered with a mass of magical paraphernalia. On floor, walls, and ceiling were dozens if not hundreds of enameled and engraved runes, symbols, and occult charms.

"Since you left the waters of the Nyr Dyv and came southward," the mage continued, "I have used my powers to mask you. No one knows your whereabouts. No force can manage to scry this chamber. Given time, some dweomer great enough to unveil your presence could be brought up, no doubt. But we shall not give . . . them . . . that time, shall we?" he finished, trying to soften his expression as he peered into the woman's eyes.

Her face now showed grief as she turned her thoughts to what was about to happen. She glared accusingly at the robed mage but said nothing. Her husband saw this and spoke in her stead. "No, my old comrade, we will not linger here so as to allow our foes to find us."

"My good apprentice will see that you two are safely away without so much as a stir," Wanno said with relief. "Just place the infant within that chest," he added, "and then— "

"No!"

"Yes, love," the dark man said to his woman. "No need for instant compliance, though. Bid adieu to our son for both of us while Wanno and I discuss a few small matters yet to be set straight. I will return in a few minutes. Then we will be off." She looked at him, tears rolling down her pale cheeks.

"Be strong," he continued, doing his best to console her while keeping a rein on his own sad feelings. "It is a separation, merely a parting for a little time. He will be back with us ere his first year's natal day is celebrated."

As the robed spell-binder and the black-clad man went through an archway into an adjoining room, the woman's sobs were still audible. "I wonder if my own mother cried thus when I was bound to the 'craeft at birth." Wanno's words were not meant as a question, but voiced as a detached speculation. "No matter. . . . What do you wish to say?"

"What news have you of the ones who sought our downfall?"

Wanno shrugged. "Little, but I can say that it seems that none of the clans now actively work against you, prince."

"And can the same be said of my grandfather?"

"Who can speak with certainty of that one? Still, even though he never supported you, neither did he encourage your . . . noble cousins in their efforts to bring you low," the mage said slowly. "If I had to hazard a supposition, I would tell you that his hand has been more with than against you, prince. It is surprising to me that the six greater clans have not been more active against you and the heir," Wanno added, slowly stroking his wispy chin whiskers.

The dark-garbed man pondered the mage's pronouncements for a moment. Then he smiled suddenly. "The luck of the seventh, perhaps. Those evil ones who have combined cannot long remain in union, and when they are sundered then it will be safe for us to reclaim our son. I charge you again — keep him safe, Wanno. We will be back for him soon. Your reward will be great indeed on that happy day. Fail, and I pledge to you that you will be cursed here and in all other realms too, as long as my kind live and breathe!"

"That I have always understood and accepted," the strange mage said with an undertone of rebuke evident in his voice. "Still, I understand your concern, I think, although parent I am not nor will be. Tell your lady that he will be kept safe and secure, given all I have power to provide, so that upon your return the heir will be strengthened and ready for whatever might come."

"You speak as if the time will be years, not weeks or months!"

"Who can say? Not I, prince. Know you well that I have tried to pierce the future, but there are veils upon veils which surround you three. Not even I could lift more than a few of these shrouding layers. The time did seem long, though," Wanno added in a conciliatory tone, not wanting to offend this man but also not wanting to leave him with a false impression of what lay ahead.

The dark man let this last remark pass uncontested, then seemed to mellow as he gave the spellbinder a hearty clap upon his thin, narrow shoulder. "You have always been a friend, old one, even in this city of hawks and double-dealers."

Wanno looked somberly at the shorter man. "City of hawks? Indeed. Yet, it is a place which has suited you and yours for some time, prince. Never have rules and regulations been meat and drink to the Lord of— "

"True enough," said the man, his face and voice imbued with rising anxiety. "Now, let us speak no further, for I mistrust even the strong wards you have used to hedge this sanctuary of yours, Wanno. I am uneasy, full of foreboding."

"What father would not be? Far and fast you and your lady must travel now. This is your one chance — and the only hope for the heir, too."

"What if we . . . do not return?"

The mage did not flinch at this; as always, he was ready with an answer. "I will tell him of his parents, his heritage, and his duty. I will equip him, aid him, in whatever manner I can."

The black-garbed man pulled a ring from his finger, then took a small wooden box from a pouch that hung at his belt and handed both objects to the mage. "Forge a chain for this ring, Wanno, so that he might wear it round his neck when he is old enough to walk. Keep this box and what it holds safe for him so that he may have it at the right time."

"The ring I recognize. But what of the coffer?"

"A dweomered container given to me by mine own

16

sire, Wanno. It appears normal and empty when first opened, but when the magical false bottom is discovered . . . inside are likenesses of my parents, and my lady and I too, plus a little scroll telling of who and what we are — his heritage and more, it seems. Nine black sapphires are inside as well, beneath a second secret panel. They are said to have some greater significance, but in here they serve simply as a store of wealth in case of dire need."

An odd smile played briefly over Wanno's face. "Considering the amount of gold you have managed to get into my possession over the last few weeks, old friend, I somehow doubt your son will lack for resources."

"As it should be," said the man solemnly. "Yet material wealth is not as important as physical health . . . and both of these are insignificant compared to wellness of the spirit. So long as my son's spirit is unbroken, I have a feeling that health and wealth will be his in due course. Keep his body safe from harm, Wanno — but beyond that, make his spirit strong so that he may conquer danger when he must face it."

In this short speech, the infant's father sounded very much as if he knew he would not be coming back. Wanno, grasping the man's elbow to lead him back into the main chamber, said nothing to discourage this impression.

* * *

Gone at last! Wanno breathed a sigh and set about his work. He liked the prince as well as he liked anyone — indeed, more than most. And his lady was a fine woman, as females went. Why, then, had he been so ill at ease when they were here? And why was he now so relieved to have them away?

17

Could it be simply the responsibility of seeing to the young lordling, the prince's infant son? No. That part was easy. Although he had never been a parent, Wanno had most of the skills and resources he would need for the job, and could easily afford to procure those he did not possess.

Perhaps it was the danger. Certainly there was much at hazard in this business. But Wanno had been involved in perilous undertakings before, and had never felt quite like this.

Finally, the mage decided that it was simply a matter of his not liking any company very much, not even that of other dweomercraefters. For a moment, he absently wondered if he was deluding himself by allowing himself to come to this conclusion. Then Wanno gathered up the sleeping bundle that was the little prince and headed for his private chamber. As he entered the room, a figure who had been seated on a stool near the door rose to greet him.

"All is done?" It was his apprentice, Halferd, who spoke.

Wanno only briefly turned toward the one who queried thus. To the mage, Halferd was a stripling whom he retained to perform services and instruct. This apprentice was held by many others to be a powerful spell-caster in his own right, but to Wanno he was a mere pupil. Had he gazed at Halferd's face at this moment, looked into his eyes, perhaps the mage would have reconsidered his estimation; but after no more than a sideways glance at the other man, Wanno placed the child in a crib in a secluded corner of the little bedchamber and laid the magical box at the infant's feet, covering it with part of a blanket. Only then did he bother to answer Halferd's question.

"Yes. Both parents are gone away for a time, and there is much to be done if I am to fulfill my oath.

First, I must arrange for the nurse who is to have care of the babe."

"I'll fetch her for you straight away, Master Wanno," Halferd murmured deferentially as he stepped toward the exit from the room.

"No."

Halferd's heart sank at that short utterance. Did the crusty old bastard suspect him of something?

"Yes, Master Wanno? Is there something I have neglected?"

"You don't know who I have decided upon to be the infant's maid," the hollow-eyed mage said as he began to fuss over the circle of runic inscriptions chalked on the floor around the cradle where the princeling slept. In fact, Wanno had some time ago made his decision on a guardian for the child, and had made many preparations concerning that subject without Halferd's knowledge. Unfortunately, he had also been forced to deceive the woman he had chosen to care for the child, but this was certainly a case where the end justified the means. "That is a matter I will see to myself. While I am gone, you will do a second and third ward around this one's place."

"Of course, master," Halferd answered quickly. "May I ask who you have selected?"

"You may not," Wanno said without rebuke. "The less you know, the easier it will be to mask all of this from those powers who seek to undo my protection. That would be a hot fire for us both now, wouldn't it, boy?"

His lips pressed into a tight line, Halferd bobbed his head just as if he were an apprentice lad, not the able sorcerer he actually was. "I will complete a three-fold warding, master, and stand alertly on guard until you return."

Wanno looked briefly at him, then nodded. "Yes. Keep a sharp eye out for hawks. . . ." the mage said, his words trailing off as he suddenly brought his arms up in a sweeping gesture and spoke a word that sounded impossible to speak, even for one so skilled at dweomers as Halferd was. At its utterance, Wanno was gone with a popping sound, followed by the whoosh of air rushing in to fill the space where he had been a split-second before.

Hawks? The man really is beginning to slip into dotage, Halferd thought. Demons or devils, yes; perhaps some horror from Tarterus or Gehenna; but . . . hawks? "Bah!" Halferd muttered aloud. "This is for you!" he added, making vicious strokes as he drew a precise set of sigils and strange marks on the stone floor. Instead of scribing the lines and shapes with tenderness and deliberation, Halferd worked as if he were wielding a sharp instrument upon exposed flesh.

*   *   *

When Wanno eventually returned, his apprentice had done all he had been charged with and was alertly seated near the infant, an old, gnarled staff held in his grasp. When his gaze fell upon this, Wanno spoke sharply. "What are you doing with my staff!" It was an accusation, not a question.

Halferd tightened his grip on the ebon-hued wood. "I carry out my duty to guard the babe," he said, letting his eyes meet Wanno's for only an instant before sliding away. The old one could work magic simply through his gaze meeting with another's, and Halferd had no intention of allowing himself to be caught by some trick — not now!

Then something seemed to alert Wanno. A strange light shone in the old man's deeply set eyes as he looked at his apprentice. The realization came to him at that moment that Halferd was near middle age, even for a dweomercraefter. And he was also a spell-worker of considerable ability — so why had he been content to remain an apprentice? There was only one answer. . . .

Wanno stood with his spine straight. His staff was in the hands of an outsider, a man he didn't really know after all, despite their years as apprentice and master. Halferd's brief glance into Wanno's eyes had betrayed something that the old mage liked not. There was a smell of duplicity in the still air, a sense of something malign that hovered in the shadows overhead.

"I see," Wanno said, meaning something entirely different from the way Halferd took the remark. "Exemplary, Halferd, exemplary!" he added with a bluff heartiness that he hoped didn't seem as forced and insincere to his apprentice as it did to him. "However, I have other, more important things for you to see to now. Hand me my staff, and I'll instruct you as to their nature."

Halferd coughed and shuffled his feet. He didn't hand the twisted length of ancient yew to Wanno. Instead the apprentice raised the silver-bound tip of it, so the staff pointed with veiled menace in the general direction of his master. "There is a matter to be cleared up ere I give this to you, Wanno."

Coldness suddenly flowed through the mage's veins. Here was vile treachery unmasked! Wanno had anticipated the possibility of some trouble; indeed, he had built in some protections around the infant that no one else knew about, just in case something beyond his control should occur. But he had not suspected that Halferd — loyal, quiet Halferd — would turn out to be one of his enemies!

Smiling slightly, Wanno set his steel-hard eyes upon the man before him. A word was locked just behind those iron orbs as he stared out upon Halferd, a terrible word of magical force ready in his forebrain. Before his foe could do aught with that fell instrument, the syllable would roll from throat to tongue and out into the room. Halferd would be blasted where he stood. Perhaps he was more than an apprentice, but he was no great binder of dweomers. It was madness indeed for one of his poor strength to challenge Wanno — especially in the old man's own place of power!

"Place my staff most gently upon the floor, boy," the mage commanded, "and then I will permit you to speak." He saw Halferd break into a sweat and begin trembling slightly.

"No!" Halferd shouted, but at the same time he started lowering the staff. Then he began to shake more, and his body was wracked by a fit of coughing and gasping. He tried to talk, but explosive bursts of air and desperate indrawings of breath between the hacking coughs prevented meaningful speech.

This was very odd, Wanno thought, for he had used no spell upon the fellow. What was going on? Then a faint rustling from behind betrayed the presence of someone else in the room. It was an act! Halferd's fit was a contrivance, intended to distract him while more danger came at him from the rear. Without another second's hesitation, Wanno allowed the word to thunder forth. The syllable rolled up and was shot forth in an eyeblink — and Halferd was no more. Greenish bits of ash floated in the place where he had stood. Gone too was the staff. Too late to mourn that now, the mage thought, as he started to direct his attention toward the trespasser who had slipped in at his back.

Too late indeed. . . . As Wanno turned his head to look over his shoulder, the last thing he saw was the face of his killer — and the last thing he felt was the blade of a dagger as it sheared through his spine.

"That's done him!" The voice was jubilant, harsh.

"Shut up, you silly blaster, and do the same for the sprat!" the other man ordered. The bigger and meaner-looking of the pair held a long, wavy-bladed dirk whose metal glinted with an ugly purple sheen where it wasn't smeared with bright red blood. The man he spoke to was slighter and uglier. Both were clad in deep gray and wore felt-soled boots. Any resident of the city could have identified them instantly — assassins of the guild. Denizens of either the lowest dives of Greyhawk or of its high places might have been able to do more than tell one what they were; these were two of the greatest assassins in the whole city. Alburt, known by some as Goodarm, was the dirk-wielding leader of the pair. He spoke to Slono Spotless, held in only slightly less awe than Alburt himself by those who knew of them.

"Futter yerself, Alby," the small, ugly killer growled back. "What about Halferd?"

"He don't have nothing to fret about now, Spotty. The geezer got him before I stuck the dagger in. Now cut that little brat's throat while I check this place for valuables."

The child in the strange crib was wailing, and Slono thought it would be a good idea to off it quickly. No sense in taking a chance on having its noise alert anyone to what was going on. "Here, my wee bunny," he muttered with a horrid grin on his crooked face, "Uncle Spotty's got a nice little s'prise fer ya. . . ." With this, the assassin stepped toward a place where he could reach down and ply his own sharp blade — and suddenly his eyes stopped working!

"Godsdamnit!" Alburt cursed. "What in the Nine Hells are you doing?"

"I can't see a thing. . . ." was all Slono managed to reply. The man's voice, although panicky, was barely audible.

Alburt hurried to where his compatriot crouched, still a few steps away from the crib, with his hands clutching at his face. He had seen no flash, heard no sound, yet the chalked marks upon the floor burned with a smokeless, almost lightless flame. He felt weakness in his bones, sickness in the pit of his stomach, when his gaze went to those dancing lines of flame.

"Here, jerk," Alburt said to his smaller associate as he roughly yanked the assassin out from amidst the magical markings burning on the stones. "You stay put until I finish the kid — I can manage everything." With that, he picked up the lifeless body of Wanno, dropped it across the magical lines, and used it as if it were a bridge. He stepped gingerly, careful to put his feet only on the corpse or on the places where Wanno's robe was splayed on the floor. Alburt made his way to a location from where he could peer over the side of the high-walled crib and view what was inside. His eyes grew wide instantly, and then he reached down and stabbed repeatedly, viciously.

"Crap!"

"Wazwrong, Alby?" Slono was still swiping at his eyes, but it was evident that some vision had returned to him already, for he was peering in the direction where the bigger thug stood.

"The li'l fart's gone!" Alburt growled. "Jus' plain vanished!"

The smaller man suddenly realized that the infant's crying had stopped at the very moment his eyesight had been lost. "Some rotten magic trick," he suggested.

"Naw," replied Alburt. "I stuck the damn blade all over the whole crib and didn't feel it sink into nothing but the mattress. Magic maybe, but it sure as shit ain't invisibility. The flamin' sprat just ain't here any more."

"What'll we do, Alby? This could be big trouble for us. . . ."

"Not by a long shot, Spotty. Remember what that geezer did to our customer, so who's to know the same thing didn't get the brat too? I'll check the place out, and check it good too, but I think the kid's gone to wherever Halferd got blasted to."

Eventually the smaller assassin managed to regain enough vision to assist his comrade in the search for loot. There was a fair haul that included gold orbs and several potentially valuable items of interest to those who dabbled in the arcane arts. Alburt claimed the lion's share because he'd slain Wanno the mage and would have had to do the job on the child as well due to Slono's temporary blindness. Because the smaller assassin valued living, he didn't argue too loudly or too long. And neither did he enlighten his partner when he discovered a heavy ring of pure gold with a big, green cat's-eye chrysoberyl set in the yellow metal. That he scooped up and slipped into his pocket without Alburt noticing. Whatever the cut he got, Slono would have a little something extra as his just compensation for this botched mess.

"Get your ass moving, Spotty. We been here too long," Alburt ordered as he stuffed the last of several small crystal flasks into a bag.

"You know it," his associate said, heading for the place in the wall where a secret passage led to and from Wanno's hideaway. "Nice of that spell-binder to set up his quarters so near the Thieves' Way," Slono observed as the two went along the narrow passage in the walls of the Citadel.

"Yep. His sort always stick themselves up in some high tower or down underground. Never does 'em any good, either way." He fell silent after that. In a few minutes the pair left the known passage and went into the even more secret way beneath it, the adit

25

built by Greyhawk's vaunted Thieves' Guild. None of the members of the latter group knew that it was now a regular route for the assassins. Silence was complete in the passage and in the rooms it led to.

It was not until days later that Wanno's body was discovered, and the news caused a stir in the Citadel that lasted for days thereafter. Finally, the apprentice Halferd was held guilty of murder and flight to avoid paying for his crime. Word was posted that he was a wanted man, and the matter was all but forgotten.

Chapter 2

THE BEING WHOSE NAME AND TITLE was Infestix stood as a misshapen pillar before the silent assemblage. If likened to a court on Oerth, this gathering would be an imperial parliament, or perhaps a council of royal sovereigns. The masters of the many planes of Gehenna, Hades, and Tarterus were ranked before Infestix. These terrible beings stood in a semicircle before that one's dais, those to the left diabolic in appearance, those to the right demoniac, those in the middle resembling Infestix.

Other royal assemblages would show magnificence, splendid robes, glittering gems, bright gold. But the court of Infestix was the nadir of squalor and decay; where other courts would display beauty, grace, and life at its finest, this one showed instead ugliness, clumsiness, and the everpresent threat of death. This grand court existed in the deepest Gloom of Hades, lowest of the Lower Planes, evilest of evil realms. "Nightmare" would be far too pleasant a term to describe this place, considering both the gathering of creatures and their overlord, Infestix.

"Is there nothing more?" Infestix asked accusingly. His voice was hollow-sounding and sepulchral. Sickly yellow slime dripped from his lipless mouth as he spoke, and his tongue was a fat, gray worm.

A muted rasping and creaking issued forth in re-

sponse, sibilant whispers mixing with harsh croak-
ings. Here a figure shuffled, there another shifted.
Ghastly heads bowed, clawlike hands clasped, but
none of the Lords of Netherevil spoke in reply to their
overlord's query.

"What is forewritten can be altered." This statement from Infestix, for all the self-assurance of its
content, held a note of doubt, perhaps desperation.

A warty dreggal from the fuming pits of Gehenna
drew itself up to its full height. "Who can oppose Infestix?" the monster shouted metallically.

"Better to ask who does," a massive demodand
crackled in retort.

The Masters of the Horde gabbled back and forth
at that remark. Deviloids and dreggals screamed in
rage while demodands and demonkin yowled their
laughter at the caperings of hordlings and night hags.

"Stop." The dead, toneless voice of Infestix somehow filled the vast chamber. The assembled horrors
became instantly silent and still. Riot had been averted. "You, Haegresse. What became of those fools who
were Our dupes?"

The queen of night hags made a terrible face,
something between a smile and a moue. Perhaps she
was being charming. "They have withdrawn, all of
them, to their domains," she simpered. "They will re-
spond to no coaxing and are beyond ken."

"What is the rede of the hells?" Infestix put this
question to a huge fiend towering over the wart-cov-
ered dreggal who had begun the near-chaos.

The horned head of the great devil tilted slightly in
perfunctory obeisance. "The writ has changed, fearful
lord," he replied with a sharp clashing of his tusks
and fangs, "but there is still the last portion which is
nebulous. We have increased the probabilities in our
favor, but at the last there is still a small chance of
risk, a modicum of doubt. . . ."

Infestix's terrible visage grew even more awful to behold. "Why did the eight sons of . . . that one . . . withdraw, hag? They had already given over their brother into Our hand."

"They are a suspicious lot at best," Haegresse replied in her strange voice, "and much bent toward the weakness of weal. Suspicious the eight were from the first, and their part in the fratricide caused much argument amongst them. Usurpation of the right of lordship was no longer a sufficient prize. He of Lions demanded to see the whole of the prophecy. Of course I demurred, seeking the sympathy of the one representing the hot-tempered Ancient Tigers, but even that stupid lout was no help," the queen of night hags said, spitting to emphasize her disgust.

"They know, then, that there was less than total success." Infestix looked slowly, his gaze moving from left to right, over the group that stood before him. "It is our mission — more than that, our duty! — to reawaken the Greatest One, free Him, and assist in His triumph over all. . . . You have failed me, though, and that will not be forgiven." With that the Netherlord's burning stare fell squarely upon the night hag. Haegresse's form cringed under the gaze. She bowed her head in fear, expecting the worst, but Infestix looked away and spoke on.

"Fortunately for all of you fools, I have personally brought forces to bear on this affair. I have discovered what you could not: Others have learned of what we plan. They dare to interfere. It is their power, their meddling, which caused you to bungle."

At those words, Haegresse dared to look up again. She saw a bony finger pointed straight at her, and the leering visage of the terrible daemon looking along the digit's path. The night hag opened her mouth to protest, but a pale ray of putrescent green hue struck her full in the face before she could utter a sound.

The leathery flesh of her face bubbled and ran as if it were wax. In seconds Haegresse was nothing more than a vile-smelling puddle on the black basalt flags of Infestix's court.

The others looked warily at the Netherlord. "She it was who gave our enemies the clue. Her stupid mouth is now silenced forever in nothingness," Infestix informed the assembled horrors. "Bunglers cannot be tolerated."

Those on the side of chaos shuffled and leered at what had just occurred, enjoying the spectacle, while the more ordered sovereigns of Gehenna merely stood taller and gave slight indications of approval. After a few seconds, the ambassador of the Nine Hells spoke up. "Lord Infestix, does this mean that my master will be called upon to play his proper role in this?"

"All of the Dukes Infernal will be . . . welcomed," the overlord of daemons replied in his chill, hollow voice.

"Of course, Overlord of Gloom, the great Asmodeus will be chief—"

"That is between your master and I!" Infestix's glare was sufficient to silence the pit fiend, and the devil bowed his head in recognition of the daemon's power. "No mere mortal, regardless of potential change, can stand before the united might of the nether planes. Haskruble," Infestix said, fixing the demon of that name with his icy gaze, "you must bring the rulers of the Abyss to us now."

The steel-blue scales of the demon rippled as Haskruble shrugged. "No one can do that, mighty Overlord of Hades — not even Orcus, my own lord. The monarchs of the Abyss do as they choose."

Although the daemon knew full well the truth of that statement, he trembled with rage at its utterance all the same. The demon emissary's voice had borne an unmistakable tinge of sarcasm when he had spoken in reply. This was not missed by the other beings in assembly, and they awaited the results of this breach with varying degrees of anticipation.

No retribution came. The overlord of the nether planes swallowed his umbrage. The demon hordes of the Abyss, their many and puissant rulers, were needed. "Leave now, servant, and tell Orcus and the others that the time has come for all to rally to the Everdark Banner of Tharizdun. He alone can overthrow all Good and bring Evil to a place of supremacy for eternity!" There was disappointment plainly written on many of the vile countenances at so meek a rebuke, so straightforward a command. The demon Haskruble, needless to say, was not among the disappointed ones. He knew all too well the situation.

"I shall inform Prince Orcus," he said loudly, and without formality spun on his scaly heels and strode toward the chamber's exit with a swagger. Then Haskruble howled in agony as an ulcerous growth sprang from his head, sprouting upward in corrupt nodes. The demon spun to face Infestix, a mixture of indignation and terror on his visage.

"That will remind you, niggling, to pay homage to all above your station — and to Me, Infestix, in particular. Your master can remove it or not, as is his whim. It won't destroy you, only turn you into a gibbering mound of boneless flesh in due course. You have hours, so there is no need for you to hasten your departure. . . ."

Haskruble disappeared with a shriek, gating himself from the chamber instantly. There was a chorus of yammering, barking, yowling approval at the Netherlord's justice — one in which even the diabolical monsters of the lower regions joined in, for Infestix's punishment had been swift and masterful. Here was strength and power that could not be mocked!

"Strugne, return to the Infernal Regions and inform the dukes of Our decision. You others are also dismissed," the daemon added, "save for you, Utmodoch, and you, Weyzeneal." The master of demodands and the king of dreggals bowed to their emperor and stood still. The rest of the attendants slithered or strode, flopped or flew from the massive chamber after paying homage appropriately. None cared to test the power of Infestix again.

After all had departed, the daemon motioned the two remaining beings to join him upon the dais, and when they had complied the whole vanished from sight, leaving only a bubbling pool of nauseating filth where the platform had stood but an instant before. By whatever means, the trio of monstrous denizens of the nether regions were now elsewhere. Their abode was a circular room suspended in nothingness, a chamber with no entrance or exit. It was an otherworldly place, but it was not strange to them.

"Thank you for the honor, overlord," the demodand Utmodoch boomed.

Not to be outdone, the sovereign of Gehenna, Weyzeneal, also hastened to murmur his appreciation. "My emperor shows much wisdom by his generosity."

"Cease this stupid pandering," Infestix snapped. "We are all but pieces to be moved by He of Utter Evil . . . although our ranks do differ. You are here to supply me with information, not waste time on useless flattery. I know your black hearts and your festering brains too well for that!"

"The parents of the whelp were assuredly slain, overlord," the pocked and warted dreggal said without being asked. He too had certain abilities, and a small show of strength could not harm his position. "Before we could take the corpses, though, someone or something intervened. The bodies vanished without a trace, and probing failed to discover the cause of the disappearance or where they went."

"You, Utmodoch?" the daemon asked after nodding at Weyzeneal.

The gigantic demodand rumbled his response instantly. "My human servants on the material plane have sought in vain for some clue to the mystery which Weyzeneal just told of, emperor," he said. "But not a trace of the whelp can be found, not an inkling from Greyhawk to a hundred leagues outward. It is as if that one no longer existed."

"Kill your servants, you feces-headed vessel of dog vomit! Were the whelp not alive, the rede would not show uncertainty as to the success of My plan!"

"But one small child cannot—"

Infestix's sneer silenced the dreggal, just as the daemon's harsh rebuke had stilled the gaping maw of the master of demodands. "You dare to suggest that My understanding of this is flawed?"

"Never, great lord," the pair muttered in unison.

"I will forgive you . . . this time. Think on this. Long and long have I worked and schemed to bring back the Evil of Evils. Centuries have passed since the time I commenced the plan, and now this! A miserable human threatens Our success. Unacceptable!"

"My agents will continue the hunt," the demodand said with assurance. "It will not be long before his skinny soul whimpers in the nethermost depths."

"His?" The word, drawn out by Infestix's bubbling growl, spoke volumes. "Not even I know if the whelp is male or female! Speculation will prove your undoing, Utmodoch, if you persist in this."

Weyzeneal grasped the opportunity to curry favor for the forces he controlled. "I will serve, emperor, without the use of idle statements. My dreggals and our human slaves too will keep at it until the cryptograms are broken, the cipher revealed, and the secrets known. Recall, it was Gehenna that discovered the arcanum of the Tripartite Artifact."

"And the hells whose servants gained the Initial Key," scoffed Utmodoch. "Tarterus alone can—"

"Enough, both of you," Infestix admonished without force. The poxed creature was not growing soft; he was merely distracted by his own pondering of the problem. He had strived for an eon to locate the three parts of the artifact that kept Tharizdun slumbering, chained, and prisoned in somewhen, some nullity in dimensions. The wardings around the secret were of incredible potency, but with tenacity equal to the task Infestix had broken them, one by one. Then the information had somehow slipped out, and servants of the Infernal Dukes had managed to gain the only known portion of the key that the forces of Good had fashioned to bind the Evil of Evils, Tharizdun. There was no help for that now. The rulers of the hells would have to be given appropriate merit when the Darkest One arose and again sat upon His throne. Perhaps their devils would be of some assistance now, the greatest of daemons mused.

The problem was actually a simple one. A prophecy had been scribed, and its rede was ominous. There was the inkling of failure in it. One chance in ten thousand — a seemingly insignificant factor. It had been one chance in a thousand but a short time before. Then Infestix had caused the netherlords to become active. The packs and the human hounds of Hades and its dependencies had gone out, and they had brought down their quarry as expected. No, that was incorrect. They had torn the throats from two, but a third had somehow escaped, and that third little one was the most important of all. Somehow that one was connected to the Final Key. The rede implied that Evil would gain the Middle Key soon enough, but also that the fates of the Final Key and the human would intersect. If they did indeed come together, then all would be lost.

Getting this far had not been simple, but the forces of darkness were accustomed to having to work hard for what they gained. By the use of treachery, beguilement, lies, deception, flattery, and all the other tools of the lower planes, the denizens of Evil had managed to discover the identities of those who threatened to defeat Infestix's purposes. The instigator was the half-human offspring of a minor lord of the concordant existences. He and his woman had brought forth a child who might become a factor in the matter.

Now, father and mother had been betrayed and slain thanks to the cooperation of their siblings — the father's siblings, more correctly. They were a jealous lot, that litter, and each was anxious to inherit the domain of his sire. The mere hint of one gaining an edge over the others was sufficient incentive to keep all of them working on behalf of Evil for a time, but then their realization of the enormity of their treachery had caused the eight dupes to withdraw from the cause — a major miscalculation on the part of the night hag to whom Infestix had entrusted the responsibility of success. Just as well, the daemon lord rationalized — Haegresse had grown too ambitious anyway. It was high time that the night hags had a new queen. Infestix would inform them of his choice later.

"Emperor?" The hesitant word came from the lord of the dreggals, reluctant to interrupt his lord's musings but anxious to know if his continued attendance was required. Infestix set his gaze on Weyzeneal for a minute. Then he turned away and stared at the massive, hideous face of the demodand. "It is not so much a matter, one in ten thousand. It is the Abyss which troubles me. Those brawling tubs of excrement will never be useful!"

"I am a demodand, overlord, not a sovereign lord of demonkind," Utmodoch replied defensively. "I have much influence amongst the strongest of the princes of the Abyss, of course," the ghastly being hastened to add so as to assure Infestix of his value, "but the stupidity and worthlessness of demons is legendary."

"See that you maintain your influence, and use it correctly," the overlord of the nether planes replied in his hollow, menacing voice. "One way or another, I will succeed. Fail me naught, either of you." Nothing further needed to be uttered, for both knew the consequences of incurring the wrath of this being.

"Gehenna will be unrelenting in pursuit of your purpose," the dreggal king intoned.

Utmodoch dropped to his knees, saying, "Tarterus will serve by sussing out and destroying all who attempt to stand in competition to you, overlord."

The cadaverous daemon seemed satisfied with that homage and those promises. "I will send you to your respective places now. Report the least thing to me personally. Nothing regarding this matter must escape my scrutiny. Hear me and obey."

Before they could reply, Infestix touched a diagram before him and spoke a word. The demodand and the dreggal king vanished.

Weaklings, both of them, thought Infestix. Better that He should be served by the Infernal Dukes, despite their machinations. Let Tharizdun come, and He, Infestix, would gladly stand to be weighed in evilness and ability against any of those order-headed devils. In the interim, their strict routine and meticulous methods would serve well to promote the one worthwhile goal that would end the factiousness of Evil for all time and make it paramount in the multiverse forever.

Chapter 3

"YOUR HAIR IS LOVELY this evening, mistress," the serving girl said as she held up the mirror.

Meleena peered into the glass and turned her head slowly from side to side, scrutinizing every detail of her coiffure that she could see. The sapphires in the comb that adorned her rich, chestnut-hued tresses matched her eyes perfectly. At last she smiled and motioned the girl away, completely pleased with herself and her situation. New servant, new wardrobe, new jewelry . . . a new life!

"Fetch my fur-trimmed cloak, girl," Meleena said, trying unsuccessfully to maintain an attitude of aloofness and not give a hint of the secret pleasure she felt inside. "I will be going to the Citadel tonight," she added, every word exuding happiness and pride. Thanks to Wanno, there was every likelihood that young Lord Roland would notice her this very evening. In addition to providing her with clothing, jewelry, and a great sum of gold, some of which she had spent to attain her new station, the mage had promised to use his power and influence to bring her to Roland's attention. Although she had not seen Wanno for several days, she had no reason to doubt that he would be true to his word. Meleena was certain that she would soon be someone in the city.

"Here is your cloak, my lady," the serving girl said

happily. It was evident she shared the glory of her new mistress this night as she spoke. "There is a litter waiting outside too," she gasped breathlessly, "with two linkboys and a guardsman!"

At that Meleena could no longer help herself. She smiled and hugged the thin girl. "Isn't it wonderful?" she said with a little giggle. Then, recalling her new station, Meleena quickly released her servant and stepped back, once again a cold and important lady. "Sleep on the rug by the hearth, for if I happen to return late tonight I might need you."

"Yes'm," the girl replied as she opened the outer door for her mistress to depart. She was pleased at the prospect, for her usual bed-place had no warm fire to add comfort to the hard floor. After shutting and latching the door, the girl quickly tidied her new mistress's bedchamber and went to her assigned place by the embers. Thinking that no one would notice, she added a few big chunks of coal to the fire and snuggled down on the thick rug.

She felt a bit guilty about using the coal, for she was a devout person and the deity she worshiped would not have condoned such an action. But she did, after all, deserve what little comfort she could procure for herself, so long as she did not hurt someone else in the process. She would be able to sleep for several hours, undisturbed and toasty. This was luxury indeed, she said to herself as she drifted off to sleep, clutching the symbol of her faith that she wore around her neck.

Meleena was thinking similar thoughts as the bearers carried her hooded chair along toward the fortress that was the governmental heart of Greyhawk. Before her great good fortune of the last few days, she had been merely one of the many maids-in-waiting amid the welter who served the oligarchs. As the orphaned daughter of a petty landowner and unsuccessful merchant, she had been fortunate to get even so lusterless a position as that.

Wanno, the Master of Magics to the Oligarchs of Greyhawk, had first seen her by chance at the Halls, when she had come to protest the annexation by the city of her father's property upon his death. Initially Meleena had thought the weird old man was lusting after her, but the mage had not so much as laid a finger on her. Wanno had simply silenced her useless protests to the unsympathetic clerk, taken her to another building nearby, and informed the functionary there that he should give her immediate status as a waiting maid to the oligarchs. The fellow had done just that after Wanno had presented him with the mage's own writ, and hied himself quickly to the task too. Spell-binders were not noted for their patience with petty bureaucrats.

Although he had spoken to her seldom over the next few months, Wanno had certainly kept track of her. This Meleena knew because of the little hints given to her by others in the same station within the Citadel. Like her, they were quartered in dreary lodgings in the Halls District and had to come to the fortress center of the city every day to await instructions as to their duties. Usually there was nothing to do save attending some oligarch's wife, seeing to an important female visitor, or serving dainties at a feast or function. In truth, she and the others were nothing more than glorified serving wenches themselves, and but slight the glorification at that. Meleena flushed with indignation as she thought about how she had been ordered about, humiliated, and often degraded during that time.

Then, one day, Wanno had summoned her to his own quarters and questioned her at length. There were many bubbling retorts and smoking pots and braziers in the place. The fumes muzzied her, Meleena recalled, and the bloodshot eyes of Wanno had bored into her brain.

Afterward the mage had been kinder still, and certainly friendlier. During this meeting, Wanno had informed Meleena that she was soon going to have to care for the little son of her deceased cousin Ermantrude. Try as she might, Meleena could not recall ever having heard of Ermantrude — nor, for that matter, of her mother's sister, someone whom Wanno referred to as her Aunt Una. However, Wanno convinced Meleena that he had researched her family history, through means that only an accomplished mage such as he could command, and he had found that she was assuredly the infant's only known relative. Meleena could hardly remember her own mother, who had died when she herself was a babe, so she scarcely wondered that she had trouble recalling her Aunt Una and her cousin Ermantrude. Once she had gotten over the surprise of hearing all this information for the first time, Meleena readily assented to taking charge of the child — and Wanno had been mightily pleased at that.

As part of his final preparations for Meleena's assumption of her new responsibility, Wanno had sent word to another official in the Citadel, and soon she had been moved from a waiting maid to a position as Lady and Ward of the Lord Mayor. No more daily drudgery, only occasional summonses to official functions where Meleena would sit at table with those of rank and high station. This very night was her first such occasion — her coming-out, as it were.

Good things come in threes, it was said. Meleena was convinced that, for her, it was so — the babe, her newly exalted station, and the means to maintain and enjoy that status. And all of it revolved around the efforts of the kindly old mage. Wanno told her that he had taken the time and trouble to personally investigate the circumstances surrounding her cousin's death, and the case was worse even than her own, where property rightfully hers had been taken by the powers that governed Greyhawk.

In Meleena's own case, Wanno told her, he had come on the scene too late to help. But luckily, he had found out about Ermantrude's demise in time to act swiftly. It seemed that the woman had been very wealthy. The officials of Hardby had meant to seize that wealth and make the infant a ward of the state, but Wanno's intervention had saved the situation. The mage, being one whose abilities and influence were respected even where his name was not known, demanded to be recognized as the infant's official guardian, and could not be refused that right since he had come forth before any judgment had been rendered. To the dismay of the court officials, Wanno's status also carried with it the right to administer Ermantrude's considerable fortune, so long as it was disbursed with the infant's welfare in mind.

Fortunately for both Meleena and Wanno (whose life was not one that could easily accommodate the raising of a child), he was permitted to delegate the responsibility for the day-to-day care of the infant. Since he was later able to identify and then locate Meleena, the babe's only relation, she became the logical — and from an ethical standpoint, the only — choice for a nursemaid.

Getting a chance to be a mother was wonderful enough in itself. Having her station in life elevated (in the interest of giving the babe a decent upbringing) was an exciting additional benefit. And there was more: As long as Meleena cared for her cousin's infant son, she would receive a maintenance stipend — stipend, mind you, she thought to herself, was how Wanno put it — of five golden orbs each month!

As if that wasn't enough, then the goodly old dwe-

41

omercraefter had produced a chest filled with beautiful clothing and jewels — a part of the estate of her poor, dear cousin. Meleena regretted that she couldn't recall anything about Ermantrude, for she must be . . . must have been . . . a very sweet and wonderful person.

"Please alight, m'lady. We are at the Grand Palace," the guardsman said deferentially as he swept aside the heavy plush drape to enable Meleena to leave the sedan chair.

The sound and the motion snapped her back to the present. "Thank you, my man," she said with a detached tone, emulating the women she had waited upon until recently. "This is for your services," she added, drawing a silver coin from her purse and holding it out to the brawny man. "Please make certain that all is well until I return."

The affair was as splendid as Meleena had imagined it would be. Many a handsome young gallant noticed her. Many of the older ones saw her too, and they were more aggressive than the less experienced or less secure younger fellows. Yet she managed to fend them all off while awaiting her chance at Lord Roland — and it finally came. He even danced with her, and they laughed together at his missteps in leading her through the complicated tracery of the pompous rite. "I am hopeless, I fear, dear lady," he apologized. Meleena quickly blamed her own lack of grace for his blunders, then nearly stumbled and fell over his wrongly placed foot. When he caught her and clutched her close to keep her from injury, and in doing so looked so concerned as to be near comic, Meleena laughed in combined happiness and mirth. That was enough to provoke the nobleman to laughter himself, and the remainder of the night, which she spent almost entirely in his company, was a dream come true.

"May I call on you tomorrow, Lady Meleena?" Lord Roland asked at the close of the evening.

"Yes, m'lord. It will be my pleasure," she replied then, consciously appreciating that just days before she had received her first stipend and taken more suitable quarters pending the arrival of her orphaned infant cousin.

"Just off the Street of Silks, you said?"

"Your lordship has a good memory. It is the house at the very end of Vertwall Close, just off the middle of that very street you named."

"I shall call in the afternoon, then. Perhaps we can stroll the Gardens?"

"We shall see, Lord Roland, when the time comes." She had overheard enough of such banter to know precisely how to reply.

Despite the damp chill of the night air, she insisted that the curtains of the litter be left open on her way home. Meleena needed the cold air to clear her head of wine and calm her dizzying state of excitement. Every time she thought hard about what had occurred this night, it made her head swim — and, at other times, it positively ached with sadness and sympathy when she thought of Ermantrude and the poor little waif she was soon to become foster mother to. It occurred to her, during one of these musings, that she had never been told the infant's name. But as soon as she realized that, it ceased to concern her. No doubt Wanno, or someone he had designated to deliver the babe, would tell her what to call her newfound child. By the time the bearers had carried her up the Processional, along the Street of Silks, and to her own apartment in Vertwall Close, Meleena was cold to the bone and weary too, but still floating on a cloud of joy.

Lambent eyes watched Meleena as she climbed stiffly from the chair and entered her apartment.

They were slit-pupiled and red, the evil eyes of a monster not of this world. As the door closed behind her, the fiery orbs became disembodied and floated upward. Where they had been was empty space, and neither the porters nor the guardsman noticed anything as they trudged wearily away.

The attendants had not been gone many minutes before a pair of black-garbed figures entered the close. Silent, no more noticeable than shadows in the darkness, the two men took up stations a short distance from Meleena's residence, and the evil eyes of the nether-plane watcher seemed to narrow in pleasure at the sight of the pair.

"Up, lazy wench," Meleena said cheerily when she found the servant girl fast asleep before the embers of the fire. "You must help me undress, for I am utterly exhausted!"

Despite her sleepy state, the serving girl detected her mistress's mood immediately. "You look radiant, m'lady, and your voice is filled with happiness."

Meleena stopped and smiled at the thin girl. "Thank you. It was a nice evening. Now I must rest, for I am tired, and my head throbs so when I try to think that it makes me dizzy! Be a dear and hasten me to my bed."

Clad in a warm nightdress and ready for sleep, Meleena was just about to dismiss the girl from her bedchamber when a sudden gust of wind shook the house. The shutters rattled, timbers creaked, and the wind howled and groaned and shrieked in chimney, eaves, and cracks. Both women were frightened by the onslaught. Then the wind suddenly entered the chamber in full force, and all the candles in the room were instantly snuffed out.

"My lady?" The servant girl's voice was small and thin, but its tone was nearly hysterical.

"I'm fine, girl," Meleena managed to quaver from

where she sat nervously on the edge of the bed. "Light a candle, quickly now." The wind had let up somewhat, the sounds had lessened in intensity, and through the darkness she thought she heard a baby crying.

"The shutters blew open, ma'm. I'll close and latch them first, for if I don't the wind is likely to come again and put out whatever I light."

"Well, hurry then," Meleena said urgently. She was beginning to feel terrible now. The gladness and exhilaration that had filled her was being replaced by an awful feeling of foreboding and a malaise that sickened her to the core. "I must lie down quickly."

The girl trod carefully around the room, the sound of her passage occasionally punctuated by the banging of shutters — and then, finally, the scratch of steel on flint. A tiny flame blossomed into warm light as it climbed eagerly down the wick to consume the tallow below.

"Look!" The servant's tone was one of amazement, with a tinge of happiness.

Meleena turned toward the sound, and saw what had prompted it. There, a few feet away from her on the floor, in a tangled bundle of wrappings and a sigil-embroidered shawl, was a tiny baby. Its little arms were waving helplessly, and its legs were kicking as it let out a wail of distress. "This can't be," Meleena managed to say weakly. She had expected an infant to arrive, but not like this. . . .

More than shock was affecting her now. Waves of sickness and excruciating pain were sweeping over her body. Nevertheless, she tried to reach the infant and see what was wrong. The instinctive desire was not strong enough, and blackness claimed her just after she got to her feet, before she could accomplish more than a single small step. She collapsed back across her bed.

45

The two black-clad watchers outside had heard a keening wind but noticed nothing else, for they were staying at a safe distance to avoid being detected. They were uneasy but remained still, eyes upon the house. Above the steeply angled rooftop of the building, however, another sentinel reacted quite differently. The slit pupils of the thing's eyes widened as the roaring gust of air came sweeping toward it. Whatever the thing was, it gathered in upon itself, lambent eyes turning into mere slivers as the wind howled past and down. Then the thing expanded and followed. As the rush of wind shot off into the night, the fiery-eyed creature floated slowly down to where light glimmered from the cracks in the shutters covering a window.

"There, there, little one," the servant girl crooned as she picked up and held the infant that had so suddenly appeared in her mistress's bedchamber. "I am here to protect you. It's all right now."

A splintering crash brought another wail from the baby. The shutters of the high window broke inward as if struck by a giant hammer. The servant girl's eyes grew round with terror, for in the gaping space where the shutters had been a moment before she saw a terrible visage, a thing barely discernible, with shadowy fangs and burning orbs that fixed her evilly. Without thinking, the thin girl dropped the infant on the bed so that it lay next to her unconscious mistress. Then the girl stood so that she was between the tiny baby and the awful thing at the window.

A fiendish laugh issued from the near-invisible monster that hovered there, a sound both mocking and anticipatory. It was followed by a hissing sound, a billowing, and then the thing was inside the chamber, slowly taking shape — bloated, reddish-black, ugly, with a mouth larger than the span of the thin girl's shoulders. As the monstrosity formed, the girl shrank back but did not panic. Instead, she reached inside the neck of her smock and drew forth a silver object that hung from a leather thong. Without hesitation, she tugged, and a portion of the object came free. From the cylinder she had extracted, she shook out a spray of liquid. The stuff splattered over the creature with the huge mouth and the burning eyes, and wherever it touched the thing, flesh steamed and hissed and became insubstantial once again.

The thing voiced a nearly inaudible scream when the tiny shower hit it. Its evil eyes shut tight, and its great maw snapped open and shut convulsively as it shrieked its pain and agony. There was but a small amount of the liquid, though, just the single splattering. The monster recovered and reshaped itself once more. Now its eyes were more wicked than before, and it relished the way this confrontation would end.

Then, through the intervening space, the silver cylinder flew. The monster saw it and tried to avoid the missile. But, not fully corporeal yet, it was too slow. The silver tube struck the thing squarely in its leering face, and the malign visage contorted in agony at that blow. When it opened its eyes again, only the right one glowed with the evil fire of the nether planes; the left was a blank, black space.

The liquid and the cylinder were gone now. The thin girl stood unmoving. She had no more defenses against the creature. Strong, sinuous arms with taloned fingers reached out. Before she could move to avoid their grasp, or even utter a scream of fear, those fingers were upon her and tearing. A gout of red spurted forth, and the thin girl's head sailed across the room while her lifeless body toppled to the floor in gory testimony to the rage of the thing that she had dared to oppose. With fury and disdain, the creature picked up the body and flung it into a dark corner. Then, moving its talons greedily, the mon-

strous thing turned to where Meleena lay unconscious with the now-silent babe next to her. Despite
the pain that continued to assail it, the creature gave
voice to glee as its single remaining eye saw the pair.
Its long arms stretched forth, ignoring the woman . . .
intent on the child.

"Yeeeraagh!" The cry came from the thing, and it
was very substantial this time, for the monster was
fully formed now. The rusty-black body was being
buffeted, the leathery folds of its gross, misshapen
body were torn and rent, its bulk spun and wrenched
by unknown forces it could not control or combat.
The one-eyed thing tried to react, did its best to fight
off the attack and reach the baby, for its ultimate
duty was to rend the infant into shreds.

But a spinning circle of bodies kept the thing from
its goal. Shapes that moved in blinding speed, forms
that were blurred but held weapons that sliced and
gashed the thing mercilessly, were always before it. It
could not remain still, let alone advance upon its intended victim. The monstrous beast was spun and
turned, driven backward, and all the while slashed
and torn. In moments the battle, such as it was, was
over. The nether-plane thing rotted and decomposed
into a slime, which itself vaporized. One burning eyeball rolled, flickered, and went out. Where it had been
there was a charred mark on the floor, nothing more.

The awful sounds of the struggle awakened many
of the other residents of the area. But even before the
first of the neighbors' lamps were sputtering alight,
the two dark-clad men were racing toward the house.
They arrived at the door to Meleena's dwelling, kicked
it in, and entered with drawn swords.

"I don't see no gods-blasted brat!"

"Ain't even the bitch here," his companion said,
peering under the bed.

"Somebody was here, fer sure," the other one remarked, noticing and pointing to a pool of blood on the floor.

"The window?"

"Only if they had wings, pal. No couple of wenches could get out that way with a squawling brat in tow."

They looked blankly at each other. Then they heard sounds from below. "Looks like we'd better take off. We're already in it deep. . . . What in the hells are we going to report about this?"

"Bugger it! Let's get moving. It ain't our fault if the misbegotten daemon they sent screwed things up . . . or didn't. All we were supposed to do is watch the entrance and kill 'em if they tried to get out that way."

Still bantering back and forth, the two men slid over the window sill and away into the darkness. The climb down was easy for them, and the two were already away when the first head poked into the room to discover what the matter was all about. Save for the gory mark and the mutilated body of the girl that was discovered in a dark corner, the mystery had no clues, and those who were interested could only speculate about what had occurred.

Chapter 4

THE LIGHTLESS TEMPLE, the place where vile and degenerate and wholly evil folk came to pay homage to Nerull, was still and dark that night. Since that condition was usual for the place, no passerby who dared to look would have noticed anything out of the ordinary. But no one passed by anyway — not after dark. This place was shunned by all who walked abroad after nightfall. Even the humans and humanoids who considered themselves among the "faithful" normally stayed well away after sundown, for they were afraid of being sacrificed to the evil deity they professed to venerate.

But every rule has an exception. Tonight there was a stream of traffic to and from the place. Rushlights flickered and cressets flamed deep within the cursed place. In the maze of passageways and rooms below the temple, there was certainly life and light.

Colvetis Pol eyed the two figures who stood before him. "That is the sum total of your report?" The maroon-robed cleric put the question forth as if he were disgusted at having to ask.

"Both apprentice and babe were blasted by the crazy old fart of a mage. Took care of our work, so to speak," Alburt added with a conspiratorial wink. He didn't fear this silly priest, and he was intent on letting Colvetis Pol know that.

"And you, Slono Spotless? Have you nothing to add?"

The smaller assassin wasn't as cocky as his mate. After all, clerics were spell-weavers, too. They had unnatural powers, and their sort was never to be trusted — or taken lightly. Slono wrinkled his brow, thinking hard. "Nope," he finally said. "Jus' like Alby tol' ya, we checked out everything real careful. Only took us a couple of minutes. Wanno was stone dead, that asshole apprentice of his gone to flinders, and the kid blasted too. We buggered outta there quick as ferrets and come right here to tell you."

"And now we want our coin," Alburt added to his comrade's statement. "The job's all done, and you owe us another fifty orbs."

"Is that so . . . ?" Colvetis Pol asked, allowing the query to trail off as if it weren't really a question at all. "You saw the child blasted and came here right away to tell me, is that right?" The words were like little darts aimed at the two assassins.

"Well, we sort—"

"Shut yer yap, Spotty!" Alburt glared at the smaller man, then turned to face the priest with a belligerent expression plainly written on his flat, hard-lined face. "We did as we said, and that's that. Both the mage and the kid are dead, as contracted for. Now hand over our gold, or else."

The cleric's robes rustled as he made a small gesture. An arras covering the far wall swayed, and several men emerged from the area that the hanging screened from view. Alburt and Slono Spotless were shaken at this, for among these arrivals was the master of their guild. "You heard their own words," the great priest of Nerull said flatly. "Your servants are quite unreliable."

The chief of all assassins in Greyhawk was pale. His pallor was partly due to rage, partly fear, and the combination was evident to any observer. "I heard, Lord Pol, and I will make amends."

"Not to me," the priest said with a sly smile.

The master of killers looked sideways at a cloaked figure beside him, involuntarily moving away from it as he did so. "No, Lord Pol . . ." he murmured.

Now Alburt was becoming more than uneasy. No longer belligerent, the big assassin was close to panic. "Wait! I was only covering for Spotty. It wuz him who futtered up things, and that's so. The stupid little bastard blundered right into the geezer's runes, and—"

"Rot yer tongue, you big bag o' shit!" Slono was not going to go down without a fight. "You were the top dagger, Alby, an' you tol' *me* to go and orf the kid whilst you was checking things out. You took all the loot, too!" The last accusation was the most damning one the little assassin could think of.

A hollow, rasping voice came from the cloaked figure, cutting through the air inside the stone vault where the scene was transpiring. "How long was it after the infant vanished before you came back here?"

"Maybe a half hour," Alburt stammered out, but almost at the same time Slono also spoke.

"About an hour or so," the smaller man blurted.

The raspy voice sounded again. "Was it a half hour or more than that?"

"Longer . . . I guess," the big assassin admitted, with a murderous look at Slono.

"So," the strange voice choked out. The figure lurched suddenly, and then, without seeming to traverse the intervening distance, it was standing before the two assassins. Hands covered with rotting flesh shot out of enveloping sleeves and clamped firmly upon the two heads. Alburt was held by the forehead, Slono Spotless atop his pate. "For your actions I give you my special blessing," the figure said. Then it seemed to convulse again and was suddenly standing back where it had been before. Both Alburt and Slono stood dumb. Then they began trembling as if with the ague.

"No . . . please . . ." Alburt whimpered. Then a fit of coughing wracked his big frame and he was unable to speak further.

"Had you reported at once, as you should have," the sallow-skinned priest of evil said slowly, making certain each word got through to the two assassins, "none of this would have happened to you. I — we — could have known what device was used to remove the child from our ken, and the matter would be a simple one to correct."

"Dispose of those two carefully, priest," the hooded figure said in its sickness-tinged voice. "Their infestation is one which could be spread to many weakling humans."

The maroon-gowned cleric shrugged in indifference. "What is a little disease to me? Still, there are some hereabouts who might be affected." He stared at the slowly dying assassins thoughtfully for a moment and then said to them, "Remove yourselves to the tunnels and sewers below. You have but a little time left to live, and there is no sense in befouling this place."

Alburt fell to the floor, blubbering and pleading for mercy. He knew that the priest could remove the plague that was slaying him as easily as the assassin himself could snuff out a life. Slono reacted in a different manner. Despite the terrible disease that was filling him with deadly weakness, the small murderer proved true to himself. Cursing all present, Slono managed to snatch out a handful of wickedly tipped darts and hurl them, broadcast, at those who were serving as the tribunal condemning him to death.

One struck the strange figure, the feathered butt

of the dart alone visible, the remainder out of sight within the facial opening of the shadowing hood. The thing reached inside its hood, pulled out the missile, now lacking its metal point, and displayed the headless dart before the gaze of the dying Slono. "Fool! Poison is as honey to me," the figure said with a laugh as it slowly chewed up the metal and swallowed it.

One struck the wall near the hooded creature and fell harmlessly to the floor. The thing bent down, picked up the dart by its tip, and with a deep chuckle casually flung it back the way it had come.

One sunk its length into the fleshy thigh of the wizard who served Nerull's house in Greyhawk. That worthy shrieked in pain. "Neutralize this venom," he called, seeing the reddish flush spreading from the puncture, "else I shall be felled and no use to you!"

One poisoned dart struck the arras and hung there.

One grazed the clean-shaven head of the priest, leaving a bloody trail on Colvetis Pol's shining, yellow-tinged scalp. "Be silent, Sigildark," he called to the mage, "and I shall tend to you in due course." Even as the priest spoke thus, he was preparing to treat the injury done to him by the missile. Above all, his own life was the most important concern.

One ricocheted off a stone pillar and buried its nose in a nearby chair.

And, scant seconds after he had initiated the attack, Slono Spotless became the only real victim of the outburst as the dart hurled by the otherworldly thing buried itself in the assassin's chest. It was a cleaner death than that which he would have experienced soon anyway. In the end the small murderer proved to be a bigger and better man than his compatriot Alburt.

Within minutes Colvetis Pol treated the venom in

his own system and that of the mage Sigildark so that its toxin was harmless. The corpse of Slono and the gibbering, near-corpse of Alburt were hauled off to a cistern and unceremoniously dumped therein, to be carried off into the labyrinthine system of ducts beneath the city. Rot and rats would soon leave nothing but bare bones. Of course their valuables were first removed. One of the guards found the chrysoberyl ring hidden in Slono's boot. It was hidden in a hollow heel, so he didn't see any reason to mention it to anyone.

"The guild will make amends for this, my lords," promised the city's chief assassin as his former minions were carted from the chamber.

"That I am certain of," the priest replied dryly. "You will begin by sending two reliable men of utmost competence to this address late tonight," he went on, handing the guildmaster a slip of parchment. "All they need do is watch a doorway for a woman coming out, with or without a babe. Both or either are to be slain should they emerge."

"Consider it done, lord priest."

"You may leave us now. See that your men go immediately to the place I have indicated." When the man had departed, Colvetis Pol waved the guards out as well and spoke to the two who remained — the wizard Sigildark and the hooded thing from some other world than Oerth.

"Can we now be certain of success?" Pol asked.

The spell-binder took on a doubtful expression, cocked a thick eyebrow, and gave his head a small shake. The cloak-hidden figure spoke loudly in its hollow voice, however. "I will send one of my own trusted hounds to see that there are no further mistakes made. Mortals are bumbling and untrustworthy, while daemonkin are quite the opposite."

At that the wizard seemed annoyed. "May I point

out to you, Lord of the Pox, that it was I — a mere mortal — who discovered the whole web, who set his spies to work, and magically traced the skein of power which enabled the destination of the babe's sending to be found!"

"We admire your work, Sigildark." The voice of the priest was so sardonic that even the hooded creature from the nether planes gave voice to a ghastly chuckle. "The merit of your efforts is well known to Great Nerull. . . . What more could you want?"

Sigildark, steeped in evil as he was, knew that the deity just named was but one of the avatars of the nether emperor, having a form somewhat less repugnant to humans than that of Infestix, for instance. "He knows, or will know, Pol, because you or Poxpanus there will so inform him. Honor to the Image, dedication to Tharizdun."

Colvetis Pol made a hasty sign. "Be it graven."

The daemon-thing too made a gesture of formal obeisance. "Each serves and will be measured by his Master," he intoned in a dead voice. "But now let us deal with what matters remain."

The priest nodded. "We need information, lord. We are reacting as you instruct, but we will prove more useful instruments if we are told of things."

"That is so," the wizard agreed. "If you will share with us, Lord of All Pox, we can serve you, Nerull, and great Tharizdun better!"

"My liege has given me liberty in this matter, so I shall inform you as you request," the nether-thing replied. "But for the sudden change of heart, the vile little sprat would be destroyed ere now. His own kith and kin it was who gave him and his parents over into our hands. Their reversal came too late to save the sire of the babe, and the dam too we found and expunged. They had not gone far from where they had left their cub for safekeeping, and our agents were hot on the trail. It was a petty dweomercraefter named Wanno who sought to confound the writ of Hades. You know him, Sigildark?"

"Yes. I knew him from our Society." The mage said no more, for if anything, Wanno had been perhaps a more potent spell-worker than Sigildark himself.

"Please go on, lord," Colvetis Pol urged.

"The sudden withdrawal of support from the cousins of the infant enabled his sire to elude our clutches for but a short time. It is passing odd, though," and here the rotting, hollow voice and the bearing of the thing seemed all too human, "that no augury, no divination, not even of the lowest magnitude, could pierce the curtain which hedged the three." The shadowed opening of the cowl swung to face the two, and priest and mage pulled back just a little. Yet the daemon spoke in a low, conspiratorial tone, imparting knowledge as if to equals. "Had we not been so close, all would have escaped. Much of the contest will be played out on the material plane, and some different, unknown force has aided those who oppose us. . . ."

"I have detected nothing of the sort," Sigildark stated flatly.

"Do be still," Colvetis Pol admonished the spell-worker. "I have seen some slight change in certain castings," the priest of evil said to Poxpanus. "When your hound has devoured the infant, will the interference dissipate? Or will it not?"

The daemon studied Pol. If ever was a mortal bound for lichdom, this one was. Ambitious, powerful, skilled, and dedicated to the malign might of Hades. Unlike the upstart Sigildark, a paltry factor, Pol had served on the highest councils of Nerull for decades. Poxpanus knew him to be two centuries old.

Although the man's outward appearance had changed little in the last several decades, the daemon could see into the inner creature, and it knew that the spirit there glowed with unnatural light and black force. Pol drew upon the negative energies already, and soon enough the priest would pass from the status of a mortal human to that of an eternally undead lich-lord. All the better, for Colvetis Pol was a useful servant to Hades.

Poxpanus noted that the priest was studying him, even as he gazed upon the man. Pol had the power to see clearly in darkness, and no shadows or even dweomered darkness could prevent his vision from working. It made the daemon a little uneasy to realize that the assessment, the weighing, that was going on was mutual. "The interference will be weakened. That is certain. And what is weak can be made to disappear."

"What if your hound should fail, lord?" The priest was not inclined to take Poxpanus at his word.

"That would be my failure, and such a condition is not possible," the nether-thing said with hauteur.

The mage seemed satisfied at that, but Colvetis Pol slightly raised one of his thin, sharply arched brows. "You can predict the unpredictable, know the unknown. I am impressed, lord." His tone was perhaps the tiniest bit sarcastic.

"You will see in a short time, priest!" Poxpanus spat the words out in his anger at being japed at by even so powerful a man as this priest, for Pol was still but a human. There could be no doubt that he was also one who was growing overly ambitious. He would be dealt with in stringent fashion, Poxpanus assured himself, soon . . . soon. "Now I grow weary of this puerile banter. I shall retire to my private chambers."

* * *

"Virgin's blood, lord — fresh and warm." The servant set a flask on the table next to Poxpanus and backed out of the room hastily.

Now within the deep enclave that was the special guest chamber of the temple, the nether-being was preparing for what he must do next. He quaffed the satisfying refreshment quickly, for it gave him the energy and power he would need to execute the task before him.

The words of the priest had caused Poxpanus to consider. His queries were too pointed. The daemon had spoken hastily, and now it was time to make certain that what he had said was no mere boasting. First there would be a sending of sickness. Although the daemon did not know exactly those whom it would visit, their locale and general descriptions were sufficient, for he was near and full of vigor. Some of that strength, however, had to be saved for the second part of his effort.

The ritual of the sending was similar to the complex incantations and conjurations often practiced by mages. Sigildark would have seen much he recognized. So would Colvetis Pol have recognized certain ceremonial portions used by those who invoked clerical powers. Poxpanus worked with speed and deliberation, but he did not rush. Even a netherlord could make errors, and the daemon knew that well. Soon enough the sending was completed, and then he turned his attention to Rheachan.

Although that creature served as his hound, Rheachan was his own offspring, a thing sprung directly from Poxpanus. The beast was therefore controllable, loyal, and totally predictable. If it drew upon the daemon's own strength, it also fed him when it fed. The relationship was complex, symbiotic in a sense, an unbreakable extension of the vilest portions of Poxpanus's mind and body too. Rheachan had never failed. Still, something in the priest's words had made the daemon uneasy. The unknown was, after all, just that. Better to be too cautious now. Cautious, that is, in assuring the strength of his hound-offspring as it did its work.

There was no mystery involved in Poxpanus's calling down sickness and disease upon an enemy. Pol and others steeped in the arcane knew well that such powers belonged to daemons of stature. Rheachan was an altogether different matter. Something that was strength could also be weakness if enemies were aware of the resource. To avoid any possible spying on what he planned next, Poxpanus set about cloaking this innermost cell of the temple. With drawn glyphs and murmured chants, the nether-being began to build layer upon layer of wardings. First was the shield against the mind, then the prying forces of magic, and finally came the guards that prevented priestly scrutiny of any sort — even that assisted by beings of other sort than humans.

When the triple protections were set, Poxpanus added to each, strengthening here, tightening there, until he was satisfied that each was sufficient to withstand even a major assault for the time he needed to do his work. To be even more sure, however, the daemon then wove the three wards together, meshing them so that each supported the other, and over all three he built a screen of such stuff as to make the whole invisible and undetectable except to the most exacting scrutiny. No sweeping search would discover his carefully built fortress of energies. To have it otherwise would invite the attention of all sorts of unwanted intruders, evil as well as those who fought against it. None could be trusted, none could know. The axiom of Hades, perhaps of all the lower planes, was a simple one: Strength is mastery; the weak are ruled.

In the web of energies, the complex tapestry of magic and planar powers, there was yet an opening. The mesh allowed Poxpanus a place where his own

particular psyche, those vibrations that were unique-
ly his own, could pass into and move out of the con-
finement of the fortress. It was but a small opening, a
tiny weakness in the structure. In time a being of
might would find and exploit such a tiny flaw, but
time was not a factor. Poxpanus would use the protection for but a short duration — a few minutes, a
few hours, a day at most. After that, it would be finished. With success, the daemon lord would return to
the nether planes. Then there would be a reordering
of the ranks, and only Infestix would be greater than
he. Long had he contested with Anthraxus and the
rest to assume the second position in Hades, Viceroy
of Glooms as it were. Soon that struggle would come
to an end.

"Rheachan!"

"I watch, and I wait, as you instruct."

The reply was crystal clear. Poxpanus sent his
force out along the channel. "Good," he thought, as
he saw in his mind what the daemon-hound saw with
its eyes.

"It is pleasurable to me that you find me suitable,
Paterfamilias." There was no lie in that, no deception.
Rheachan was unsatisfied and incomplete without
contact with Poxpanus.

That was true to a lesser extent for the daemon as
well. When he brought his force into attunement with
the force of the nether-hound, Poxpanus was not only
whole but more than he had been without the pro-
creation, his hound, Rheachan. "The one we will devour — where?"

"Not yet come. But now that we are conjoined I
can sense that it will happen soon, soon. . . ."

"Yes, that is so. The humans who are assigned to
the one?"

"But two weak females, Paterfamilias. Even now
the second has entered."

"Wait! Something comes from another place." Pox-panus felt the waves washing outward into the material plane as some force from elsewhere made its way through planes and dimensions. That force bore with it the unmistakable emanations of humanity, small but strong. The infant was being brought from its otherworldly hidey-hole to where the stupid mortals imagined it would be safe and secure. "Upward, hound-child. You must be ready."

Of course Rheachan had anticipated the command. Even as the thought formed, the thing was well above the cobbled lane and heading toward the shuttered window that was its objective. "The two assassins charged with securing the escape way are arrived, Paterfamilias."

"Unneeded, now!" The daemon was exhilarated by the prospect of the conclusion of his hunt, the kill and the feeding. The ether was torn just at that moment by the arrival of the force. "Now, my dear hound! Into that place, and we will have our sport!"

With the vital energy of its procreator filling its body and mind, Rheachan, hound and child, felt as if it could conquer the multiverse. How great and all-knowing the Paterfamilias was! Perhaps if it did well this night, that one would consent to mingle with Rheachan always, so that Rheachan would be as strong and smart as Poxpanus. It sent its desire to the Paterfamilias, along with its hound's lust for savage killing and devouring of blood . . . and soul, too. This primordial urge swept through Rheachan and into Poxpanus, and both were one and glad.

"I have it now," the daemon crooned mentally to its hound-child. "The life of the sprat, the vibrations of the bitch who was to care for it — so easy to read, to know, to find anywhere now."

"No need to think of future hunts, Paterfamilias. I will rend them both for you now."

Then the liquid stuff struck Rheachan, and the agony of its burning made Poxpanus writhe in his hidden cell as if the Netherlord himself had been subjected to the assault. In the confusion of the pain, the daemon allowed his hound free rein. The pain drove Rheachan into a murderous frenzy, of course, and the thing forgot all caution in its desire to avenge itself upon the miserable human female who had dared to so harm its corporeal form. Then the cylinder too went home, and the nether-hound and its father were suffused with even greater torment as the blessed silver struck, vaporized, and destroyed the eye of the hound.

"Revenge!" The mental scream shook Rheachan and infused it with new strength and purpose. So too the assurance that followed: "Slay, feed, and then I will bring you to me, hound-child. Your eye will grow again, your vision be better still, for I will suffuse your being with more of me!"

It was a fleeting communication, one that scarcely required any consideration. Rheachan reached forth, and the offending female human was no more. There was no reason for feeding, not on such a puny force as that one offered. Neither was the other female worthwhile . . . at least not immediately. A tiny human cub was there before Rheachan's remaining eye, and its vitality belied its diminutive size. That one's blood was ten times more desirable than the others'. The nether-hound reached greedily for the babe.

"Wait!"

The mental cry of warning reached the hound-thing too late — or perhaps Rheachan ignored the call. Rage and hunger had driven it beyond thought. This made it quite unaware of other forces that were suddenly impinging upon the space it was in. More than impinging. The forces were indeed in the room almost instantly. They attacked Rheachan then, and it baffled the hound-thing. All it desired was to devour the infant, and there was something in its way, something that tore at the hound and prevented Rheachan from its evil desire. Then the nether-hound howled and ravened and died.

The very web that Poxpanus had woven to protect himself prevented the daemon from assisting his offspring. The netherlord could have been with Rheachan in a split-second, using his powers to prevent what occurred, but his own wards prevented that. Only the mental link was possible, and that was now unbreakable as well. When Poxpanus tried to disengage the bond he found that something interfered.

The umbilical connection between daemon and hound-child was affixed by some outside force that Poxpanus could not fight, locked just as the netherlord was kept tight within a fortress of his own construction. As Rheachan howled and ravened and was destroyed, a similar fate befell the daemon sire of the hound.

It wasn't actually death to Poxpanus, of course. The netherlord suffered pain and loss, but at least here, on this plane, it could not be slain. Not so the hound-child. And when Rheachan shed its ichor and died, a portion of Poxpanus, progenitor of the monstrosity, was annihilated. The shock of the loss was traumatic in many ways. The daemon lord tried to see its tormentors through Rheachan's dying eye. The glaring orb revealed nothing to him, and when it flickered into nothingness, something within the daemon snapped. Poxpanus raged round his carefully created fortress, destroying it as a maddened boar would tear the earth when wounded. With occult forces went wood and stone too, until the chamber was a gaping wreckage of rubble and slag.

Colvetis Pol's personal servants found the place in this state the next day and reported the fact to their master. The priest pondered long on it thereafter, when servants of his master informed him that the daemon lord was now chained in Hades until his madness could work itself out and Poxpanus could assume some minor role in the hierarchy of the nether planes once again. Pol disappeared shortly after that. Some said he went to Hades to serve Nerull, but others whispered that the once-priest was now a hermit seeking holiness in the wilderness.

Chapter 5

"EAT THAT GRUEL, you miserable little bastard, or I'll thump your gourd!"

Leena the crone was in a fairly cheerful mood this morning, so she didn't bother to carry out her threat. Satisfied with a sharp pinch that made the toddler yowl, she went off to see what she could discover in the refuse heaps along the Old City's nearby wall. The day was warm, and that made her feel less irritable than usual. Cold made her old bones ache and her temper more foul than was usual even for Leena.

Why did she bother to care for the nasty little runt? The question bothered Leena, for she couldn't honestly and fully answer it. Somehow she felt the brat had something to do with her luck, or perhaps her very existence. She wasn't certain of that — but then again, she was not certain about a lot of important matters, including who she really was, where she came from, or why she didn't just end her misery by ending her own life.

Leena thought she knew one important thing, though. The brat's presence seemed to have something to do with her being able to continue to stay alive . . . at least, as long as she was inclined to do so. Some benefactor of the little bastard must watch over the place they lived in. Sometimes when Leena returned from one of her forays, when the hovel she and the runt shared had been empty for a while, she found evidence of that. One time a small sack of meal would appear, another time a pot of soup, and sometimes even a few small coins or a nice piece of woolen cloth.

"Stay out of here, witch-crone!" The warning came from a stick-thin drab who had taken up residence near the Slum Quarter's refuse dump. Leena didn't see the woman's old man around, so instead of trying to avoid trouble, she stopped and stared at her.

"Shrivel your teats!" Leena shouted, and then she cackled loudly as she continued to glare at the drab. The whole display wasn't much of a threat, but it did seem to have the desired effect, for the skinny woman covered her face and ducked inside the decaying old structure that housed her and the hairy old ragpicker who lived with her. A rock came sailing out of the doorway, but landed ineffectually a few feet away from where Leena stood.

Still cackling, Leena shuffled on her way. Being old and ugly had its advantages, yes indeed. When had she been young? Lovely? Leena knew that there must have been such a time. Deep inside herself she was sure of it. But she had no conscious memory of being anything other than Leena the Crone, no recollection of a time when she had done anything other than care for the skinny brat who shared her slovenly home.

The gangs of boys from the Labor Quarter and the Beggars Quarter were her worst nightmare. Sometimes Leena dreamed about them, and they took the shapes of terrible monsters as they came near. Then a noble warrior would intervene, or the brat would come into her dream and change into a giant who frightened off the dirty pack of boy-demons. Some laugh, that. Leena kept a long knife under her dirty old blanket, the same wrap that served her as a cloak when she went out. That way she was certain that she had real protection. The witch stuff, the shouting and cackling, didn't work as well with the gangs as it did with other sorts of adversaries. But they usually only bothered her when she strayed from the area between the rubbish dump and her place in the abandoned tannery, so with care there was no problem — other than finding food and a few little things to add to her comfort.

"Glory!" The exclamation sprang unbidden to her lips. A whole bundle of wax tapers had been discarded along with someone's garbage. The breaks in the candles weren't too bad, and the oiled cloth they were rolled in was a minor treasure in itself. Leena bent down and began scrabbling around in earnest in that particular pile of debris. Perhaps there was more good stuff to be had.

* * *

At an earlier time inside Old City, even within the slums, and outside in the New Town as well, others conducted their own searches even more carefully than old Leena scavenged for the means to stay alive. The word had gone out, and who had put it forth mattered not a bit. Beggars and thieves were alert. Petty clerics and city guards kept a watch on all they saw. Peddlers, shopkeepers, barmen, and ostlers too knew and sought to gain from their knowledge. Merely seeing a pretty woman named Meleena, and being able to prove it, was worth one hundred gold orbs. If she was seen with an infant, then the sum would be doubled. Should both be taken by those who sought them, then the informant who enabled that to happen would have a thousand of the fat discs of gold for his trouble!

Every young woman in Greyhawk was viewed critically. Every mother with a baby was a potential fortune. A thousand eager informants turned the city inside out seeking the two, and a thousand false claims were checked and proved to be nothing more than that. The word was out for weeks before the offer was finally cancelled. By then, nobody much cared anyway, for avaricious expectations quickly turn to other and easier prospects.

Other agents, ones with non-monetary motives, also sought the woman and the baby. Men and women with position and power used magical means or discreet inquiries to try to locate them. Strange creatures roamed the city at night searching for the two.

No magic succeeded, no inquiry uncovered a clue, no occult observer saw anything of consequence. It was as if the earth had swallowed up Meleena and her charge, or the pair had been removed to some other plane. After a time the hunt was, in fact, transferred to likely places other than Oerth, places where the pair could have found refuge. Only a few of the nether plane's operatives remained to continue the search in Greyhawk, and then only because those individuals had other duties there as well. Weeks became months, months rolled into years. By then even those agents had forgotten Meleena and her ward. Certainly, by now, both were long dead.

"No one as weak and insignificant as that one could have avoided the sending of Poxpanus," Sigildark observed when the subject came up in conversation one day.

"Agreed," said Arendil, the new Great Priest of Nerull now presiding over the Lightless Temple.

"Our lord and master placed potent curses upon both woman and babe as well, did he not?"

"Most assuredly. I assisted with minor portions of the whole complex of dooming which was cast," the cleric said slowly.

The mage was at a loss. "Five years now, near enough, and there has been no sign, no trace, no clue anywhere. There is only one possible answer. The pair was vaporized, blasted into nothingness. That must have happened long ago; so why do we still search?"

Arendil gazed at the mage without expression. Sigildark was already above his true mark, and before long he would have to be replaced. "That is why I summoned you," he explained. "Other, more pressing concerns now demand our attention. There is no longer to be any search for either of the two."

Sigildark looked satisfied at this, as if he had been influential in the decision and was receiving long-overdue praise for what he had advocated. The priest didn't inform him of the fact that the redes of both Hades and the Nine Hells were unchanged. Perhaps they bore on an altogether different individual anyway. It didn't matter, for the spell-binder had no need to know.

"What urgent matter am I to attend to now?" Sigildark asked pompously.

"It seems, dear mage, that there are clues to the whereabouts of the . . . objects we seek, the portions of the ancient relic we must reunite, hidden somewhere in the grimoires to be found within the very library of the Savants of Greyhawk. You are to . . ." and the priest thereafter proceeded to explain to the mage his task in regard to that matter. That was the conclusion of the whole affair of Meleena in the city.

* * *

". . . thump yer gourd!"

The crone was at it again, and the little boy leaped to get clear. Leena's cackle of mirth was sufficient to send a wave of hatred through his skinny body, but he scampered even faster. "Fetch me wood, brat, and don't come back without enough to keep old Leena warm all night, hear?"

Safely outside, beyond her reach and secure that her crooked stick couldn't touch him, the boy turned and made a terrible face. "Go scratch, you old bag! I'll never come back and you'll freeze to death!"

"I'll *smash* yer gourd!" Leena cried, raising her stick threateningly and advancing toward him. The small boy ran off immediately, and Leena cackled her ugly laugh once more. An empty threat from an empty little gourd. The boy was useless, but somehow she would manage to make him of some value. She'd work him to death if necessary, pound knots on his head in the process. She knew that the dirty little bastard was the cause of all her troubles, and she meant to even the score. Meanwhile, he would be made of use.

Spitting after him, Leena shuffled back into the still-standing portion of the old warehouse she called home. It was small and dirty, but rain didn't come in and there were no other people around to threaten her. She liked this place better than the dozen or two others she had lived in since leaving the abandoned tannery. Old Leena crooned to herself as she went, smiling at her wisdom. An inner voice always told her things like that — keep moving, speak to no one unnecessarily, keep the boy alive because one day he must be made to pay. Oh, yes, indeed! Old Leena was smart and wise, and no one would ever catch on to her, never.

There was a place for a fire. It was near the rear wall, and above it was a hole in the ceiling. The hole went above to where the upper storey was collapsed. There were, in fact, floors above that one even. No rain found its way down the hole, but the smoke from the fire went up through it, drifted around above, and escaped skyward in wisps and wafts that were hardly noticeable by day, invisible after dark. "Smart," Leena said aloud. She talked to herself, naturally. Who else was there to talk to? "Very smart, and getting younger and prettier too!"

That bit of self-delusion made her recall something she hadn't thought of for a while. She looked around carefully to make certain the dirty little brat wasn't spying on her, then pried up a loose flagstone beneath her pile of ragged bedding and took out a small box. She lifted the lid and looked at a scrap of parchment she had found inside the box long, long ago. "How long ago was it?" she asked absently, scratching her filthy gray locks until they became even more straggly and tangled than before.

She recalled how she had found the parchment, an event that mystified her to this day whenever she thought too hard about it. She had found the box under her bedding one day, and had no idea where it had come from — but all she really cared about was the fact that the box was hers. Then she got angry when she opened the box and found it empty — no food, no coins, nothing. Frowning at the container, she had growled, "Who would play such a bad trick on old Leena?"

Then, to her amazement, the bottom of the box seemed to disappear, revealing some items beneath it — but still inside the container! She reached in carefully and withdrew several sheets of parchment. Some of them contained writing she couldn't read and didn't care about anyway; on other scraps there were pictures of people, and Leena was immediately drawn to one of these portraits in particular.

It was a picture of a girl. Leena wondered if she was a princess. After all, princesses had their pictures drawn, didn't they? "Not like this," she said aloud. "How do you know?!" The response was cross.

The ink markings on the scrap were carefully drawn, and the detail showed a young and pretty face, a face without lines and wrinkles, framed by long, flowing hair. "I wish I were that lady!" she said, continuing to converse with herself. "You will be, silly girl, but it takes a long time to grow young and pretty. . . ." Tears made marks on the leathery cheeks of the crone, washing away the dust and grime of Old City's slums.

"I didn't wait for so long when I grew ancient and ugly!" she sobbed. Then a thick veil came over her thoughts. Leena toppled over onto her heaped rags and slept, still clutching the drawing of the beautiful girl. At the bottom was written a word, but only the first two letters — "ME" — were legible. Below that pair of letters was written the number "100." Perhaps, the crazy old hag imagined, she would become like the drawing when she reached a hundred years old, or a hundred years from now. . . .

* * *

Finding wood or anything else to use as fuel was no easy task. Old City was a vast place to the little boy. He didn't dare venture very far from his home. Even though that location changed every few months, he soon exhausted all the ready sources within a quarter-mile of where he and Leena lived at the moment. This was now the case. He could find not even any dried horse-apples to use for fuel, so it was time to begin exploring some of the dark and dangerous old buildings on the fringe of his territory.

"Hey, sonny!"

The boy nearly jumped a foot at that, and he began running away from the sound immediately. A hand grabbed his garment, which was merely an old sack converted into a one-piece outfit.

74

"Don't you remember me?" The voice was rough but bore no hint of menace or threat of punishment.

The urchin gathered his courage and turned his narrow face toward the voice. "Oh," he finally managed to say.

The big, bearded face split into a friendly grin. "A clever lad like you can say more than that. I'll give you a little something to help you speak — here," the man said, producing an apple. "Try eating that up, and I'll bet you'll be able to say a whole lot more after it's inside. It's a magic apple, you know."

The lad didn't care if it was magical or otherwise. He was always, always hungry. He grabbed the little red sphere and bit into it without a word to the man. Eat it up first, then see what happens afterward. The fruit was soon gone, core and seeds included.

"Well?"

"Gotta nuther one?" the grubby boy asked seriously through the last mouthful.

The fellow took him gently by the shoulder, smiling and chuckling. "That and more, lad. My place is just there," he informed the waif. "Let's you and I go there for a bit. You can eat all you want, and I'll just talk a bit — sort of fill in the gaps until you're ready to take over. Sound all right?"

The man was big, much bigger than Leena, so undoubtedly he could hit very hard. His laugh was nice, though, not like the old hag's. Besides, this was the same man who had saved him from a pair of bigger boys who had been pummeling him just a couple of days ago — and so far the two hadn't come back to beat him up again. The boy was grateful to the man for that, too. He still didn't trust him completely, but getting food was worth a risk. His large, gray eyes met the man's merry blue ones, visible above the bushy beard.

"Yes," the boy said after a moment's hesitation.

The man walked off. The little boy had to hurry to keep up, and this fact was reassuring to him. He reasoned that if he had to work to get where they were going, the hairy-faced man wasn't setting a trap for him. They went into a small, narrow building through a stout door the man opened with a key. Not many places in this part of the city were so guarded, but there were a few. Leena had told him to watch such places closely, because if he ever found one left unguarded, vast treasures would be found inside. But he had never before been inside such a place, and the little lad was instantly impressed.

"What's your name?"

"Don't know," the lad said without thinking too hard about the question. His eyes were busy roaming over the place. It was a treasure trove. There was a real rug on the floor, dishes on a table, all sorts of wondrous things.

"Sure you do," the fellow countered. "Everyone is called something. Now, I'm called Bru, see? That's my name. What are you called?"

He thought for a moment, then said the first thing that came to mind. "Dirty little bastard."

"Nope, that's not a name. Think some more."

It seemed evident that the man would keep at it until he had a name from him, and then perhaps he'd give him more to eat, so the little boy thought carefully. Almost everything that old Leena called him was like "dirty little bastard," not really names but nasty things. That much the lad had understood down deep for a long time. Then something came to him. "Leena always says she'll thump me . . . gourd!" It was an exclamation of near triumph.

"Gord. . . . Well, then, that must be your name. Glad to make your acquaintance, Gord. Sit down on this stool here, and I'll ladle up a bowl of soup for you."

The lad's big eyes grew bigger when he saw chunks of meat drop from the ladle into the big wooden bowl. "You got meat?"

"Sure, lad . . . I mean, Gord. A hunk of bread to soak in the soup, too. Now eat that up, and we can talk a bit. See, I been looking 'round for someone like you to talk to. There aren't many folks in these parts who are worth talking to, of course."

"Why me?" the newly named boy managed to ask through a food-stuffed mouth. Nobody ever wanted to do anything with him except pick on him or make him work. Maybe this hairy-faced man was a crazy — a dangerous man after all! He wanted to get out quickly — but not so quickly that he would leave any of this wonderful soup behind. Eyes darting from the bowl to the man and back again, he began shoveling the stuff into his mouth as fast as he could.

Bru noticed the sudden tension in the skinny little body, the suspicion plain in the child's eyes. The big man let the child eat in silence for a couple of minutes, then got up slowly and went over to his cupboard. "That's it for the soup, Gord, but I think you're about filled to the top anyway. I'll give you a piece of cheese to take with you when you leave," he said slowly as he pulled a package off a shelf.

Gord was relaxing more with each passing moment. If the man meant to do him harm, he wouldn't have let him fill his stomach first. As hard as it was to accept, Gord had to admit to himself that maybe this bearded stranger really did want to talk to him.

"I guess I like talking to you, lad, because I've got a sharp eye — 'most as magical as that pippin I let you gobble up."

Now that was just too much for Gord to pass up. "That old apple wasn't magic!"

"Look at how blue my eyes are," Bru countered. "Ever seen anything like that?"

"No," the boy admitted slowly, "but I don't see hardly anybody. Does a sharp eye hurt?"

That made the man laugh. "Hah! Good question, though, Gord m'lad. See how much you're talking? That proves the apple was magic, I think. And see how good your question was? That's what my sharp eyes spotted! Not everyone can tell a good lad who can talk so well and ask sharp questions. That's sharp thinking, a sharp mind. Like my sharp eye, it means it gets to the point of things."

Gord belched contentedly and gave a small smile. This was kind of fun. Not the eating — although that was enjoyable, it was done more as a matter of survival. The fun was in having someone like the hairy-faced man . . . Bru . . . to talk to.

"Do I really have a sharp thinker?" Gord asked, not quite convinced of what Bru was saying. "Leena tells me I'm a—"

"Never mind her — not for the time at least. Poor old woman is a little off her noodle," Bru explained, tapping the side of his head to enable the boy to understand what he meant. "Maybe you'll want to give her some of your cheese when you get home."

"No! Anyway, maybe I could stay here with you, Bru. I'm pretty sharp at finding stuff. . . ."

The big man shook his head ponderously. "Love to have you for company, Gord, but I'm not around most of the time. Tell you what, though — I'll make a point of looking for you whenever I am about. Then we can have eats and a good talk. There are many things I can show you, and you'll think it's all fun, too."

That seemed like a lot of empty promising to the boy, but he was too accustomed to disappointment to bother trying to argue. Things were as they were, and he had learned long ago that someone as small and weak as he was had to accept the pain and sadness that came along with lack of size and a shortage of strength. "Sure. . . . I'll go now."

"Not just yet, Gord. I have to put my knife to the cheese for you. What were you looking for when I saw you, anyway? Something I can help with?"

That brought Leena's warning back to mind. "Shit! I gotta find some wood in a big hurry!"

"Hold on, Gord, hold on. Here's your cheese," he said, handing over a hunk of the stuff as he finished wrapping it in a bit of cloth. The piece was bigger than the small boy's fist. "Well, look at that, will you? You've no pocket to carry this back in, and I daresay you wouldn't get far holding it out in the open. Say, would you maybe like a little sack to use? That way I could dump in a few bits of charcoal and some splinters of wood, too. That would sort of take care of things for you, I suppose." He looked at Gord with his kindly, blue eyes, and the boy was happy.

"That would be . . ."

"Great! You got a deal, Gord. Now, just say 'Thank you' and that'll make us even. Then we can be true friends."

"Thank you," Gord said quietly, humbly. He knew the word "friends," but he had never heard it used to refer to himself before. Then it occurred to him that friends should help each other, and he became more animated. "Can I get the sack for you? I'm good at getting things."

The big man considered the offer for a moment. "Well, you gather up some of the charcoal there in that box by the fire, and I'll fetch the sack. Look around for the kindling wood — the broken stuff that's in small pieces. You can take as much of that as you like."

Bru produced a bag from the bottom of his cupboard. It was old and had several holes, but it was a prize nonetheless. They loaded the black sticks of charcoal into it, added handfuls of wood bits and ends, and then plopped the chunk of hard cheese atop the lot.

While all this work was going on, Gord kept thinking about something that puzzled him. Just as the cheese went into the sack, he looked at Bru and asked, "Was that apple really magic?"

"Do you feel any different?"

Gord smiled and nodded. He felt far, far different. He even had a name now. "It *was* magic. . . ."

"Magic is funny stuff, Gord. It isn't anything to talk about, and what's magical for one might be something different for another. Let's you and I keep the secret of the apple magic to ourselves, and that way it will stay magic." Then Bru picked up the sack, hefting it to determine how heavy it was. "I'd say you can just about carry this halfway to your place. I'll tote the load that far for you, but then I'm heading off for a while."

"Will you be off a long time?"

"Not a chance, Gord my friend, not a chance. In a day or two or three I'll be bumping into you again. You keep a sharp eye out meanwhile for stuff you and old Leena need to stay alive — and for the dangers hereabouts too, right?"

"Right!"

Chapter 6

A DOUBLE WALL ENCIRCLED the city. All of Greyhawk — Old City, the larger area called New Town,
and the Citadel too — were within it. The outer curtain was some twenty-five feet high. This wall splayed
out at the base where it met a ditch, or moat, or some
other watercourse, and was topped with serried mer-
lons and crenels to protect defenders in time of war.

Between the outer and inner walls was a relatively
level sward a hundred or more feet broad. The outside edge of this strip of grass was level with the battlements that topped the outer wall. The crowning
stone of the inner wall was much higher. The city had
been built on a large hill — not especially high, but
large in area. Those on the sward between the walls
could look upward forty feet to where machicolated
battlements stood topping the massively thick curtains of the inner wall. At intervals there were bas-
tions on the outer wall, and matching them on the
inside one were tall towers.

Wherever the walls were pierced by gates, the
sward was broken. Every way that led into the city
resembled a road at the bottom of a canyon. Travelers
from the outside would pass through a gatehouse
first, then a long passage, open above, but flanked by
walls on either hand; then a tunnel that bored
through another, bigger tower. Only then was one

actually considered to be within the city of Greyhawk. The place was thus well protected. If a portion of the outer wall fell into enemy hands, the other segments could still be defended, and there was still, of course, the great inner wall as well.

The eastern curve of the metropolis followed the slope of the hill and the bank of the Grey Run. When Old City was the extent of Greyhawk, an island that stood opposite the stretch from Hillgate to Midgate was fortified as a first line of defense against attack. As the city expanded, the works of the island were strengthened. Eventually it became the Bastion, a fortress so strong that a major siege would have to be mounted to take it before the city could be assaulted. The Bastion was connected to Greyhawk by a pair of causeways, with appropriate bridges, and was both a garrison and a village in itself.

New Town was built to link the military fortress that overlooked the Selintan River to Old City, while in the process sufficient additional land was enclosed to provide for a larger population. There were villages there already, and eventually the engineers made the rambling walls follow the entire complex of ridges and hills that rolled from the northern tip of Old City to where the Grey Run and the Selintan flowed together. The walls that hemmed in the original city were left standing. They were not, of course, nearly so vast as the new outer wall that was built around both Old City and New Town, but they would serve to divide the place and help protect it too, just as the walls encompassing the Foreign Quarter were kept in place when it was the lower third of the entire city. The military fortress was strengthened and became the governmental heart of Greyhawk, the Citadel, while the old moat became a canal, with new ones added, for barge traffic up, down, and across the city.

As Hutsham and The Shacks huddled at the base

of the outer wall along the broad Selintan, so too did buildings abut the inner works. The inner structures, however, were tall and substantial places of brick or masonry. The hovels outside Greyhawk were quite the opposite. Thus the whole place was defined and segregated, Old City from New Town, outside from in.

Each portion of Greyhawk was clearly defined and relatively ordered. This was especially true of the original part of the metropolis. There, because that part was made of older buildings crowded closely together, the less desirable elements of Greyhawk's population were confined.

Old City's southern third was, as it had long been, the Foreign Quarter of Greyhawk. This area was connected to the rest of the world by four gates, one going to the outside, two leading into New Town, one northward into the northern portion of Old City.

Two great gates led from the northern two-thirds of Old City to the outside, and two others gave access westward into New Town. Because Old City was quartered into sections for thieves, beggars, laborers, and brewers, and one portion known as the Slums, the whole place was shut up fast after dark. Walls can be used to keep enemies out, or undesirables in . . . at least in theory. Passages under the wall were numerous, from aqueducts and sewers that were part of common knowledge to those built for escape or more nefarious purposes. So too were there forgotten postern gates now masked by one building or another, and carefully made ways to allow a route between New Town and Old City after the gates were closed and barred. Yet if a thief or an adventurer could move about with relative freedom, not so the ordinary residents of Old City — especially not denizens of the Slum Quarter, and certainly not small urchins dwelling therein.

"What are all those horses doing here?" Gord's

eyes were big at the sight of a herd of about two score of the animals.

Bru explained. "Those are the mounts of a troop of the Greyhawk Guards, lad. There aren't many cavalrymen in the city, of course, because mounted men aren't very useful inside a crowded place."

That made sense to Gord. He'd seen the carts and wagons typical of the place, vehicles drawn by massive draught horses or broken-down old nags. Mules and donkeys there were aplenty, as well as the occasional riding horse of some well-to-do visitor to the quarter. Someone on foot could easily elude a mounted man, thanks to narrow gangways, walls to scramble over, steep steps and narrow catwalks, and more. "Why have any . . . cavvary-men . . . at all?"

"Well, here on the Green they can be useful — no buildings. If an enemy got over the outer wall and up here, the cavalry would be used to drive them back. Every section of the Green has a troop or two of mounted men. If enemy troops ever actually got inside the city, all the cavalry would be withdrawn to defend the threatened part. See?"

They approached the big horses, and as the two did so Gord was pondering what he'd just been told. "Uncle Bru, if horses are not good inside the city, then why take them inside? That doesn't make any sense to me."

The big man laughed as he often did when Gord questioned him. The boy was used to it by now, and knew it was not meant as an insult. After all, he and the man he now called Uncle Bru had been good pals for a long time — about a year, he reckoned, although his childish mind didn't keep track of time very closely. Bru helped to make sense of a lot of things for Gord. "There are places where the cavalry can be used. Along with men on foot, they can be a big help in defeating an invader."

"When will we be attacked?"

"Never, I hope. Everyone should hope the same, because in wars there is a lot of suffering and people get killed."

"But lots of people are pretty miserable now, Uncle Bru, and I've seen big fights where people get killed — like when the gangs fight each other," the small boy explained.

"Those fights are like wars, Gord, but very little wars. Put 'em all together, every one you've ever seen, and that's just a bit of what a real war is like." Bru went on to explain why wars were fought, doing so in simple terms.

"Then we are free here in Greyhawk?"

"Pretty much so, Gord."

"Then how come I can't go anyplace?" That was phrased as an accusation and objection, not really a question. "Every time I try to go somewhere I get chased by someone, or the soldiers at the gate tell me to go away back home."

"There are things about freedom, Gord m'boy, which you will understand only when you're older. Let's see if we can't talk the soldiers into letting us climb up to the top of the big tower there now. Won't it be fun to be able to see all over the city?"

"You bet!"

The big man led him over to the little gate they had passed through to get to the strip of grassland between the walls. There was a guard slouched there, and after the exchange of a few words and a coin, the two were permitted to climb to the top of the tall structure that loomed over the gate. Gord had never seen anything like that view. Bru pointed out where they lived, the inside wall that bounded Old City, and the distant places beyond. Wind tousling his dark hair, the little lad gazed off into the distance for a long time.

"When I'm as old as you are, Uncle Bru, I'll live way over there," he finally said, pointing to a place where big trees and a park could be seen.

"You just might at that, Gord. You just might."

Leena hardly ever bothered him any more, thanks to his friend. All the old woman ever wanted from him was food or some similar commodity. Scavenging for sustenance was the fate of the poor of Old City, especially in the decaying slums. Garbage and refuse were the mainstays of life for such folk. Occasionally something of worth would be found, and then it could be sold and the money gained used to purchase the stuff of dreams — beer, wine, and the like usually, but sometimes real food, a warm coat, or something else worthwhile.

The smallest coin used in the city, the iron drab, was a treasure to Gord. It would buy a stale bun, a turnip, or something of similar worth. Four drabs together equaled a brass bit. Uncle Bru had taught him that. A bit would buy a sweet, a juicy red apple of monstrous size, even a thick tallow candle. Next came a coin called a zee. Gord had found one once, and with it he had hoped to buy a pair of old shoes at the ragman's shop. Leena had found the bronze disc, taken it, and beaten Gord soundly for trying to conceal it from her and keep it all for himself. Of course, she then used the whole thing for her own benefit.

He still had to scavenge, but not as much as before. If his friend was around, then Gord didn't have to crawl around in garbage piles or put himself in danger to get loot, and Leena never cared where the stuff came from anyway. If he brought home fuel, food, or some old shirt, all she expected was to have most or all of the booty. Uncle Bru made him do work for him, or else Gord had to learn things — that was sometimes a lot harder than the chores his friend gave him.

In return for his efforts, Gord would get to eat wonderful stuff and sometimes have something else bestowed upon him too. The old clothing didn't fit well, but it helped keep the skinny lad warm and dry.

Uncle Bru even taught Gord to wash himself and his garments occasionally. "Why bother?" the boy had asked his friend.

"Because if you ever want to get out of this place," Bru had told Gord, "you'll have to look like something other than a guttersnipe." Thereafter, Bru had given him a lesson on language, including what the word "guttersnipe" meant and what one of that sort of boy was like. Gord knew from Bru's description that the boys in the Slum Quarter were all guttersnipes, or worse. He feared them and hated the way they were, so he then and there determined that he would never grow up to be one.

Without his knowing it, the young boy's reckoning of time was very accurate. The big man who called himself Bru had been Gord's friend for almost exactly a year before they went out on the Green and up to the tower top to view the city from a bird's perspective. After that, the two saw each other pretty frequently as well. Sometimes his friend would be there every day for a week, then again Uncle Bru might be gone for twice that long before coming back and searching out the urchin within the twisting streets and narrow alleys of the slums. Once Gord wondered aloud why, if Bru knew he was going to be gone a long time, his friend didn't give him extra food and maybe a few small coins so that Gord wouldn't have to search and scavenge to stay alive.

"That wouldn't be fair to either of us, Gord," the big man had said. "Don't you have to earn what I hand over to you?" Gord admitted that was the way of things. "Then how would you be earning it if I just gave you things because I was going to be away?"

"Well, who says you have to earn stuff?" Gord was cross and quarrelsome. "You've got lots and lots of food and money and everything else too. If you can't be my father and let me live with you, then you could at least give me enough so that old bag Leena doesn't hit me and be mean to me. You could give me stuff to eat so I wasn't hungry all the time until you came back." After the last accusation, Gord could restrain himself no longer, and he burst out in tears.

Bru turned away so that the boy couldn't see the tears in his own eyes. "Maybe I could, boy, maybe I couldn't. That's not really the meat of the matter. I'm your friend, and I'm your teacher too. I say that everything anyone gets he earns, or he pays for. Sometimes earning means working the way you work for me, doing little tasks I give you. Other times it means giving up something to have to learn a trade, working at it, and then collecting earnings. And sometimes people earn what they don't want to get."

"What does that mean?"

"You've seen the gangs of prisoners from the workhouse, haven't you? Bet you've seen the gallows there by the prison, too." Little Gord murmured his assent, but he seemed uncertain what that had to do with earning. "Well, lad, we don't always get the right wage for what we do, and sometimes folks collect a lot for doing wrong things. Then again, there are those bad folk who finally earn what was coming to them."

"Oh . . ."

Bru's eyes were sparkling again, and he smiled at his small friend. "So, you see, you have to be able to earn a living here, no two ways about that. What's more, Gord, you can't count on me either. Not because I don't want to be a friend and help you," Bru went on with a rush, "but because you and I don't know for sure that I'll be here tomorrow and all the days after that."

There was still doubt in Gord's eyes. "You can do whatever you like."

"I would that were true, little friend, but it isn't so. Think of it this way. What if a runaway wagon ran over me? I'd be dead and gone. Suppose bandits attacked and killed me? That is hard for a lad to think on, I know, but you have to be hard inside and deal with the world as it is." At this last part, Bru took the small boy by his hand and grinned. "We've had more than enough of that sort of talk for a long time! Let's you and I take a prowl around the neighborhood, and we can see if there are any interesting prospects for you to go back and investigate later."

More months slipped by, and Gord and his friend were often seen about the district. The gangs hated both of them, for the big man was not to be threatened and in fact ran them off if they attempted extortion. Perhaps the members of these bands of young toughs secretly wished they had such a friend and protector, but whether from envy or for some other reason they vowed to get Gord whenever he was without the hairy-faced fellow. The little lad had to be very cautious indeed when he ventured forth on his daily rounds, for the older and bigger boys did watch for him and stole whatever he had.

When Gord complained to Uncle Bru about this, the big man nodded sympathetically and told Gord that he could teach some things to him, but some things Gord would have to learn on his own. That way the lad would be fit to survive in the harsh environment of Old City.

"Do you remember how to count?"

Gord proudly counted to twenty, and he was ready to go on all the way to one hundred, but Uncle Bru raised his hand. He asked Gord to show him how to make the numbers he'd just said. "Easy," the boy replied, and using his finger he began drawing lines in the dirt. "That's a one . . . and that's a two . . . and here's a—"

The boot struck him with fair force and sent him sprawling in the dust. The carefully made numbers were obliterated by Gord's skid as he fell from the kick.

"Get away from me, you filthy little beggar!" Uncle Bru spat in Gord's general direction and then turned away and walked off. "If I ever catch you trying to steal from me again, I'll break your scrawny neck!" he called back threateningly over his shoulder.

This couldn't be happening! Gord's mind was racing. Leena would do something like that, but not his friend, not Uncle Bru. He could trust nobody but the big man, and his friend would never betray his trust! Bru was walking away with long strides, not even looking back to see if Gord was injured. Perhaps it was a new game or a lesson. . . .

Thinking that, Gord scrambled up and started to call after Uncle Bru. Then he saw two mean-looking men come out of a nearby alley. They had a huge mastiff with them, and their appearance was sufficient to still Gord's words in his throat. The little boy swallowed hard and shrank back. He knew the trick of becoming invisible. It is a skill all children have, and it worked only with adults, of course. In the slums, it was a vital part of survival.

Neither man looked at him at all. The huge dog glanced at the boy, then stared at the figure of the man walking away, for that was the object of his master's attention. "Dat's 'im," one of the two said. "Round the corner, then, and we'll take 'im," the other agreed as Uncle Bru disappeared down a lane. With that the two men ran off, the mastiff on its rope pulling the one on the right. They too rounded the corner and disappeared in seconds.

Gord's skinny legs pumped. His heart racing almost in time with his running feet, the boy dashed after Bru, the two bad men, and the fierce dog. He managed to get to the lane in time to see the pair chasing his friend turn into a side passage, a gangway too narrow for them to walk abreast. The one with the mastiff's rope went first, with the dog straining ahead. Gord slowed and crept closer, because the second of the two pursuers had stopped and was standing just inside the narrow passage.

Then a horrid growling echoed from the gangway. The mastiff was attacking Uncle Bru! The ferocious sound suddenly changed to a rising howl, however, and it ended with a high-pitched whine that was cut off suddenly.

"Shit!" The man still waiting near the entrance said that loudly. Then he produced a small sword from beneath his jerkin and rushed into the passageway. As soon as he did that, Gord was able to run up to the place to see what was going on.

He heard sounds of the struggle as soon as he got to the opening between the buildings. Gord peered around the corner cautiously, wanting to run right in and help his only friend, but knowing that he was far too small and weak to do anything except get in the way.

The passage was short, no more than a dozen paces long. After that the space between the two structures widened and was open to the sky. Gord could see the shapes of three men beyond the gangway's end. One was surely Uncle Bru, judging from his size and his beard. He was locked in a hand-to-hand struggle with one of the smaller men. The other assailant was dancing around the pair, sword in hand, trying to find an opening to strike with his weapon.

It was evident to him that nobody would notice him now, so Gord scurried up to where the passage opened, staying back just far enough to be hidden by the shadows. Just beyond the end of the tunnel lay the mastiff. From the way its head was positioned, Gord knew that its neck had been broken. The boy noted that fact in a quick glance; then his attention was redirected toward the trio of fighters.

Although Bru's clothes were torn, and his cheek was bleeding from a couple of long gashes, the hairy-faced man seemed to be unhurt otherwise. Perhaps his bushy beard had saved him from the jaws of the dog, for there seemed to be parts of the thick mat missing now from around his throat. The smaller man was holding a dagger, but Bru had the fellow's wrist and arm locked in his viselike left hand, while he clasped the killer in a bear-hug with his strong right arm, using the man's own body as a shield. The dagger was moving back, away from Bru, because his friend was slowly bending the attacker's arm upward and back. Gord thought that it would have been an easy thing for Bru, except for the other bad man with the narrow sword.

"Stab the sonuvabitch!" the man with the dagger cried. There was pain in his voice, and as he spoke the last word, the wind rushed from his mouth with a gasp, for Bru had used the opportunity to tighten his grip around the man.

"Hold 'im still," the other one panted, trying to circle so that he could get at an exposed portion of the big man. Bru kept shifting and circling at the same rate, however, seemingly able to anticipate every move the swordsman made. The sword-wielder made a tentative stab, then shouted, "Hol' 'im still, godsdamnit, else I'll never get to stickin' 'im!"

"The bastid's tryin' ta break me arm, ya shithead," the one caught in Bru's grasp managed to choke out. "Do sumpin'!"

Just then the arm holding the dagger moved farther back, and the man's mouth opened in a grimace of pain. There was a funny, snapping sound too, and the knife flew from his open hand. That seemed to make the other killer act with more quickness and less sense. The man with the sword fairly flew as he circled, and the sword shot out with terrible speed and force.

"There!" the evil-faced man cried as his blade sank into flesh. Then the man's face went very pale as he saw that he had driven the weapon through his comrade's back. Bru and the stabbed killer were between him and the gangway. The man simply let go of his small sword, turned on his heels, and fled through the courtyard and into another passageway at its end. He was gone in a matter of seconds.

"Uncle Bru! Are you all right?" Gord called from his hiding place. His friend was just standing there, still holding onto the man with the sword sticking out of his back.

"What are you doing here?" Bru's voice sounded strange to Gord's ears. The man turned slowly, still clasping the dead attacker. His face changed from its hard expression to a smile, however, as the thin boy advanced hesitantly out of the shadows. "Never mind me, Gord," he said softly. "You're a friend indeed, and I thank you. Take hold of that sword there and pull it out — real careful like."

It was a terrible thing to ask. Gord didn't want to do it. He stood still, looking uncertainly at Uncle Bru. "I don't want to touch it. . . ." Gord managed to say.

"Do as I tell you, you little fool!" Bru's eyes were narrowed, and his tone was hard. "Do it now, and do it carefully. If you don't, I won't be your friend any more!"

After the kick and the strange behavior, Gord wasn't so sure that Bru was really his friend anyway, but he had to do what Bru said because the little boy still wanted the man's friendship, even if the feeling was no longer mutual. His hands reached out and touched the sword's hilt.

"Grab hold, boy, that's right," the big man said with soft encouragement.

Gord grabbed hold and his thin arms tugged. The weapon came slowly at first, then all the way out at once. Gord toppled over from the sudden end of its resistance as it pulled free.

"Aaaah," Bru sighed as he let the dead man topple to the cobblestones. "That's a good lad! I feel much better now."

Now the boy suddenly realized what had happened. When the man with the sword had stabbed his friend, the thin blade had gone all the way through the fellow and stuck its point into Uncle Bru too. Gord had pulled the sword out of his friend as well as from the dead attacker's back. "Are you hurt bad?" He saw his friend pushing a wad of cloth against a place on his side where blood stained his jacket.

"Yes, of course, lad. I'll be just fine, but I'll have to have this wound tended to soon. That was a stupid thing you did, Gord, following me," he added with a mock scowl at the worried little face that peered up at him.

"Those men were after you. I saw them and the bad dog chase after you, and I had to see what was happening. I think you're my friend even if you were mean to me, and friends got to help each other — you told me that." Gord's expression was a mixture of uncertainty and challenge. Would Bru now contradict his own words to him?

"Ah, you are right again, Gord. But come on, we have to get away from this place quick. It won't do for anyone to see us here — particularly together." The big man picked up the sword, wiped it clean on the dead man's clothing, and hid it under his jacket. "Did the one who ran away see you?" he asked as he guided the boy back the way they had come.

"No, neither of them saw me, but the dog did."

"That's no matter. Are you sure the men didn't, though?" Uncle Bru's tone was urgent.

"Oh, yes, I'm very sure of that. Both of them only wanted to see where you were going, so they were too busy to spot me following them."

"Good. Very good. This is far enough, though. You go back to your place now, and forget what happened. Forget all about me too! You must never mention what happened here to anyone — not Leena, not a new friend you might find, not anyone. The same goes for me. From now on, you never knew anyone named Bru, never saw anyone who even looks like me. Understood?"

Gord shook his head. "No. I can't say that. Friends don't forget each other . . . even if one is mean and kicks the other."

"That was necessary — I'm sorry I had to do it, Gord. You are still my good friend. But, you see, those two men who tried to kill me were watching. I saw them, and I knew they had seen us. If they had thought you and I were pals, they would have killed you first, then come after me."

"That's why you did it!" Gord was jubilant at the revelation. Now he understood the sudden change from friend to enemy. "You did it so they would think I was just another guttersnipe trying to steal from you." That made the little boy feel very good. Then something else came to him. "You really and truly saved my life. . . ."

"Perhaps, perhaps. That's no matter now, for the whole thing is done and over." Bru sat down and leaned back against the crumbling bricks of the old building. There was pain on his face, and he groaned

95

just a little as he tried to get into a more comfortable position. "That fight sort of tuckered me out, Gord. Your Uncle Bru needs to rest a second. Sit down here by me, and I'll give you a last lesson."

That didn't sound good at all. Gord wanted no last lesson, but he did as Bru said anyway. "What do you mean?"

The big man patted Gord on his tousled head, ruffling the dark hair fondly. "Those men after me were killers. One of them is still a killer, of course. He got away. Soon he will be coming back with more of his kind, and this time there will be enough of them to do the job. I have to be long gone when they come back, and you don't want them to see you, either — you can never be certain that the one who lived didn't notice you. If he remembers you being with me, even if he saw me kick you, then he'll try to get you, and ask you questions."

"I'd never tell him anything," Gord said stoutly. "You and I are friends, and friends don't rat on each other."

"That's for sure," Bru said with a grin, but then his face grew very serious. "But his kind have ways of making you tell. They would use knives, hot coals, anything they could to hurt you so bad that you'd have to tell them to make the pain stop. Those are bad, evil folk. That's why I have to clear out and never come back again. That's why you have to lay low for a week, and thereafter be very careful for a long time."

"Won't I ever see you again?" Gord couldn't believe this was happening. "Take me with you when you go away!"

The big man compressed his lips. "I've got to move fast and travel far. You couldn't manage it, and you'd slow me down. Even alone, I'm not so sure they won't find me. They, or their lot, are determined once they decide to go after someone and kill them." He looked at the thin face and the sad eyes. "You don't want me to get killed, and I don't want that to happen to you, either. The best thing a pair of friends can do in this kind of situation is to part company, so that each of them has a chance to live."

Gord could understand that. "You're really a very smart man, Uncle Bru. You have to get away for sure, and I'll be a mouse here, and nobody will see me at all."

"Good. It's all settled, then," Bru said with a sigh of relief. He managed to get back to his feet, the lad assisting him in the effort. "Now I'm off to get this hole in me patched up. One thing more, old friend. Don't ever go back to my place — never! I'll not go there again, and you mustn't do so, either. Don't even go near it. They'll watch it for weeks, maybe months."

"But all of your things are there, Bru! You can't just leave so much."

"Things don't matter a bit. You know that, don't you? What good is money, what use finery, if you're dead? None, of course. Let those devils have what's there — we need to stay alive!"

Gord couldn't restrain himself. "You must be a very important man to have those killers after you. Are you a prince in disguise? You have to tell me, please. You're going away now, and who knows when you'll come back? I have to know, Uncle Bru."

That made the big man pause. "You're right in a lot of ways, Gord. It isn't likely you and I will be meeting again for a long, long time — if ever, to be honest, and I must be honest with a friend like you, boy. You're right about those who seek me. Most folks don't have murderers hounding them. You're right about them thinking I'm important. I'm not a prince, though, not anything even near it. I'm just a common man, sort of a soldier in a good cause. I have something those bad ones want to know, though. If they get it, then their side gets stronger and can do terrible things to good people. I must see that they fail, and then we have a chance of defeating their evil in the end."

Gord hugged his friend around the waist, and Bru gave his narrow little shoulders a squeeze with his free arm. "I'll think about you when you're gone, Uncle Bru. You will beat the bad guys, I know it! No one's as big and strong and tough as you are."

"Luck be with you, lad," the big man said. He gave Gord's shoulders a last embrace, then went off.

Gord watched him walk away through misty eyes. Bru never faltered in his step, never looked back to where the small boy stood watching. In a minute there was no man in sight, but the waif stood as still as a post, staring along the street where his friend had been. The sense of loss was overwhelming. Far beyond his years in understanding, Gord realized that a part of his life, the only good part, had just gone. It was a permanent loss. From now on, it was Gord against the world, and he had no friend to help him, no teacher, no benefactor, no protector.

When he came back that evening, old Leena was furious that the boy bore nothing with him. None of her abuses or threats drew a response from him, so she finally seized him and shook the thin boy until his teeth rattled. At that a small leather bag dropped out of his smock.

"Eh! What's this?" the crone said as she stooped over and snatched the thing up. It clinked in her hand, and her fingers shook in their haste to undo its tie and open it. "Holdin' out on old Leena, were ya?!" She clouted Gord on the head with her fist, and the force of the clenched hand with the coin bag inside it knocked him flat.

He managed to lift his head and shake it a little so

that the stars before his eyes went away. Gord saw
Leena pouring a dozen silver coins back and forth
between her hands, crooning "lovely nobles, pretty
silver nobles" as she did so. Gord knew then that Bru
had slipped the purse of coins into his blouse when
they'd parted. Now Leena had them, but that didn't
matter — it was knowing that his friend had cared
and given them to him that counted. Leena couldn't
take that away from him.

Chapter 7

HOW LONG HAD IT BEEN? Three or four years? Gord couldn't remember exactly, nor could he recall much about his long-gone friend. In fact, the boy seldom even thought about Bru any more. Staying alive was difficult enough, and it demanded all the attention he possessed. All he had going for him was his speed, agility, and cunning. Everyone he met was bigger, stronger, and deadlier than he was. Gord hated it. He hated to think that even his foster mother, Leena, was tougher than he was, but the facts were inescapable. An old alley cat, or even the rat it hunted, was better armed to fight than he was.

"Get out and find us some food," Leena would command. If Gord didn't hurry to obey, the old hag would thump him with a stick, and he could do nothing but take it and then run off to do as she told him. Gord didn't dare to try surviving without Leena. Most folks in the slums thought she was a witch, so they shunned the two of them, and that kept Gord safe to some extent.

"Hey, ya little runt! Get the hells outa here!" Other children of the district always yelled something like that at him, and Gord got away as fast as possible. A couple of times he'd tried to stand up to bullies instead of running, but he was too small, too skinny, and too weak.

"Watch that dirty little guttersnipe there — the dark one!" Most adults he encountered said something like that, especially when they had something to protect. Being honest with himself, Gord had to admit that their attitude wasn't surprising. The only reason he would even approach other people was if they had food or something small he could grab and run away with.

A friend? There was no such thing in Gord's life, really. Leena used him, and Gord used the crone, too. He was ready to admit that to himself. Had he really ever had a friend? Bru was but a hazy memory, and Gord actually wondered if he had imagined the whole episode with the big, bearded man. It didn't matter. Now he was getting older and more sure of himself.

He might be little, Gord told himself, but he could use his wits and his speed to show them all. He needed no one but Leena. Through no generosity on her part, she provided him with a safe haven. One day he'd grow bigger and stronger, and then he'd leave the nasty woman to fend for herself. Gord would have a weapon, a big knife or something like that. He'd be fast still, but also tall and strong. Then he'd show them all, and pity the bully who dared to call him a runt or a coward!

"You lazy little dogturd! Why are you sitting there making faces at nothing? Get out of here and bring back something good for Leena to eat!"

He got up quickly and went out. He considered hurling insults back at Leena, but why bother? He was hungry, too, and anyway, when he came back she'd remember and make him sorry for his brash words. Gord decided to take his gathering-pot and head over to the brewers' area to get their leavings. The walk was a longish one, and there were many places to avoid, but the boy managed to get there and back to his part of the slums in two hours.

The scratched and dented metal pot was about three-quarters full of the grain mash the beer makers had thrown out. The stuff wasn't good to eat, but it was useful for another purpose. Using some of the sloppy mash as bait, Gord set a trap for the pigeons that were everywhere in the slums. A pair of them made a good meal, and Leena couldn't eat more than the breasts of two, so there'd be plenty for him to have also — if he got them. The rest of the stuff he saved for rat bait. He hated to eat the dirty rodents, but sometimes he managed to trap one, or drop a big stone on one. Then they had rat to eat. Leena would skin it and gut it and toss it into the iron kettle to boil. The slumgullion of rat and near-rotten vegetables was one of the better meals she made.

Bubbling coos brought his attention back to the here and now. A half-dozen of the blue-gray birds were on the ground nearby, pecking at the soggy mess that Gord had set out for them. Gord peered out of his hiding place around the corner of a shack, holding a long piece of leather thong in his hand. That item was one of his prized possessions. The thong was tied to a short stick. The stick supported an old door, so that the structure formed a lean-to. Under this "shelter" Gord had placed most of the bait. The birds were working their way under the trap now, having first pecked up all the mash that was not directly beneath the door. Gord waited impatiently, and when it looked as if four or five of the pigeons were inside the trap, he jerked the thong with all his might.

Squawk! Thump! Flap-flap-flap-flap. . . . Only four birds were winging away!

Gord ran over to the door and levered it up after jumping on it to make sure the two pigeons beneath it would not be able to get away. He twisted each neck thereafter, just to be certain again. After tucking his prized catch into his baggy outer garment, a poncho-like thing that was tied with twine around his waist, Gord headed for home. Tonight, at least, Leena would be happy, he would have a full belly, and all would be well. Maybe he was a runt, and he was weak. But he was smart, and that made up for it. Let them call him a coward, but inside Gord decided that it was better to be gutless and alive than brave and dead.

So the days slipped past in this way, one by one. Each brought its own load of troubles, its own little triumphs or petty tragedies, into Gord's drab existence. With each incident his perspective changed. The difference was minute, so infinitesimal that it couldn't be noted. Only when reflecting back from one season to the last could the boy begin to detect change. He wasn't growing much in height. There was no great increase in Gord's girth of bicep. Yet he was growing better fit to survive. A year passed, then another. Things were becoming harder and harder in the slums. More crazy folk were dwelling in the district these days, and there were more homeless boys, wandering scavengers, more competition.

"Why are you trying to starve me to death?" Leena whined that question frequently these days. Gord was having trouble finding food these days. It was early winter, and in addition to being hungry the crone was feeling the cold and damp. Gord almost felt sorry for the poor old woman in her endless suffering — only he suffered too in his own way.

* * *

"Wake up, Leena," Gord said one day as he entered the little shack the two of them had moved into at the start of the cold season. "I found a half-loaf of dark bread and a store of winter apples someone must have forgotten about!" He was proud, because the sum of what he'd brought home was sufficient to feed both of them for several days. "The apples are in a burlap sack, and the sack in a box." Firewood and food in one fell swoop! Leena remained still, lying under her rag-heap by the cold ashes of the little stove of tin and stones they had fashioned.

In his eagerness to share his good news, Gord didn't worry about being punished for waking her up. The boy grabbed her by the shoulder and shook her gently. "Come, on, old woman, your provider has plenty to keep you from starving to . . ." Leena was cold to his touch, and her normally gray color was ashen. "Leena? What's wrong? Leena!" The old woman made no response. There was no movement, no flutter of the eyelids, no breathing. Gord released his grasp and shrank back.

Her death was a terrible blow to Gord. The crone had been mean and miserable, and had beaten him, but only as an expression of her own despair. For all her faults, and for as little as Leena had taken care of him, she still had been his only parent, his foster mother, his one human constant. Her protection was a key factor in Gord's survival, too. All that she was, and all that she was to him, had disappeared in the space of an afternoon. Gord was only twelve, but his reaction to Leena's death showed that he had understanding beyond his years.

Two tears ran down Gord's cheeks as he sat back on his heels and stared at the corpse. He quickly wiped them away with his sleeve. He was a man alone now — or he had to try to be that. He had to deal with the reality of things here and now, and it was necessary to do so immediately. There was no such thing as burial, not in the Slum Quarter. Many a body he had seen simply tossed out into the street. Some were removed by the carts of the cleaners, most were dragged off by mongrel dogs to provide their food. Rats ate what dogs left, people killed some of the dogs and rats, and the cycle of life went on.

"I must take your valuables, Leena," the boy said as he shifted the old woman's body this way and that. All he found were two near-worthless iron coins. "Even this tiny wealth I must have," he said to her earnestly, as if she could hear. "I am alive, you are dead, and I might need it." Although the boy knew it was foolish, he carefully wrapped the frail body in the worn blanket Leena had treasured as shawl and cloak. That done, Gord set his jaw and moved the corpse out of the shack. Well up the narrow lane, in a place where there was a rubble-strewn yard, he finally let go. Leena's funeral was over. There was no more to it. Gord went back to the hut, closed and wedged shut the small door, and carefully made a little fire to warm himself by. The night was frosty, and the thick scattering of bright stars in the sky indicated it would get colder too.

"You won't need these rag-blankets any more," he said aloud, as if old Leena were still there to hear. "I'll take charge of my inheritance now too," he added, as he lifted the old wooden box out of the hidey-hole Leena always made under where she slept.

Gord had known about the box for several years, ever since the day he had accidentally discovered Leena's current hiding place while groping around under her bed for a scrap of food he had dropped. She wasn't in their shack at the time, so he took the opportunity to leaf through the pieces of parchment he found inside. None of them had meant anything to him or even interested him, so he had simply put the whole batch back in the box and replaced the container in the hole. Leena had cuffed him soundly and cursed him viciously when she realized the box and its contents had been handled — and threatened to do much worse to him if he ever touched the box again. Since he didn't have any use for the thing anyway, it was not at all difficult for him to leave it alone, but he had not forgotten about it.

Clutching the small coffer, and with a thick mattress of rags around him, Gord crooned himself to sleep beside the slowly dwindling flames of the fire.

The next day he moved from the hut to a cellar beneath the ruins of an old building, fairly near the old site where he and Leena had dwelled. Gord thought it would be a good idea to move, because as soon as the rest of the neighborhood found out that Leena had died, the other boys would terrorize him even more than they did already. His new place was small, dark, and difficult to enter for anyone or anything larger than the size of a small boy. An old chimney provided ventilation for a fire, and the little space was easy to warm. It suited his needs perfectly, and he was happy at having found such a good place so quickly.

But if Gord had been very lucky on this day after Leena died, his fortune turned round thereafter. He had to be very careful when he went out, because the gangs had heard that the old witch with the evil eye had looked in a mirror and killed herself. Gord didn't realize how much indirect protection Leena had provided him until he had ventured forth on a few expeditions after she died. The boys that used to beat him up and take what he had salvaged still did that, of course, whenever he couldn't avoid them. The difference was in the slum-gangs that formerly had merely cursed him from a distance and thrown rocks at him. They too were now confronting him directly, roughing him up, and stealing from him. It became harder and harder to garner anything worthwhile anywhere, and finding food was becoming a major task. By spring Gord moved again, seeking better pickings.

The gangs of the sprawling slums stayed within

their own confines. Within the crumbling district they were virtually supreme, because nobody outside the slums cared. The place was home to the homeless, the insane, the flotsam and jetsam of the city. If the local economy ever began to flourish again, then the Slum Quarter would shrink as laborers increased and property was rebuilt, refurbished, repaired for those who contributed to the city's wealth. In truth, the slums were a preserve, a place for the misfits and useless to dwell within the walls of Greyhawk, but the place had not been intentionally provided for that purpose. They existed simply because nobody cared about the area at the time. Many of the constructions therein were abandoned now because of slow trade, a weak economy, and lack of demand. No one stayed there if he could go elsewhere, unless he was a crazy person or a wanted criminal.

Of course there was an economy, of sorts, within the quarter. There were food shops, peddlers, stores selling old clothing and used things, places to buy small beer and sour wine, and all that. There were three relatively thriving places within the Slum Quarter, but they were the haunts of those forced to dwell there because of being wanted criminals, or else the territories of those who chose to deal with the slums for some related reason. If a denizen of the slums had money to spend, he could enter these three islands of activity, but when his coins were gone he had to leave. There was no safety in these places of activity, no safety anywhere in the quarter, unless you bought it or were strong enough not to be threatened by roving gangs of boys, muggers, crazy men, and the rest of the feral folk of the place. Needless to say, Gord stayed well away from the active parts of the quarter.

Three gangs claimed territories that virtually surrounded the place where the boy dwelled. It would be no use to go elsewhere, for no other place would necessarily have fewer threats. Gord had to deal with the threats, the predatory neighbors of all sorts, as a matter of course. Without Leena to frighten off the gangs, Gord was in trouble. Although he had become very clever and wise from having dwelled in the slums since infancy, the prospect of his staying alive was dwindling. Without allies or a protector, he was nothing more than prey for the other boys.

Not only was he small for his age, but Gord was also not very strong. It was more a case of late development than innate weakness, but the harsh environment made no allowance for that. Because he was subject to being bullied by virtually any gang boy, Gord was an undesirable potential member as far as the gangs were concerned. He might be clever, but that threatened the leadership of the gang. He might be fast, but speed and agility weren't considerations in the society of a group of homeless boys, unless these characteristics were associated with toughness and fighting ability.

Gord's nature denied him membership anyway. He was a loner, and the very idea of having to be the lowest on the scale, the butt of all others in a gang, was sufficient cause for the boy to stay away from a gang even if he would have been accepted. He was known to many of the other lads in the area, and because he fled from them or was caught and trounced by them, these boys despised and derided him. He was never simply called "Gord" — gutless, chicken, or a similar term always accompanied Gord's name or was used in place of it. The nature of the slums was for the strong to pick upon the weak, and there was no question that Gord was physically weak.

"You live in our fief now," a member of the gang called the Headsmen told him at the start of low summer. "You give us half of everything you get, or else we'll take everything — and beat the crap outta

you in the bargain." Gord told the boy he would do as
he was told, but he didn't actually comply unless circumstances compelled him to. He could be physically
bullied, and he cried from the pain of being beaten,
but mentally Gord had plenty of courage. Threats and
beating made him agree then and there. But once he
was away, it was an altogether different matter. He
did try cooperating once or twice, voluntarily going to
the gang's headquarters to split some haul with the
other boys — only to discover that they took all of his
loot anyway. After that, he never sought them out
and decided to take his chances instead.

The Headsmen soon caught on to Gord's defiance
and lurked in ambush for him. Whenever they caught
him, these bullies seized whatever Gord had, pum-
meled him, and then let him loose again. It was diversion, amusement, and profit all in one, for Gord usually had something worth taking. The gang profited,
but Gord grew weaker still, for he could manage to
amass no store of things against the future. Each day
he had to find enough to eat, devour what he found
immediately, and then attempt to carry anything remaining back through the hostile territory to his own
den, without revealing the location of his hideaway
either coming or going. Most of the time the return
was a disaster. Gord would throw his prizes away, if
the opportunity allowed, to avoid being beaten; or
else he would be caught, his booty taken from him,
and then he would be hit and kicked in the bargain.

There was no other place for him to go, so Gord
had no choice but to put up with it. It was a humili-
ation and a shame. It began to prey upon his mind
even as the conditions ate away his strength and
stamina. The very names of Chopper, Jot, Snaggle,
and the others of the Headsmen were enough to
make the boy furious inside. Finally, after living this
way for the better part of a year, Gord decided he had

to do something. If he were still in the same area when another winter came, the lad knew that he'd die as Leena had.

"I'll never manage here in the slums," he said to himself as he gathered up what little he owned. Not wishing to risk the well-crafted box with the parchments inside, the only thing he possessed that had any real and lasting value, Gord hid it away in a place where no one but him would ever find it. Carrying his few remaining items, the boy went off, headed for the workers' district. Although he was nabbed in the process and stripped of even what little he held, Gord remained determined. He would leave the Slum Quarter regardless.

Wearing clothing that was barely presentable, and feeling frightened inside, Gord managed to make his way from the upper part of Old City all the way into the Foreign Quarter, a far-off and exotic place he had only heard of. Nobody seemed to notice him or, if they did actually see Gord, pay any attention to him. That bolstered his spirits and encouraged the boy. There were riches everywhere in this fabulous place. With his skill and daring, Gord was certain he could take some of the readily available wealth and soon be set up for life in such a place.

But self-confidence and speed weren't enough. The experience of stealing in the slums was certainly insufficient training for this place, where real artistry was required to defeat the guardians and sharp-eyed protectors of goods displayed for sale in the Foreign Quarter's marketplaces. Gord tried, of course, and then he was caught, taken before the authorities, and sentenced to penal servitude all in the same day. The boy didn't realize it at the time, but that calamity was a turning point in his life.

Chapter 8

"YOU SAW HIM?"

"I think so. He fits your description pretty well. Who can tell for sure? All those little guttersnipes look pretty much alike."

"He's been sent to the Old Citadel?"

"For three years — imprisoned and working off a theft."

"Will he survive it?"

"Not very likely. The boy's too small and weak to manage there for more than a few months. Between the labor, the abuse, and the food, I'd say that the coming of winter solstice should see him dead."

"That can't happen."

The nondescript man scratched his leathery cheek. "I never did understand this whole business anyway, Markham. If one little urchin is important, why in the hells didn't we pull him out of the slums long ago?"

Markham was a fat trader who made his living buying and selling goods brought into Greyhawk from foreign parts. He didn't really care about politics or meddling in affairs of states and governments. Matters of tariffs and taxation interested him, as did profits and costs.

Still, the obese trader had some other concerns. He was an agent for an association that covered the whole of Oerik, from the Flanaess to the distant West. Markham was a small cog in a complex organization that sought to keep the balance between Evil and Good while promoting the status of the neutral group that viewed all as a necessary part of existence. If the trader was a small cog, then the shabby-appearing Tapper, to whom he spoke, was a mere tooth on the gear.

"Who can say, Tapper? I don't make the decisions, I just carry out the directions given to me. Now I'll give you yours."

It paid to listen and follow instructions. Markham got cash from someplace and passed it on to Tapper and others. Tapper was one who believed in balance, of course, but he believed in seeing to himself first, too. The coins were worthwhile, and the strength of the group was persuasive too. Although the group didn't flaunt its power, incurring the enmity of the shadowy organization would mean trouble indeed. Tapper knew that his life wouldn't be worth a drab if he crossed Markham. Still, after hearing just the beginning of his instructions, he couldn't help being frank about his reservations.

"No matter what, I can't manage to get the little bugger out of the workhouse — not without arousing a whole lot of suspicion!"

"Relax," Markham said. "Neither you nor I will be required to do anything stupid or dangerous. You just have your friend at the prison keep an eye on the kid . . . Gord, is that his name? Be sure that he isn't worse off than any of the rest of the lot there. Sooner or later an opportunity to get him out of there might come; then your associate is to see to it that the boy gets it."

"Gord's the name all right, Markham," the nondescript man said. "Sharp Clyde is my contact there. The warden doesn't realize he's a member of the

Thieves' Guild, and the guild doesn't know he's an agent of the Balance."

The fat trader knew everyone who worked for Tapper, whether or not they were dedicated members of the organization or knew not a whit about the Balance and merely performed small services for the money paid to them. Markham was careful and thorough, and kept tabs on everything. That's why there was a lot more to the fat man than met the eye. "Right, then — look up Sharp Clyde now, and give him the word."

"That alone isn't going to guarantee that the boy survives."

"I know that," Markham said with a sigh. "My instructions are to give the lad whatever help can be given without revealing it is being given." Whatever those who run things were thinking, Markham didn't know, but his own orders could be interpreted, on the surface, in only one way: The organization's interest in the boy was not to be exposed, even if refraining from this meant that he might not survive. When Markham tried to reason one step deeper, he ran into speculation and uncertainty. It seemed that whatever value was placed on the orphan, it was only marginal, and not worth risking the organization in any way. Or possibly, the reason that no attention must be focused on the boy could be that his value to the organization was actually much greater than Markham could perceive. That made for a whole different set of probabilities. . . .

"Just a moment, Tapper, I want to read something again." Markham pulled out a small sheet of thin paper, unfolded it, and read the tiny markings on its surface again, very carefully this time:

"The loop of fate may pin some small part
of our web squarely on this urchin's dirty
collar. Then again, he might stem from those

who seek to disturb the scale, tip it a bit one
way or another. Watch for him, assist without being evident, but do not actively interfere. His value is uncertain, and better to lose
him than imperil us in any way."

Markham decided to share his information with
Tapper. "Here, take a look at this and see if you notice anything."

Tapper took the letter and peered intently at it for
a long time. His lips moved as he went over the passage a second time.

". . . loop . . . pin . . . web, that's it!" Tapper looked
at the fat trader with a grin of pride. "The parts of a
key are named in the first two sentences, Markham!
See? Loop, stem, collar, pin, web — that's even
named twice, 'cause bit is another name for the web
part of a key. Hells, I make enough of 'em myself!"

"Very perceptive, Tapper, very perceptive indeed!"
Markham looked at the semi-retired thief with new
respect. Tapper was still a member of the Thieves'
Guild — one big reason why he was so valuable an
operative. The guild allowed him to be semi-retired
because he operated a locksmith shop. Only the few
who ruled the guild knew that Tapper was a still-
active part of the organization. In fact, most thieves
had no idea that the man had ever been a fellow of
theirs. "I'll take that piece of paper back now," said
Markham with a smile, "and here's a lucky for your
work."

The coin spun through the air, and Tapper
plucked it from space with an easy move of his hand.
"Thanks, Markham," the thief replied as he handed
over the paper, regaining his composure but finding it
hard to suppress his pride and excitement. "I'll inform Clyde to keep an eye on the kid." Tapper had a
clear idea that Markham's masters were in fact taking special notice of the urchin boy Gord, notice be-

yond what either of them had perceived before Tapper discovered the hidden message.

"Do more than that, Tapper," said Markham with new vigor in his voice. "Tell Clyde that there's a lucky in it for him, too, if he gets the boy out of the workhouse without attracting attention. Wait a minute," the fat trader added as Tapper started to leave. "Perhaps I should speak to Clyde myself. You two meet me at the Four Pots tonight."

"About nine," Tapper said as he left. He knew the little tavern well, and knew that Sharp Clyde would have no objections to going there either, for it was out of the way and safe for meetings of this nature, since thieves seldom went to it.

When the nondescript Tapper had gone, Markham took the note and burned it, then broke up the ash into powder.

Finding the parts of a key in the message told Markham all he needed to know. No matter what the note seemed to say, the boy was very, very important to the Balance. Of course, this fact could not be conveyed directly in writing, in case the paper intended for Markham found its way into the wrong hands. But it was now obvious that, for some reason, the skinny little urchin from Old City's slums was thought to be so vital that no hint of his importance must be revealed even if the boy's life was at risk.

Markham knew that his duty was to do everything possible, short of revealing the organization's interest in him, to get Gord out of the workhouse and located elsewhere, preferably in a place where he could be overseen and would not be so vulnerable to other sorts of outside influences and threats. No, that last was too much of an assumption. . . . Markham decided that before the meeting tonight, he would seek more detailed instructions as to just what he should do in this matter. Cursing himself for not having deciphered the message without Tapper's help, the fat trader hurried out to atone for his stupidity.

* * *

"I've made a small fortune this day, barkeep! Ale or wine for all of these good patrons gathered round the bar, and for yourself too!"

The stolid proprietor of the Four Pots nodded and touched his forelock in thanks and respect. "Thanks, Trader Markham. Right happy to hear you've done well . . . as are the fine souls here who will be glad to drink to your health and prosperity — right, lads?"

"Aye!" came a chorus from the seven or eight others in the immediate area. "To your health and fortune, trader!" they added, quaffing the drinks that the tavernkeeper hastened to deliver to them.

Markham beamed, swigged a good portion of his dark beer, and casually looked around the place. He noticed two men sitting at a back table idly playing a game of plaques. The fat trader ambled over to the pair and watched the play for a minute. "May I join the game?" he asked amiably.

"Why not, friend?" one of the men said, barely glancing up from his study of the tableau on the stained wood. "We can use some fresh coin."

"Barman! A round for me and these two here. They'll soon be making me richer still, and I'll want them happily oiled before that."

Nobody in the place paid any attention to the three gamers thereafter. Markham was well known as a drab-pincher. Although his largess tonight must mean he had indeed managed to cheat some unfortunate customer out of much silver, he'd never spend that much on drink nor lose it in a game of chance. The plaques game would involve nothing more than brass and bronze coins, perhaps a copper in a big

118

pot. Watching such a contest was about as exciting as viewing the wet rings on the table as they were slowly absorbed by the wood and dried away by the air. For all the other patrons were concerned, Markham and the other two didn't exist after the first flurry of excitement.

"Two zees on that one!" The fat trader said this loud enough for anyone nearby to hear. Then, under his breath, he added, "The lad has promise if we can train him. Can you manage to get him out?"

"And another!" Clyde cried out in the same loud tone as he tossed three bronze coins onto the table in answer to Markham's bet. "In time, I am sure of it," he said softly.

Quietly, Markham said, "Do so, and you've earned a lucky." Then, loudly, looking at Tapper, "And what about you, friend?"

"I'll match the three zees, never fear!" Tapper replied, then whispered, "What's the boy to be trained as, a thief?"

"Can't be done," Clyde said in a hushed voice. "He has to be sponsored, and that'd attract attention." He revealed his plaques then, and the three talked loudly about it, for he had won the hand. Between plays, however, the undertone of conversation progressed. Clyde was to get the boy apprenticed to the Beggars' Union. That was the best prospect any of them could come up with.

"Enough!" Markham rose with a sour look. "You two have managed to reduce my profits to nothing in the space of an hour. I'm for home and bed, a poorer and sadder man."

"Bah," Tapper said, looking at the coins in front of him. "You lost but a copper or two in total."

"I'm an honest trader, not some rich noble. Besides, I swear I'm down twice that sum," the fat man said as he stumped from the tavern. Several of the customers laughed at his display, but Markham didn't mind. All had occurred as he'd hoped. Tapper and Clyde thought that they had determined the course of apprentice beggar for the boy. All the while, however, Markham had steered them to it — as instructed by the man he took orders from, the learned sage . . .

. . . No. He mustn't even think of that name. In any event, it was out of his hands now. Sharp Clyde would manage things from here on. If he succeeded, then another would take over. Who that was, even Markham didn't know. It was enough that his part had gone smoothly and as planned.

Tapper and Clyde spent a little more time and money at the Four Pots so as not to arouse suspicion. The place was frequented mostly by laborers and the common workers from the brewery nearby, but there was no harm in avoiding unnecessary risks. One could never be certain who was a spy, an informant, or the like.

"I cursed my assignment to the workhouse," Clyde said quietly to Tapper. "Now it seems lucky indeed that I pissed off the captain and got the Old Citadel assignment as punishment."

"Not much there in the way of income for a thief, though," Tapper observed.

Clyde grinned. "I thought so at first, but there are plenty of coins to be picked up — bribes for adjusting the work schedule, bribes from the better-off inmates for special treatment, and good money for selling off prisoners."

"Selling prisoners?"

"Sure. Change identities with some corpse due for discharge soon, or a falsified death sometimes. Then the former prisoner can be sold into indenture. Of course," Clyde added thoughtfully, "it's more profitable to have a long-termer buy freedom that way, but not many with that much money need to use such means to escape."

The nondescript locksmith looked at his associate with new admiration. "So you'll sell the kid as an indentured servant, take Markham's coin too, and be paid as a guard in the bargain!"

"None of which will make me a wealthy man, Tapper," the thief said as he nodded agreement. "I still need to get out and about in order to make ends meet." He referred to his trade, naturally.

Tapper, older and less interested in carousing, managed quite well on his fees for services from the Balance to augment the income from his trade and kickbacks from thieves. He understood what Clyde remarked on, though. High living in Old City cost plenty. If it was done in New Town, it was even more expensive. "It's hard to keep a full purse," Tapper agreed.

"True, friend, in more ways than one . . . when I'm about," Clyde said with a wink.

Laughing together, the two then departed the tavern. Tapper headed toward the secret thieves' portal that would enable him to return to his place in the Foreign Quarter, and Clyde turned north to go back to the prison where he was barracked.

Next morning Clyde made a point of finding out where the boy was. Gord was the kid's name, and he was a skinny, weak-looking little urchin. His group was a mixed lot of weaklings, children, and the aged. They were quartered together in a common cell and taken out six days of the week to work off their crimes against the city and its honest citizens. Their assignments were fairly light ones, considering they were being punished. Toil was the lot of the poor anyway, and what the gang of criminals had to do each day was no more strenuous than what many free persons had to manage. Of course, they did get the dirtiest and most dangerous work, but that could be expected as well.

Clyde found out that Gord had been on the workhouse roll for only five days. "They certainly are keeping close tabs on this one, and acting fast," he murmured to himself, thinking that he had good cause to ask for more than a hundred zees for getting the lad out. He'd demand two luckies for the accomplishment, twice the sum promised, and expected he'd get it, too.

It was just after sunup, so Clyde headed for the prisoners' section of the massive old fortress. He wanted to get another first-hand look at the boy as he was marched off to work. Tomorrow was a day of rest for the prisoners, an opportunity for Clyde to pull the lad out of the cell and get him away. No really careful body count was kept, so it would be easy to forge a document saying that the child prisoner known as Gord of the Slum Quarter of Old City had died accidentally while serving his term of imprisonment.

Clyde was in for a surprise.

He arrived in time to see that the lad had taken things into his own hands, so to speak, by using what meager means he could devise to make himself appear stricken with some sort of contagious plague. The trick was one that any good thief or accomplished beggar would see through immediately, just as Clyde did. However, the stupid clods who were the regular guards at the prison were completely fooled.

"Now that's very clever and considerate," Clyde thought to himself. "He's saved me a lot of work and taken away the risk, too!"

Clyde got the "body" out, and the records of the workhouse showed Gord dead of disease, type unknown. In reality the boy was indentured, just as his secret benefactor, Markham, had instructed. The fat trader was glad when he heard the news from Clyde (although he already knew the truth from his other sources), but not quite so elated when he heard what followed.

"You expect twice the pay I promised?" Markham asked with a tinge of angry incredulity in his voice, repeating the request so as to give his irritation a chance to die down.

Clyde smiled serenely. "Yes, Markham, I do expect just that."

The fat trader paid, grumbling loudly, but was actually very satisfied inside. It was a cheap price to pay for the lad's safety. Safety? Well, more like a better chance of survival. Markham knew well the master of beggars in Greyhawk, and the fat trader also was aware of the clandestine thieving activities of the group. One of the trusted masters of the place was also one of Markham's agents.

Theobald's ascension from leadership of the Beggars' Guild to the head position of the recently formed Beggars' Union made the already egotistical man full of hubris. Obscenely fat, lazy, and a dangerous psychotic, the Beggarmaster was not one to trust or cross. Now the guild of beggars had allied itself with peddlers, tinkers, actors, and similar riffraff to form the Beggars' Union, and Theobald sat haughtily atop the entire organization.

It was an odd association, but one that actually worked. The beggars brought goods they found, expropriated, or were given and dispensed them to peddlers for sale, or to tinkers to repair and then sell. They also traded with these groups for goods. Actors, the lowest of society save the beggars themselves, were paid to assist the latter in their performances on the streets, and when out of work the actors could then likewise earn a living with a bowl. Certain street gangs were also brought into the association, as were wandering folk and traveling entertainers.

Theobald had forged the union in order to increase his own power, of course. It combined all of the elements that the Thieves' Guild disdained. The gross master of beggars hated the thieves, for they had both respect and wealth. Theobald was bent on gaining both as well, and at the expense of the more prestigious guild of thieves.

Chinkers was as skillful a beggar as any in Greyhawk. In the process of perfecting his art, Chinkers had learned petty thievery and the craft of convincing others to become part of a scheme that resulted in their being fleeced. Certain thieves would employ him as an assistant, a cloyer to enable them to pick pockets or cut purses more easily. These fellows taught Chinkers more skills. Soon the beggar could sham merchandise, switching real for fake or actually making the shoddy seem otherwise. He could counterfeit coins, forge, and cheat at games such as dice and plaques. Why, thereafter, he still chose to practice begging as well, even Chinkers couldn't say, but he did.

Then Theobald decided to displace the thieves of the city with his own beggars, found willing teachers, and began to arrange instruction for his most trusted minions. Chinkers was one of those trusted souls, and in a short time there were a half-dozen trained beggars able to perform as well as any cutpurse or robber belonging to the Thieves' Guild, with Chinkers better than the rest.

One day soon thereafter, the three outlaw thieves who had agreed to take the treasured gold orbs of the Beggarmaster in return for teaching his lieutenants the craft of thievery were invited to a banquet in Theobald's own quarters.

"Chinkers, Furgo, Jenk!" It was the squeaky voice of Theobald summoning them to him next morning. They hurried to him at once. "Our dear friends are no

124

longer with us," the gross beggarmaster told them blandly.

"You mean they ran off?"

"Of course not, Jenk. Don't be a bigger dolt than you are! We all supped together last evening. I think some vile assassin must have made an attempt on my life."

"No!" The three lieutenants chorused disbelief at that.

"But yes," Theobald retorted without force, his fat face still emotionless, jowls hanging placidly. "Fortunately, I had no taste for the wild mushrooms grown in our own cellar by Bellytimber Jane, so I passed the dish. The three instructors loved them — devoured the lot. When you have finished disposing of them — the old cistern will do nicely, I think — bring the cook to me."

"Jane wouldn't try to poison you, Theo—"

The greasy visage of the Beggarmaster instantly grew livid. "Never contradict me!" he screamed at Furgo, making the one-eyed man flinch. "Now get on with it, and make certain nobody knows about it, either. If anyone dares to inquire, you say the three simply moved on to some new city where the pickings were thought to be easier."

Chinkers and Jenk managed to dispose of the stiff corpses of the dead thieves, and Furgo went off and brought Bellytimber Jane to her audience with Theobald. Chinkers made a point of eavesdropping from a place in the cellar where he could hear what went on above.

"Furgo seemed very nervous, Theo," he heard the voice of the cook say clearly.

There was a high-pitched titter from Theobald. "Three stiff bodies are sufficient to make most men a trifle edgy."

"I made the whole batch just as you ordered,"

Jane said slowly, "and those three will never be able to tell now. Are you pleased?"

"Of course, Jane, my dear cook and assassin. It turned out just as I had planned. But . . ."

"But?" Bellytimber Jane's voice sounded strained. "What else am I to do?"

"Come here, my dear, and I shall whisper it in your ear." Chinkers envisioned the woman approaching Theobald. She was youngish and rather plain, but she fancied herself a favorite of the beggarmaster. Suddenly a shriek sounded, but it was cut off almost immediately. He could hear a hammering sound accompanied by the high-pitched giggle of Theobald. After a minute or two all of the noise stopped, and then there was a thud.

The beggar made haste to leave the cellar then, for Chinkers had no wish to be discovered spying on Theobald — especially not now!

What happened to Jane's body he could not guess. Theobald had taken care of that himself. Chinkers never said a word about it to anyone in the place, and the beggarmaster never spoke of the cook again except to say, "Find me a new chef, Furgo. Our old one is no longer with us." Furgo asked no questions, either. Next day Bald Jim was made official cook. Soon his nickname was changed to Batcrap in honor of his cuisine, but despite the man's seeming ineptness at preparing meals for the inmates of the place, Theobald seemed satisfied with the decision. Chinkers, and others, supposed that this was because the beggarmaster ate different fare from what they were forced to settle for.

Because Chinkers believed strongly in certain things, the beggar-thief served as an agent for the Balance. Everything that went on in the Beggars' Guild, and the Beggars' Union thereafter, was noted and duly reported to Markham. When the news of the boy arriving as an apprentice was transmitted to him, Chinkers was pleased that he had been selected the safest bet for the child's survival.

"I won't actually work with him myself," he assured the trader. "I'll see to it that those who do are the best, though, and that young Gord is treated fairly. That'll be hard, with that monstrous bastard to contend with, but I'll manage."

Markham was confident he would, and Chinkers did.

Chapter 9

MOST OF THOSE WHO PURSUE BEGGING as a vo-
cation are lean. Certain devotees of deities that allow
the asking of alms by begging can be robust and
rotund. But poor and hopeless individuals, or those
seeking to give that appearance, are not well-fed
monks or devotees. They are thin, starved-looking.

Chinkers was neither of these things. That is, the
fellow was plump even though he was not a religious
man but a master beggar. He sat now at the Silver
Shield, an inn typical of those that bordered the
street dividing the Beggars Quarter from the Thieves
Quarter as it wound its way to New Town.

"And a bumper of ale for the mendicant cleric
there!" A roar of laughter and many jibes were directed at the robed figure — none other than Chinkers, in
the grimy attire of a wandering priest of Fharlanghn.

"Perhaps a bit or two for the good work as well?"
The suggestion was made so piously, and with alms
bowl so politely extended, that anyone who did not
know the brown-robed man would have thought he
was earnestly begging contributions for his deity. Of
course, begging was indeed his trade, although as far
as anyone familiar with him knew, the fruits of his
religiously sought donations went only into his purse,
with the requisite share to the beggarmaster and
various barkeeps.

There were more rude jests and roars of mirth at this. "Here's a drab, but I expects a special blessin' fer it!" The bawd who said that then thrust out her rump suggestively.

"You are amply blessed already!" Chinkers said, giving her a loud whack. "Be off now, or there will certainly be lightning gathering above."

The beggar-cleric quaffed his newly come tankard while the latest round of laughter ran its course, and then he rose. "I have more of the good work to do yet this night," he announced. Then he headed for Theobald's massive headquarters.

It was a fair hike from the Silver Shield to the central place where the newly created union had its headquarters, but no one he encountered along the way troubled Chinkers. This was the Beggars Quarter, and he was a prince among the folk dwelling here. In fact, a fair number of thieves and various sorts of other scallywags frequented the tavern he had come from, and all knew Chinkers well. He was one of the few of his kind who dared to pose as a clerical beggar or some sort of otherwise sanctioned raiser of donations and get away with it successfully for years. Thus, Chinkers could be plump and remarkably different from the vast majority of his ilk.

For a beggar, Chinkers was both renowned and respected. A good part of that status came from the fact that the Thieves' Guild officially sanctioned his activities. Even though he was not a member of that group, Chinkers occasionally had to pay it a tithe too because his activity was of that class of operation that was normally performed by a member of that guild. As additional compensation for his unofficial license to "steal," he fed information to Arentol, the master of the Thieves' Guild.

It was a dangerous game, but Chinkers enjoyed it. He spied on both beggars and thieves on behalf of the

Balance. Now he was involved in yet more duplicity, for there was young master Gord to see to as well — and beggarmaster, thieves, and boy were all to be kept totally unaware of what was going on. That was a challenge.

"Top of the night to you, Emmit," Chinkers murmured as he passed the hidden sentry guarding the rear entrance of the old building. "Get on with ya," the fellow replied just as softly, moving to the side of the narrow door but not coming out of his shadowed alcove.

Chinkers entered and went directly to the narrow stairway nearby. He managed to climb the steps without a sound, despite his bulk and the decrepit condition of the wooden construction. He and a score of the masters who served the Beggars' Union had quarters on the second floor.

Just as Chinkers did, each of the other masters knew well the craft of thievery. Unlike the normal thieves of Greyhawk, though, the beggar-thieves performed almost exclusively in broad daylight, the normal time of day when beggars ply their trade. The vast majority of their illicit thievery was performed when the sun was above, while the reverse was true for those serving Grand Guildmaster Arentol, who only robbed and stole with full sanction of the city's governing officials. Thus, Chinkers could go to sleep each night without worry. The newly apprenticed Gord would be locked up fast until dawn.

The boy had been with them only about three months now. At first Chinkers had thought him hopeless; why anyone involved in the Balance should concern himself about such an urchin seemed inconceivable to the plump beggar. Gord cringed at the sight of Theobald, but that wasn't the way he behaved at other times. Chinkers soon saw the significant difference in Gord's makeup. The boy wished to

131

excel, to prove himself better than, not just as good as, any of the other apprentices being trained.

"Here, you!" Chinkers had called to the lad one day after observing him for some time. The boy had looked at Chinkers uncertainly, so he reinforced the command. "That's right, you. Come with me. I have a special drill for you."

Gord had gone along without comment, and when they were alone Chinkers had grilled him on his past, what he thought of the present, and where the lad thought he would go in the future. That had been only a few weeks into the training. Then and there, Chinkers had been suddenly aware of the involvement of powers greater than he. The facts of Gord's previous existence in the slums, his adaptation to life in the headquarters and the rigorous discipline and training, and the carefully veiled, evasive answers Chinkers received regarding the future the lad saw amazed the master beggar. Here was one to keep an eye on indeed.

Just months later, Gord had proved exactly what Chinkers had suspected. He was far and away the brightest pupil any of the masters had ever seen. The skinny boy, weak from deprivation and hunger, had turned into a lean little powerhouse, full of questions, brimming with energy and enthusiasm — all masked, naturally, so as to protect himself. The others who served in Theobald's cadre suspected the true measure of the boy. Chinkers was very certain of it.

It was all he could do not to take a direct hand in the boy's training. Somehow Chinkers resisted the urge. He kept back and even glowered at Gord now and then so that the lad would not suspect he had the favor that Chinkers was determined to employ on his behalf. It was also difficult to fool Theobald. The vile beggarmaster was none too fond of Chinkers anyway, for the beggar-thief was plump. That was the mark of an exceptional beggar. Perhaps that was the reason why Theobald had originally become fat. It applied no longer, of course. He was gross and obese and thoroughly given over to his appetites. Still, it did provide a remarkable contrast between master and beggar, save in a case such as Chinkers, where the contrast was not so extreme.

"What do you think of that skinny urchin I purchased, Chinkers?" the gross man asked.

He looked at Theobald and shrugged. "I see him at his work with the other apprentices, Beggarmaster Theobald. As you know, I work only with the journeymen these days, but it seems that the boy . . . Gord, is it? . . . shows occasional bursts of rebelliousness. I'd watch that, were I his master."

"Hmm. . . . A point which Furgo himself has mentioned. One-eye says the boy is quite superior to the rest, however. I told him to work or beat the rebelliousness out of him — or I would do so, with pleasure!" Theobald laughed at his own joke, and Chinkers had to smile as if he enjoyed it, too.

"Should the little upstart ever gain journeyman status, master, rest assured I'll see to his discipline."

"You are a good servant, Chinkers, despite your airs," Theobald said then with a secret smile. "Your peculiarity won't be so notable soon, and then perhaps you and I will become better acquainted once again." He paused and stared into space for a minute, during which time Chinkers imagined Theobald was envisioning his soon-to-be-realized empire of beggar-thieves and a position high in the ruling oligarchy of Greyhawk. Then the Beggarmaster dismissed him, saying, "Don't concern yourself with the apprentice boy, Gord. Furgo and the other masters who have him tell me he will not be a journeyman at beggary."

That remark puzzled Chinkers all evening and into the night, the time when he usually forgot all concerns as he enjoyed drink and the companionship of other lowly rogues at the Silver Shield. First thing in the morning, he meant to get Jenk or Halfway aside and see if he could discover what was afoot. Surely they didn't mean to drop Gord from his training! Then sleep overtook the master beggar's thoughts, and Chinkers worried no more for the night.

* * *

"More of that tea, Batcrap," Chinkers said as he broke fast with several of the other masters. "What were you saying about the apprentices, Jenk?"

The latter had his mouth stuffed with bread crusts soaked in stale beer, so Halfway filled in for him. "The latest lot is 'bout average, save for three or four."

"Then I'll be expecting those three or four soon for advanced work, I suppose."

"Nope," supplied Foxy Lon. "Furgo tol' me all but one will be needin' another few weeks o' hard work afore he sends 'em on t'you."

Jenk was about to say more, but Furgo himself appeared in the cellar kitchen and sat down. "Talking about the new crop?"

"Yeah, Chinkers wants to know how many to expect and when," Jenk informed the one-eyed beggar-thief. "Lon just told him not to worry for a bit."

"Who are you drumming out?"

"Drumming out?" Jenk shook his head at that. "Did I say that?"

Furgo was readying to eat, but he took a minute to explain. "That little one, Gord — he's a real find for us. Never seen anyone take to either trade, begging or stealing, so well as him. A duck to water, and that's a certainty. I've put it to the rest here, and we're all agreed. It's up to the master in the end, but the six of us who train apprentices all say that Gord should be promoted right on up to master as soon as possible. With what's going on now, we could use an army of lads like that one!"

The pockmarked face of Halfway was serious. He saw Chinkers take on a concerned look and mistook the expression for doubt. "I know that's unheard of, Chinkers, but we all agree with Furgo . . . even if he only can see half what we can!" Furgo was too busy with his breakfast to bother replying to the needling, so Halfway continued. "The boy is a whiz at things. Works his skinny little ass off to be the best at whatever we give him to do. You won't be able to believe it until you see him in action."

"I'll do just that and then let you know," the stout beggar said as he slid off the bench and headed upstairs. "Next time you take him on an outing, tell me beforehand."

"Right."

And soon enough the opportunity came.

For the next week or two, in fact, Chinkers made a point of observing Gord as he plied his trade, but being careful not to let the boy know he was under such scrutiny. Even Chinkers was surprised. Had he not known the boy, and been looking for him in a disguise as well, the master beggar-thief would never have recognized him.

The first time Gord was a one-legged cripple whose tale of woe was sufficient to cause an iron-bearded dwarf to part with a bronze coin. On the next outing he was a drooling half-wit — a fairly common sight, and one not likely to gain more than a few iron and brass coins for a whole day's effort. But Chinkers was surprised to see that even while Gord was feigning idiocy, the boy was busily filching coins from the unwary. The lad was an excellent pickpocket, and the disguise made marks less conscious of the possibility of being had by a thief.

The third and last time Chinkers saw Gord in operation was the best of all.

Gord was obviously in charge of a squad of beggar-boys and girls who were probably meant to operate as a group to surround and harangue likely-looking folks. Sheer weight of numbers and the impact of the all-too-evident misery of so many hapless children was meant to melt the hearts of otherwise stolid individuals. It was a tried and true means, but it took careful control so as not to underwork or overdo it. The lad got the hang of it quickly after a few trial-and-error runs at passersby going through the Foreign Quarter. Then Gord worked the gang for several hours to near perfection. During one episode, however, Chinkers suddenly lost track of him.

"Now where has he gone off to?" he muttered, seeing all of the apprentices but Gord break from their whining, pleading knot surrounding a trio of well-equipped outlanders, their actions indicating that the three men had broken down and tossed them coins.

A flinty-eyed merchant came into view, leading a mule-drawn cart whose cargo was secured under a sheet of canvas. Chinkers noticed that the two biggest of the lot, a gawky, stringy-haired girl and an even uglier boy, were watching a narrow alley nearby. Suddenly they rejoined the other children and rushed off in a pack toward the merchant. He was as unlikely a mark as any the pudgy expert could think of. Nonetheless, the band of urchins quickly crowded around him and began their begging. The hard-faced fellow simply ignored them at first. They persisted. He then cursed the lot soundly. The flock of filthy beggar-children was undaunted. This infuriated the merchant, and he began to berate them in earnest as he struck out with fists and feet to teach these guttersnipes a lesson.

"Eat shit!" the gawky girl cried, picking up a lump

of horse dung and hurling it at the man. It was a well-aimed shot.

The merchant had a short, heavy whip, and he began to lay about him with that instrument. The urchins howled plaintively when struck, but those out of range threw more filth at the raging man. He was incautious with his whip and struck a passerby, who promptly punched the fellow. At this point a full-scale brawl erupted, with an eventual chase of the beggar-children as its climax. During the confusion, Chinkers was almost too distracted to keep watching for Gord — almost. But the man was, after all, a master in all respects of begging and thievery, so he spotted the boy just as Gord was setting knife to canvas at the back end of the cart.

With uncanny speed and deftness, especially for one so young, Gord slashed, grabbed, loaded the loot into a sack, and faded away at a casual stroll down the street without a backward glance. Best of all, Gord was no longer in the filthy attire of a beggar. Chinkers saw what appeared to be a typical apprentice boy of the lower class toting a heavy burden on some errand.

It was robbery, pure and simple. Beggars were involved, but no witness would incriminate them in any reported loss of goods. Anyone could have decided to take the foolish merchant's goods. To chase after urchins and brawl in the streets is to ask for loss, and no sensible man would do it. In Old City, everyone was a potential thief. Protect yourself and your property at all times: that was the axiom of survival here, and all knew it.

"Did you hear about it?" Squiddle asked excitedly when Chinkers entered. Before he could reply, the old fellow went on. "That apprentice, Gord. He came back here with a haul which would have made the master of thieves proud. He's a lad to watch, all right!"

"Is that so?" said Chinkers dryly as he pushed past the man.

Not a month later there was a minor fete in progress for the newest master cadger and thief of the union, Least Master Gord. Not a few of the others at the celebration, especially the others the lad's rank, and some of the Associate Masters as well, were displeased or jealous of one not yet fully grown being elevated to the status of master of thiggery and expert thief, the agreed-to ranking of a Least Master of Theobald's new union.

That brought up something else that bothered some of the members. They were proud of being beggars, and they knew that soon the gross beggarmaster would disdain that name. He favored cadger or thigger over beggar, and when he became head of thieves in the city, Theobald would certainly wish himself to be called something like Archmaster of Thieves and Thiggers. Such was the gossip at the party.

Chinkers talked with Gord, congratulating him in a reserved way that was genuine because the man would now never have a chance to supervise the lad personally. Gord affected great happiness, but inside he felt something else — a sort of vague anticipation tinged with uneasiness and dread. Chinkers couldn't determine what was on the boy's mind, but considering Gord's aptitude, the plump beggar was certain that all of his talents and desires would come out soon enough and surprise them all.

In a few weeks' time thereafter a great war between the thieves and the beggars commenced, and Chinkers lost track of the boy during this uproar.

Chapter 10

DILLOR WAS A RIVER RAT — a nasty scavenger who lurked along the banks of the Selintan, looking for anything worth taking. Greyhawk was built on hills and ridges, just as most cities of its sort were. The various drains that lay beneath the place eventually ran down into the waterways that virtually surrounded the walled city. Some few drained into Bubbly Mire and the Grey Run, but most came out on the western side of the city. Dillor haunted these places, searching through the various effluences for valuables. It was a filthy and vile existence, but it kept Dillor alive, and he didn't actually mind the work at all.

"That's gold!" he exclaimed aloud as he peered into the mouth of a broad drain. The illumination was dim inside, but the setting sun glinted off something yellow and shiny. The drain was barred, of course, but the object was just on the other side of the great metal poles that prevented entrance beneath the city. "Dillor, you've finally struck it rich!" he babbled, clambering through the shallow outflow and debris to get to the object.

After using his hooked pole to drive off a half-dozen rats and get right up to the outside of the bars, Dillor saw that the glittering object was indeed a piece of gold — and it was set with a gem, too. It was on the bony finger of a partially eaten corpse. Nearly eaten, more like it, and soon to be finished by rats, beetles, and the rest, but not before Dillor jerked free a skeletal digit and the ring attached to it. He snared the golden object with the hook on the end of his pole, thrust the ring onto his own dirty finger, and set off quickly to find a buyer.

He couldn't know that the bit of jewelry he now sported had recently been in the possession of a hired killer who had taken it from the corpse of yet another assassin. Because its most recent former owner had no need of immediate cash, he had kept it for quite some time and on occasion sported it on his hand, even though it fit his finger rather loosely. He had been in the process of escaping from a botched assassination attempt while wearing it. In his haste to flee, the wearer had tried to push the ring farther back onto his finger as it began to slip off. His attention divided, the fellow had slipped and fallen. His head struck a corner of the ledge above the subterranean duct he had just climbed down into, and that was enough to cause his drowning. That incident had happened but two days before.

"What's this worth to ya?" Dillor asked the Rhennee bargeman.

The dark-skinned water-gypsy whistled in surprise at what he saw. "Where'd you get that, Dild?"

He hated to be called that. Dild was a contraction of his nickname, and Dillor didn't like it at all. "Call me Dillor! That's my name, and you'll call me that if you want to buy the ring from me!"

"Sure, sure, Dild . . . Dillor, I mean. Come on ze barge, an' we'll talk."

Eventually they agreed that the Rhennee would give him five hundred zees for it, payment to be made in copper commons and silver nobles. Dillor knew that having coins of greater value, such as luckies, would not only attract unwanted attention to him but also be hard to change in the places he meant to frequent shortly.

"Done," the Rhennee said with a grin. The dark man rummaged around in a low cabinet and drew out a box. It was filled with an assortment of money — bronze, copper, and a sprinkling of silver. "I got only five nobles, so you'll have to take the rest in commons, Dild. Got a bag to load 'em een?"

The dirty gypsy had dared to call him that again. Suddenly it struck Dillor that he could have even more than five hundred. He could have both the ring and more money than that easily. He and the river-man were alone. . . .

"Ah, yeah. Sure thing, Streebul. I got a poke here," he said, reaching inside his filthy jerkin.

Dillor was not very smart, and he telegraphed his intention to the wise and wary Rhennee even before his fingers had closed around the worn haft of the heavy, broad-bladed knife he kept hidden inside his clothing. Streebul was on his feet in an instant, his own dagger out and in motion even as the clumsy river rat dragged his own blade out in his "surprise" move. Dillor was stabbed twice before he even knew it. "You eediot!" the gypsy bargeman hissed. "Don't you know you're a dead man?"

The thick blade struck wildly, cutting Streebul's cheek. "Yaagh!" was all Dillor could manage to say. Then he groaned and grunted as the bargeman's dirk went home again and yet again. Those were the last sounds that Dillor ever made.

"Well," Streebul said as he wiped the cut on his cheek with a rag, "Dildo, you always were a poor one at bargaining." At that the bargeman laughed wildly. "Giving a lousy life for a leetle cut ain't half bad, but you threw in the reeng to boot!"

A few months later Streebul was killed by a wag-on-gypsy. They were arguing over whether the Rhennee or the Attloi were the true folk, and the bargeman was too slow with his weapon. Naturally, the victorious Attloi gypsy took the gold ring set with its precious stone as part of the rightful spoils of his victory.

The new owner of the ring made it all the way to central Urnst before a group of particularly fierce brigands attacked the train of wagons he was with. A pitched battle was fought, and the Attloi made the raiders pay dearly. In the end, however, all the gypsies were either killed or carried off as slaves. The captain of the outlaw band took the ring as part of his share of the spoils.

"Why'n hells name we heddin' norf?"

"Shut yer flappin' lips, Dogteeth," Renfil Leed said without bothering to look at his lieutenant. Even that fool should be able to tell when things were too hot for them. "The duke's horsemen are after us, and I'm goin' to head for quieter places and easier pickin's."

There was no argument, of course. The captain was too tough, too mean to contest with — at least for now. He brought Dogteeth and his troop of seventy or eighty bandits through border provinces and wild lands in a long sweep that went through parts of both the Duchy and County of Urnst, then along the contested strip that ran between the Pale, Nyrond, and County Urnst. From there it was an easy swing into the safety of the Bandit Kingdoms, where the brigands could rest and their leader could plan fresh forays.

Disaster struck when the company was raiding in the Shield Lands. Leed and his surviving men were forced to flee westward, and a tribe of humanoids ambushed them there. The humans were eaten and their possessions either discarded or used to adorn the trappings of the great goblins that had killed and eaten the bandits who had previously possessed the articles. A heavy ring of gold set with a strange green stone now decorated the braided sidelocks of the trib-al chieftain.

When the head of that humanoid monster was taken by a knight of Furyondy some time later, he salvaged the ring and took it for his own. Not long thereafter the warrior was bested in a joust with a knight errant who had challenged him. To redeem his armor, weapons, and steed, the Furyondian paid over all his other wealth, including the ring.

Eventually the wandering knight who now pos-sessed the gem-set ring took service with a marcher lord. Nothing untoward happened to him thereafter, although he did eventually lose the ring to a dwarf with whom he was gambling.

After roaming the mountains for a long period, the dwarf passed along the Kron Hills, heading eastward in search of a lost gold mine said to be there. He found the mine, but in his avarice, the dwarf entered the place incautiously. A great she-bear was denned therein, and she had two cubs to protect. The dwarf died quickly, and the bear devoured him, ring and all.

Hunters from the estate of a lord of Dyvers took the old brown bear when she came into their pre-serve. The animal had been driven there by swarms of humanoids who had moved into her territory and forced the bear away by their presence. The hunters shot her with arrows as the she-bear was held at bay by their hounds. One of these men discovered a ring lodged in the creature's stomach. After washing it clean, the fellow donned it happily, considering him-self a rich and lucky man.

The lord of the manor who employed him was not inclined toward mercy. When he caught the hunts-man dallying with his daughter, the noble had the unfortunate fellow hanged without ado. Not wishing to soil his hands, the lord told the executioner that whatever the criminal possessed was his by way of payment for his work. So, the executioner got the ring along with some other, petty items.

In time the executioner took service in Dyvers proper, since the officials there were offering a good stipend for a headsman and torturer. When the fellow was discovered taking bribes to free certain political prisoners, he was himself sent to the block. His ring was seized and placed in the city treasury.

A spy who had just returned from a particularly successful mission was allowed to take the ring as a bonus for his services. In due course the agent went to Greyhawk on behalf of the Lord Mayor's secret police, masquerading as an ally of that city. His true identity was discovered, and the Lord Mayor of Greyhawk hired the Assassins' Guild to deal with him. After all, it wouldn't do to have the city's own agents involved, for that breach of etiquette might precipitate serious difficulties between Dyvers and Greyhawk. Possessions found on the victim were always part of the payment for services rendered, so the assassin who did in the spy happily added the ring to his fee.

* * *

In this way, after a half-score years and several thousand miles of traveling, the ring had come full circle back to Greyhawk. Not one of the men or other creatures who had owned it in the meantime had ever found it worthwhile. To call the ring ill-omened was to be kind, only not one of those who gained it knew of its nature, for the previous owner wasn't around to inform the next, or else didn't actually know. It made no difference either way. Eladon the assassin would not have blenched even had he heard of the ring's history. He liked the stone's color and the way it appeared to wink in the right light.

In celebration of his success in disposing of the

spy from Dyvers, and because he had gained so valuable a jewel as he now wore on his finger, Eladon went on a drunk of considerable proportions. He ended up in a bawdyhouse at the end of the Strip, and being what she was, the whore he was with rolled him for his purse and other valuables, for the assassin was too far in his cups by then to resist. Unfortunately for her, she had taken the precaution of bringing along the valuables she had stolen rather than leaving them in the room where she obtained them. This turned out to be a mistake because Red Mel, the doxy's pimp, caught her trying to sneak the comatose form of Eladon from her crib to a place in the alley.

"Hey, ya stupid bitch! What are you up ta?" he hissed.

She dropped the fellow's limp legs and ceased trying to drag him along. "He passed out on me, and—"

Smack! Red Mel hit her hard on the side of the head. "Don't lie to me, not ever, else I'll give you a second mouth right where your windpipe is. Yer rollin' 'im, ain't ya?"

The doxy held her throbbing temple and nodded while her other hand went protectively to the sash at her hip.

"Hand it over," Red Mel ordered, and the woman did exactly as she was told, loosening the sash and then pulling the man's purse from where it had been hung on the cloth.

"Wow! You're one fine worker, Flos," he said with real admiration as he saw the stack of coins and the ring. Who could have such wealth? Red Mel rolled the drunken man over with his booted foot to get a better look at him. "Shit! This bird is a killer!"

"Whadda ya mean, Red, honey? . . ." The woman's voice trailed off as her victim suddenly sat up and stared bleary-eyed at her and her pimp.

"Whass goin' on here?" Eladon was beginning to

recover from his alcoholic stupor, adrenaline starting to surge through his system as he realized that something was very wrong. "You dirty—"

Red Mel used his heavy boot to shut the man up. He kicked him as hard as he could, and Eladon's head snapped back with a crack. Just to make certain, he felt for a pulse. The assassin was stone dead, his neck broken. "Now, woman," said Mel in an even tone, "help me get the body to the alley."

Flos complied without saying a word, glad that the pimp wasn't angry any more but worried about what would happen when the body of the assassin was found. "What'll I say if someone from his guild asks about him?" Her voice was nervous.

"That does it," Red Mel said, not bothering to answer her until he had pulled the corpse out of sight. He turned then to the whore and smiled. "Don't worry, Flos, you won't have to talk to nobody at all." She looked relieved until the dirk stabbed her. It was in her heart almost instantly, however, so her expression was one of mingled relief and shock when they discovered her body in the morning, next to that of the dead assassin. The crime was of no interest to anyone, not even the Assassins' Guild. Eladon had not, after all, been on assigned work when he died, so the matter was of nothing more than passing concern, and even that faded when it seemed probable that he and the whore had done for each other in a disagreement of the sort often had between purveyor and client.

*　　*　　*

Red Mel's fortunes took an upturn after that. Ladav Idnorsea, one of the greatest members of the Thieves' Guild, took a liking to him and added Red Mel to his henchmen, which meant that he no longer had to maintain a string of trollops to make a living. For the next year everything went so well that the thief couldn't believe it. Whatever Ladav Idnorsea set his hand to seemed to turn out right. Even his small portion of the take was sufficient to make Red Mel wealthy, and Mel was soon regarded as a figure to watch in the guild, one destined to rise high in the organization.

One warm night his boss took Red Mel and three others with him to work the Strip. They spotted a likely-looking prospect soon. The mark was a riverman, probably the owner of one of the small ships that carried cargo from the lake to Greyhawk and then took goods from the city on downriver to the lands below. The man was winning big, and he and the two sailors who accompanied him were drinking in proportion to the gains being made on the table. Idnorsea sauntered out, and as he went he signed for Red Mel to follow. After a little time, the thief did as his master indicated without anyone in the place noticing his movement.

"What do you think, Red?"

That was very flattering. Red Mel smiled and replied, "You always pick 'em right, boss. That riverman will be a pushover!"

"I'm not so sure of that, but he's worth taking." Idnorsea liked to deflate his henchmen now and then just to make sure they understood who was the top man. He was gratified to see Red Mel wilt at his words. He stared at the man a moment as if weighing his worth. "You and the others can take his two bully-boys, can't you?"

"With one hand tied behind us," Red Mel assured him eagerly.

"See to it, then," the richly clad thief said, adjusting his blue velvet doublet and brushing off his sleeve where he saw a little fleck of dirt. "You get the others

147

and wait across the street. We'll try to get them between your group and me, so that at least one of us
can take them from behind. . . . And leave the captain
for me!"

"I'm at your service as always, boss," said Red Mel
as he hurried to get back inside the gambling house
and carry out Idnorsea's instructions.

It was an easy matter to round up the other three
and drift back outside. Just as ordered, Red Mel and
the others loitered casually across the street from the
dive, awaiting developments. Idnorsea knew his trade
well. The captain would soon be too drunk to continue gambling, so the four of them would not have to
wait long. In fact they didn't.

"I'll tap my bladder in yonder passageway," the riverman said in a loud voice as he and his pair of sailors crossed the half-empty street and passed by Red
Mel and the others. Red Mel saw Idnorsea exit the
place too, and his master gave him the high sign immediately. He and the boys were to get around to the
back of the building and catch the mark while he was
pissing. With a quick gesture to his mates, Red Mel
entered the structure, a seamy tavern with rooms
above and various vices offered in its cellar. Without
hindrance the four thieves passed through the bar-
room, the kitchen, and a storeroom. The little alley
beyond was feebly lit by light from windows. The illumination was sufficient for them, however, and Red
Mel led them silently and quickly around to the left
where the captain and his guards would be relieving
themselves.

Hilgar happened to round the corner first, and he
let out a yell as the sailor waiting there let the thief
have it with his knife. "At 'em!" Red Mel shouted,
knowing that the boss would soon come up and take
these damned rivermen from the rear. He drew a pair
of daggers and suited action to command. The sailors

were quicker still, however, and came out to meet the thieves before the latter could bottle them into the gangway. Hilgar managed to grab one of the guards by his leg, and that took the fellow from the fight for the moment. Big Suggill had the other sailor by the throat and was trying to hit him with his cosh, but the riverman was tough, and somehow managed to avoid the blows while slashing the thief badly.

Trant jumped in to help his wounded pal Hilgar, which left Red Mel facing the bull-like captain. "Come on, killbuck," the riverman taunted. "Have no taste for fightin', do yer, yer slimy barstid?" Just then Idnorsea came up and ran the dolt through with his sword.

"Great work, boss. . . ." He was going to say more, but something stuck him from behind at that moment and sent Red Mel sprawling. The thief saw Hilgar's dead eyes staring into his own, while Trant sat atop the sailor who had done for Hilgar, driving his knife into the riverman again and again. The sounds from behind indicated real trouble, though, for the ring of steel on steel meant that others were now involved. Red Mel staggered up, saw Idnorsea and Big Suggill engaged with three sword-wielding men, and did the only logical thing he could do. Leaving his comrades to their fate, Red Mel clapped one hand over his wound and ran off down the passageway leading back to the Strip as fast as he could go.

Two scrawny boys were heading for the passage from the other direction, but Red Mel disregarded them. "The stupid little farts will get quite a lesson there," he was thinking to himself as he went past the pair. Just in time he noticed that one of the kids had a slender blade and was trying to stick him. Wounded or not, Red Mel was still fast. He caught the arm and almost had the offending knife free from the filthy little bastard's grip when a bolt of excruciating pain shot through his brain. Too late the thief realized that both of the small boys had weapons, and while he was stopping one, the second had killed him.

"You hurt, San?" The boy who had first tried to stab Red Mel said he was fine. "Good! Then let's see what this lousy thief has on him," his friend Gord said to him. The two boys, beggar-thieves in service of the union, quickly frisked the body. Gord found the ring that the thief wore and slipped it easily from the dead man's finger. A warm tingling shot up his arm when he held the object, but Gord said nothing. Slipping it into his shirt, Gord pointed into the alleyway, where the fight was in its last stages. "Let's see if there's more for us to do."

Events had run their course by the time the lads got to the scene. The riverboat captain and his men, who were not nearly as helpless as they had led the thieves to believe, had killed all but two of their assailants — and since the boys had done for one of the others, they were congratulated and welcomed into the group.

Soon thereafter the two lads were accompanying three sell-swords and a captive thief, a master named Idnorsea, to a place where the prisoner could be secreted for transportation to Theobald's headquarters. Not one of them was aware of where the ring had originated, how it had come into Greyhawk, left the city, and made a circuit of the Nyr Dyv before returning to the one who should have possessed it always in the first place. Even Gord regarded the thing only as a valuable trophy. It would be years before he knew differently.

Chapter 11

"THAT'S THE LOT, TAPPER. HOW MUCH?"

The locksmith gazed at the array of mechanisms before him. There were a dozen locks there, all as good as new. "Gord, you are a wonder! How about taking a position as a journeyman with me?"

"Journeyman?"

"Master, then. I'm getting to a point where I'll want to spend less time working anyway. I'll split the profits with you if you become a master and my partner here."

The young fellow shook his head. "Nobody would believe that a locksmith my age was a master. Besides, the work is too . . . quiet for me. I need something more exciting. Too bad my chum, San, has gone to try his hand at other work. He might have enjoyed the opportunity, and he's a better man than I at all this."

Tapper shook his head as if in disbelief. He knew very well that San was the better of the two when it came to solving locks. Because he was still associated with the guild of thieves, Tapper also knew full well where San had gone to and what he was doing. He pretended ignorance, though.

"Hmmm. Perhaps I can understand your position, Gord. I was rather inclined toward excitement myself when I was your age. . . ."

"About the locks," Gord said with a smile. "Are you interested in buying the lot?"

"Oh, of course. Let's see now," Tapper said, and he began a careful examination of each device, recollecting the price for which he had sold them to the lads and assessing their current value now that they had been opened and repaired. "A bronze each."

"Hah! They'd sell for a silver each."

"Two!"

"Ten!!"

"Done at five, then, and it's a hard bargain you drive for one so tender in years, master Gord of Grey College." Tapper was secretly pleased, proud of the boy. Gord knew the actual worth of things and held fast to his knowledge. Now Tapper would install these locks and charge about a noble for the lock, plus his work. He'd make a few zees on the lock, and extra money for his time would bring the bill to a nice profit even after accounting for overhead. As he rummaged around to find the correct coins to pay Gord, Tapper asked, "Is your mate, San, doing well?"

The boy shook his head a bit and shrugged. "I never run into him any more, Tapper. I suppose that means he is fine."

"Probably for the better," the locksmith said encouragingly. "You'll have more time to study now that you two aren't out and into mischief all the time. Say! Do you need another batch of old locks?"

"No. Thanks, Tapper, but I'm too busy with studies to manage the work on them now." That wasn't exactly true. Gord simply didn't find enjoyment in the work any more. He knew about all he could learn, or at least cared to learn, on the subject, and without San there to encourage him, the effort was sheer drudgery.

Tapper studied the boy for a moment. He'd grown some and filled out well in the last few years. There was lean muscle on the lad, and there could be no doubt that he was nearing full manhood. Gord's voice was deep and his cheeks showed the darkness of a heavy beard that the boy hadn't bothered to shave today.

"Sorry to hear that, lad. We had a nice little business going, but all things come to an end eventually, don't they?" The question was obviously rhetorical, and Gord didn't bother to reply. "You will come and see me now and again, won't you?" That was not a question to be ignored.

"If I happen to be around here, Tapper — but I doubt that will be very often," Gord said in straightforward fashion. "Not much reason to come to Old City — at least other than the attractions of the Foreign Quarter."

There was some wistfulness in the boy's tone. There was also pain hidden underneath, but not so deeply that the other man could not sense it. Tapper could understand him not liking to refresh his memories of childhood in the slums or of his stint as a beggar-thief.

"Not much excitement hereabouts, that's true," the locksmith supplied. "Here's your payment, Gord, and luck be with you."

Gord seemed a little hesitant about leaving. He hated to sever this link with his most recent and enjoyable past, for it was so unlike all of his previous experiences. He took the little heap of coins from Tapper, set them down, and clasped the man's hand. "You have been a good friend, Tapper. I'll miss seeing you. . . . Thanks, and you have good fortune, too," he added in a serious tone.

"If you don't come to visit me, I'll drop in at the university to see you."

The boy grinned. He knew very well that wasn't likely to happen. "You do that, Tapper. I'll show you

how we students toss off bumpers of ale while singing!" With that, Gord departed.

*　*　*

The whole of the city had altered greatly in the last
few years. The Beggars' Union had been soundly de-
feated by the Thieves' Guild, and a new beggarmaster, Chinkers, ruled the re-established organization
— called the Beggars' Guild, of course. As far as Gord
knew, he was the only master beggar-thief to have
survived the debacle. The thieves and their hirelings
had done for the rest — all but Theobald. The hunt
was still on for the ex-king of beggars, but Gord knew
that the obscenely gross devil would never be found.

Quite a few thieves had been slain in the brief war.
Now the number of beggars in Greyhawk was slowly
increasing again, but after the last fight — the inva-
sion of Theobald's headquarters — so many beggars
had died that hardly one in six of the old union survived. Even those who only tithed to Theobald's organization had suffered. The citizens of the city were
indeed pleased at the overall result: fewer thieves and
not half as many beggars, street gangs nearly wiped
out as well, and honest folk the better for it all.

Gord had changed in appearance sufficiently so as
to no longer fear recognition as a former Least Master
of the Beggars' Union. Other than San, there was no
one alive to recognize him anyway. Well, he thought,
perhaps Chinkers also might be able to, but Gord
had serious doubts about that. The wily old fellow
had been too busy with his own schemes, certainly,
to notice a boy beggar-thief; otherwise he wouldn't be
beggarmaster today. Any thieves who had encountered Gord two or three years ago would never recognize him now either.

He and San had feared a hunt for them at first.

They had fled from the Beggars Quarter when the end came. First they'd hidden here, then there — Foreign Quarter, Craftsmen's Ward, and even the Low Quarter briefly. Then they settled down below the Halls District in the University's precincts, just south of Clerksburg. They insinuated themselves into the academic community and took up formal studies, primarily as a means of concealing themselves. In the throng of students, the two boys were as invisible as they could be to any search — and probably there had been none at all anyway. Both of them had overestimated their importance, but that was part of being boys.

Of course, being a student had other advantages, too. The time he had spent studying under a tutor and then in a college had served Gord well. He had matured, grown, changed. He was far better educated now and more capable of dealing with the world as it really was. Being able to survive in Old City was by no means a measure of viability anywhere beyond those circumscribed limits.

Gord was pleased with recent events, all in all, yet he missed San. He was near manhood, but the part of him that was still a boy needed and wanted a companion of the same sort. He had been denied that luxury throughout most of his life, and the feeling of being close to another was something that Gord now comprehended and appreciated more than ever. But now San had left, feeling a need to follow his own path, and Gord was on his own again.

Gord paid over a small iron coin, toll for passage from the Foreign Quarter into New Town. Suddenly it occurred to him that he was halfway back to the apartment that he had, until recently, shared with San. He had been so lost in thought that he couldn't recall most of the walk. Alone again. . . .

"I am meant to be that way," he murmured to

himself as he strode through the streets on his way south to the university area. "I'm a loner, and that's another reason why San left. I'm pretty poor company." No, he told himself in the next instant, that wasn't really true. Gord's estimation of himself went from one extreme to the other as he tried to take stock of himself and decide what to do next. He knew that when he felt like being so, he was excellent company, always ready to banter, desport, or devise some new prank. Much of the time, however, he did prefer to be on his own. That wasn't being selfish or reclusive, considering his skills and his lot in life. Study, weapons practice, exercise, and thinking all required time alone.

And being alone did have its benefits. A solitary person was not burdened by responsibility for anyone else's welfare or safety. And there were some things he could do by himself that would be impossible, or at least more difficult, to do as one member of a team. If there was treasure to be gained, and it could be gained without someone else's assistance, was it not better to undertake the project as an individual?

Snatches of thought began to come together in his mind, and as they coalesced he began to feel better and better. Soon Gord came to his own neighborhood, his loneliness submerged beneath the excitement of a new plan he had conceived.

* * *

"Doctor? Doctor Prosper, are you there?"

The old sage was getting crotchety these days, and when he came out to answer the call he didn't look too pleased at first.

"What? Oh, it's you, Gord. Now what is it?" The boy started to reply, but the old fellow cut him off. "Don't stand out there. The draft is going to be the

death of me! Come in, come in. Talk inside where it's
warm."

The day was balmy, the season spring. Gord noticed the woolen shawl wrapped around Prosper's
narrow shoulders and understood. Leena had always
been chilled — not because of the temperature, but
because of old age, poor circulation, death creeping
closer day by day.

"I brought you a bottle of nice brandy, doctor,"
Gord said as he entered the old sage's little cottage.

"Pour a glass for me, and bring it over by the
hearth. Have a jot yourself, but not too much, mind
you! Growing boys must avoid ingesting quantities of
spirits, you know."

Having done as the old sage instructed, Gord
brought two glasses to where Prosper sat by the fire-
place. Parchment sheets and several quills nearby indicated that the old fellow had been writing when
Gord had interrupted him.

"May I sit down?" he asked respectfully.

"Of course! Take that stool there and draw it
close," Doctor Prosper said, and as the lad did so the
old man carefully straightened up the mess, placing
the pages face down. "Are you in trouble again?" the
sage asked as Gord sat.

Gord couldn't resist the urge to grin. He was still
half-boy at best. He and San had found it necessary
to beg intercession from Doctor Prosper several times
to get out of scrapes and worse at Grey College or
with the university officials. "No, sir," he said through
his smile. Then he put on a straight face again and
added, "I came to seek your assistance in a scholarly
matter."

"That's a relief, then," Prosper said, sipping the
fiery brandy and giving a little grunt to acknowledge
its quality. The old man very much appreciated
Gord's thoughtfulness. He had tutored Gord and San

for a year before using his influence to gain them entrance to the University. He had found the other lad bright and capable, but Gord was his favorite, for never had Prosper taught a more natural student. The doctor didn't know quite how to define Gord's mental ability — remarkable recall, strong logical reasoning, maybe simply overall genius. At any rate, he was always pleased inside to have Gord call upon him, even if it was only to have him help the two rascals out of trouble. He did his utmost to keep his pleasure a secret from Gord and San both, for he didn't want to make the former too self-confident or the latter jealous.

"And what might this be about?" Doctor Prosper added in a gruff tone when he realized that the youth was waiting to be prompted for his request.

"I am interested in the city, doctor."

"The city? That's a lot to be interested in — you must have in mind something more specific than that. You know its history, politics, and demography, don't you? I've given you lessons on those subjects myself, and the college hasn't neglected your learning, I am certain. Come now, boy! What exactly is going through that fertile mind of yours?"

Of course, Gord did have something specific in mind, but he wanted to ease into the subject so that he didn't give away any more information than necessary. Gord suspected that if the doctor knew the full extent of his plan, he would not only refuse to give him the information he wanted but might even turn him in to the authorities. The doctor never would have done anything this drastic, but Gord had no way of knowing that for sure.

"I'm interested in planning — the planning out of Greyhawk, the way the early engineers built it," he ventured.

Prosper's wrinkled brow became more furrowed

still. Try as he might, though, the old man couldn't discover anything actually nefarious in Gord's expressed desire. "Are you considering becoming an engineer, then? An architect?"

"Well . . . no, not exactly. I haven't ruled out those professions, of course," the boy added quickly. "This is my city, my only home. I need to comprehend it better, know it more fully, in order to be knowledgeable and understand its history and its future." That was a broad and ambitious claim. Would Prosper let it go at that?

In fact, the old fellow could relate to such a thirst for knowledge. The broader the base of information from which one drew, the better the decisions one could arrive at. Information along with understanding were keys to success in any endeavor or calling.

"So, why not simply consult the library at Grey College? They have material of the sort you need." Prosper pretended annoyance he didn't feel.

"That's just it, doctor. I've searched through the entire library and found nothing to really satisfy me. I want to see the old plans, the original drawings of the city, its water ducts, walls, sewers, the whole works! Do such plans exist?"

Still no clue to give away what Gord was after. Perhaps the boy in truth was becoming a dedicated student, as Prosper had always hoped he would. The old professor pondered the question Gord had posed. Where would such stuff as original plans exist? Possibly the Lord Mayor's archives would have them, but no student would ever be allowed access to such information as would be contained there. There would be secret escape tunnels, means of defense, and other secret stuff not for the eyes of any save the rulers of the free city. That left only one possibility.

"Landgrave," the sage muttered.

Gord understood instantly. Landgrave College was

159

the oldest of all the schools that made up the university. It had originally been located in what was now the Labor Quarter of the Old City. Centuries ago, when the New Town had begun to take shape, Landgrave had acquired the land and buildings of a monastery whose sect desired seclusion, not inclusion in a burgeoning metropolis. The college was moved to the place where once monks had been and now stood in the very heart of the whole district of learning. "That is a most respected institution, doctor. As a mere student at Grey, I'll never be allowed to enter Landgrave's library."

"Don't be hasty, and don't say 'never' — too negative and restricts the thinking accordingly. There is always a way." Doctor Prosper looked around, found a clean sheet of paper, and began scratching away with a quill pen, pausing only to dip the instrument into a pot of sepia ink now and then. "Should your chum . . . San, is it? . . . have access to the facility as well?"

"Ah, no, Doctor Prosper. You must have forgotten, but he has left college."

The elderly sage shook his head, covering his irritation at having forgotten. He hated to face the fact of declining memory. "Yes, yes, of course. No matter. You alone will have the means, then." He added a few more words to the letter, signed it, and sprinkled sand on it to dry the ink.

"You can give me a letter which will enable me to use the library of Landgrave College?" Gord's tone was properly deferential, and his awe, though subdued, was genuine.

"Of course," Prosper said, concealing his pride in his status. "You are a student engaged in research on my behalf — I've stretched things a bit by telling an old associate of mine at Landgrave that I am no longer able to manage such strenuous work myself." He gave the missive over to the boy with a bit of a flourish. "Go right over to the college and seek out Doctor Bizzell. He is a senior don, you know. He will take care of all you need."

"Thank you!" Gord was excited and eager to be off on his new quest. "I'll remember this always, doctor, and you can bet— "

"I can bet you'll forget it almost as soon as you're outside my door," the sage interrupted, saying what was probably true but which Gord would never admit. "You'll stay right here for a while yet, boy. I have a few chores for you to do, and then you can fix me some eggs for supper. While you're at that, I intend to ask you some questions. As a former pupil, and one for whom I have just done a considerable favor, I am entitled to at least that much."

Grinning, Gord acquiesced to the old fellow's demands. He did the work as instructed, whistling as he went, then started preparations for a special meal. It was an honor to be able to serve the good old sage thus, after all, and despite the quizzing that he knew Prosper would give him afterward. Time was always precious, but he could certainly put off his plans for a few hours.

It took longer than he had anticipated to find the facts he needed. Gord had entered the sanctum of Landgrave's ancient library thinking that it would be a simple matter to find what he sought. Many days, many pages, and much dust afterward, he finally discovered the drawings he was looking for bound into a great, flat book. That tome, along with similar works, was stored in a section of the library that probably had not been visited in years. That was no surprise. Not even scholars had much interest in the aqueducts and cisterns beneath old Greyhawk. The boy was happy to have it remain that way. Only San would know the real reason for Gord's interest, if he had been aware of the young man's current search for knowledge.

Gord recalled the whole incident from his past with crystal clarity. It was one he would never, never forget. The young lad paused a moment, reflecting on what had taken place nearly three years ago to the day. He and San had been part of the roving force of the Beggars' Union that had brought the war to the Thieves' Guild. In one of their "illegal" thieving excursions, Gord had obtained his cherished ring by slaying a vicious killer in hand-to-hand combat. Thereafter, he and San had roamed the Low and River Quarters, hidden among the Rhennee bargefolk, and done everything else they could to defeat their enemies, even though both young boys had despised Beggarmaster Theobald. It was a matter of sheer survival, and despite their lack of years, both of them understood that all too well.

Suddenly a summons had come to them. The war was over, a peace was about to be negotiated. Gord and San had no choice; they returned to the vast old warehouse that Theobald had made his headquarters and palace. Gord laughed inwardly at the term. Palace, indeed! The building was a gross exhibit of shabbiness and decay, a monument to the sick and perverted mind of the beggarmaster and his hubris.

The slaughter of the beggar-thieves and all who associated with them occurred the very night of the boys' return. Perhaps Chinkers had been in the old building, but Gord doubted it. He imagined that the chubby rascal had slipped away beforehand. Considering his current position, there was no doubt in Gord's mind that Chinkers had served as a spy for Arentol and the Thieves' Guild.

Gord and San had been very lucky indeed not to have been murdered in their beds when the assault came. Fortunately, San had fled his quarters on the top floor of the building when he heard noise from below. Gord, who had been sequestered on a lower floor, was assaulted in his room and had been forced to kill a man who was bent on stabbing him to death. That brush with death still gave him nightmares occasionally. It had also earned him a superb short sword to complement the dagger he had won from his very first fight to the death.

Gord had tried to escape by going into the bowels of the building, where he met up with San and Theobald, who promptly forced the boys into carrying out a load of treasure for him. It had been poetic in a way. . . . Gord had driven the fat devil to his demise with his own metal strongbox — a coffer containing coins of unguessed value, used to smash a disgusting monster of no worth whatsoever.

What had been the beggarmaster's plan after commandeering the two boys to assist him in his flight? Gord thought there could be no doubt. Theobald certainly would have stabbed or strangled both of them, dumped them into the cistern, and pleasurably gone on his way. Ironic, then, that the gross murderer had gone to his end in the very place he had intended to dispose of Gord and San, the hundred-foot-deep well hidden beneath the secret subcellar of the beggars' headquarters.

The scene floated before his eyes, the memory clear enough even now. "Give me that box!" Theobald roared. He had been poised, waiting, just a little below the rim of the cistern's mouth, expecting Gord and San to ease the heavy coffer down to his waiting hands. Instead, Gord had hefted the great metal box all by himself. It took all of his strength for him to raise it all the way up to his scrawny chest — not the muscular torso he now had; in that respect, as in most others, the change in him had been great. The uncomplicated but difficult act of lifting the chest,

Gord thought later, had been part of a catharsis for him, part of the purging of boyishness to make way for the man to develop.

Why did he do what he did? A flurry of thoughts had raced through his mind as he staggered with the chest over to the rim of the cistern. Gord had despised Theobald. But beyond that, he feared the man, as one would fear some ravening demon — only more so, for this monster was there to threaten the boy day and night. The beatings and torture of his early days as a beggar-boy had not been repeated after Gord's skills had become noticed and appreciated, but Gord always knew that the gross beggarmaster could resume such punishment at will, and the likelihood was strong that he would do so one day when the mood was upon him.

As his way of proving this assumption to himself, Gord recalled the day that Theobald had killed Violet. Like himself, she was a young member of the union with much promise. But she had incurred the wrath of her master and had paid the ultimate price — not that anger had been the man's only emotion at the time of her murder. Gord was sure that Theobald had actually enjoyed the act.

In retrospect, Gord found consolation by telling himself that the girl had been unworthy of his admiration, which may actually have been love. That assessment was not meant to fault her; "unworthy" was a poor choice of word. It was simply that her mind-set, her ethos, everything about Violet was very different from what he had become. At the time when they worked together, though, the difference had been less sharp. She had erred in greed, possibly helped to undo one of Theobald's schemes — unwittingly, Gord was sure — and the beggarmaster had killed her for it, strangling, beating, and assaulting her slowly, methodically, with relish. Oh, yes, he remembered that all now . . . and then. It was for himself, for San, and for Violet too that he did what came next.

As Theobald demanded his cache of money, Gord had hurled the heavy chest down with all the force his puny arms could muster — quite enough to do the job. The fat man's outstretched hands could not absorb the force of the downrushing iron box. The metal struck his bald head, hitting it sufficiently hard to cause the beggarmaster to topple off his precarious perch and plunge to his death in the depths below.

Only Gord and San knew of Theobald's fate, and that fact they kept strictly to themselves. To speak of it would be to implicate themselves as part of the organization that had been expunged from Greyhawk. Even this much time thereafter, it was likely to mean a death warrant if the thieves or city officials should learn of it. So afterward they almost never discussed the execution even between themselves. Perhaps San still thought about it, but Gord knew his former companion was not the sort to take unnecessary chances. To San, he suspected, a chest full of coins was not sufficient reason to risk one's life when plenty of less perilous ways existed to make an income. Gord had other thoughts, however.

Since becoming a trained thief, Gord had utilized his skills to make his livelihood. In fact, he and San had managed both by exercising and by putting their talents into play, as it were, not to just retain their skills but improve upon them too. Now his former comrade had gone off to become a member of the Thieves' Guild, and Gord recently had worked strictly alone. He rationalized that he had to be an independent thief, a rogue, since he had no other means of supporting himself as a student.

"Don't kid yourself," Gord said aloud, startling himself out of his reverie temporarily by the sound of his own voice. Fortunately he was alone in the little storage chamber that housed the plans he was memorizing. He didn't dare try to copy them here, but at his own place he drew from memory each night, carefully duplicating the information gained that day.

He tried to refocus his concentration on what was before him, but his mind wandered once more. . . . Gord knew he had become a thief by force of circumstances, and he also realized that he remained one by choice. Other avenues, such as that Tapper had offered, were open to him. Gord wasn't interested in such opportunities, though, partly because he liked the thrill of illicit thievery, the excitement of planning and executing a theft. He felt that the city owed him much while he owed it, and particularly its Thieves' Guild, nothing but his revenge. Perhaps this was rationalization, but he thought not.

Once, shortly after the incident, San had wondered out loud why Gord had wasted the treasure in the strongbox. Gord explained that it had been his only weapon under the circumstances. He had simply utilized the best tool at hand to accomplish a much-desired result — and that was that. The ledger wasn't closed yet, though. To be fully even with the ghost of Theobald, Gord needed to do one more thing. He intended to recover the chest of coins from Theobald's wet grave and have the treasure for himself.

It was a challenge in many ways, and the gathering of the information was by no means the greatest. Finding where the cistern was required a lot of research, but Gord was steeling himself for a far more exacting demand than that. He had to face the dangers of the subterranean maze under Greyhawk by himself. He had to go where the bones of the beggar-master lay and take from them their treasure. The very thought of what he would have to do made the boy shudder, but the man in him was determined to see it through in order to prove that there was no longer a weak and frightened child in his body, no more gutless coward. Alone he would prove that once and for all time, and in the proving he would gain much more than monetary reward.

With that, Gord finally forced his mind clear of such thoughts and returned to his study of the ancient drawings. A vast complex of tunnels and drains was shown on the maps, but repeated exposure to the information had made Gord a virtual expert in deciphering the different features. Sewers were singled out easily now, and drainage tunnels too. The cisterns and aqueducts stood out clearly in his mind as he scanned the map. Tonight his own map would be complete, and his adventure ready to begin.

Chapter 12

THE HAND-DRAWN RE-CREATION spread out before Gord showed the deepest layer of tunnels beneath Old City. A network radiated from a place under the old citadel, with ducts running to it from the far reaches of what then had been the whole of Greyhawk. From the notes he had managed to decipher, Gord knew that the whole system had been carved out of the solid rock that lay under the place. Beneath the upper layers of the limestone, the stuff that the higher tunnels ran through, there was harder rock. Into this the original builders had cut shafts and passages for water. But most of the old collection points had long ago been filled and cemented over for other buildings to stand atop.

The reason for this was that times, and needs, had changed. The sprawl of the city now was so great that getting water during time of siege was of no concern. When Greyhawk had stood far from the Selintan, and the damming of the Grey Run by enemies was a possibility, then the need had been a real one. Far beneath the surface was a huge cavern intended to hold a reserve of water against an eventuality that would never occur now. The ducts that once had brought rivers of rain from above down into the deep pool two hundred feet below the surface sent only a trickle of liquid that way now. The rock was not permeable, yet the reservoir was not dry — of that Gord was certain. The splash that Theobald and the chest had made when they fell had told Gord that.

He studied his carefully made map again. Four main channels sloped gently down to the place where the big cavern was. A dozen smaller ducts fed into each of the underground canals. Each of those ducts, in turn, was fed by a half-dozen conduits from collection points. The place where the strongbox lay was in the western canal. All Gord had to do was to find one of those old openings that wasn't fully closed up. He couldn't use the secret subcellar of the Beggars' Guild to gain access to the canal, but one of the conduits would do as well.

What seemed an easy matter proved to be quite the opposite in practice. Gord spent most of his free time during the following three weeks searching the streets of Old City for one of the places where the drains had been. Changes made over the centuries were difficult enough to determine, so that locating the correct areas in itself proved most trying. The task was complicated by new layers of cobbles, plazas, dwellings, and all forms of other things that had been built upon what had been there before. Perhaps a collection conduit still remained somewhere, but Gord couldn't find it. He was only temporarily stymied, however. Giving up was not in his nature.

Returning once again to Landgrave College's hallowed repository of scribings, Gord managed to convince the doddering old custodian that he was still involved in the project for Doctor Prosper and that the good sage desired him to garner more from the dusty archives the librarian warded. Again with the great folio before him, Gord located and studied successively higher layers of the works beneath Old City. He had to go back several times to find what he was looking for, but it was eventually uncovered. Then

Gord had to search through yet more of the old plans to get what he wanted. That was the military plan of the subterranean complex.

When he finally thought of the answer to his problem, he was astounded by his own stupidity. It was simply this: Well openings alone weren't sufficient to manage the reservoir — there had to be passages leading to it for maintenance!

These ways would be regarded as secret, naturally. But somehow the college had gained copies of the military plans despite their secrecy. That probably had happened in that long-gone time when the masters of the complex that was spreading forth to become a major metropolis of the Flanaess, instead of the out-of-the-way trading center that the city had been, realized that the former concerns of the community were no longer applicable. Gord imagined the long-dead officials of the college receiving the gift of the plans from the equally long-deceased city officials with great ceremony; and sometime shortly thereafter, the lad mused, the whole batch had been quietly consigned to the oblivion of an ordinary storage room. Surely that was as good as, if not better than, locking them in a strongroom that every spy would seek to penetrate to discover what it held.

Once he knew what to look for, Gord quickly found what he needed. The plan wasn't identified as a secret military one, but he recognized it as such immediately. Routes for movement of troops beneath the city were shown, and so were the means of getting to the reservoir. All he had to do now was to get to the passages that lay about midway between the sewers and the drains, and the rest would follow.

Because of his own experiences, especially his apprenticeship as a thigger-thief, Gord was familiar with the maze that existed just beneath the streets. From deep cellars, sub-basements, sewers, and the like, one could enter a network of hidden pathways that could be taken to bring the adventurous individual unseen from place to place within the entire city. Beggars used this lowway, as it were, and thieves and assassins also utilized it frequently and extensively. Wild cats, huge rats, all sorts of vermin, and who knew what else made the complex their home. Gord had heard stories of desperate and mad individuals who dwelled in the subterranean realm under the city. Recalling that thought made him shudder. Such an environment would make men into something different and more terrible in a short time, for to survive there would mean that an individual would have to become more ferocious, more vicious, than the other beasts that resided there.

What equipment would he require to get through the upper labyrinth, find a means of penetrating deeper to the ancient military complex of passageways, and eventually go all the way from there to the western canal wherein the coin-filled strongbox lay? The list was not difficult to make.

First, he needed dark-colored, old clothing that fit snugly so it wouldn't get in his way when he had to climb or go through a tight place; solid boots, well-greased to keep out water; and, of course, his weapons — boot knife, long dagger, and short sword.

Then he'd have to have a strong line for help in climbing up or down sheer surfaces, plus a spike or two to use as an anchor for the line; a pair of small pouches to carry the money he would remove from the iron box; and a waterproof container to hold his map, some spare sheets of parchment, and a charcoal stick for writing on them.

Next, a couple of good pieces of chalk for marking the walls with. That, and the rough map he would have along, should assure he wouldn't become lost in the black mazes. Perhaps it would be a good idea to take along a little flask of brandy too, and a bit of food. It might take longer than he thought to find his way down and get back up again.

That was just about it. He had or could easily obtain everything he needed except for one thing: What would he do for illumination?

If Gord had comrades with him on this expedition, he would certainly have opted to bring some good, long torches. These would have provided both light and protection from whatever lived down there. The things dwelling there would not be accustomed to light or flame; they would shun the former and fear the latter. But this was a solitary endeavor, and he could not carry a supply of torches by himself. And, a regular lantern would also be of no use. It would require him to hold it or affix it to his body. That arrangement would be too cumbersome, the lantern too likely to fall or break.

He decided that what he needed was an object enspelled by a cleric, one that the priest had treated to make it give off strong light for a long time. Gord had seen such things occasionally. Wealthy people used them to light their dwellings and the areas around them. Rushlights, fat lamps, and candles were also used for this purpose, but only the poor folk had to employ such expensive and temporary means of illumination exclusively. Expensive, indeed . . . . Perhaps the priest-lights were more dear than he supposed. He had to find out.

Temples and similar places of worship were absolutely foreign to the boy. He had studied theology in school recently, but outside that, he had no experience at all with religion. The small amount of knowledge he possessed allowed Gord some advantage in selecting a potential place to seek one of the special lights. He went to a little chapel of Fharlanghn nearby. The wanderers who tended to profess the deity were few in number in any city. The sect was broad-minded, accepting all sorts of folk. It also seemed likely that the priests there would be less oriented toward money. There were possibly other reasons for preferring this sort of place somewhere in the back of his mind, but Gord didn't take time to ponder them. It was time to get on with his work!

* * *

"Pardon, good priest, but may I speak with you a minute?" he asked politely upon entering the small building and seeing a brown-robed man therein.

"You may, boy. I am here to help all the faithful."

Gord was forthright. "I am no follower of your god, sir, just an inquiring student seeking something."

"If you seek knowledge of Fharlanghn, then this is certainly the place. If there is something other than such knowledge which you expect to find in this chapel, I fear I cannot help." The priest looked steadily at the boy.

"I am here to ask if it is possible to obtain an item which your clerics are known to fashion with your powers," Gord said plainly, looking the tall man in the eye as he spoke, returning the priest's gaze without blinking, but with a friendly expression. This was not difficult, for the cleric seemed a good fellow.

"Then perhaps I'll be able to serve after all, young scholar. What manner of thing do you seek?"

"A light of the sort you priests enspell on things. The kind that the gentry encompass in stout cages and employ to make yards well-lighted and their homes as bright as day."

The tall priest smiled. "So, the demands of your studies require much reading and scribery at night, do they?"

"Well . . ."

174

"Never mind the reason, boy. I am able to provide such an object as you wish — a small stone, smooth and regular, with the powers granted to me from my service to Fharlanghn employed according to his desire so as to make the stone glow as bright as day, and for a long time too. That is possible, if that is what you wish."

"Yes," said Gord with a sigh of gratitude, and his relief evident on his countenance. "Please give me one of those stones you just described, and I shall give you whatever coin you require for the favor."

At that the cleric actually gave a gentle laugh. "Of some of the students at the university I could believe it — but that you'd be able to simply reach into your purse and count out the money is doubtful. You are no rich young noble, that is evident. You are likely the son of a merchant or a military officer from the look of you, boy. Where would you get so large a sum as three thousand zees to pay for the item?" The fellow chuckled again, but in a kindly way.

Gord resisted the urge to reach into the secret place in his belt and take out three of the gold coins he had there. The tall cleric was right. A lad such as he would have no business possessing that sum of money. "Perhaps I could give you some now, and then pay the rest in weekly installments until the whole were delivered."

"What? And have your irate father down upon me? Not likely. I think you had better settle for candles and lamps, boy. They are bothersome and have to be replaced, but you can purchase many of them for the cost of the lightstone you seek."

The priest was about to leave, but Gord was by no means ready to admit defeat. "Wait, sir! . . . Ahh . . . Please, good priest, may I have yet one further word with you?"

"Be brief," the fellow said politely but firmly.

"If I became a student of . . . Fharlanghn, studied the teachings you profess, and became a member of your faith, would you then perhaps make the lightstone available at a price less than that you named before?"

Now the cleric stopped and assessed the boy before him more carefully. There was more to the lad than he first thought. This boy wanted the thing as more than a novelty, for some other reason than a light to study by.

"Perhaps you and I should go into my personal apartment and have a chat. If you explain to me exactly why you have need of the lightstone, we may be able to strike a bargain. What say you . . . ?"

"Gord, sir," he supplied without thinking. "I have my reasons, and I'll be honored to speak further with you, but I don't think I will actually be able to explain fully."

The tall man smiled again, taking a closer look at the lad. "Well, Gord, you are certainly honest in your statements. Perhaps I won't have to hear a full explanation. Still, let's you and I have a chat to see about this matter." With that the priest led the way to the rear of the place where various administrative offices and lodgings were located.

After perhaps an hour the two emerged again, the boy talking as they did so. ". . . and you see, sir, that I have reason to search out this thing because of need!"

"It is a foolish undertaking — typical of youth!"

"With or without your help, I will do it." Gord's voice was firm, his face a study in determination, but he was neither wheedling nor imploring. The youngster simply stated fact.

The cleric was a good judge of character, and he read Gord easily.

The lad had admitted no details, but did tell the

cleric that he planned to seek treasure in a place where difficulty, not danger, was the major obstacle. Wise in the ways of the world, the tall cleric knew that where one factor was present, the other would likely be encountered as well. Still, he was not inclined to belabor that point. And there was something about this boy. . . .

"You shall have my help," the cleric said after a brief pause, "in the form of a lightstone and a blessing too. Give your contribution over for those in need, and both will I then bestow. When you return with your treasure, you will pay the agreed-to fee and also again contribute to the needy."

Gord presented his hand. The cleric noted ink stains, a sure sign of bookish pursuits. He also found the hand calloused and hard. The lad did physical work as well! There was certainly more to the small student than first met the eye.

"Happily agreed, good priest!" Gord said heartily.

The tall man smiled. "And gladly done, Gord. May all be well with you."

The boy waved farewell. "In two days I'll be back to see you. You are truly a fine man to understand this matter so well!"

The cleric smiled wryly at that. He doubted that his decision would meet with approval from on high, but he was subject to mortal weaknesses too. The lad had him caught up in adventurous nonsense.

As promised, Gord appeared in two days, and the lightstone was ready.

Chapter 13

HE ENTERED THE SEWERS from the Moat Stream
Canal, where a narrow strip of warehouses and shops
existed between the waterway and the wall that sepa-
rated Old City from New Town.

Gord chose a place where he would come under
the beggars' section of the ancient portion of Greyhawk, rather than farther south where the passages
would take him under the Thieves Quarter. The reasoning was simple. The more southerly sewers would
be heavily trafficked by thieves, while those to the
north, where the beggars held sway, would be virtually unused — particularly now that the business of
stealing was the sole province of the thieves. Because
of his training, Gord was able to detect the secret
signs of both thiggers and thieves. Any concealed ad-
its would be marked, and Gord needed to find some
means of getting lower in the subterranean maze.

He had used his mechanical skills, those gained at
locksmithing principally, to fashion a small case for
the enspelled stone. It was a tight cube of sheet tin,
each of its six faces only a few inches square. The
lightstone was tightly wedged between the top and
bottom of the box so that it would not move or even
rattle. One of the side faces was solidly and perma-
nently fastened to the top and bottom for added rigidity, and a handle affixed to it, so that half of the sides

of the cube were set. Each of the other three faces was flanged at the top and fasteners were placed there to allow locking. Along the bottom each side had a hinge. Flip the hook, shove the flange with thumb or finger, and the face would drop away to allow light to spill out.

The face opposite the handle was, by definition, the front of the lantern — the gadget, for all its distinctiveness, was actually nothing more than that, all in all. Gord had made a small hole there and added a flat piece of tin that could be slid aside to uncover the aperture. That allowed the light-box to send forth a thin, bright beam of light without illuminating all the space ahead or nearly around him, as was the case when all three sides of the device were allowed to drop open.

He was pleased with his work, even though he had been unable to keep the cube from emitting any light at all when he closed it. Try as he might, Gord could not stop the bright light from being visible along the cracks where the moving faces met the frame. Finally he decided to use the side-face openings only in an emergency and plugged the light leaks there with beeswax blackened with soot. Because there was no help for the other glimmerings, from where the front face met its four neighbors, Gord carried the box inside a baggy jacket where he could easily conceal its illumination by the cloaking effect of the dark, thick cloth.

He wore a long cloak over his other garments as he walked northward to arrive at the place where he planned to enter the sewers. Having set out just as the sun was sinking, Gord timed his arrival so it was just fully dark when he came to his destination. The boy was small enough to be able to slip through the side opening in the grate that covered the entrance, and being familiar with such places enabled him to find the iron rungs of the ladder leading down without using any illumination.

At the bottom of this first shaft, some fifteen feet below street level, Gord blinked and looked around. His eyesight was excellent, his night vision superb according to those who knew about such things. The faint light from above was sufficient to enable Gord to discern the walls and the places where the vaulted drains ran from the conjoining point of the shaft. After orienting himself, Gord chose the one going north and carefully proceeded up the tunnel for several yards. Then he took out his magical lantern and allowed a little light to spill out from the hole in the front face.

"Just a trickle," he said aloud, satisfaction evident in his tone, as he viewed what was before him. The old drain had a concave bed in which a small stream of waste ran. The stuff was mostly water, and it was flowing in the same direction the boy was headed. Gord stood on a narrow ledge some three feet above the channel. The stones were enslimed and worn, dangerous unless one was careful. The odor was nauseating, but not so horrible as to make breathing painful.

"It could be worse," Gord said as he slipped a wrapping of black cloth up from around his neck to mask his nose and mouth. At the last minute he had thought of this added bit of gear, as well as a small flask of vinegar to douse it with, but that would be used only if the air got really foul. Off came the cloak, and in a trice he had it rolled, slung, and tied over his right shoulder.

Pacing carefully ahead, Gord found no secret sign to indicate that there was any concealed means of egress from the sewer. Coming to another junction point, he decided to turn right, into the system that ran under the center of the Beggars Quarter. This tunnel was about a foot above the north-south one, so he had to step up. The concave drain on the floor in this conduit was absolutely dry. There were heavy webs and a few scurrying beetles, but nothing else. The existence of the webs confirmed his judgment. The sewer he had been in was not one that had been used by anyone coming from Old City, else these webs would have been mangled and torn down before now.

Using his sword to clear away the webs, and being careful to avoid the spiders that hid within them, Gord walked quickly along his route, covering ground at a good pace because the ledge was dry and easy. Soon thereafter that changed.

Several openings here released effluent into the main tunnel. Those that opened onto his side made going difficult, and Gord had to use his athletic ability a few times to avoid being drenched by the noisome outpouring of one pipe or another. There were glitterings ahead, and nasty chitterings and squeakings that told the boy that there were rats here.

Just as he was becoming discouraged, Gord saw a series of marks on the opposite wall. They were barely discernible and to the untrained eye would have appeared as nothing more than worn places in the stone blocks. Gord read a sign that alerted the initiated to the fact that there was a means of leaving the sewers just ahead.

"Damn!" he said under his breath. The exit led upward, not below. Where there was a means of leaving the maze, however, there might also be a way deeper as well. Gord forged ahead.

About half an hour later he came to a place where several sewer tunnels met. The effluents formed a deep pool in the circular chamber where the various drains converged, and there were flying bridges built to span the noxious pond. Gord flashed his light atop one of the spans, and when Gord's light struck its greenish-black body a reptile shot off its perch to land with a splash in the pool below. The tail of a huge rat was hanging from the side of its mouth. Gord saw that clearly before the thing vanished under the scummy surface.

Shuddering involuntarily, the boy paused a minute to make certain than some even bigger monster wasn't lurking about. The stench here was practically unbearable, so while he was pausing, Gord decided to douse his scarf with vinegar. Again he changed directions, going right to parallel his initial route. After carefully traversing the flying bridge that led in the desired direction, he was again prowling along a passage, this time walking southward.

He saw a narrow opening about a hundred paces from the pool. It didn't seem promising, but something urged Gord to investigate it just in case. The corridor was not more than twenty feet long and terminated in a flight of steep stairs . . . upward. He turned away in disgust, using that emotion to fight off his despair, when something caught his eye. It was another marking on the wall, one he had overlooked at first because of the narrowness of the passage and his rush to find out where it led. The sign indicated access to a lower pathway!

With a sigh of relief, Gord began searching along the wall opposite the marking. He knew from experience that such signs were often used to mark location as well as give information. Thanks to his sharp eyes and with the help of his light, Gord was able to discover the hidden door in just minutes. It took much longer for him to discover how the mechanism worked that enabled the doorway in the stone blocks to open. Eventually he found the place where a knife blade could be inserted to release a catch, and a low section of the wall swung inward to reveal another passageway going off at a right angle to the narrow passage he was in. Gord entered the place without hesitation, pushed the door shut, and smiled to himself in triumph.

The low tunnel led to more stairs, but these spiraled down. It was impossible to discover if this was an oft-traveled route, because the damp stones would not leave traces of passage — at least not to one who was not an expert at tracking. Gord was many things, but no expert at discovering such signs. He merely looked as he progressed, checked to see if he could notice his own trail behind himself, and shrugged. Whether or not there were other users, Gord meant to go downward now and take his chances.

The circling steps took him down and down. By counting Gord was able to estimate that he was at least another twenty feet deeper when the staircase ended in the corner of a small room with four passages leading from it at right angles to one another. All well and good, but thanks to his spiraling path Gord now had no idea of direction. There was only one way to get his bearings, and that required that he go back up the stairway and mark the wall on the way down using his chalk, noting every time he had made enough of a turn to leave him pointing in a different direction. Eventually Gord determined that the little room at the base of the stairs was hewn eastward from where the steps ended. That meant that the narrow, arched exits from the room led off in the cardinal directions. Excellent!

Gord stopped to catch his breath and to take a sip of the brandy he had. This was exciting stuff! As he rested, the enormity of what he was doing, where he was, suddenly struck the boy. Even though he had been in the sewers previously, this excursion was more than a bit frightening now that he stopped to think about it. When he had pondered this mission during the planning of it, the thought of risk had simply added zest to his undertaking. This was an altogether different situation. Now Gord was actually in the totally unknown, where great dangers probably lurked, seeking a place he was uncertain of, and as alone as any boy could be. Despite his best efforts, Gord's rate of breathing increased until he was panting, and his heart raced. Fear was getting hold of him.

"Calm down, or else they'll be calling you 'Gutless' again," he said aloud. The sound of his voice helped to reassure him, and the epithet he hated so much was sufficient to do the rest. Unknown monsters were one thing, but the fear of being thought of as a coward was stronger than the apprehension of facing hidden perils here. Gord slowed his breathing with conscious effort, took a pull from the little flask of brandy, and spoke aloud again.

"That's better now, isn't it? High time we showed everyone that there is no more little boy to shove around!" The fiery liquor spread outward in him, and he reassured himself further by touching his hand briefly to the sheath of his dagger and the hilt of his sword. Then, getting back to business, he took out his waterproof case and flipped it open. He checked his three sketch maps carefully, trying to locate his position on the second one by guessing where he had been on the first when he found the spiral steps that led to this second tier of ducts beneath Old City.

"Then I must be about here," he muttered to himself as he made a small mark on the second map. "South will take me to the place where the canal runs below, and then I'll need to head west, so it's a right turn at that point. . . . Anyway, the flow will be east, toward the great basin of the reservoir, so it'll be easy to know direction."

Despite his returned confidence and bravery, the

185

boy stopped to listen, his lantern dark and sword at the ready, at each of the room's other exits before he ducked through the one that went to the south. He was now in the system of tunnels and passageways that the assassins and thieves held as their own secret highway. Gord had no desire to disillusion the likes of them, or to stumble unwittingly into some creature who dwelled in this labyrinth, and caution was not cowardice! There was a faint dripping sound from the shaft he had just come down, but otherwise the stillness was absolute. Gord held his breath, quieted himself as completely as he could. Nothing. Carefully moving the slide on his light-box to allow a tiny shaft of illumination to spring ahead, Gord set off once more on his quest.

He came across side openings at regular intervals. Gord's light showed that there were empty chambers beyond. He couldn't guess why these had been chiseled out. Possibly to store food or weapons or both, possibly for some reason that could not be guessed at now. The passage was dry, and there were no living things along its way. Both of those facts changed, however, as he went farther.

The air went from cold and chilly to actually damp, and Gord noticed thick webs stretched across an opening on the right-hand wall. He paused and looked carefully at the walls ahead and to the rear. They had not been immediately obvious, but there were certainly wisps and small fragments of web clinging to the walls. This passage had been used by someone, and not very long ago! Whoever had come along its length had cleared the way of most of the webbing, but traces remained.

As he took this in with his eyes, Gord also used his ears. The sound of trickling water came first, then he heard voices somewhere ahead, their words indistinguishable in the echoing tunnel.

Dimming his lantern to its lowest illumination, the boy sank down to the stone floor and used his sword to make as small an opening as he could in the curtain of silken strands that covered the archway on the west wall. He then slithered through the hole and tried to replace the strands of web he had sliced away, to partially hide the space he had passed through. The effort was clumsy at best, but it was the best he could manage. Then he crept quickly along to where this entrance tunnel opened up into a chamber beyond, slipped around the corner, and tucked the light-box into his jacket. All of this was done in utmost haste, and he didn't stop to consider what might be in this place with him. Gord simply sat very still, his back pressed against the slimy stone of the wall, and waited. Something scuttled across his hand. Gord nearly shrieked, then bit his lip, huddled tightly to make himself even smaller, and held his breath.

There were footfalls in the passage just a half-dozen feet away. Rough voices spoke in hissing tones punctuated with guttural sounds and sharp barkings. Were they ogres? Trolls? Then the sounds became clearer.

"Dat was a nasty bunch o' creeps we had ta take out," one deep voice said. There were a score of others discernible too. There was a whole platoon of men going past the place! At least they sounded like men, and the rattle and clink must have come from armor and weapons. "Who needs duty like this here?" another voice said with a questioning whine. Most of the troop had clumped past where Gord was hiding when one must have seen the break in the webs.

"Hey, lookit! Sumpin's been 'round dis!" The flickering light of torches shone dimly through the veil of spiderwebs, and a dark shadow made a long shape stretching into the place where he crouched. "Shove yer torch into 'em, and frazzle da ettercaps. Den we have a little look-see, huh?"

The sounds of feet were fading off northward. "Whaddya, crazy? Who gives a rat's ass what's been goin' in dere anyway? C'mon!" The second man's voice trailed off.

"Hey, wait up, Albie!" shouted the first voice. The light faded as did the sound of feet and voices. Gord let out his breath with a gentle whoosh. Relief flooded over him. The passing group apparently had been no more than some sort of patrol, probably a branch of the city watch — men that normally stayed above ground. Whoever sent the soldiers down to this place, and why, was beyond Gord's understanding. But no matter what the reason for their presence, the realization was comforting to the boy. He was accustomed to ducking squads of the watch, and the soldiers' presence here meant that this part of the maze wasn't filled with dangers.

There could be some perils, of course. The fact that Gord could avoid such groups meant that others could also, and that the boy understood. One man had talked of "taking out" something called "creeps." Gord figured that this meant the patrols of men did come here once in a while to keep the place relatively clear of dangerous threats. This subterranean system of passages was used then, and used frequently, by those powerful enough to employ men-at-arms to police it.

All sound was gone now, so Gord decided to take a look around the chamber he was in before venturing back into the passageway. He nearly dropped his lantern when he saw the place.

Not more than twelve inches from his feet was a yawning hole in the floor! He was sitting on a ledge that encompassed the well, but the portion along the wall next to the entrance tunnel was the only place the stone floor didn't slope steeply, funnel-like, into the great opening. If he had taken one more step into the chamber, or even crawled a short distance in the darkness, he would have gone over the edge and fallen to whatever lay below!

A big, pale-colored spider froze into motionlessness as the beam of light from Gord's lantern centered on it. It was as big as his fist and had wicked-looking mandibles. Perhaps that was what had run across his hand. "Ugh!" he said aloud. Gord's voice echoed strangely in the room, and he was instantly silent, wishing he hadn't made such a noise.

The spider scuttled off when Gord brought his sword's point near. Ignoring it thereafter, the boy stood up and looked down into the well. It was deep, but his light illuminated its bottom well enough. Then Gord played the lantern upward, found an opening in the ceiling as well, and instantly knew what he had stumbled upon. Here was one of the drains that used to send water from ducts and conduits, from collection points above, down to the system below for storage in the great reservoir. He had found a passageway to the lowest level at last!

The chamber was indeed similar to a well. It must have been meant as a place where the besieged defenders of old Greyhawk could come to draw up water from the canal below — the very same canal in which Theobald had plunged to his doom. Red stains and bits of corrosion on the sides of the shaft told him that there had once been iron rungs set into the sides of the well, but time and rust had had their way with the metal.

"Well, now," he whispered to himself, smiling at his own pun, "it's time for me to shimmy down and have a look." The boy unwrapped his stout cord from around his waist, put a few knots at regular intervals along its length, and then took a flat piece of steel out of his belt pouch. The metal wedge was pointed at one end and had an eye at the other.

Gord jammed the pointed end into a crack, then pounded it in farther with the pommel of his boot knife. After assuring himself that it was firmly set, Gord ran an end of the thick cord through the eye and knotted it securely around the spike. He dropped the loose end over the side and heard a tiny splash when it hit the water below.

"That's about forty feet," he said to himself after shining his light over the edge and counting the knots that were visible in the line. The cistern in the subcellar at Theobald's headquarters had gone down a hundred or more feet, but the place where he stood now was farther below the surface. Gord was certain that the water below was what he sought. After thonging the lantern securely around his neck, Gord opened the front face fully and slipped over the ledge. He used his feet to push off from the wall and slide down the rope without banging into the stone. Centuries of erosion had made the shaft smooth and slippery. "It'll be a bugger to climb back up," he said through gritted teeth as he carefully lowered himself hand over hand down into the well-like shaft.

After about thirty feet there was no more wall. Once his head was beneath the place where the shaft pierced the ceiling of the canal, Gord used his feet to grip a knot, hung swaying, and grabbed the little tin box with his right hand. The black water below was impervious to his light, but Gord knew from the ancient plans that the depth of a canal such as this was only fifteen feet — ample volume for any flood of rainwater or diverted stream being sent to the waiting reservoir. From the place where the well shaft entered the tunnel to where his boots rested was just about seven feet, and he dangled at least five feet above the inky surface of the water. This meant that there could be no more than four feet of water at the lowest portion of the curving conduit. Where he dangled there would be no more than a foot or so between the surface of the liquid and the rock beneath. Gord lowered himself on down the line, allowing his feet to sink below the black surface.

The water flowed sluggishly away to the right. Gord balanced on the slippery, sloping stone beneath his feet, the black liquid covering his boots to a point midway up his shins. Still clasping the rope, the lad tried a few small, sideways steps, first away, then back to where the line depended from above. The footing wasn't terrible, and he gained confidence. Still grasping the line, he walked cat-foot, one step just ahead of the last. If he went cautiously and leaned slightly to the left, toward the curving wall of the tunnel, he could move along fairly well. Leaving the lantern where it was hanging at his chest, Gord decided the time had come. With his sword drawn and held toward the inky surface of the channel, and casting sideways glances suspiciously there, Gord loosed his hold on the cord and headed off to his left. Somewhere up that way, certainly no more than a few hundred yards distant, lay the bones of Theobald and a rusty iron strongbox!

The effort required to keep from slipping toward the center of the canal and falling into the lurid water, combined with the necessity of constantly checking ahead, behind, and above, was exhausting, and Gord's progress was agonizingly slow. He refused to panic and rush ahead, though. He deliberately went over and over his routine in his mind as he performed the steps. Look back and to the right . . . and watch for ripples approaching or the gleam of feral eyes. Now look ahead, search carefully for the same danger. Now flash the light's beam above. No openings. Check ahead before you move on, go slowly when you move, and stop before you repeat your scan for potential danger.

At about sixty paces Gord chalked a mark on the wall. After three such marks the boy went through his search procedure carefully again, took time for a sip of brandy, and pressed ahead. The squishy feeling inside his boots told him that they were beginning to allow the water of the subterranean canal to penetrate their oil-soaked and greased exterior. Well, that was bound to occur, and the discomfort wouldn't stop him.

After making a seventh chalk mark on the wall, Gord was starting to become disheartened. Perhaps he had misjudged the eastern orientation of his location when he entered from above. Could Theobald's former headquarters lie off in the other direction? It seemed unlikely, but the cold and dark and silence were beginning to tell on him. His nerves were frayed, and his mouth opened and closed with each breath. Why had he ever done anything so stupid and crazed as this anyway? No treasure was so great as to risk all this for.

"It isn't the treasure, dolt, it's the need to prove yourself that drives you on!" That thought made him pause and regroup. "Do I need to prove myself to myself?" That answer was clear, but he verbalized it to himself anyway.

"Who else is benefitting from this exhibition? We are alone in our head, you and I, and if we are not brave now, only a coward will remain hereafter. . . ." Stop! He was mumbling to himself, just as old Leena used to talk to herself. The thoughts were true, nonetheless, and they served to urge Gord onward.

Where he would have made his ninth mark there was no wall. Gord had come to a basin, a widening in the canal. As in the sewer above, the canal was enlarged to form a chamber where two smaller ducts met on either hand to empty into the main conduit. His light was strong, but it barely enabled him to see the distant walls of the chamber. The near wall was only about twenty feet away. The eastern one, where the water of the canal flowed from, was not less than sixty feet away, and the far wall seemed to be the same distance as well. The domed ceiling above was smooth save for a small hole. From that aperture hung the remains of what apparently had been a ladder. This had to be the place — the cistern into which he had precipitated the beggarmaster and his strongbox three years ago.

By racking his brain Gord could recall seeing basins such as the one before him drawn in the ancient engineering diagrams. They were spotted along the course of each canal to serve as waterholes, more or less, for those not able to tap the central pool, the reservoir far beneath the old citadel. Gord berated himself mentally for not considering the possibility that the cistern might plunge into such a basin. What had the drawings indicated? The basins were dish-shaped and had a central depth of twenty feet . . . which meant that bones and box were twenty feet below the black water!

"Godsdamn you, Theobald!" Gord screamed this out, and the echoes gave it back to him in a broken taunt: ". . . damn . . . damn . . . damn . . . you . . . you . . . you . . . Theobald . . . eobald . . . bald . . . ald . . . ald." As if in answer to the cry, the dark surface of the circular basin rolled and heaved — and something rose above the inky waters.

Gord turned at the sound of it breaking the surface, and the full beam of the lantern fell upon the thing that was there. What the monstrosity was he couldn't tell. If ropes and rotting seaweed were intertwined and covered with the black ooze found at the bottom of a stagnant pond, a correct picture of the

thing would begin to take shape. Add to that the
trailing tendrils of a monstrous jellyfish and the thick
tentacles of a great octopus. Finish it off with en-
crustations of things, vast bumps like rotting anemo-
nes, broader patches that resembled nothing other
than masses of exposed intestines, and excrescencies
that might have been putrescent mollusks without
their protective shells.

That is what reared up from the black waters of
the basin, and Gord wanted to flee at the sight of it.
But there was no place to run.

Gord stood, more paralyzed with fear than stead-
fast because of bravery, and the light of his lantern
brought the creature into stark relief as it heaved its
way through the water, making the inky liquid dance
under the illumination, drawing closer by a yard with
each heave of its rotten, stinking body. The horror
made him cringe, and his feet moved instinctively,
taking him back along the conduit, but only one foot
for each yard the creature was covering. There could
only be one end to this encounter.

As the monster thrashed toward him, beating the
ebon waters into a dark froth with its furious passage, Gord kept his eyes fixed upon the thing, backing still, sword now pointed at the ghastly abomina-
tion. As if hypnotized he watched the scene before
him, and was quietly amazed to see that parts of the
horror were breaking off as it advanced.

A massive tentacle broke into writhing pieces as it
came. Bits of stuff, the rotted growths and adhering
pieces, flew away or slid off the mass with audible,
sucking pops. The thing was disintegrating before his
eyes! At the same time, its rush was slowing, but it
still gained on him. Now it was within the canal, and
its bulk was evident. Its congealed mass of a body
was vaguely seal-shaped, as large as a great walrus,
and had a necklike protrusion that thrust toward the

oy, snaking ahead with each convulsion of the mon-
ter's body.

Gagging in terror as much as from the fetid stench
hat arose from the mass, Gord kept backing. Soon
he monstrous thing would be upon him!

Smack! The form heaved up and came down closer
till. Splash . . . plop . . . plop, plop-plop. The waves
f displaced water struck the walls and his own legs,
early knocking Gord off his feet, as pieces of rotten
tuff continued to drop off.

Schlooop! It was drawing its body up again, this
me with the long neck rearing as if it were a serpent
oiling to strike. As if in slow motion Gord saw it all,
nd he finally realized what was happening. Under
he bright light from his magical stone, the foul sub-
tances that composed the body of the thing were
nelting away, but the horror seemed totally unaware
hat it was dwindling, unaffected by its parts slough-
ng away in hunks and bits.

The reptilian forepart was high above Gord's head
ow, its end bulbous, its neck melting away to show
hite beneath the blackness of rot and muck. But
he thing was still coming on, and there could be no
urther retreat. The creature was upon him.

As the snakelike neck began to move forward and
own, Gord grabbed the hilt of his sword with both of
is small hands. Despite the chill, both of his palms
ere sweating freely. Holding on with all his might,
ord swung the puny blade to meet the terrible head
s it swung down to smash him. Steel met corruption
ith a disgusting sound. There was a spray of putrid
tuff everywhere, and then the head and neck were
ring in the water just in front of him.

"Oh, gods!" The boy cried the words so loudly that
hey nearly deafened him, but at the same time he
as comforted by the fact that he could speak — that
neant he was still alive!

The horrible body, meanwhile, deprived of its fore-part, flapped and writhed. Tendrils and tentacles continued breaking away, or simply dissolved in the waters. Great sections of the unnatural agglomeration of stuff similarly disappeared, falling into bits, washing away, going into nothingness.

Gord watched this, his teeth chattering, eyes bulging, until there was nothing of the horror left to see. It took only a very brief time even in the slow current of the canal. In minutes the black water was as placid as a quiet pool, and even the noisome reek of the monster had wafted away along the great pipeline. Gord shook himself, reached into his shirt, and pulled out the small container of brandy with a trembling hand. Using his teeth to pull the cork, the boy downed the remaining liquor with a gulp and tossed the empty flask away without a thought.

"Hollering hags of Hades!" he uttered with a long, whooshing breath thereafter. Too weak to stand any longer, Gord put his back against the curving rock of the conduit and allowed his knees to buckle. Slowly he sank to a sitting position, the cold flow of the dark water washing his body all the way to his ribcage. He didn't notice, for his eyes were riveted to something discernible in the water nearby. There, just under the surface, picked out by the light of the enspelled stone of his lantern, was a globular object, white and familiar somehow. Then he recognized it. The thing was a human skull!

With a shriek Gord rose, water flying from him as he stood. He still held his sword, and he used the weapon to strike at the grinning sphere of bone. There wasn't sufficient water between skull and blade to lessen the force of his blows. The third time the edge struck bone, the thing broke into bits.

"There, Theobald, there!" Gord cried as he delivered the last stroke. "This time you'll die forever!"

With that, he used his boot to kick the fragments, and they washed away into the deeper channel and out of sight, just as the other parts of the unnatural thing had done but a short time before.

The trauma of what had just transpired was gone. He had proved he was able to stand up to Theobald, both as a human and as a monstrous horror of the worst imaginable sort. The thing he had just fought had to have been fashioned from the remains of the beggarmaster. No other will could have been strong enough and evil enough to collect rottenness and filth into a congealed mass and make it have semblance of life and a purpose.

Oh, yes, the monster had had a purpose. It had lurked there by the treasure, waiting, growing, knowing that some day Gord would come there to find the iron box and take the wealth away. Then the thing that had been Theobald would strike. Revenge, assimilation of his body into its own bulk, and . . . and what? The thought made him shudder again, mentally and physically: unlife as a conglomerate thing, a lurking horror seeking other lives to consume, a oneness with Theobald.

"It was the lightstone that did it," Gord said aloud as the realization came to him. The enspelled brilliance of his lantern destroyed the corrupt creation born of hatred, darkness, and vile stuff.

"I did well enough, Theobald, for I struck the blow that finally ended you. But the light weakened you, ate your form away, and made it possible." He was exhilarated, almost satisfied, by what he had accomplished. He was almost ready to turn away then and there, forget about the treasure, and go back the way he had come. But he stayed — not out of greed, he told himself, but because to leave without the strongbox would be to give the beggarmaster a last triumph. Small it might be in relative terms, but the treasure was what the thing had held dear, and that too must be cleansed.

Hours later, Gord was back in the sunlight. It had taken a long time to find the iron container, even with the help of the light that water didn't extinguish. When he located it, he fixed his leather thong to one handle and dragged it out of the muck that covered the bottom of the basin and into the channel of the canal that it fed. That finally done, he had broken the lock and seen the contents of the chest for the first time.

It was disappointing. But, all things considered, Gord supposed it had to be. Most of the coins were corroded brass, bronze, or copper — corroded because the chest was not waterproof. But there were some of more precious sort, enough silver, electrum, and gold too to fill one of his small pouches. Like the man, Theobald's treasure was shabby and mean for the most part. Only cheap jewelry, glass, and valueless stones remained in the chest with the stained coins. Gord left the lot standing in the dark waters of the canal beneath Old City. If any others should ever find it, let them wonder.

Rather than try to climb back up by using the knotted cord, Gord decided to find an easier means of leaving the subterranean realm. He was too tired physically, too drained to face a climb like that, but his mind was still keen. In a short time he found a way upward, just as he remembered seeing depicted on the old plan, and after that it had been an easy matter to get to the clean air above. It was a long slog home, but he managed, cloak pulled around him to hide the bedraggled condition of his garments.

One thing more remained to be done before Gord could go to his apartment and sleep for a whole day. He was determined to accomplish that last thing before allowing exhaustion to have its way. . . .

"What's this?" The tall cleric was astonished at the glittering coins he had just found in the chapel's poor box.

His sole acolyte was uncertain. "A young student was here briefly an hour or so ago. I didn't pay attention, because I had duties to perform. . . . Could he have given so much?"

"If he was a slight, dark-haired lad of about sixteen, I think he just could have," the priest said, letting it go at that.

Chapter 14

WHAT IS A CITY? What makes it singular? Memorable? A place regarded with affection or distaste? Gord knew the city of Greyhawk. Industry and trade made it what it was. Its location and government made it a singular entity, similar to other cities, perhaps, but distinctive too . . . perhaps.

Gord was beginning to hate the place, hate his existence in it, and the questions in his mind had no final answers. Was it eighteen or nineteen years he had been dwelling within Greyhawk? He didn't know exactly. What was important was that he had never been farther than a long bowshot from the double walls of the place. What was the city of Dyvers like? He had heard about it, read its history, but beyond that the other great free city of the Flanaess might as well have been on one of the moons for all Gord had experienced of its reality.

"Bring me another bottle of the black wine of Pomarj," the young man called. There was no friendliness in his tone, and the harassed serving wench shot him a look as dark as the wine he had just demanded. Gord returned her look with hard eyes, and the girl went off quickly to comply. She and Gord had been on other, more pleasant terms not long ago, but she knew he was moody and thought him strange.

"Why do you drink this filthy stuff?" the girl demanded crossly as she banged the heavy bottle down before him.

Gord regretted being sharp. After all, it wasn't her fault that he was thoroughly discontented. "Because it reminds me of you, dear Meg — dark and tasty," he replied with a small smile, handing her several large coins as he did so.

"Liar!" Despite the compliment and the overpayment, Black Meggin was having none of Gord's overtures. "You swill it because of the stuff they put in it. You're an addict!"

"Keep the change, love," Gord said as the girl spun around and went to answer the call of another patron. She had a point. At two hundred a bottle, the inky stuff was costly. Its bitter aftertaste did grow on one, and its effects were at least habituating.

"Do I drink to dispel the dark mood? Or is it the drink which cloaks me in such a state?" He asked these questions softly aloud. No one was near enough to his little table to hear. "What does it matter? I like it, and I can easily afford it. Drink it I shall."

A trio of men sat and conversed among themselves several tables away from Gord. They were strangers to this tavern known as the Man in the Moon, and from their garb it was evident that they came from another place — Urnstmen, possibly, and surely merchants or traders. Without being obvious about it, the three had been keeping a close watch on Gord's every move. Black Pomarj wine was rare, especially costly since so little was made now due to the humanoid occupation of the territory.

"He gave the wench the value of a full silver piece," a hawk-nosed man murmured to his two associates.

"That's nothing," a man with small eyes next to him said. "I saw the gleam of yellow when he reached in and fetched his payment forth."

The third fellow, a bull-necked man with a closely

trimmed beard that only partially hid a sickle-shaped scar on his cheek, merely nodded and called, "Come, girl, more ale here!"

Sunk as he was in his own mood, Gord gave no indication that he was noticing the men's attention. Since he had abandoned his studies in favor of a more active life, the young man had changed considerably. Even after his friend and companion, San, had gone off to pursue membership in the Thieves' Guild, and also to pursue the daughter of a member of that association, Gord had remained pretty much unchanged. For a time he had remained a carefree student, a seemingly normal member of the large group attending one or another of the various colleges of Greyhawk's university.

Certainly, he was different in that he managed to provide for his living all by himself. He did informally and without the sanction of the guild what San now did with its approval . . . thievery. By using his considerable talents and skills, Gord earned a comfortable living and put himself through college nicely. Discovery of that knowledge would have shocked the authorities of the august institution. It also would have brought the young man before the tribunals of the city. To practice the trade of thief without guild membership was forbidden.

It was almost six months since he had left his old apartment to begin a new life. Gord still read whatever he could get his hands on — and books were not common — and maintained his active work learning the art of fighting with dagger, sword, and the two weapons in combination. He and San had determined to learn fencing skills as a key to their ultimate survival. Being boys alone in a city filled with predatory adults, their decision had been wise. Now that Gord was away from Grey College, he still took instruction. Currently, he went weekly to learn from a retired mercenary who lived in the Foreign Quarter. That would have to change soon, however. Because Gord actively pursued thievery now, as a gambler, confidence man, and burglar principally, it was necessary to change his identity and residence frequently. Still, he knew he could always find instruction, for the city was filled with capable warriors willing to accept coin in return for lessons in weapon-play.

Tonight would be his last at the Man in the Moon tavern. It was time to relocate his dwelling, change identities, and thus effectively disappear. When it came to being a lone thief in Greyhawk, one couldn't be too careful. Every hand was against the rogue — city police, guild, and citizen alike. Gord idly twisted the drooping end of one of his moustachios. Although young, he had a heavy beard, and his fast-growing facial hair made changes of appearance easy.

"Will more changing help?" He asked the question mentally. "No," he mused to himself. "I am what I am."

He didn't like that conclusion, inescapable as it was. Whether residing in the slums or the High Quarter, he was still an orphan. He knew not his parents or his heritage, nor did he have a friend. As a student he had used his thievery to maintain himself in the sheltered world of the university. There he had felt a sense of meaning, had believed his life had purpose. That had been a delusion, of course.

Now he was using his larcenous and acrobatic abilities to strike out at the place he grudgingly called home. It was only fair that this city filled with hawks be preyed upon by another. His gains would help to repay him for his own suffering in this place. It was long past time that the score be evened, time for Gord to live high at the expense of the other folks of Greyhawk. There were, he knew, other young rebels like himself in the city. Perhaps if he joined forces with some of them he would find satisfaction and companionship — and best of all, peace of mind.

The bottle was nearly empty. Gord spilled the last of the ebon wine into his goblet and quaffed it off at a toss. "Shall I wait for you tonight, Meg?" He already knew the answer she would give, but the banter was part of his game, related to the art of vanishing without being thought of as having done so for suspicious motives.

The black-haired Meggin stopped and looked at him without smiling. "Leaving so early, Gord? No wonder, what with the amount of that drink you've swilled down! That will keep you warm and content, I'm sure, so as not to be needing my company." Then she softened a little and came close, looking straight into his eyes as Gord stood up. "There's no use our being together, you see. You're unhappy, and I can't change that no matter how hard I try. Ask me again, Gord, when you know yourself."

Gord gave her his best boyish grin, grabbed her around her narrow waist, and planted a kiss full on her pretty lips. "I love you, darlin' girl, but you're right as always! It's time I was off to see the lands about this great world. I'll seek my fortune — and myself, too. When I come back a rich man you'll marry me, now won't you, Meg?"

"That'll be the day," Meg said, pushing him away with mock anger. "You'll be back here tomorrow, drinking that nasty wine again and trying to seduce every lass with a well-turned leg," she snapped, and then hurried off to attend to her work.

Meg didn't allow Gord to see the moisture in her eyes. She knew he wasn't just talking — indeed, he wouldn't be back. That she had sensed the moment Gord had come into the tavern this evening. He was going away, possibly never to return, and Meggin truly cared for the young man, scoundrel though she believed him to be. She would have preferred him to stay, under different circumstances, but Meg was no fool. Gord could never love her, or any other, until he came to some decisions inside, found something he sought after. That was why he drank the black wine of the Pomarj. "Goodbye, Gord," she whispered as the young man strode out of the Man in the Moon.

A minute later the three nondescript men left the tavern also. They didn't bother finishing a nearly full pitcher of ale that was at their table. Meggin wondered about that later as she cleared their place, but she thought nothing further of it.

The trio followed the young man as he headed toward the southwestern portion of the quarter, with every step taking him deeper into the dark, quiet byways of the district.

"See, he reels like a sodden sailor," hissed the pig-eyed man.

"Better still," the man with the thick neck and the scar on his cheek said with a tone of satisfaction, "he goes to where there will be none to witness what is about to occur!" It was evident that the bull-necked fellow was the leader, and he made a point of letting the other two know this by his words. Scarface had the last and best always.

"As usual?" The query by the hawk-faced member of the trio brought a quick nod in affirmation from Scarface. Without further instruction the questioner strode purposefully across the narrow street. He walked quickly, paralleling the path of their target, and was soon ahead of Gord on the opposite side of the way. The drunken young man paid him not the slightest attention, intent as he was on simply making his journey home without falling.

"As near as I recall . . ." Gord sang softly to himself as he went, occasionally using his right hand to steady himself against the front of one building or another. "'Twas an evenin' . . ." he caroled out, loudly now, as if pleased with his performance, ". . . in the fall. . . ." — and at that point he actually lost his balance and toppled to the ground in the darkness beside a building.

"Take him now!" Scarface called out to the man with the hawk face as he and the pig-eyed fellow ran toward the fallen youth. The lead man was already crossing to get to the victim when the command was shouted, for he had been watching and waiting for the right moment. The three thugs converged on the prone victim as vultures swoop down to feast upon the carcass of a dying animal.

The hawk-faced man was the first to arrive, his dagger poised to strike — and an instant after he lunged toward the fallen figure, a scream sounded along the lane. No shutters flew open to shed light on the happenings, no doors cracked to allow the inhabitants of the street to see. Nobody cared to investigate late-night events in the Foreign Quarter. Even the watch patrolled only the main thoroughfares and the streets along the walls. Those who dwelled within or dared to walk through this neighborhood were fair game.

"That blaster is already looting him!" This came from Pig-eyes as he and his companion ran up to where the two shapes were mingled in the deep shadows. They had seen their comrade fall upon the prone fellow, and assumed he must certainly be going for the victim's purse even now.

"You'll get yours!" Scarface growled at the hawk-faced man through his panting as he lumbered up to where the assault had taken place. The threat was obvious and certain to be carried out. The thick-necked leader would brook no attempt at grabbing spoils without his approval. Scarface bent over the two bodies, grabbed his comrade by the collar, and flung him off the victim. A second too late, he realized what he had done.

"He's already gotten it, friend!" Gord said loudly as he lunged upward to a kneeling position and rammed his short sword into the man's paunchy gut. Now it was Scarface's turn to yell. He let out a roar of pain, for the blade had sunk into his vitals. Clutching his belly with both hands, the bull-necked man reeled and staggered away, moaning.

Pig-eyes had been a few steps behind when his boss got to the scene, which gave him time to stop and pull out the weapon he hadn't thought he would need. The momentary delay did Gord some good as well. The man cursed as he ran at Gord and drove a wickedly aimed blow at him — but the curved blade of his knife sank into the back of his dead associate instead. At the last instant, Gord had pulled the hawk-faced fellow's corpse between himself and his attacker, using it as a shield.

"Gods—" Pig-eyes began to sputter another oath as his blade sank in, but he got no farther, for the body suddenly sailed upward and outward, striking him. As the would-be mugger stumbled backward, trying to get free of the sprawling corpse and pull out his knife at the same time, Gord sprang up and went over to press a full attack.

Drunk he was, but not so much as he had put on. Further, this trio of thugs was inexpert. Gord had figured them for bandits when he had first entered the Man in the Moon, before he had fully sunk into his black mood and black wine. His young age and heavy purse had made the three incautious. That pair of mistakes, taking him for an easy mark and having overconfidence in their own ability, had cost two of them dearly. Now the third member of the group had to face the same possibility. As Gord advanced toward him, sword held before him in his right hand, the man had finally figured out how to get the leverage he needed to yank his curved blade out of his comrade's body.

"Free your knife," Gord said to him, "for this must be a fair contest." He laughed as he said that, for such sport made him forget his own discontent.

"Help me, Baldor!" The fellow called to his bull-necked leader, but that man had no more stomach for the fight . . . in more ways than one. Seeing that, Pig-eyes crouched low, knife before him. His stance was good; it was evident that he had fought this way often enough to feel comfortable and act instinctively. His renewed confidence showed as he addressed Gord. "Fair? You lying little shit! Sword against knife is never equal."

As a mugger the man left much to be desired, but Gord sensed his opponent to be a skilled fighter as he cautiously edged closer to the small-eyed man. "Perhaps, perhaps not," Gord replied, flicking his blade out to observe how his adversary reacted. He knew that the contest was not as unequal or unfair as Pig-eyes would have him believe. A good knife-man was a terrible opponent, if he could close.

Pig-eyes saw his opportunity when the tip of the short sword moved slightly to the young man's right as Gord edged around the body he had thrown at the small-eyed thug. To make matters even more promising, the young punk had thrust his left hand behind his back at the same time, leaving his torso virtually unprotected.

"Yaah!" the man shouted to distract his enemy as he swung his left arm outward to knock the sword wide and away. As he did that he leaped forward, and in a second Pig-eyes was almost upon his target, his sharp-edged knife held before him to sink inward and slice upward in a killing stroke.

Then Pig-eyes was shocked by a sudden move-

ment, and the sound of steel on steel! Gord had met
his knife with a dagger — a weapon that until an instant earlier had been concealed behind the young
man's back.

"Not so easy . . ." Gord grunted, needing all of his
strength to fend off the stroke of the pig-eyed attacker. The man was full-grown, bigger, and far heavier
than Gord. As they met, Gord pivoted on his right
heel, turned his body, and allowed the attacker's own
momentum and straining to carry him away to Gord's
left. He stumbled, off balance, as Gord completed his
turn. The sword's blade arced upward as he spun,
then came slicing down, and the fatty neck of the pig-
eyed man was nearly severed.

". . . for you!" Gord finished as the cut went home.
Then he turned to look for the third of the trio, the
one named Baldor. He was nowhere to be seen, and
Gord didn't bother to look for him. In fact, he didn't
even bother to see what the purses of the two dead
men contained. From his assessment of them at the
tavern, he judged that the men wouldn't have more
than a few coppers between them. After wiping his
sword clean of gore, he hurried on. This was no time
to have attention drawn to him.

Gord's chambers were in a tall, narrow building
that housed an apothecary. The man and his family
lived just above the shop, while the three upper floors
were rented out to tenants. As usual, Gord had happily taken the uppermost floor. From there he could
enter and leave via the rooftop, unnoticed. This night
he did just that, ascending to the top of a nearby
warehouse and from there gaining his own rooms silently and unseen. Although he intended never to
wear his present clothing again, Gord packed all of
his belongings into a leather traveling case. When he
was finished, nothing remained behind. Leaving by
the same means he had used to arrive, Gord worked

his way back along the steep rooftops, balancing the baggage case carefully. Soon he was back in the warehouse, and there he took a few items from the case before closing it up again and hiding it in a corner. It would eventually be found — days, weeks, or months later. Someone would be a few coins richer, and nobody would care enough about the mystery to inquire.

By now he was familiar with virtually every secret route that allowed egress from the Foreign Quarter without passing under the eyes of the city's guards. His choice this time was a secret tunnel under a tower above Safelock Portal, a place where the inner wall of Old City met that which bounded the Foreign Quarter. It was too close to the active patrols on the street and the wall to appeal to clandestine parties of folk from Greyhawk's underworld community, so it was especially safe for him. Avoiding the watch had never been a problem for him, and this time was no exception. Gord found his way below the streets, passed quickly along a corridor there, and emerged just as rapidly on the other side of the wall.

Early the next day he purchased a new cloak and a large chest. Then, with hired porters in tow, he acquired a larger wardrobe, commenting that it would not do for a stranger in the city to be garbed in outlandish fashion. Because he shopped in the trade district adjacent to the High Quarter, the merchants who profited from his free spending made no note of it. Many a rich traveler did the same there, and the young man was no different from the rest.

Later that same day, as the sun was beginning to sink, Gord sallied forth again, this time without bearers. Here he purchased a hat or two, and there gloves and gauntlets. A doublet for a pair of electrum coins, a short cape of superior tailoring for a like sum. Several times he went back to the little villa he had rented, dropped off his parcels, and set forth again. By dusk, as shops were closing their doors and shuttering their fronts, Gord had completed his work. The armoire in his bedchamber was filled, as was the trunk. Clothing of many styles and of varying degree of material was on hand. He could now go forth as a noble from some nearby kingdom, an ordinary youth traveling to seek his fortune, or in any one of a dozen other guises.

"This city is always ready to fleece the unwary, to use the weak, and to pay respect to the rich and powerful," he said aloud as he donned the rich apparel typical of Velunese aristocrats. "Let them think me, then, a noble young lamb, rich and foolish, ready for shearing, too weak to even bleat a protest should I discover what is being done to me.

"In turn," he said with a hard smile after a short pause, "I shall fleece the shearers, use the strong, and employ wealth and position to gain the upper hand. By their own dishonesty and greed I'll play them for dunces, and none will be the wiser until it is too late."

With that he set off into the evening, whistling a jaunty air. The poor had no cause to fear, nor even the wealthy but honest. But woe to any of the rest whom Gord the rogue might encounter. He had come to grips with himself and decided it was time to redress his status even as he changed his attitude.

Now he still was only what he was, but the "he" of now was vastly different from the "he" of before, and the prospect of a satisfying future gave him purpose and confidence.

Chapter 15

THE CREAK AND GROAN of oaken axles and roan-wood planks made soft music to Gord's ears. As the Attloi gypsy wagon rolled along the old road heading north, he lay on a narrow cot built into its side and dozed. It was pleasant here, good to be off the water, splendid to be away from Greyhawk, far away. Flashes of memory came to him as the caravan trundled along. . . .

The years he had kept up his masquerades in the gray-walled city of hawks were well past now, although he could recall his duplicity and daring there as if it were yesterday. As gambler, swindler, and confidence man he had been successful indeed; so successful that the city now paid keen attention to all strangers who were for the least reason suspicious. A chance encounter with his old friend San, now son-in-law of the Grand Guildmaster of Thieves, Arentol, prompted Gord to decide it was time to travel. San, perhaps, had saved him from being brought into the Citadel for official questioning — Arentol was, after all, an oligarch as well as the chief of Greyhawk's thieves.

Rather than being disgruntled about his need to get out of the city, Gord took it in stride and even welcomed the change. His rakish pose and devils-may-care attitude had been naught but a bluff face anyway. In truth he had become sick and disgusted with the poses of Grand Count Sir Margus, Poffert Tyne the jewel merchant, and all the other guises he had affected. After two years and more of high living in the city, his desire for revenge on the city of hawks had been assuaged, and it was high time to get out into the wilds of the wide, wide world.

He had spent nearly a year sailing the Nyr Dyv in the barges of the Rhennee. At first this had seemed a leisurely way to broaden his experiences, but now the recollection of that thought nearly made him laugh aloud. Perils and dangers there had been aplenty, whether aboard the barges or in one port of call or another. He had faced several sea monsters during that year, fought duels with Rhennee bravos, and gone with them on forays into water's-edge communities to rob and steal. With all of that, though, nothing had compared to the risks involved with courting and winning the affections of one of their dark-eyed and beautiful women. He'd done that, and then had the devils' own time getting rid of the scheming bitch! Wondering what had become of the hot-tempered Adaz, Gord drifted back into his doze, and the wagon creaked slowly on.

*　*　*

As Gord dreamed of his past adventures, there was, in Greyhawk, a discussion of him. The individuals concerned, and their talk, would have surprised the young thief indeed had he overheard the scene; but he was hundreds of leagues distant, asleep, and totally unaware.

"I can't tarry here long," the plump lord of beggars said to the other six individuals in the small room. "There are drawbacks to having headship. . . . Who'd have supposed that!?" Chinkers looked from one to

CITY OF HAWKS

the other, as if expecting an answer to what he well knew was a rhetorical question. He smiled when the tall priest of Fharlanghn chuckled. Then another figure spoke.

"You have kept track of him, then?" It was Markham, merchant and chief agent of the Balance in Greyhawk. His deferential tone indicated that the man he spoke to was his superior. Gord would have been amazed to see that man — flabbergasted indeed, for it was none other than the one he had called Uncle Bru more than a decade past.

"To a certain extent, yes," the big man said slowly. His face was heavily lined, and his beard grizzled, but his eyes still showed a youthful gleam and twinkle. "He was being watched by our friends amongst the bargefolk, but we've lost him now. . . ."

Clyde, now a member of the Lord Mayor's Own Guards, and an officer at that, shot a glance at his companion, old Tapper. That worthy too was a respected community member, having risen to one of the council of presiding masters of the Craftsmen's Guild. He didn't comment either, however, but turned to look at the cleric as that man ventured a question.

"Lady Risteria, is there something you can add?" The priest wondered why the wizardess had been silent all this time, for although the bearded Bru was nominally the leader here, there could be no question as to which of their number was the most powerful and most easily informed.

She had been holding off just to see what the others might have to say, and because she wanted to be asked for her rede instead of volunteering facts and opinions like the other members of the group. Now she decided to take her turn.

"Thank you, Zarten. There is indeed something for me to say here." The wizardess settled comfortably in her chair and took a moment to adjust her long gown of plain gray. "We have helped the lad. . . . I'd say we have meddled, save for the fact that wiser heads than my own have directed us in the course taken . . . but to what purpose?" She took a breath and answered her own question. "Well, he is no longer a weakling, no more a coward, not a misfit dweller in the poorest places of Greyhawk. But just what *is* this man called Gord?"

This question was not entirely rhetorical. Lady Risteria paused to look at each of the six men in turn. Some of the expressions she saw showed the wizardess that the minds behind them held definite opinions, but none of the six spoke. She nodded, satisfied with their continued deference, and went on.

"I submit that we have somehow erred in what we did. Sometimes the Balance allows us too much latitude, and I fear that this is a case in point. Instead of a poor, ignorant, and useless slum-youth, Gord is a knowledgeable, skilled, wandering thief and ne'er-do-well. He shows no loyalty, no concerns for aught but his own pleasure, acts on mere whims, and now companions recklessly with Attloi gypsies, squandering ill-gotten gains and increasing his efficacy at finding more such wealth by association with those shiftless cheats and liars!"

"Thank you, Lady Risteria, we—" Before Bru could say more, the wizardess cut him off. She had more to say and would say it!

"Why didn't you act, Markham, to see that he remained at the university? And you, Zarten — as a priest, it was your duty to encourage him to study and follow useful paths in order to reach a better goal than that he has attained. Far better a cleric, even, if no suasion could be found to turn his mind to dweomercraefting! Yet you all, each and every one of you, served to keep him on course so that now he is nothing more than a wretched thief!"

216

"Madam!" Tapper sputtered, red-faced. Clyde was too angry to even manage a sputter, and the Beggar-master, Thadeus, better known as Chinkers, had great difficulty controlling his ire as well. If Risteria spoke thus of thievery, what would she say of thiggery? The very thought of her sharp tongue dissecting his profession made the plump fellow wince.

"Who here is so perfect?" It was Bru, speaking for them all, who asked that. The wizardess opened her mouth to reply, but the big, bearded man pressed on. "The Balance makes no such value judgments, lady, so by what right do you place your craft — or that of Zarten — above any other? There is no answer, lady, for there is no right. Neither you nor I may sit in judgment of Gord, or of those above us who directed our actions in this regard. We did as we were asked because we accept the guidance of the Enlightened. Shall I now contact them and state your dissent?"

The wizardess's face grew pale. "No, Master Bru, I think that will be quite unnecessary. I must apologize to you all for losing my composure and not checking my speech. It's just that I thought the boy had so much promise . . ."

"And still does — or has even more so!" It was Clyde, finally able to voice his opinion. "That one is a man now — and never has a finer practitioner of the art of thievery existed, to my knowledge! As a stripling he outshined most adults. Full grown, Gord must be a match for the masters of the guilds both east and west. Why, in a decade or two his name might be legend amongst all who— "

"Who know of the rankings of speculation and depredation," the priest filled in. "Yet we aren't here to discuss Gord's merits, either — and it needn't be said that I happen to side with Lady Risteria in regard to deploring thievery, on grounds too self-evident to go into here."

"Get on with it, man!" Markham was beginning to grow weary of this conclave. Bickering should be reserved for trading and kept out of council. His look said that plainly enough.

"Of course, of course," ahemed Zarten. "I suppose I assisted the lad's course by supplying him with the lightstone, after all. . . . To the point, then. Good lady mage, please intelligence us on young Gord's whereabouts and likely prospects now. You mentioned that he was part of a band of gypsy folk, as I recall."

"Quite right," Lady Risteria said. "When I was notified of this meeting, I took the trouble to scry out the subject, and thereafter I sought advice arcane from certain powers favorably attuned to me." She paused to allow comment, but not one of the six others present spoke, so the wizardess resumed her account.

"Gord is a very able young man, of that there is no doubt. Since leaving our city he has grown in skill, both at his . . . craft, and with the weapons of warfare as well. The Attloi he now accompanies are artful instructors, and young Gord practices diligently at gymnastics and acrobatics, rope walking, tumbling, the whole useless lot common to jugglers, wandering performers, and the rest of the gypsy lot who employ such feats to further their own—"

"Ahem!"

The loud clearing of his throat and the accompanying look from Markham sufficed to put Risteria back on track again. ". . . livelihood," she finished, doing her best to remain unruffled. "It seems he will become more able than ever to succeed, yet there are many dangers ahead for Gord, and many clouded areas. Someone, something, a power perhaps, still interposes itself if his skein is examined too closely."

"I too encountered such interference, lady," Zarten said solemnly. "I think it was no evil one who interfered, though. I cannot be sure, of course, for I dared not pry too strongly," the cleric added for the benefit of the others. "It seemed evident that he will be in peril often. One of ours should be near just in case."

"And that is why we are met here this very hour," the bearded leader of the council said. "Your words are well taken. Before nightfall I will be departing Greyhawk, and I will pass along the opinion of this group to those above me. Is that the voice of us all, then? Gord should have full attention in the near future because of impending peril?"

Nods of assent to this came from Tapper, Clyde, Markham, and Chinkers. "I concur," said Lady Risteria. The priest spoke last, saying, "It would seem to be the most prudent course for the Balance, assuming that he is still considered to be important to future events — for Gord does go into danger, of that there can be no question."

"Then that is the message I shall give to my superiors," Bru said, concluding the meeting.

*　*　*

At about that time Gord awakened. He had had a bad dream, and the sudden jolting of the wagon brought him out of it abruptly and thankfully. Wiping the sweat from his face, the young thief went to the back of the vehicle and swung open the little door at its end. It was no feat to jump out and run along beside the slowly moving wagon. His two friends were on their steeds up ahead someplace, and Gord would seek them out now. Soon camp would be made for the night, and he wanted to see what plans were afoot for the evening.

"Hey, Channos! Elo! Wait for me!" The two young Attloi gypsies had been his friends, and instructors of a sort too, since last summer. It was early spring now, and Gord was no longer a pupil. If anything, he

219

could show the two of them a trick or two at acrobatics, but boon companions they were still.

"Where have you been hiding?" Elo demanded as he turned his horse in Gord's direction.

Channos was less patient than that. "Hurry up! Get your horse and join us. We won't wait, you know! There's an inn at Karrish, the village just ahead. If we don't get there soon, the rest of the men will be there to get the best pickings before us!" With that Channos rode off and Elo followed him, leaving Gord to run back for his own mount and catch up as best he could.

Perhaps the two thought the village's only inn was a splendid place to be. In a sense it was, considering the long distance their band of wagons had traveled before coming to such a place, and the relative quality of similar places found in this part of the Flanaess. Gord, however, comparing it to the many establishments he had patronized from Greyhawk to Radigast City and beyond, found it disappointing. Even the girls here were plain or lacked vivacity, or both. Although the folk here kept a sharp eye on the visitors, they at least seemed ready enough to accept their temporary presence, Gord noticed.

Even his two friends seemed deflated after spending a time drinking at the place. "These women have no life in them," Channos observed at large.

"Shall I start a fight?" big Elo asked, a smile lighting his face.

"No," Gord said, grabbing the bigger man and steering him toward the exit. "Come on, Channos. The three of us have some thinking to do."

Hardly a fortnight later Gord rode away from the Attloi encampment in the vast prairies where the gypsies spent the summer raising, training, and selling horses. With him went his two friends, Channos and Elo. All three were heading northward to see if perhaps they couldn't find excitement and riches in a kingdom none of them had ever been to before.

* * *

Elsewhere, some distance away, a very important man was concerning himself with the young thief. "How closely can you monitor him?" the one-eyed man asked.

Three hooded figures, unbleached linen cowls shadowing their faces, sat in tall-backed chairs. The central one spoke in reply to the one-eyed man's query. "He seems to be unwatched by any others . . . at this time, at least, so we are able to follow him closely, Lord Gellor. We watch now, and will do so later too. You are needed."

"There is trouble, then?"

"Always, constantly. This young man Gord is a difficult subject!"

"Show me, please, the course you have foreseen. I will do my utmost to serve as you direct, Enlightened Ones."

The air shimmered as the three figures made small gestures in unison. A transparent set of images appeared in the air, as if the one-eyed Gellor were viewing a faint mirage or a ghostly vision. He knew it was neither, but rather what he saw before him was a projection of the future of the youth, a series of scenes that flashed past rapidly, an hour's time but a minute, with sudden blurs where the trio of Enlightened Ones caused the events to go by even faster. At one point Gellor called "stop" without thinking. The three made the images halt and didn't go on again until the one-eyed man politely, and rather sheepishly, asked them to.

Suddenly the vivid images faded into shadows, and the scene vanished. "What's this?" Gellor gasped.

The three figures rose jerkily, crying out together.

Gellor was shocked. "Have I done something?"

"No, faithful agent, it is not you who has caused this distress," one of the three said as all of them sat down again. The one-eyed man was surprised to note it was the leftmost figure, not the central one, who had spoken.

"It is some agency, a force to be reckoned with, which so discommoded us," the rightmost of the trio continued to explain.

"Yet we suffered no real harm," the central figure noted. "It was a demand for personal privacy, perhaps, but not an attack. The youth himself could never do such a thing, so we must conclude that he has other . . . friends."

Gellor wanted more of an explanation, but did not press for it. He supposed that more than privacy could be involved, much more, and the force displayed could be either good or ill. Then he was drawn from his introspection by a question from the central figure. What did Gellor intend to do?

"Alert the local lord to the fact that there are bandits in his hunting preserve," the one-eyed man replied. "The danger to Gord there is mortal unless some agency intervenes, I think," he explained, recalling what he had seen. "That change leaves but a single likely course open, so thereafter I'm off for the realms of brigandry. I'll position myself so as to encounter Gord there and keep my most watchful eye on him."

Did a slight rocking on the part of the Enlightened Ones indicate they appreciated his little joke? After a couple of moments, the central figure spoke again.

"We will not scry any more now, nor will we employ any agent whose power is such as to attract notice. A black wind has just swept through the aether — it came from the void and sends eddies even here.

Go swiftly, Lord Gellor. We will contact you again as needed."

"Thank you, Enlightened Ones. I will serve as instructed and await further instructions as I proceed," the one-eyed man said with a slight bow. Then Gellor turned and strode from the chamber and away into the night. He didn't bother to look behind, for he knew that the place he had been in was no longer there. That was the way of the Enlightened Ones.

He had much to do, many affairs to attend to in a short time. Several crowned heads employed him as an agent, and he served them well and faithfully, to the limit prescribed by his greater duty to the Balance. That gave him perfect cover, of course. When Gellor departed at first light on the morrow it would be on business of state. Elsewhere Gellor would be recognized too, and accepted as a member in good standing of groups and organizations of less savory sort. Being a spy and agent was like that, and in truth the one-eyed man enjoyed his duty.

Several weeks later, in a dirty little town in the heart of the Bandit Kingdoms, Gellor finally met Gord. It was the beginning of a long and adventure-filled friendship.

Chapter 16

"I NEVER THOUGHT TO SEE YOU HERE!"

The exclamation of the young thief was filled with joy, for before him stood his friend and sometimes mentor, Gellor. "How did you find me here? No, never mind that. Come in! You can tell me everything after you've had a chance to sit comfortably."

The one-eyed man smiled and clasped Gord's arm in greeting. "It is good to meet again, eh?" As his young host led the way, he entered the suite of rooms and took a seat on a divan while Gord busied himself getting wine and goblets. The place was well and comfortably furnished but showed no trace of riches. On the contrary, it showed ample means of only average sort. The young fellow was no fool. Gellor knew that Gord could well have taken a villa and filled it with lavish trappings, lived luxuriously, and reveled. But that would have attracted attention and brought certain downfall.

"What are you doing here in Greyhawk? I thought you'd be roaming the east, doing important things at the behest of dukes and kings!"

His face betraying nothing, Gellor replied, "Perhaps I'm doing just that, Master Gord. . . . Or perhaps there are greater lords than that directing me."

"You are here on some affair of state or another, then?"

"Let's just say I was in the neighborhood and thought I'd pay my respects to an old friend," Gellor said with a warm smile. Before Gord could ask more questions, his comrade hastened on. "Since you left the east, things there have settled down into a boring state of mundane sort. During such a lull I deemed it possible to enjoy a bit of holiday, so here I am in Greyhawk."

"I don't believe a word of that," Gord countered, pouring them both brimming goblets of wine. He handed one to Gellor and after both men had drunk, the young man went on. "Has it to do with the demon we slew? The evil relic called the Middle Key? Some war about to break out hereabouts? Come on, you one-eyed fox, tell me!"

"No, and yes. Possibly, and absolutely not. . . . I am not being frivolous, Gord. Who of us can say? Neither you nor I are capable of ordering events or determining fate." Gellor looked at his young friend, and it was evident from the expression on his face that the man's explanation would never do. Gellor sighed and took another drink of wine. It was excellent stuff, a prime vintage of golden Keoish, and he savored it, allowing it to lave his tongue, roll on his palate, and slowly make its way on down so as to enable him to enjoy the full aftertaste as well.

Appreciating his guest's savoring of the refreshment, Gord remained silent while Gellor relaxed and enjoyed, but he never took his eyes from the man. He was clearly waiting for more of an explanation, and would not waver until he got it, and Gellor was aware of both of those facts.

"All right, Gord, I shall be a little more specific — otherwise, I'll never have sufficient peace to properly quaff the remainder of this superb wine you've so foolishly provided to me."

Taking the hint, Gord put bottle to glass and filled

Gellor's goblet again. "How long has it been since you and I met?"

"More than a year — two, near enough. From that question, I take it you have needed no special amusements to pass the time here in Greyhawk. . . ."

"That's so, although I do seek some diversion now and again. Chert — surely you remember him? — went off to find more action and adventure many months ago, though it seems but yesterday. I've kept occupied, shall we say, here and about, making a modest living this way and that. But the sameness cloys, Gellor. Have you come with some momentous quest for me?" When the one-eyed man shrugged and shook his head in tentative fashion, Gord's interest was even more piqued, if that was possible.

"Well, don't just sit there supping on my wine and being as silent as a stone! You'll not lure me into more discussion of my own affairs until you recount your own."

"The druid Greenleaf is more concerned with the minions of the Abyss and malign relics of power than I am. Save your questions for that one," Gellor said with a smile. He knew that he wasn't fooling Gord in the least with his disclaimer, but he wished to direct the conversation to other matters. "Do you think often of your heritage?" he asked after a slight pause.

The young man was serious now. "Too frequently, old friend. It causes me pain, so I gain surcease through action and hazard. There is no one to answer my queries. It is a riddle with no answer. Yet, I find myself going over the matter again and again. . . ." Gord's voice trailed off, his gaze resting on the small box that, as far as he knew, was the only possible clue he had to his past, his parents, his heritage.

"That is one of the reasons why I am come here, Gord. Perhaps there is someone, something, to provide at least a partial answer to your questions." Gord

227

opened his mouth at that, but Gellor cut him off before he could speak. "No, wait, don't interrupt me now. You've been at me as a mosquito on fair flesh, and now I'll speak — only do open another bottle of that wonderful vintage!" Gord complied readily, and the one-eyed man returned to his tale.

"It is a fact, Gord, although one unknown to you until this very minute, I presume, that you have been the subject of some considerable attention. Greater ones than you and I have watched and wondered. Imagine a game of Archchess. . . ." He paused to look at the young man, and Gord nodded. He was an avid gamester, and he knew the sort of contest Gellor was using for his analogy. "Think of it as a three-sided competition, though, and not two or four. Consider also that the pieces and pawns are sometimes of unknown color and shape."

"You infer that the players do not always recognize the allegiance and powers of the men on their game board?"

"Exactly! And it would be appropriate to liken you to such a man on the field of play. What is the blazon on your coat? What rank do you hide?"

Gord waved his hand in denigration. "I am a passably good thief and swordsman. A boon companion, I trust, and a willing adventurer after prizes or against dark foes, but a playing piece in the big game? No, not I — and even were that so, I would be a pawn of lowest station at best!"

"Perhaps that is so, perhaps not," Gellor countered. "Yet you are — or were, anyway — observed by malign ones as well as those of other stances. I think that you alone can determine whether or not you are in play, and if so whether as a pawn or a greater piece. That, my friend, is tied to your past, I think."

"You speak in riddles more abstruse than that which is bound up in my own origin, Gellor," Gord shot back with agitation, rising to his feet. "I can answer your riddle as soon as I find a solution to my own, but I cannot gain even a hint of the latter, so the former shall forever remain unfathomable!"

The one-eyed man granted that with a small nod, but waved Gord back to his seat and called for calmness. "You have done deeds of derring-do, rescued ladies, fought battles large and small, and undertaken many a perilous venture without flinching. Your skills have grown, and you now bear both great magical accoutrements and a seemingly charmed life. Think you that there are many such as you? Do you truly believe that the amulets and weapons and the like which you so blithely accept as part of your existence are commonly held by mortal men? And as to your luck, what can be said? There has been some aid, granted, but how much? How many times would an end have come to other men, ones not so endowed, who were in your place?"

"Hmm. . . . There is possibly something in your words," Gord allowed. "Pray go on, and let me think on this matter as you speak."

"Very generous, your grand grace," Gellor replied with heavy sarcasm. He was not offended, simply getting in a small jibe as is often customary between comrades. "I am a man in that game, as well you know, as is Greenleaf. We joined it because of instruction, but both of us remain in it because of choice. There is something in you, Gord, which gives us hope. Perhaps one day you will find some clue to unlock the mystery of your past, to discover the significance of that ancient coffer and its unimpressive contents. I know not.

"What I do know, though, is that wherever you go, you leave in your wake turmoil and change. The machinations of nobles are foundered by your presence, wars are won, great evil sent howling back to the lower planes, and information suddenly surfaces that is vital to all. Don't you find that passing strange?"

"I hadn't thought on it."

"No, you've been too busy pursuing wenches, playing boyish pranks, pilfering jewels of incredible worth, and playing at being a mysterious nemesis here in this city! Don't mistake my words — I am not faulting you. You have done all these things from necessity and it was most natural, all things considered. My question is, Will you now turn your talents to a more meaningful end?"

That gave him pause. In truth, Gord had again become jaded with life as a rogue in the city; he was rather bored with playing at being the cat burglar, the rake, the carefree wanderer. Even though he could not determine the origin of his life, he did have a growing desire to make it a meaningful one nevertheless. Simply being a thief of utmost skill wasn't the answer, as far as the young man was concerned. He had merely been doing something at which he excelled until something better was presented. He said that to Gellor, and the man reacted in a surprising way.

"Presented? You say that seriously? Do you expect fate to come ambling along and proffer something better to you on a silken cushion?! I am speechless! Perhaps I overestimated you. As an urchin you didn't await anything — you seized opportunities with talons of wisdom far beyond your circumstances. At every turn you acted to better your position, gain, and grow. Now, as youth passes into full-blown manhood, at the very threshold of your prime, you tell me you are content to dally while you await a finer moment?"

"Well . . . that isn't put exactly right," Gord said somewhat defensively. "I am ready now to answer your call."

"Ready to answer, but not going forth to seek the

foe. It is as I said," Gellor retorted. "Only you can determine your purpose and find meaning. Use your
talents to a better purpose, I say!"

"You say much, but still too little! Just what higher goal do you direct me toward, sage?"

Gellor sat back, harrumphing. He had gotten so
caught up in his lecture, as a father might scold an
errant son, that he had gone too far. "Well, ahh, yes,
yes indeed. It is time I got to that. I am not going to
offer firm direction, of course. That would pressure,
suggest far more wisdom than I possess. Still, I can
offer you at least an inkling, and it should suit your
own desires, too."

"Well?" Gord's tone was rather cold, his expression
distant.

"It seems that you are not the only one unsure of
who and what you are, my friend. As I have inferred, I
believe that you are on the field of play, and eventually the attention of the dark players will rest full upon you. If we — and you — gain knowledge first, then
you have every opportunity of not merely avoiding being *en prise*, but being able to move to oppose evil. To
do so, you must know yourself. That might or might
not mean learning of your infancy, your parents, and
all. Whether or not you find out these things, knowing yourself is a worthy aspiration. . . ."

"You avoid the issue, beg the question, and skirt
the point," Gord said as if voicing a rejoinder. "I am a
profligate, and you are about to direct me on a wiser
course, I believe."

"Leave off. I am properly rebuked, and I apologize.
Will you truly hear this now?"

Softening a bit, Gord agreed. "Of course. It's just
difficult for me to withstand such words as you have
said. Remember, dear companion, that I had no such
counsel when I was babe, stripling, or youth."

Gord had no pity for himself in his voice, and

Gellor didn't insult him with a display of pity for him either. Life was what it was for each individual fortunate enough to live it. The man continued to explain.

"In the course of our observations and delvings — not mine, but the activities of those greater than I, in whose service I act — both evil and other interferences plagued our purpose. You, my friend, have a most mysterious skein! With care and skill, some small services were performed by means of dweomers and direct interactions. Those greater ones sought the same answers you seek even now, and they met with blanks. There is a slight something, possibly a matter of no import, but just perhaps something germane. It was detected in a scrying to foresee. That foreseeing was altered in your benefit, but I suddenly recalled something which made me come here to see you."

Now the young man stood and began to pace back and forth in excitement. "You have a clue as to my parents? My home? What? I will venture into the pits of the Nine Hells, the Abyss, or the greatest sink of the nether realm of Hades for such information!"

"Nothing so definite, nor requiring such danger, Gord. Those who probed uncovered something which even they paid no heed to, and it is only my own strange ability to recall things which prompted my visit. Have you any memories at all of your infancy?"

"Not actually . . . just what old Leena related. It was she who told me that the box, there, was my only inheritance, but this only after I discovered it by accident one day. It didn't mean anything to me at the time, but she was cruel and possessive about it. She would keep it hidden away from me and try to torture me by saying she'd burned it to keep warm, sold it for food money, and suchlike. Poor old crazy woman. How do you suppose I came into her care?"

Gellor nodded sympathetically. "From what you've

said, Gord, she was a sad one indeed. She saved that little coffer, though, and you have it. Now that you've showed it to me, I have realized that it is what I recall seeing! The connection was a difficult one, else long ago I'd have told you. In the vision I saw the box was unmarred, magnificent, and within it were nine great black sapphires!"

"You're certain you saw that same container, this very box?" Gord demanded, picking up the worn, scuffed coffer and thrusting it under the one-eyed man's gaze.

In answer, Gellor lifted his black leather eyepatch and viewed the battered wooden box with his enchanted orb, a magical eyeball of gemstone that empowered him to see close up, far away, and things invisible or hidden even by ether or astral vibration as well. When Gellor employed the device, neither illusionary concealment nor any other magical cloaking could prevail against its inspection.

"The very same, Gord. I think, with care and skill, it could be restored to the very state it was in when I saw it in the scrying."

"Nine black sapphires? . . ."

"Star sapphires of purest ebon, they were. I recall distinctly because of the circumstances."

Setting the box aside, Gord demanded, "What exactly were those . . . circumstances?"

Gellor had wanted to examine the box more carefully, to thoroughly inspect it to see if some additional clue could be discovered, but his young friend's insistence would brook no more delays. "In a scrying of the sort done by those of great power, Gord, even as the present and future unravel, a shadowing of the past manifests itself as well. Those trained in the arts can easily ignore such scenes at will, for following them wastes precious time, time better spent discovering future probabilities. I am no master of dweom-

ers, and my attention was often distracted by the
phantoms of your past — the actual and that which
might have been as well. In one of the adjunctive
shadowings, my friend, I saw a plump and happy
child. He played at the feet of a lovely woman, and
among his playthings were that box there and its
contents. The infant was you, Gord, and the box held
the stones — gems which you poured out and replaced gleefully."

"So . . . and the woman?"

"Who knows? She was none I have ever seen. Was
there a beautiful lady ever around? Can you recall?"

"No. . . . Would there had been," Gord said ruefully. "That one must have been exceptional and wealthy
beyond belief to allow an infant to make playtoys of
gems!"

"Set aside the value of the stones for the moment.
Think on this: To have been shown thus, those nine
black star sapphires must have been yours, a part of
your inheritance or a gift. The woman was what was
meant for your childhood, a governess or protectress,
I am unable to differentiate. The stones were a vital
portion of what had been meant for you as well."
Gellor looked steadily at the young man. "Do you
have the slightest recollection of those precious gem-
stones? Any memory at all?"

"None! But perhaps if I saw them, held them,
something would return. Do you know where they are
now?"

Without answering, Gellor sat back and sipped the
wine from his nearly empty goblet. "What memories
does your ring evoke?"

"This?" Gord held it up. The setting in the piece of
jewelry held a deep green emerald with a star pattern
in it that made it look like a cat's eye. From its hard-
ness he had at first taken it for a chrysoberyl, but
then he decided it was far too green and deep for

such a stone. Only an emerald of the corundum sort could be as lovely as that. " No memories. I gained it from a stupid man, a thief and manslayer, when I was just a boy. I thought I'd told you of that."

"No matter. I have a clue as to the whereabouts of the nine stones, and that is of import, no?"

"Yes! Out with it, man!"

With a long sigh, Gellor admitted his frustration. "I made inquiries here in Greyhawk as soon as I arrived. Rare specimens such as that have a way of being kept track of by gem merchants, jewelers, and those with a lust for their likes. It seems that I was but a few weeks too late in coming — blame my failure to associate the two images of the box, if you will." Gord interjected his assurance that he could never affix any blame, rather only approbation for the ability to see the one in the other, so disparate were the two forms and so tenuous the one-eyed man's connection to either.

"Thank you. Anyway, the nine are still together, it seems. They could be no other gems, for even a single black star sapphire is as rare as compassion in the heart of a hag! They are part of a necklace now — a thing of astonishing beauty, made of wrought platinum and also set with diamonds, I'm told. The piece was brought to Greyhawk a month ago by a trader from the Wild Coast. He claimed that the necklace had come from far to the west, and the merchants viewing it said the workmanship was so fine that they dared not doubt the fellow's statement.

"A work of that sort is never openly advertised for sale. The necklace was viewed privately for some few days, and then the trader auctioned it off in the company of a select private group of individuals who typically have interest in rare gems, jewelry, and works of art. It was sold to the agent of a powerful foreigner, a lord from Dyvers, evidently. Although the purchasing agent left Greyhawk only a few days ago, you can be certain that the necklace went off long before that — say three weeks past. A known dealer in such precious commodities doesn't travel with funds, or with purchases either. Thieves and brigands would soon have all, and him dead."

It was all Gord could do to restrain himself from pulling his friend out of his chair and hugging him. "And the name of the buyer?"

"Neither the buyer nor the man he bought for are known. That's hardly surprising. The agent is known hereabouts as Demming, or Sharpeye Demming. The descriptions I have heard could fit any man of middling height, common features, and average age. You can wager with assurance that the name he uses elsewhere will be different from his alias here. There is nothing else."

"Then let's be satisfied at that! Dyvers is not quite as large a city as Greyhawk, and hiding in the place is one with a clue I seek. We can ferret out him and the stones in no time at all!"

"I hate to say this, Gord, but what makes you suppose the man will be in Dyvers? If he is an active trader, and one seeking to earn a living, he'll be off again by now, looking for such things in other cities — and the whole of the Flanaess is a large place to disappear in."

After pondering that for a moment, the young man inclined his head in agreement with Gellor's statement. "Yes, there is merit to what you say. The necklace, however, is not at all likely to be making its way about the lands of the west, east, north, and south. In fact, such a treasure will be locked up safe in a special place — that I know from experience!" Gord exclaimed with a roguish grin.

"Except . . ." Gord added with a gleam in his eye, "when such a thing is brought forth for others to envy and admire. A necklace of this sort will grace the throat of some gorgeous courtesan ere long, if not already. Thus its owner shows off a pair of prized possessions at the same time. . . . Oh, yes, Gellor, my boon friend! We shall have them soon!" Gord paused, snapped his fingers, sprang up, and began to bustle about the apartment.

"How soon can you be ready to go, Gellor? It won't take me an hour to put my gear together. Allow me twice that long to settle a few other matters, and then I'm horsed and away!"

Gellor stood then too, walked over, and gripped the young man firmly by his shoulders. "All of us, you know, are not quite as free and unencumbered as you are, my boy. You propose a journey of a week in length, and possibly three times that long nosing around in Dyvers thereafter. If I could accompany you, I would, and I would that I could! There are other things for me to see to, however — duties which I can neither neglect nor pass off onto another's shoulders. I leave tomorrow on a coaster, and I'll be gone on various business for at least a month. Perhaps when those affairs are tended to, I'll be at liberty."

Gord was disappointed but determined. "It would be better with you, Gellor. But with or without, I am setting off for the west road this very day! When will we meet again?"

"This is something neither of us can know, but I will return here as soon as I am able — two months at the outside."

"If I'm not returned by then, I'll never be back," the young man said with a confident laugh. "Look for me here or at the Chessmen Tavern — now, isn't that a fitting place!"

Gellor stayed on as his young friend went about gathering and packing. They exchanged only a few words for the better part of an hour, and then Gord addressed the one-eyed man when his packing was almost done. "You'll find your way all right until your vessel departs?"

"But of course," the one-eyed man said with a chuckle. "That's something I've managed alone quite well for many more years than you've seen. Now be on your way as quick as you like, and don't waste any concerns about hospitality. This is a matter which cannot be ignored in favor of small talk and pleasantries, now, isn't it?"

"Thanks, Gellor. You are a good friend in all respects. I shall expect to see that bright eye of yours again in a few weeks. Farewell!"

Gord picked up his gear, and the two men clumped hastily down the long flights of narrow stairs and out into the afternoon's waning. The one-eyed man went off to find a comfortable place to spend the night near the docks, while Gord finished up a few errands and then made for the stable not far from his lodgings. The dust from his cantering mount made a golden plume in the last rays of the setting sun as he left Greyhawk behind on his way to Dyvers.

Chapter 17

THE CITY OF DYVERS was like Greyhawk in many respects, but the differences were significant. Dyvers was older, not quite so large in area or population, more crowded with strangers. The buildings were different, squarer, the towers squatty with even thicker walls than those of Gord's home city. The place had no new and old cities; Dyvers was one municipality. It had slums and poor sections, but none so bad as Greyhawk's, just as its finer portions were not so grand as those of its rival to the east.

The hilltop villas and mansions of Greyhawk looked out over the snaking waters of the Selintan. In Dyvers, similar palatial structures had vistas of the Velverdyva River or the endless-seeming expanse of the Nyr Dyv. Beautiful and ugly were intermixed, poor and rich, just as in great cities everywhere, Gord supposed.

His journey here had been rapid and relatively uneventful. After arriving in Dyvers, Gord had spent a day simply relaxing and refreshing himself. He chose a middle-priced inn near the middle of the city where most of the clientele seemed of middling sort. It was drab, dull, and quiet — just the place he wanted for his coming work.

Being an able scholar was a boon indeed. It didn't take long for Gord to locate a seller of books and maps, and there he found a fairly accurate map of the city. He retired to his room to commit the map to memory, using key features as landmarks. That night, his second at the inn, he ventured forth and began making the rounds of taverns and inns frequented by the wealthier folk who dwelled in Dyvers or came regularly to the city to do business. That excursion gained him nothing, but Gord wasn't discouraged. He had expected nothing, even though it was worth the chance anyway.

The detective work required several sets of new clothing and extensive drinking and frequenting of various high-class establishments of many sorts to accomplish fully. A slim lead was obtained here, a possibly false name there. There were only a handful of people in the whole of Dyvers able to afford a costly piece of jewelry of the sort Gord was looking for, and of those, most wouldn't have agents traveling around to find specific pieces.

The work would have been far simpler had he not been constrained by the need for discretion and confidentiality — his need, of course, not that of the owner of the nine sapphires. If Gord boldly inquired in the seamier establishments of the town, he could have soon come up with the name he wanted. But then, however, every government informer, thief, and assassin in Dyvers would have known him as well. The trick was to gain information while revealing none about yourself. That required more time, great skill, and considerable expense. Gord had all three commodities at his beck and call, so in a few days he had what he needed.

"I shall be departing for Veluna City today, landlord. May I please have my reckoning?" Gord made a production of it all, paying, leaving a good sum in addition for the proprietor, ordering his horse, and then departing. He was sure the landlord would not forget him for a long time. In fact, Gord actually did leave the city by its western portal, stopping there a moment to chat with the sergeant of the guard, complimenting him on his community and remarking with a wink on the looks and friendliness of the women. Of course, that last remark rubbed the fellow the wrong way, just as Gord had intended.

When the sergeant countered with a protest and demanded an apology, Gord sneered, called him an ignorant yokel from a backward city, and cantered away. "The folk of Veluna are better and brighter too," he drawled over his shoulder with a disdainful air. That man would remember him, too.

Several days later, on a different horse and garbed as a traveler from distant Keoland, Gord re-entered Dyvers by one of its southern gates. He found a low hostel where no questions were asked as long as payment was made in advance. Now his real work could begin. If by the slightest chance someone recalled his earlier inquiries about a person most likely to be interested in rare and precious gems, because that worthy soon thereafter lost the most valuable prize in his collection, the individual who would be sought after was the one who would be found to have departed Dyvers days prior to the theft.

Gord as he appeared now was older, hair streaked with grey, and was noticeably taller than the fellow he had been before. The young thief grinned to himself, thinking of how well a bit of dye, built-up boots, and a hat could so easily deceive the untrained eye. The observation of skilled eyes was another matter, but he didn't plan to expose himself to any such scrutiny.

Gord went out early in the evening and returned to the hostel before midnight reeling drunk. He sang and stomped his way boisterously to his quarters, attracting the attention of several other patrons along the way, slammed and locked the door, and collapsed noisily on his bed. In a few minutes he was cold sober, clad in black, carrying all the thieving gear he figured to need, and creeping out a window on the way to seek his prize.

A lot of trouble to go to? No — too much caution could not be used when a rogue thief was planning to invade the Temple of Nerull and steal from its high priest a necklace of inestimable worth . . . particularly when that very same high priest had announced that the nine black stones of the piece meant more to him than could be guessed!

That tidbit of information had been gained from the steward of a rich and degenerate aristocrat of Dyvers. The man's master was a worshiper of the evil deity Nerull, for whatever reasons he had. That aside, this same man, the noble worshiper, was the collector of gems whose agent had obtained the nine sapphires. Only he had not kept the necklace, as Gord had supposed he would. Instead the piece had been given to the chief cleric of Nerull as an offering. No matter — whether they were held by aristocrat or priest, Gord would this very night have the black stones from whatever repository they were locked in.

The squat temple of basalt lay on the edge of the district of the city that was given over to places of devotion. But unlike the other temples, the House of Nerull had no buildings close to it. The streets nearby were deserted, and the place seemed lifeless. Gord knew better. Night was the time for the followers of this evil being to pay their duty to their deity. Somewhere below ground, in a dark and foul chamber, the devotees of the vile god of death would be chanting their praises and making blood sacrifices. Such activity was good for him, for all inside would be busy, and Gord could operate undisturbed. He would enter, burglarize, and leave before the fools knew what had occurred.

Thanks to a dweomered blade he had gained in his eastern adventures, Gord was able to see in utter darkness as if it were dim dusk, while in starlight his vision was as sharp as if it were early twilight. Thus the low wall surrounding the grim temple and the sentries silently prowling the open ground between wall and temple were nothing to him. Any skilled thief could have scaled the wall, of course, despite the clawed spikes atop it. Wickedly planted iron spears and a dense hedge of dwarf yarpicks on the inner verge of the wall were a matter to be dealt with carefully. Still, the stationary obstacles would not have been insurmountable. His biggest problem was the padding guards with their accompanying beasts. Each sentry was matched with a black ape!

"Now there's a type of vicious killer I've never seen before," Gord said to himself as he studied the area beyond from a precarious position between the spikes atop the wall. Now he understood why the points hooked both outward and inward too. These apes were undoubtedly carnivores and man-killers. The result of one or more running loose in the city would bring severe repercussions to the temple's master priest.

"I could fall upon man and beast," Gord ruminated. His acrobatic ability was sufficient for him to clear the abatis of metal and thorny growth without difficulty, and he could land ready to fight. His short sword and long dagger were sufficient armament for the young thief to dispatch both adversaries quickly and with possibly no sound — or at most some stifled cries.

"No, the pairs meet and exchange soft words at intervals. The priests have covered themselves well," Gord reflected. So he changed his thinking. If this place was a typical one of its sort, and there was no reason to think it was not, he knew that there would be some hidden subterranean way inside, a secret passage meant to be a death trap for anyone foolish enough to trespass. Gord stayed still a few minutes longer, watching the movement of the sentries, the snuffling and peering of their apes. Then he acted.

As the guardian pairs moved away, Gord vaulted outward and tumbled into a somersaulting roll as his feet touched the sward surrounding the squatty pile of the evil temple. Quickly gaining his feet again, the young thief crouched, opened a small bag at his belt, turned, and tossed a handful of red pepper back over the area he had just been. Then he dashed toward the grim building itself, sprinkling the powder behind him as he went. The sharp-smelling stuff was meant to irritate and confuse guard dogs, but he knew it would likewise confound the nose of any ape that came near to where he had landed.

The big blocks of basalt comprising the outside of the temple were smooth and closely set, and it required his utmost effort to ascend the nearly sheer face quickly enough to avoid being seen. Gord had no more than grasped the top edge of the first tier of the temple when he heard a barking sneeze from below. Without a sound, he pulled himself up onto the ledge and flattened his body. The primate was sneezing, pawing at its nose, teeth showing white in its inky face as it did so. Gord watched as two more pairs of sentries hastened to the scene. The men exchanged whispers, the two new apes began snuffling, and then those creatures were taken with sneezing fits too.

As the men sought to discover the reason for the trouble, Gord decided it was time to move. He would have only a short period of relative safety, of that he was sure. Soon the guards of Nerull would be searching for a possible intruder. He mustn't waste the interval, or his opportunity would be lost — and possibly his life as well!

He discovered a door leading to a balconylike area, and the portal had been carelessly left open. Or perhaps, he corrected himself, the denizens of this place did not bother to lock out intruders — otherwise, how could they have fun dismembering the curious and foolish who dared to enter? That was not a pleasant line of reasoning, so Gord forced it out of his mind.

The young adventurer slipped inside the temple and hurriedly descended a nearby flight of steps. This brought him to the main floor of the place, in a location obviously reserved for the clerics. Light showed here and there from beneath doors, warning him that many of the rooms along the long series of corridors were occupied — by lesser priests, acolytes, and the like, as well as guards perhaps. He didn't bother with any doors, however. Gord kept his eyes on the stone flags, seeking a telltale sign. The temple was old, and countless sandaled feet must have walked these flagstone passages over the centuries. Such traffic would take its toll.

What had seemed to be a blank wall a moment before revealed itself as a concealed door under the young thief's scrutiny. He had been led to it by an almost imperceptible path worn into the stone, a path that ended where the "wall" began.

"Not so much a secret, now, is it?" he observed under his breath as his dagger blade found the hidden catch and the door swung inward. Here was the way — or one of the ways, anyway — that the priests of the vile god of darkness got to the altar below. "And here too," Gord said softly as he went rapidly down the steps, "is where the chief priest will have his most privy sanctum. Let us hope he is busily engaged in some foul rite."

A low, indistinct, but somehow obscene chanting came up the staircase. The farther Gord went, the louder the sound became, but he could still discern none of its meaning even when he finally arrived at the bottom of the flight of steps. Deep-throated iron horns suddenly bellowed, adding to the noise at odd intervals, while great drums rambled as an underbeat to the chant, and discordant sounds like the random plucking of monstrous harps accentuated the strange rhythm. The sounds came from his left, so Gord went to his right into a narrow passage.

The darkness was deeper than black, but he had no difficulty making his way, of course, and the enchanted vision granted to him by the sword he had gained while adventuring with Gellor even enabled the young thief to distinguish which passages were the most traveled. When he had a choice, he always selected the least-trod way. After a dozen false leads and dead ends, Gord came to a small, circular chamber at the end of the corridor he had chosen. The only feature or ornamentation inside it was a quartet of ordinary-looking candleholders, each one set into the wall equidistant from the ones adjacent to it.

"This is strange," he said quietly to himself. "A place like this has no purpose, not even benches, a lavatory, an idol. . . . What might it be?" His actions were not those of someone searching for a place to rest, wash, or worship. Gord was checking the walls, rapidly, using eyes and fingers. Finding nothing remarkable, he worked his way back out toward the corridor. He finally realized that where the tunnel entered the little circle of space, there was a gap between walls, which meant. . . .

"No stone of the passage meshes with those of the chamber!" It was an exclamation of discovery, albeit uttered in a hushed voice.

Darting back into the room, his mind working faster than his hands or feet could move, Gord turned his attention to the high-set sconces, ancient affairs with long prickets for the setting of massive candles. Bronze they were, and each of the four polished too.

"This is the one," he murmured, noticing that the one immediately to the right of the tunnel entrance was more worn than the other three. Gord gave it a tug, then a push upward, then tried to twist it from side to side. It was unmoving, solid and firmly set.

"This cannot be . . ." Gord started to lament, his hands still working, and the words were barely out of his mouth when he hit the right combination, first pressing down the spike of the pricket and then pushing upward on the sconce. Accompanied by an almost inaudible grinding, the whole circle of the chamber slowly pivoted through a half-turn. Gord was briefly disconcerted, but because he had half expected something like this, he was not so startled that he forgot to draw his weapons as the chamber turned.

"Who dares intrude in my master's sanctum?!" It was a question and a challenge at once. The voicing of it caused a foul graveyard odor to fill the little place where Gord stood, the reek nearly gagging him.

There was no choice available to him. Gord's ears told him the sound of the voice had come from his right. Not eager to be trapped inside the small chamber, he sprang out into the lefthand area of the larger room that the rotation of the chamber had revealed. He hit the ground and spun to face the direction the voice had come from.

The body he saw before him looked at first glance something like a relatively small ogre — a monstrosity with a bulbous, barrel-like torso supported by thick, bowed legs. Its flesh had the pallor of death and a charnel stench to match its appearance. In the next instant he saw an even more gruesome aspect. Long, writhing worms issued from all over the creature's head — mouth, eyes, ears, nose. They waved blindly, independently, as if offering their own challenge to the foolish human who had violated this place.

"Hells' handles!" Gord hissed, springing back in horror from the sight.

That move was fortunate, for the massive thing spat the worms out of its mouth at that moment, and where they fell to the floor the stones hissed and bubbled for a moment. Gord noted with a combination of awe and revulsion that where the things had struck and splattered, the floor was pitted. They were small holes, but if that had been his flesh . . .

"Hackkahhkk," the terrible, rotten-fleshed beast coughed. It was bringing up more of the worms from inside its massive chest. And as it did so, it began to lumber toward the young thief, its splayed feet making a meaty, slapping sound on the stone floor.

Gord whirled to his left, slashed out and down with his sword, dived into a somersault, and came up behind the monster's right shoulder. He was too far away now to strike effectively with either of his weapons, but at least he was safe for a moment.

"Plaaht!" The thing reflexively spat forth another mouthful of the worms, spraying them in an arc that was nowhere near him. Gord saw that but paid no attention. He flashed his gaze toward where he had felt his sword's blade strike home, needing to know what his slash had done to the foul flesh of the thing's thick, distended leg.

The yellow-gray flesh had parted under the edge of his weapon, all right, and a wound resembling an open mouth, with its lower lip drooping, was plainly evident there. But the cut shed no blood and oozed no ichor. The squat creature from the pits of the netherworld seemed totally unaffected by the wound. It was now shambling around, turning and hacking deep inside its throat once again.

Gord went into a circling, dancing, diving routine that kept the thing turning and lumbering. After a half-dozen attempts to splatter the young thief with the corrosive worms, the monster gave up that strategy — whether in frustration or because its innards were exhausted of the foul, writhing tubes, Gord neither knew nor cared. During that process he had managed to score several more hits upon the great beast's legs, but although bone showed when one of these attacks had scored heavily, the monster still came on undaunted.

Now Gord was dismayed, even horrified, to find that the monster had weapons other than its foul worms. From somewhere beneath its mouldering garments the thing pulled forth a pair of sicklelike weapons. Its long arms and the curved blades gave it a reach of some six feet or more on either side. Then it spoke, the first words it had uttered since its initial challenge, while holding the sickles at the ends of its upraised, outstretched arms.

"Now, human, I shall have the pleasure of hacking you into small strips before I feast on your flesh and blood and bones!" Its voice was clogged-sounding, the words slightly mushy, as if the lungs of the creature were rotted and worm-infested too.

The thing was overconfident and, for all its fearsomeness, slow. As it gurgled the last words of its threat, Gord darted in toward the monster's right side yet again, holding his dagger ready to parry a possible sickle-blow. With a backhand motion of his sword, he chopped at the bone exposed in the monster's wounded leg and then tumbled away. As he sprang erect behind the creature, he slashed at the leg again and gave a speech of his own.

"Ogre-ghoul! Fiend! Whatever your spawning, I think clean steel will serve to blot your foulness from the world."

The monster tried to pivot and slash out with the sickle in its left hand at the same time. The blade cut harmlessly through the air just above Gord's head. Then the thing fell heavily, the weapon in its right hand clattering away as it toppled down upon the stones. The leg that Gord had chopped at repeatedly had finally given way!

As the thing floundered and attempted to support itself on the bloodless stump of its severed leg, Gord leaped in and struck the creature's neck with all of his strength. The strength of his arms, coupled with the momentum of his leap, gave the short sword tremendous force. Its keen blade cut cleanly through the dead-hued flesh, sheared bone almost as easily, and still had most of its force unspent as it came out the other side of the neck to clang on the stone floor.

The severed head of the foul thing fell to the floor and came to rest a short distance away. A gush of the maggoty worms spouted forth from the body's severed neck, just as blood fountains from a decapitated corpse. The stream of vile stuff engulfed the ghastly head as the body spewed forth its corrosive contents, and worms and head vanished in a cloud of noisome fumes. The body thrashed and jerked for a couple of minutes while Gord watched it warily, but the thing showed no signs of having regenerative powers. Then the corpse was still.

Carefully avoiding the stinking remains, Gord began a quick search of the area beyond the chamber where the battle had taken place. There were several rooms nearby — in fact, a whole suite of lavishly appointed subterranean chambers fit for the habitation of a great priest of Nerull.

What came next was almost child's play to Gord. He located the secret repository of the cleric without difficulty, noted its warding signals, and effectively masked them with stuff from the priest's own sacramental coffer — blue-purple unguent and a dark altar cloth served to mask and negate the forces bound within the sigils that had been enscribed to protect the cleric's treasury from violation. Hidden needles coated with venom were even more easily blunted, and the locks on the huge coffer were a joke to the young thief. In minutes he had the chest open and its contents exposed for his examination.

Ignoring the valuables of clerical sort, and the leather bags of coins as well, Gord singled out several finely made caskets, knowing that such containers were likely to be used for prized gems and precious jewelry pieces.

"Beautiful!" he gasped involuntarily as he opened the first and viewed the array of gems within. Huge emeralds, massive rubies, great, glittering diamonds. A rainbow of colors, and a strange stone too. The latter, held in a special velvet pouch, was a round, nearly fist-sized black opal whose green flecks pulsed with strange lights and at whose heart a vermilion light like a flame seemed to dance. "This I'll have too," Gord uttered in awe, and he thrust the orb of opal into his own leather pouch quickly. Though this gem alone was a monumental prize, he didn't forget that he was here first and foremost to regain the nine black star sapphires.

By the time he had searched the last of the little coffers, Gord's mood was one of utter despair. Although he had tucked several other fine pieces of jewelry into his pouch, he had failed to locate the gems he so desperately desired.

"Gods rot you, stinking priest of a misbegotten one! I'll have them from you personally!" With that, Gord returned to the little chamber and worked the sconce again — but this time he dived into the larger chamber as the small room began to rotate back to its previous position.

"You'll come back through this portal, priest," Gord muttered. "On that I'll stake my life. And when you come from your unholy sacrifices this night, I shall be here to greet you." Then he found a chair, pulled it to a convenient place near where the secret entrance to the place would open, and waited inside his self-imposed prison.

Several hours later the chief cleric of Nerull did indeed return to his own chambers, alone and exhausted from his night of obscene rituals and debauchery. The dark stains of blood and other substances covered him, and he was busily stripping off his soiled gown even as the little chamber rotated to allow him access to his apartments. Gord fell upon him with remorseless fury, pummeling the priest into senselessness before the man could do more than utter a brief, shrill scream for help. Gord used the cleric's stained cassock to stifle that noise even as he beat the fellow unconscious.

After binding the priest's arms and legs with cords, Gord turned him face down and slid his dagger beneath the man's chin, placing the edge of the blade a fraction of an inch from the exposed flesh of his throat.

"Awaken, grave-rat!" Gord commanded, pouring some wine from a bottle he'd found on a table in the bedroom of the cleric. As the liquid splashed on the back of his head, the priest of Nerull groaned and tried to raise his face. He turned his eyes to the side and up, and even in his half-dazed state managed to get out a threat.

"I'll have your life and soul for this, intruder! Don't you know who I am?"

"Stay still, or who you *were* will be the correct terminology," Gord said, using his free hand to emphasize the point by shoving the fellow's head back down with force. "Feel the burning at your throat? That is where my dag's edge even now slices a bit of your tender flesh. Speak only to answer my queries, or that edge shall bite deeper!"

The priest became instantly motionless. "What do you want?"

"Only a bit of information. Give me that, and I will spare your vile life. Where are the nine black star sapphires set with diamonds in a necklace of wrought platinum?" The question was met with silence, so Gord brought his weapon hand up a bit and drew the blade of his dagger ever so lightly across the man's throat. That was all it took.

"Wait, wait! I recall the piece you refer to now — I had forgotten it, that's all! I'm trying to cooperate!" The malign priest whined the last piteously.

"Where is the necklace, then?"

"It's . . . I . . . not here," he gasped fearfully.

"You lie! It must be here. I know those gems are far too valuable for you to allow them to be out of your possession!"

"No, no! I lie not, I speak true to you. Precious they were, but not so precious as a great op— er, another gem which was given in exchange."

Gord was unable to believe his ears. "When? When did this exchange take place?" He brought his dagger away from the bound man's throat, feeling himself getting caught up in the cleric's explanation and not wanting to accidentally slash his quarry before he had told everything.

"But a sennight ago."

"Who did you bargain with, then? Tell me straight and quickly. My dagger thirsts for your foul life, cannibalistic rat."

"It was a being of great power, one no longer human, but grown mighty and unhuman, a dweller in shadow, a servant of my god, a devoted follower of Ner— "

253

Thump! Gord struck the cleric hard across the temple with the pommel of his dagger before the man could finish uttering the name. There was no sense in taking chances that the terrible one would hear and attend, for they were within the deity's own house and his great priest was being threatened. The fellow stirred and moaned, so Gord spoke again.

"Mind your tongue! I am not so foolish as to allow it to wag thus. Try once more, and I'll end its wagging forever. Now, say it short and straight: To whom did you give those stones I seek?"

"The Prime of evil shadows, the Lich of Liches — that is with whom I exchanged treasures."

"What made him desire to part with that . . . other stone of greater value than the black sapphires? Surely one so puissant as this Prime would recognize his loss and your gain."

"He wished to remove his from . . . let us say that my possession of the one he held pleased his sense of propriety," the priest hurriedly substituted. He was beginning to regain his senses and gather his courage as well.

"The stones are now with him?" Gord demanded. When the cleric answered affirmatively, the young adventurer then asked, "And the lick you call Prime is where?"

"In the Realm of Shadow, thief, and beyond your reach!"

"So be it," Gord said calmly. He struck the fellow's shaven pate again. "You'll sleep awhile, now, and give me ample time to leave your precincts." Gord was much distressed at the words of the priest, but he was used to disappointment. Besides, someday perhaps he would find a way to penetrate the plane of shadowstuff and seek out the lich and his treasure then. Now it was high time for him to be leaving here with his mementos. The temple would shake under the wrath of the high cleric when the man discovered that his treasury had been looted and his prized black opal was missing.

It would have been an easy escape, but for his getting temporarily lost in the maze of narrow passages beneath the temple. It took far longer than Gord had hoped it would for him to retrace his steps and find the way above. By then the high cleric had recovered his senses, freed himself, and sounded the alarm. Even so, Gord had nearly made it to a place where he could get over the surrounding wall when he was spotted.

A swarm of arrows and bolts swept around him, humming and buzzing like angry wasps as they passed close. A thick quarrel took the young thief in his left arm, and the shock of its entry made him reel. Cursing, he managed to break off the feathered end and push the tip through, but that act took time, and it was his undoing.

The shaven-headed high priest had been helped above by then, and his dark eyes fell upon the struggling rogue with evil anticipation. Uttering a singsong litany of vilest sort, the cleric called upon his dark deity to deliver the most terrible of painful deaths to the man who had dared to violate temple and priest both! The spell spewed forth from the priest's mouth even as his arm raised and his long fingers shaped themselves into a pointing sign of evil. A dark and evilly red ray of light sprang from his hand, and the lurid ray struck Gord full on his turned back, bathing his head and torso in awful radiance.

The pain was soul-wrenching. Gord tried to scream it away, but his throat was constricted. Then his heart stopped, and total blackness washed over him. The last thing he remembered was reaching for the great opal, intending to throw it over the wall so

that the foul priest would never regain it, but he acted too late. He got it into his hand, but then the ray
of death washed over him, his arm refused to obey,
and then he felt nothing.

A flare of green light enveloped the body, nearly
blinding the priest and anyone else who happened to
be looking in that direction, as the would-be escapee
fell lifeless to the ground. The great cleric of Nerull
shook his head to clear his vision, crying, "Hurry,
dogs! Bring me that body! I am not through yet!"

A score of lesser clerics and guards scuttled to
obey. Flaring torches made the yard surrounding the
temple into a scene straight from the hells, but there
was no other way. Cleric-cast illumination would
alert all of Dyvers that something serious was amiss
at Nerull's great house, and that was unallowable.
Several of the group surrounding the area where the
intruder had fallen detached themselves and came
slowly back toward their master.

"Hurry, run! I command it!" There was no instant
response, but finally one of the men shuffled forward
to stand before the high cleric, saying: "I . . . we can
find no body, master. There is but a scorched outline
where the swine fell dead. Perhaps your power
burned him to nothingness!"

The bald-pated chief priest scowled and struck the
underling across his cringing face. "Bah! Look further! Take all night if necessary, but do not come into
my presence again without the corpse of that man!"
Then the cleric retired into his temple's safe confines.

Although the matter wasn't entirely forgotten, the
search for the body was abandoned at dawn an hour
later. After all, reasoned the priest, perhaps his curse
had indeed blasted the fellow. What other explanation
could there be?

Chapter 18

"GET UP. YOU ARE NOT DEAD."

"Yes, I am. Leave me in peace."

The toneless voice continued, not bothering to point out the contradiction, the impossibility of someone dead being able to converse. "You are not dead. You will arise."

"No!" The voice was beginning to annoy him, and with irritation came added strength to resist. "I am dead! I will do nothing but remain so."

"Get up. You are not dead."

That did it. Gord would show this monotonous know-it-all a thing or two! He sprang erect suddenly, hands reaching for his weapons. A flash of pain sent him reeling — his right arm was fine, but his left was injured. Gord looked and saw a stub sticking from the gray flesh of his bicep. A broken crossbow bolt was causing the severe pain. How in the hells had that happened?

"Go to Shadowhall now and—" The toneless voice stopped in mid-sentence.

Gord looked up. The sound issued from a shapeless thing of black, a seemingly formless coalescence of shadows that floated nearby. As he peered at the phenomenon, Gord inadvertently raised his right hand toward his injured left arm. This movement partially exposed what he held clenched in his fist, and at the sight of it the shadowy thing recoiled, wafting back as if afraid.

"Shadowfire!" it said. Somehow the lifeless voice carried a note of awe in it.

Now Gord looked down, wondering what the strange being was going on about. He saw a glimmering in his own hand, a play of blackness interspersed with motes of deep green, all made vivid by what seemed a tongue of flame that appeared and disappeared within the great gem's heart. What the dancing devas was this?

"This?" Gord inquired, thrusting the orb out toward the thing of shadows as he spoke.

Now the creature jerked backward as if yanked by a rope. Fully twenty feet rearward it flew before it came to a shuddering halt. "No!" the shadowy speaker intoned loudly. "Keep it from me and I will not tell the master anything about you," the creature called as if pleading.

Gord sat down on the silvery-black grass, feeling tired and weak. The black thing remained distant, but Gord was not satisfied at all. "What are you talking about? Who is the master? Where are we? What do you mean, I'm not dead?"

As he addressed the thing of shadows, Gord had placed the massive black opal in a pouch. Noting this, the creature again drifted nearer as it replied. "I speak of your half-existence, once-man. The master I speak of is the lord of this place, Shadowrealm, the place where we both must dwell eternally. You thought yourself dead. . . . I read the thoughts plainly for a time. You are not, of course, nor are you undead. You are in Shadowrealm, so you are half-living, half-dead, neither and both."

The lack of intonation, the flatness and droning quality of the thing's voice, made Gord grind his teeth. He did not like the creature, whatever it might be. "What are you? Where is this so-called master of yours?" He stressed the last word of the second question in order to let the dull monstrosity know that what it considered to be its lord did not affect Gord's status.

"I am important. Don't you recognize an adumbrate when you see one?"

"Don't answer a question with another," Gord admonished the black, formless thing, "and pay attention too! I also asked where your lord was."

Now the thing somehow managed to sniff, and the mass of shadows grew thicker and distended, as if it were drawing itself up. "His Umbrageous Majesty, the Lord of Murk, is my master — and yours too, now that you are consigned to Shadowrealm. His Gloominess just happens to be nearby at this very moment, for the Chiaroscuro Palace is readying for the Great Celebration."

The self-proclaimed adumbrate had continued approaching as it spoke. While its toneless voice betrayed virtually no emotion, the posture the inky monster assumed, if such could be determined in a creature like this, seemed to indicate extreme hostility. Gord read it as a desire to attack and harm him, so he reacted accordingly. As the thick clot of shadows wafted nearer, the young adventurer gathered his strength and sprang to his feet. His sword's short blade rasped forth even as he gained his footing, and the silvery steel darted out to come within a foot of the creature.

With a sound like wind stirring dead leaves, the adumbrate darted aside from the threatening point, little streaks of silvery light arcing within its body as if the thing were a miniature stormcloud filled with lightning. "So, manling," it now boomed, its voice taking on a tinge of emotion. "You think to threaten me with a mortal blade?" Still venting the dusty, stirring sound, it shot a short distance sideways, then came toward Gord as if to envelop him.

The sword seemed to react of its own volition. One moment it was elsewhere, the next it was a bar before the adumbrate's near-lightning advance. The glistening metal seemed to glow, become molten, as the thing of shadows touched it. Gord felt a shivering surge of force flow up his arm as the blade contacted the creature. There was a rush, the sound of a gust of wind venting down a chimney, and a faint, nearly indiscernible keening. Then his sword was plain metal again and the thing was gone. "Good riddance," Gord murmured, giving his full attention to his wounded arm once again.

Withdrawing the shaft was painful, but Gord knew it had to come out, and he managed to endure the hurt. A gush of black-looking blood came from the wound as the wooden shaft was pulled free. Then Gord clamped a clean strip of cloth from his shirt against both sides of the bicep, slowly winding it to make a tight binding around the injury. It wasn't pretty, and the cloth already showed dark stains of blood, but Gord thought the bandage would suffice. He had taken far worse wounds and still lived to speak of them.

As he rested and regained his strength, Gord rummaged around in his belongings, trying to find a small flask of spirits he was sure he had tucked away somewhere, and also to see what else he had. Perhaps something he carried would jog his memory. As it was, the young man had absolutely no recollection of how he had come to this . . . this Shadowrealm, as the now-vanished and presumably dead adumbrate had identified this place.

It certainly wasn't home. Gord glanced around and saw nothing that even vaguely reminded him of Oerth, let alone Greyhawk. The sky was a velvety canopy the color of old charcoal. There were spots in it all right, but they were gleaming points of black, and a sphere of deep metallic hue cast a faint, mercuric light upon the world over which it floated. The world, Gord noted, was of all blacks and grays. There seemed to be vegetation, grass and trees, bushes and flowers too, all of dun coloration, some opalescent, some actually translucent. Furthermore, the landscape seemed to be a dance of shadows that shifted and flowed almost as if he were ambling through it rather than sitting quietly observing the scene. "Shadowrealm indeed!" he muttered to himself as he went back to examining his belongings for some clue.

The huge opal that the creature had called . . . Shadowfire? An appropriate name . . . was not of help. Neither was the small heap of gem-studded jewelry Gord discovered secreted here and about his person and in his old pouch. Nothing else helped, but eventually he located the silver flask and took a healthy swig from it, shuddering as the fiery liquid burned its way over his tongue, down his throat, and into his gut. Feeling better, Gord steeled himself and poured about half of the remainder of the flask's contents on the rag that bound his arm. That burned worse still, but at least the stuff was cleansing the outer portions of the wound. The bleeding had certainly taken care of the inner part, Gord thought. One more jot for himself, and the nearly empty flask was tucked away again along with the rest of his gear.

Now, back to the other matters at hand. He knew who he was — that was no problem. But where he was, why he was here, and what had recently happened in his life still remained unknown to Gord. Was there some place he could find to refresh himself and rest? He stood up and carefully examined the surrounding terrain, letting his gaze sweep from near to far, scanning outward in segments, until the whole of this shadowy place that surrounded him had been viewed.

Now that he was somewhat used to the place, Gord could detect traces of color. There were hints of purple, suggestions of brown, deep ultramarine, and some hue like verdigris, only darker and more intense. His eye caught pearlescence, opalescence, brilliancies, and iridescence in the blacks and grays of the place that did not exist elsewhere. Black was no longer just black; the word legitimately could be used to describe a dozen sorts of colors so subtle in difference that the eye could scarcely discern them unless one concentrated. Grays were twice as varied, even if the many metallic sheens and crystalline permutations were discounted.

"It moves!" Gord exclaimed aloud. In his examination of the strange world around him, he had become so absorbed in the minutiae of things that the larger scope had escaped him for several minutes. When he suddenly realized that a low hummock in the distance that had been in front of him was now off to the right and somewhat behind him, Gord understood that the seeming play of shadows in the place was more than that. The terrain actually flowed as if it were a vast, shadowy river.

"Yet this place I stand on does not move," he murmured to himself, continuing to speak aloud because the sound gave him a sense of security in this strange land. "Let's see what occurs when I move elsewhere," he said softly, and then he left the spot he had been resting upon and trudged through the shadows and the tall, black grass to the mound he had observed earlier. He sat atop it for a time, observing the scene. The hillock became a stationary islet, while all else drifted away or across his field of vision. Eventually Gord tired of the experiment and decided this place was as good as any to rest in. He curled up under a low bush with leaves of jet that hid him from casual view, and despite the strangeness and possible dangers was soon in a state of blissful sleep.

A susurration awakened Gord from his rest. Even a slight sound was sufficient to arouse him from deepest slumber, and in strange surroundings, the young thief slept even more lightly than usual. The sound disturbed him, alerting his senses on a primeval level. Without moving, Gord opened his eyelids a crack and peered out between the long, shiny-black fronds that screened him. What he observed was sufficient to cause him to grab his sword and spring to his feet, ready to fight for his life. Once he was clear of the ebon shrub and erect, the scene was far more startling. Gord was fully ringed by a circle of creatures, the strangest collection of beings that he had ever witnessed assembled in a single place.

He immediately recognized several of the congealed-shadow things he now identified as adumbrates. These were scattered here and there among a throng of other shadowy creatures — things with faintly glowing eyes that resembled snakes, men, hounds, badgers, moths, owls, elk, and a host of other, unidentifiable forms as well, all facing the hummock he was upon and looking toward him. Gord's eye fell upon a huge, maned lion, one of umbral mane and penumbral body, with silvery eyes that gazed back at him without winking.

"Go, friend, and take all of your kind with you," Gord said to the weird cat. "I have no desire to harm you." To his surprise, the monstrous creature turned and bounded off, and when he did so, shadowy shapes similar to that of the huge male shadow-lion likewise left the strange circle for parts unknown.

"You are a nonesuch!" a murky form said from behind him — too close behind!

Gord spun to confront the speaker, sword ready. A

man-shape of somber tones and insubstantial form drew back as the sword of magical metal neared it. "And so are you," Gord retorted. "Come not near, or I shall have to send you to some yet-darker plane!"

There was another shushing sound, collectively from the strange assemblage of creatures, individually voiced by the murky man-shadow. "Brash!" the form hissed in a rustling shadow-voice that Gord had grown to expect now. "Never threaten . . . especially what might be beyond your power to perform."

The leaden eyes of the shadowy figure searched Gord's face, and, detecting uncertainty, the thing smiled at him, a translucent yawning that showed gray teeth and the suggestion of what was behind at the same time. "But be at ease, stranger, for unlike the others, I have come to assist and befriend you, not seeking any special gain."

Of course, such a statement put Gord on instant alert. "Why is that, man of shadow?" he inquired calmly but cautiously.

"Shadow? Nay, though there be some here," the dusky form replied. "I am Smirtch, the Gloam Imprimus. . . . Is that not sufficient reason for my special accommodation?"

"Shadow, shade, or spirit — what matter?"

"Are you of dwarven ilk? Or giantish?" rejoined the shadow-figure. "As readily as you deny such heritage, so too know that there are those named shadow or spirit, shade or phantom, who are as different, one from the other, as pixie and ogre are in the world that was once yours."

This piqued Gord's interest, disarming him slightly and confusing him considerably. "Ever since I awoke from what I thought was death to find myself in this odd place, I have had questions answered with queries, riddles with conundrums. I will bargain with you then, Smirtch-the-Gloam. You may remain close and converse with me without threat, but you must pledge two things."

"Two? Pray speak fully, for no oath can be made without full disclosure of the terms and conditions of such a binding act."

Relieved, Gord named his conditions. "First, you must swear that you will not attempt to harm me . . . or cause another to do so."

"Agreed, readily accepted," Smirtch said eagerly.

"Second, you must answer each question I ask honestly and fully, without any misleading or confusing elements in such answers."

Smirtch shook his inky locks at that. "Not so fast, stranger. You demand much and offer naught save nonaggression. I will gladly agree to answer your questions, but in return you must likewise consent to answer those I might have of you."

"That sounds acceptable," Gord said after a brief pause to consider the ramifications of the pact. "But what of these others? This benighted bestiary of shadow-creatures?"

"Not one of them will linger if I tell them to be gone," the gloam assured him. "This throng is naught but a collection of ordinary denizens of this plane, all curious, some perhaps curiosities to you, but all of no great power or peril to us. Why not let such harmless beasts be?"

Again a question with a question! Gord stepped back from the gloam and used his sword to wave off the encircling array. Those nearest the blade moved backward, seeming to float, making no sound except for the strange susurration. No wonder they had succeeded in ringing him while he slept. These things not only looked like shadows, they conducted themselves as quietly as shadows.

"These are shy and weak things," Smirtch said. "As you proved, since your threat sent them scurrying; and this proves my veracity as well. They pose no threat to you now — though they can be used at times. . . . Now, let us begin our discussion."

"At your insistence," Gord said briskly. "What is this place called?"

"Shadowrealm," the gloam replied abruptly. So, thought Gord, the creature he had encountered earlier used the name that must be the generally accepted one for this place. "What have you done since you've arrived here?" Smirtch continued, getting in his first question.

Gord noticed that the manlike shapes of darkness, spirits, shades, and shadows, the smaller, dwarflike murks, and the tall, gangly fuligi, were gliding nearer as he spoke with Smirtch. The young thief knew some of these creatures from chance, violent encounters in the past, and he had heard tales and seen depictions of both the murklings and the skinny, fuliginous humanoid things of coalesced shadow-stuff. Pretending not to see this encroachment, the young man answered the gloam's counterquestion blandly. "Me? But little, I fear. A rest, a look around, and then this chance meeting."

Smirtch followed up with another question, perhaps hoping that Gord wouldn't notice the impropriety. "Do you know what an adumbrate is?"

"No, I'm quite uncertain as to the nature of an adumbrate," Gord replied politely. "Now, since you spoke out of turn, you must answer two questions for me. First, what is the nature of Shadowrealm? Second, how does one such as I come to this place?"

"It is a place much as any other of its sort," said Smirtch, grinning at the way he had sidestepped the first of the two queries. Then he added another equally vague answer. "One such as yourself comes to Shadowrealm by various means, including those of magical nature, but I am unable to say with certainty how you arrived until you give me the details of what transpired just prior to your arrival here . . . which was when?"

"Time in this place is difficult to measure," Gord countered. He didn't really want to give a direct answer, but the question intrigued him for his own sake — how long had it been, anyway? — and he paused a moment to reflect before responding further. Watching the slowly advancing shadowfolk out of the corner of his eye, Gord continued, "I was . . . asleep when I arrived, and I also took another rest later, so I could have been here an hour or a day, or even longer. Now, tell me, what race rules this realm?"

Smirtch seemed to scowl a bit at the question, but it was difficult to be certain. "We gloams are the most potent of the folk who dwell here, just as duskdrakes are the most fearsome of the great beasts inhabiting the plane — I mean, place," the gloam corrected hastily, but not before Gord noted the first noun. Smirtch hastened on, perhaps hoping that the human would forget the slip if he covered it with a flood of interesting information.

"The phantomfolk are next, although we easily defeat them, then there are the shadowilk and the murklings and the fuligi. As the adumbrates aren't really more than monstrosities, I leave them off the hierarchy of folk. But I ramble! When we first met, you mentioned that you had recovered from what you presumed was death — indeed, I see a wound there on your arm. What do you recall of the circumstances which brought you to such a sorry pass?"

"Little . . . little if anything," Gord admitted sincerely, meanwhile pondering in another part of his mind the information he had managed to glean from the gloam's statements. Shadowrealm apparently was, as he had suspected, actually the Plane of Shadows, a plane that connected to the real world as well as to the planes of Yang and Yin, the positive and negative. He also had good reason to think that this Smirtch fellow was doing his best to keep Gord ignorant of the true nature of this place and its politics.

Smirtch had claimed to be the principal gloam, and from the deference given by the other shadowy denizens around, this seemed quite possible. Yet it was obvious that the creature desired something that Gord possessed, thus indicating that Smirtch was not the lord of much of anything. Similarly, his remarks regarding the adumbrates seemed to indicate that there was enmity at best between such things and Smirtch's race. Enmity exists where there is competition. Adumbrates were as powerful as gloams, at least in certain aspects, it seemed, although the scale of power was uncertain.

Gord reasoned that the rivalry between the two species was a matter of concern to Smirtch, and he seemed to think that Gord might be useful in tipping the balance in favor of his own side. Interesting . . . but what means did a new-come human possess? The sword seemed potent here, but still . . . . Resolving to listen most carefully, Gord asked his next question. "What king or kings are sovereign here?"

"There are those who proclaim a Shadowking. We gloams do not recognize his suzerainty. I, as Imprimus, am as great a lord as any," Smirtch added, still frowning slightly as he droned on, but obviously drawing himself up with what seemed more than a touch of hubris. "That is of no great import at this moment, for you have a problem which I can assist you with. You said that you could remember virtually nothing of what transpired prior to your awakening in this place, did you not? Perhaps if we inventoried and examined your possessions, there would be some clue, something which would restore your mnemonic functions. . . ."

At this, Gord smiled. "Yes, I did in fact say that I could not recall the time before my entrance to the Plane of Shadow. Now, are the gloam-folk then at war with the Shadowking?"

"You have not allowed my question!" Smirtch said with irritation.

"But I have, dear Smirtch, I have indeed. You asked if I had said a certain thing — that was your question. I affirmed that I had so said — my answer. Now, pray, answer mine!"

"No. We do not *war*."

That told the young adventurer much more than he was sure the gloam suspected. The slight inflection on the last word made it probable that there was strife between the factions. That there was no war indicated that the gloams were not powerful enough to openly contest with the Shadowking, despite Smirtch's boast that he was a lord of equal stature; certainly, this being was less puissant than the king — perhaps on the order of a powerful baron. . . . Just then Smirtch spoke again, forcing Gord to concentrate on his words.

"What did you bring here?"

"Oh, not much. What I wear and carry is all," Gord answered lightly. "And whereabouts is the capital city or castle of the one who is called Shadowking?"

"Location is always relative here," Smirtch supplied, meanwhile making a tiny gesture that the gloam undoubtedly thought would be indiscernible to Gord. "Just be in the right place, and the palace comes to you. Now, would you be so good as to display your possessions?"

"Certainly not," Gord said matter-of-factly. "How would you describe the so-called right place?"

"Briefly, if at all," Smirtch shot back at the young man. "Do you have any amusing trinkets with you?"

"Amusement is a matter of taste and perspective,"

Gord replied as a group of the shadow-men drew near behind him, with a clump of murklings and fuligi trailing behind. Gord decided that he had played this game long enough. It was time to test his theory. Should he be mistaken, his fate could hardly be worse than what the gloam undoubtedly planned in any case. "However," Gord said, casually reaching into his pouch with his injured arm, "I do have a trantle which you might regard as meriting some diversion," he smiled. Fingers grasping the sphere, Gord suddenly withdrew the stone that the adumbrate had called Shadowfire, exposing its surface to the gloam as he brought it forth.

"Put that back in the pouch!" Smirtch groaned in a scratchy whisper, sliding away slightly as he hissed the command.

Ignoring the creature for the moment, Gord spun rapidly, gem held at shoulder height, short sword suddenly sweeping in a glistening circle as he turned. Green and scarlet motes danced along the blade, colors he never had seen before in this place.

It was more than the mere sight of those colors that made the menacing creatures who had been about to fall upon him from behind moan and whimper as the young thief confronted them. The force of Shadowfire swept them backward as a gust of chill air sweeps away the dry leaves of autumn. Not all of them were quick enough; where blade touched shadow there was a coruscation of glittering black and lambent maroon. As if formed of these flickering, burning flashes, each shadow so touched became a thing of whirling sparks for an instant, then disappeared entirely, leaving only a little sound, a noise like the whine of a receding mosquito, behind for a moment.

After four shadow-things were thus touched and made gone, Gord completed his circle and again faced

Smirtch. "What is wrong, most helpful of beings? Don't you care for pyrotechnical displays?"

"You'll pay for this!" the thing threatened, safe at a distance many feet beyond the reach of the still-ful-gent blade. Then Gord advanced, and the gloam sped away, making an evil susurration as it glided rapidly out of sight. With that, all the remainder of the other shadowy creatures fled as well. Moths and birds flut-tered and flapped to escape, while animals of other sort scuttled or ran to be clear of the spot. In a short time Gord was quite alone.

Chapter 19

"MOST ENLIGHTENING!" Gord said to himself heartily after all the creatures had gone.

To test his newfound power more thoroughly,
Gord then brought the opal's sphere into contact with
the pommel of his sword. The motes brightened and
grew larger, each particle seeming to spin and whirl
more rapidly. Then the whole multitude of coruscat-
ing flashes merged into twin halos of color. One nim-
bus was coraline, shot through with weaving tongues
of snapping scarlet; the other was of peridot hue, and
similarly filled with darting arcs of bright emerald.

The transformation took but an instant, and Gord
scarcely had time to note the sudden change before
the hues intensified and dual bolts shot from either
side of the blade to strike a fat-trunked, treelike
growth at which the sword happened to be pointing.

"Zow!" Gord exclaimed as he viewed the results,
hastily withdrawing Shadowfire from contact with his
weapon. Where the shadow-tree had been there was
nothing, and the shadow-ground where its roots
must have spread was now a gaping hole, a place of
deeper blackness from which faint tendrils of silvery
stuff wafted upward and away.

"No wonder, then, why Smirtch and the menagerie
were attracted to me," Gord murmured as he carefully sheathed the sword. "This gem is more precious

than one might suppose — at least in this realm of shadow!"

With the potent black opal safely back within his pouch, Gord set off to locate the Chiaroscuro Palace of the Shadowking, confident that he could handle any chance encounters along the way. His dweomered blade was more potent here than elsewhere, it seemed, and in combination with Shadowfire something much greater was at his disposal.

"Perhaps this plane is due for a new ruler," Gord said to himself as he strode along. "No, I take that back. . . . This drabness and gloom is not for me. When I discover how I came here, and how to leave, I shall ask no more than an emperor's ransom as a parting gift!" Then he tried whistling a jaunty air, but somehow all he could manage was a rather mournful tune in a minor key.

After what seemed several days, Gord had trekked across many miles of the Plane of Shadow. During the course of his journey he had been left alone — whether by chance or through avoidance, he neither knew nor cared. During the time so spent, however, the young thief had found opportunity to think and observe.

For one thing, he recalled that his flesh had been gray when the adumbrate had forced him to awaken. He remembered assuming at the time that the light had made his skin appear that way. But after his experimentation with the gem, Gord's complexion had become silvery and he had felt more alive. Then it turned grayish again, and lethargy crept into his body.

Application of the huge opal to his skin seemed to restore the bright sheen to it, so periodically Gord rubbed himself with it. Somehow he had been consigned to this plane, but there was no sense in allowing any transition of his normal self to the stuff of shadow if he could prevent it. He hoped the gem would negate or at least stave off such a metamorphosis. That posed another problem, though. When he was radiating the sheen of argent tone, then the shadow-water and shadow-food he foraged was useless to him. Gord found it slaked not his thirst nor assuaged his hunger.

As he became more like the substance of the plane, the dim waters of sable streams became more substantial, and quaffing them did ease his parched throat and cool his brow. In like vein, the fruits and berries depending from shadow-tree and shade-bush were as nourishing as smoke unless he allowed himself to become shadowy. Gord chose a middle course. Thus he was always somewhat thirsty, his stomach never quite full, his step slightly weary, but it was not difficult to keep going and remain alert. He was no stranger to hardship.

It interested him to note a subtle change that seemed to be occurring as he made his way. Gord thought of the plane as having essentially only two axes of direction. One was parallel to the flow of the terrain, the second was across the current. The first was easy to observe and verify. If one waited in a certain spot, it seemed that all of the plane's landscape would eventually flow by. The second direction was assumed, but it seemed logical. The landscape slid by, getting more and more distant downcurrent, as he moved along at right angles to the flow.

The longer he traveled on the same path perpendicular to the flow, the faster the shadow terrain slipped by him, before and behind. Therefore, it seemed there were backwaters, of a sort, and a main stream. Gord was certain that if he backtracked on his path and trudged long enough, he would eventually come to the relatively slow-flowing portion of the plane again, and then by continuing he would come once more to the swiftly flowing main portion. This indicated that Shadowrealm had but a single surface and one edge. How broad the surface? How long the edge? Those questions he had no desire to speculate upon. He decided that such thinking could only bring disheartenment.

After more time, the movement of the terrain seemed to slow its pace. How long a period had elapsed there was no telling, but the time had certainly come to alter his course. Gord found a likely spot, a place where there was a hill dotted with berry bushes, around which a little pond spread to cover three sides of the elevation. Trusting that his presence upon the high mound would suffice to hold the shadow-water in place too, Gord sat down and waited. Rather than traversing the entire plane on shank's mare, he would let the realms of shadow come past his vantage point.

He had been sitting, staring dully upflow, for an interminable period when something began to nag at his consciousness. A corner of Gord's mind sent alarm signals along nerve paths, but his brain was so occupied with other thoughts that he hardly recognized the signals. He did shift uncomfortably and begin a slight unconscious jiggling of his crossed leg. This reaction so annoyed him that Gord forced his body into absolute stillness.

Sitting rocklike, he assessed what had caused the sudden burst of twitching and unease. That's when something clicked, and the warning flashed through him in a prickling wave. Too late . . .

"Greetings, man!" a basso voice rumbled from behind, and a chilling rush of damp, fetid breath wafted over his shoulders as the words were spoken. Another man might indeed have been as good as dead then, but not so Gord. Even as the first word sounded, he was diving and rolling in a somersaulting maneuver that brought him out of range of immediate danger in a fraction of a second. The salutation was punctuated by a loud snap, as if great teeth had closed suddenly. As this sound occurred, Gord was cartwheeling off to the right so rapidly that a mortal eye could hardly follow his gymnastic performance.

With a spring that brought him to a position that flanked the spot he had rested in a moment before, Gord crouched and drew forth his blades. Before his gaze was a long, wormy shape of near-transparent shadows. The great head however showed very substantial-looking teeth, and the monstrous thing's eyes glowed with a baleful, opalescent light as it swung its horrid snout toward the place its intended victim now occupied.

"My fondest regards, worm!" Gord managed to utter. Then he was moving again — just in time, it seemed, for from the monstrous creature's mouth gouted a stream of utter darkness that shot forth to engulf the area where Gord had been but an instant previously. The gray vegetation flickered with colorless fire, and was gone everywhere the ebon gout touched.

The shadow-dragon hissed angrily as it discovered the inky gout had not touched this agile little victim after all. Well, there were many ways to handle men and their kind, the creature decided. The dark worm had many means of attack in its arsenal, and a potent magic spell seemed quite in order now, for the man now dared to stab at his precious hindquarters with his puny sword.

"Ffaaahh!" The sound of pain issued forth unbidden as the silvery blade actually pierced the worm's thick scales and sunk a foot into its body. Now the human would suffer!

Deciding to save its pitchy breath for later, the monster began to hiss forth the sounds that would create the magic of ribboned hues here upon the shadow plane — a weapon that never failed! While the insignificant fool gazed stupidly at the weaving stream of color, he, Vishwhoolsh, would rend the offending one into tasty bits to be devoured casually at his leisure.

Then the streamer appeared suddenly, actually entwining itself around the stupid man! Vishwhoolsh was ecstatic, and writhed round to finish his work, taking his gaze away from his quarry for a couple of seconds.

"You lend brightness to a drab world," Gord laughed as the massive head of the shadow-dragon turned and once again came snaking toward him. Certainly the thing was startled, for the rainbow now formed a flowing figure-eight around the young thief's sword, and as the colors played they changed and altered to become but two hues, mossy green and magenta.

The sword's negation of his magic was bad enough, but quickly the ebon-hued worm's lambent gaze fixed on an even more upsetting sight. Gord held Shadowfire now so that the orb rested lightly against his weapon's dark pommel, and the flame within the heart of the black opal seemed to pulse and sway in rhythm with the dancing band of colors made from the dragon's own magic.

"Spare me!" the thing hissed, transfixed, as the bicolored band suddenly became a darting tongue that shot out and twisted around the worm's long neck. The colors were no longer touching the sword, but were still controlled by it.

"Why?" snarled Gord. "You would not have showed me the same kindness!"

"I have a rich hoard. Spare my life, greatest of men, and I will bestow all my treasure upon you in return." The creature hissed forth its plea in a voice laden with evil despite its attempt to sound pleasant and promising.

With a twitch of his blade, Gord caused the twin-colored strand to tighten suddenly, making the black worm gulp and swallow the gush of foul stuff it was about to vomit forth upon him. "I grant you mercy," Gord said with a grim face. "The mercy of a quick end!"

As he spat out the last words, the young adventurer raised the sword's blade so that it pointed directly at the worm. The mossy hue suddenly changed to glowing bright green, and the magenta turned to brilliant red. The monster stiffened as if its head and tail were being pulled in opposite directions by a colossal titan, rising parallel to the shadowy ground as it did so. The two colors infused the shadow-dragon's entire body, inculcating the gloomy substance with twin hues of brightness before turning dim. As the colors faded away, so too did the monster.

"And I never learned its name," Gord remarked in mock sorrow.

A single huge scale lay on the ground nearby. The metallic thing must have come free from the shadow-dragon's hide when Gord had struck it with his sword. He pierced the plate twice, a laborious process even with his enchanted dagger, and then ran a thong through it. The glittering bit of dragon's armor was as broad as both of his palms and long as his hand. Gord hung it around his neck as if it were a gorget, thinking it was a suitable memento of his encounter with the beast. Then he resumed his seat on the flat boulder and waited once again.

An indefinite time later, the young thief was startled from his reverie by something new. This time there were no flashes of warning, and he was uncertain what it was that caused his numbed thoughts to suddenly become alert. Then it came to him. Penumbral rows of shadow vegetation had flowed into his vicinity and were standing, so to speak, to either hand. Shadow-crops to feed shadow-folk and phantom-kine. . . . Without moving a muscle, he had come to the outskirts of a town!

The village could have been transplanted from Oerth — from someplace near to Greyhawk, in fact — save for its deep shade and insubstantial-seeming stuff. Gord thought that if he made himself glow with the silvery radiance bestowed by the great stone, he could walk through shadow-brick and umbrageous stone as if it were gossamer. He did nothing of the sort, however. Choosing to remain looking as much a native to this plane as he could, he strode toward the village, knowing that his former hillock perch would be slipping off into the distance behind him as soon as he abandoned it.

"Ho, stranger! What want you in Dunswych?" The challenge came from a large, bow-armed fellow wearing what Gord assumed was a jack of shadow-leather sewn with horn plates. Shadow-stuff was still rather difficult for him to distinguish. When Gord hesitated in replying, the big fellow slipped his long bow from his shoulder and casually nocked a sable-feathered shaft, whistling loudly as he did so.

"Peace, stalwart!" Gord called at that, showing open hands. "I am but a lone and friendly wayfarer seeking a place to eat and rest, a little drink to refresh myself."

The arrow remained aimed halfway between the ground and Gord as another half-dozen shadowy folk hastened to join the first. Each was armed in some fashion — axe, hunting spear, flail, fork. Common but efficient weapons, used by freemen everywhere for both work and defense.

"You are no phantom!" the bowman said in a tone half awestruck and half accusatory.

"Quite so," Gord laughed in response, "but I daresay we have other things in common."

What had been meant as a jest seemed to have the desired effect, setting the minds of these folk at ease. Ready arms were eased from striking positions, and the bow-armed fellow reslung his weapon. "Yes, of course. You expected naught but shadowkin, did you?" At that there was a little ripple of uneasy mirth. Then the big one saw what graced Gord's neck. "Where came you upon that dragon scale?" The query was both suspicious and curious at once. The others crowded closer to see what their comrade had spoken of, and there were whispers of awe as they viewed the makeshift gorget.

"This?" Gord responded with a negligent pinch at the tar-hued scale. "An obliging dragon, one of shadow-stuff like all round here, was kind enough to leave it for me ere I sent it to its just end."

"You lie!" This sentiment, in several specific forms, came almost simultaneously from the assemblage.

That provoked him a bit, and the young man's face darkened with anger as he retorted. "Lie!? See if you think this blade lies," he snapped as his sword seemed to spring into his hand magically. The villagers started to raise their weapons for an attack, but their anticipation proved wrong. "See here, fellow," Gord said to the bowman, presenting him the blade. He had not bothered to wipe the shadow-dragon's blood from it, for the silvery metal was enchanted and never seemed to corrode. "Is this not the dried gore from the very sort of monster I speak of?"

The big phantom, as he had called himself, examined the sword, carefully picking off a bit of the crusted blood and examining it. After sniffing, feeling, and even gingerly tasting a flake of the stuff, the fellow decreed it to be dragon's blood indeed.

"Stranger, you are welcome in Dunswych!" he said

happily. "The longer you choose to stay with us, the better, in fact," and the others echoed this feeling to a man . . . or to a phantom.

Later, seated in a chair at the village tavern, Gord learned more of Dunswych. The community was one of only a score or so that existed on the Plane of Shadow. All of them were populated by the phantom folk. There were decayed towns and vast, ruined cities too, but gloams and their servants, the shadow-kin, inhabited these desolate places. While phantoms sought to dwell in peace and behaved very much as human commoners would, husbanding and farming, hunting and fishing, the gloams were baneful and destructive parasites that preyed upon the community of phantom folk.

When Gord inquired why their lord didn't protect them better from such depredations, the locals were quick in defense of their sovereign, the Shadowking. "The gloams are quite like rebellious nobles," the elderly master of the village explained. "Our king has not enough strength to subdue these marauders. . . . Such slipped from his grasp long and long ago. Why, my own grandsire couldn't remember the time when the Great Gloams were faithful — although he told me that in his younger days the lesser of their sort were still vassals of the Chiaroscuro Palace."

The monster he had slain, the shadow-dragon — Vishwhoolsh, as the phantoms named him — was an ally of the gloams. Had been, rather, Gord corrected himself mentally. One of the reasons for the paucity of hamlets and villages in the realm was the dragon. Each year he would select a place to terrorize, settle down nearby, and proceed to devour all of the livestock and phantom folk dwelling in the vicinity. When the place became deserted, the dragon simply moved on. Vishwhoolsh had been able to scent out his prey from leagues distant.

"Even with the dragon's demise, lesser minions might be sought out and enlisted by the gloams," the village leader said with grim satisfaction evident upon his shadowy features. "But such puny things as will come can be dealt with by dweomered shafts and the Shadowking's spell-binders!"

Score one for justice for a change, Gord reflected. These phantoms were human enough to make the young thief feel comfortable, to enable him to relate to them as if they were flesh-and-blood humans. Perhaps they would be, or were once, on his own world. "I seek the Chiaroscuro Palace," he told them. "I believe that your lord and I might transact business to our mutual satisfaction."

"That is indeed too bad," the bowman said quietly. "It passed us not two leagues distant but a day ago, but it flows rapidly, and by now it must be a score or more miles beyond."

"How soon will it approach again?"

"Hmm . . . It is a difficult problem, reckoning time here," the bowman said with a shake of his ashen-colored locks. "It comes perhaps four times in a hundred sleeps. This time was just before the Festival of Twilight, when the heavens brighten and Mool's disc grows penumbral and waxen — a time of great merriment! You must stay for our own celebration here in Dunswych!"

"No, I fear I must find your king."

"No good now, friend," one of the villagers assured him. "After Twilight, these lands grow most livid indeed, and thereafter the Shadowking sets forth on his rounds. He is but seldom in his hall at such a time, and when he is away, you'll not be welcomed there. Gloams creep in, you know."

"When is Twilight?" The question seemed odd, here in this place of near darkness.

"Any time now, stranger, any time! We make

preparations even as you ask. Let us eat, drink, and then go abed for a bit. There will be those to awaken us when the time is right."

Gord was making rapid mental calculations. There was a chance he could pull it off. "Can anyone here guide me to the place where your king's palace was yesterday?"

"Of course! I will gladly do so right after Twilight," the bowman said heartily, swigging his black ale.

"No, I mean now, this minute! I wish to be taken to the exact spot, distance-wise, where the Chiaroscuro Palace was last seen. Can and will you do that?"

The big phantom took only an instant to consider the request. "It is easy, for I am a hunter. If we hurry, I can have you there in about a quarter-sleep — sooner if you mind not jogging as the dingewolf does."

Pleadings to hurry back, mixed with good wishes, followed the two as they trotted from the village into the black and gray of the land. Now that Gord was aware of what was coming, the face of the strange luminary above did seem lighter, the illumination it provided less dim, and the faintly glowing black specks that were Shadowrealm's stars were hardly visible in the gloom above.

Gord was a tireless runner, and he pushed his guide hard. They came to the spot the fellow was sure was the right one within about an hour and a quarter by Gord's reckoning, based in part on his heartbeat, in part on an inner time sense. The ever-paling face of Mool hung motionless overhead now.

"I must say goodbye, stranger," the bowman said. "Luck in all you undertake!"

"Thanks, phantom friend," Gord called back, already jogging downcurrent. "My hopes for prosperity in Dunswych henceforward!" Then the phantom was out of sight and Gord was running hard in the direction the palace had been seen flowing. When he grew winded, he paused, rubbed himself with the flame-hearted opal, and then dashed on again, covering ground as does a dark wind blowing fiercely from the north.

The terrain of Shadowrealm flowed, of that there was no question. Yet, when one moved along the flow, up or down, or even across, the movement altered somehow. Thus, the destination Gord sought was not moving away from him — at least not as rapidly as if he were not coming toward it from behind. Under the ever-lightening disc of Mool, Gord raced. When his muscles again grew tired, and that occurred all too soon, he renewed his vigor with the opal and trotted onward. His pace ate up yards, and yards grew quickly into miles. When he became truly weary, Gord pulled out Shadowfire a third time, concentrated, and pressed the opal sphere to his flesh. Tingling flowed into him, and his skin began to shine with the luster of ancient silver. That was enough — more, and he might actually sink through the fabric of this place!

Like quicksilver he ran, and that suited his looks well. The luminary above was just becoming the color of old tallow when Gord spied a massive structure on the gray horizon ahead. It was a huge place of towers, turrets, spires, and flying buttresses — the Chiaroscuro Palace of the Shadowking at last!

Chapter 20

"I AM CALLED SMOKEMANE," a deep voice rumbled at him in the language common to men.

Gord swung quickly at the sound. There, as if conjured from the vapors, was the largest lion imaginable, one whose shaggy head was of smoky hue, just slightly darker and less sleek than his dove-gray body. Near this great beast sat another maned male lion of shadow, seeming to be the soot-maned one Gord had seen in the throng of creatures that had encircled him shortly after his arrival on this plane — the one that had left, taking other shadow-lions with it, when Gord had requested it to leave.

The cats smiled at him, a gesture perhaps meant to put Gord at ease but one that had the opposite effect. "I go to the place where the Shadowking holds forth," he managed to stammer to the pair. "Do not inhibit my progress," he added, not feeling very threatening to such great beasts as these.

The younger of the two, the huge lion with the sooty-shadow mane, actually laughed in lion-fashion as Gord said that. Smokemane, an even larger creature, cuffed him with claws sheathed. "When that one speaks," he roared, "you listen!"

The old male then turned to Gord once again, saying, "Your destination was told to us by our liege lord. It was he who commanded us to await your arrival,

287

and we are to accompany you as attendants — if it pleases you."

Despite the pressure of time, Gord allowed himself to stay still, staring at the two shadow-lions with interest. Perhaps great cats could speak, in a language of their kind, but how was it that these shadow-lions could converse with him in man-speech? Animals of this sort weren't supposed to do that! But, beast or no, Smokemane was indeed speaking in human tongue, and in a manner that indicated that he and his young companion had intelligence far above that of the felines of Oerth, for instance.

Gord had to know just what these creatures were. "You mentioned your liege lord. . . ." he ventured.

"The Mastercat, of course!" the sooty-maned one supplied. The older lion seemed disturbed at his companion's disregard of protocol but growled a note of assent at the identification.

That seemed believable, even fitting. Shadowrealm was as appropriate a place for felines as the material plane, and it stood to reason that cats here, as elsewhere, would have but one lord.

"How came it to pass that your lord knew of me?" Gord asked.

"When you sent Hotbreath, there, and his pride away from the circle of shadowfolk who had come because of the compelling force you emanated, he spoke of it to me," Smokemane rumbled in reply. "I would have done nothing in the matter, for such things are beyond the ordinary course of our folk. In any event, it was taken from my claws by the Mastercat. He came to me, asking about any unusual events here, and I related what Hotbreath had said. Thus we are now at this place awaiting your instructions, lord."

Lord? The gem he possessed must have powers he still did not fathom! "Thanks to you, bold pridemaster. . . . Thank you both," Gord said to the two huge lions. "As it is the wish of the Mastercat, evidently in return for my regard for his own, I accept your service. I must enter the Chiaroscuro Palace and have audience with the Shadowking. You two will be my attendants in this matter."

Hotbreath stood and stretched, flexing forth his long claws and displaying his massive teeth. Above and beyond their extraordinary brainpower, shadowlions, it seemed, were nearly as amply endowed with fangs as the archaic smilodons, the saber-toothed proto-tigers.

Smokemane too exhibited his arsenal of teeth in a relaxed yawn that followed Gord's words. Then he snapped his maw shut and rasped, "The Shadowking loves not cat-kind."

If that is true, Gord wondered, then why would the Mastercat command these two to intercept him just as he was about to visit the hall of the ruler of the shadow plane? But that was not quite the question he wanted to ask. First it was important to get to the heart of the matter.

"Why does the lord of this plane bear enmity toward you?"

"You? Better think of it as us," Shadowmane purred. "That one would have it that all who dwell in shadow either serve him or strive against him. Being able to classify creatures thusly seems to satisfy Shadowking in some perverse way. But we are cats, and our ways are our own. Our lord is what he is, and we honor and serve in our own particular ways as we choose. If others are princes or peasants, what matters that to cat-kind? Alone we stand, go our way, do as seems fitting. Such independence is disturbing to the ruler of this plane, for it seems he would have control, as the puppeteer pulls the strings, for good or ill. You too are independent, aloof, and your own being."

"Are you saying that Shadowking is malign?"

"Nay," the big cat said, shaking its massive head in manlike fashion to emphasize the response. "He is not a servant of Evil. Not even I would so designate Shadowking. His self-will goes beyond the acceptable — for us cats, this is condemnation enough. That one desires to remove liberty from others through control, but in fairness it was not always thus."

"Wise pridemaster," Gord said with real respect evident, "I am in your debt, for had I gone alone into the hall of Shadowking, I fear nothing beneficial would have occurred — if, as you say, I would have been treated in some way as a lone representative of cat-kind. In the company of two such as you, I see my chances of a fair audience much improved. Time fleets, and we must press on, but one thing still remains uncertain in my mind. You say that the lord of this realm is changed. What brought such ill?"

"That, lord, I cannot say, for the workings of the minds of such as he are beyond my poor reasoning. You are far more competent at such than I, of that I am certain. Perhaps Shadowking himself will say his own rede to you, for he deals more frankly with peers than with other beings."

"Me, a peer of his? Not quite, doughty one, not quite. You see in me a false might, a puissance lent by what I bear . . . no more. Still, into Shadowking's palace I must go. Let us proceed!"

Both mighty lions seemed to smile at that, as is the wont of such great cats when they choose to express feeling and opinion. "We stand beside you," Hotbreath coughed in a vigorous assent that ended with a chest-vibrating roar. Smokemane too sent forth the deep sound of lionkind. The two were heralding the approach of their charge.

The Chiaroscuro Palace was a rambling affair, part fortress, part pleasure-place. As they neared the mas-

sive pile, Gord loosened his weapons in their scab-
bards, feeling small and insignificant even with Shadowfire in his pouch. He put the feeling aside and motioned to the great cats. Stepping from the cover of
the copse of silver and black foliage, he and his flanking escort strode boldly to the principal entrance of
the Chiaroscuro Palace. The entrance was made of
obsidian and gray marble, with soaring walkways and
pennoned domes high above the broad steps leading
to the ornate gates that stood open in invitation to
the Festival of Gloaming now getting underway. Sil-
very-sounding trumps competed with thundering
drums as the trio approached. Whether in challenge
or salutation, the minions of the Shadowking were
responding to Gord's lion-hearted arrival.

"Why are the walls untenanted, the battlements
unmanned?" Gord asked the lions softly.

"My nose says this whole place is filled with many
two-legged ones, and the formless things as well,"
Hotbreath rumbled in response.

Now that he thought about it, this seemed a far
more reasonable way to guard a shadow-palace —
not with openly visible sentries, but with gloomy, hidden wards. Shadows cloaked, obscured. They were
the stuff of nothingness, yet shadows could mask
substance. They aided and betrayed and were everywhere and nowhere at once. They were the stuff of
illusion. . . . Of course!

Having hit on the likely solution, Gord determined
to accept nothing his eyes told him, and he paused
and peered upward at the tall facade of the sprawling
place. What he saw made his mind reel for an instant. The palace was not so grand and ornate as it
had seemed. More a stronghold than a whimsical
mansion — the court of a warrior, not the palace of a
poet and dreamer. Pillars and columns were actually
armed soldiers, stone bartizans were actually great,

griffonlike guardians of inky feathers and pearly beaks, perched to plummet upon unwelcome visitors.

Gord pretended to have something in his eye, going through a series of blinkings and rubbings as he scanned what he could. "Do you see any creatures on the battlements? Warriors on the parapets?"

Neither cat responded, although both of the massive lions had swung their maned heads this way and that as Gord had continued to pause and seemingly remove a speck from his eye. The silence confirmed his assumption. Shadowking masked his palace in illusion; layer upon layer was possible, in fact. The young thief determined to do his utmost to penetrate the veils and discover the true nature of the Lord of Shadowrealm and his chiaroscuro stronghold. "Come, my friends," Gord said jauntily. "Let us pay our respects to the King of Shadow." Then he ascended the translucent steps of whorled agate, the huge, maned lions pacing him on either hand.

A shadowy figure in swarthy and insubstantial-seeming robes of voluminous sort was standing against a great pillar of stone, a veined column of polished marble that stretched the height of five men to support the arched ceiling of the long antechamber. When Gord and his lion guard neared the silvery doors at the end of the hall, the figure spoke, but the voice seemed to issue from a marble statue forming part of the opposite support. "A noble man, unproclaimed by bearing or device, save for two male lions as guard and escort!"

The lions shifted their eyes toward the statue, so effective was the ventriloquism of the magical major domo who announced them. The metal valves parted instantly at the words, swinging silently and smoothly inward to reveal a seemingly boundless space beyond. Were those real stars? Mool's ivory disc, too? No, the phantasm was penetrable when Gord concentrated. The chamber was huge, no question, the ceiling of its dome no less than sixty feet above, but it was no more than a massive room in a mighty palace despite the design of Shadowking to have guests see it otherwise.

"For revelers to be welcomed at Twilight-tide," a soft voice said sweetly, "they must provide their name and nature. Prithee, my lord, favor me with this dear information so that I may proclaim it first to our sovereign."

Gord saw a darkly beautiful woman, one he judged to be a phantom lady of the court by her dress and demeanor. "An honor and privilege, m'lady. You may state that Gord, High Citizen of Greyhawk of Oerth, has come to pay his respects to the Shadowking," he told her, trying not to overtly stare as he sought to determine her real nature.

"As you wish, honorable gentleman," the lovely lady of shadow replied, switching honorifics smoothly and giving a tiny and appropriate curtsey suited to Gord's announced status. "But I must say you are too modest," she added with a fluttering of long, sable eyelashes. "Your bearing and manner proclaim far more of you than the humble rank you claim aloud, and no simple citizen of a free city anywhere comes accompanied by pridemasters as guards."

A game of words was afoot, so Gord rephrased his status, but played it down instead of exalting it, which would have given the woman more information than she deserved. "Very well. Let us change it then. Say that Gord, a wanderer and rogue, comes to call."

The woman started a full obeisance, having anticipated something more glorious than she was told. Then, flustered, she halted, recovered herself, and hurried off into the throng populating the ceremonial hall to report her news. Gord smiled to himself. Illusion could be countered with misdirection and simple truth as well. Those who sought to delude were more often confounded by plain speaking and obvious realities than the stuff of which they were masters. Odd, however, that this inquisitress was as she seemed. A lesson, he supposed, to not expect everything to be masked. A subtlety used by the Lord of Shadows that would not be lost upon him.

"Gord, a worthy personage, accompanied by two pridemasters of our realm," a hushed but pervasive voice intoned. Eyes suddenly turned toward him, and Gord felt a trifle uncomfortable. The company he saw watching him and the two lions included the creatures he knew as adumbrates, plus what were surely gloams with shadowkin retainers trailing after, all interspersed with phantoms, fuligi, shades, murklings, spirits, and humans too. There! That was a small company of drow! Gray-skinned dwarf beside deep-brown gnome, and a smattering of humanoids of unusual sort — beings who recalled to Gord's mind the ehjure Pinkus, a memorable creature who had accompanied him long ago on another adventure involving illusion and deception.

A square fellow with jutting brows over a broad, honest face approached them with a swaggering gait. "Hello, Gord. You haven't any idea who I am, I know, but I've heard tell of you!" Then the man turned away, and was about to head elsewhere when he turned back and winked a merry eye. "Don't worry — I'll not say a word. . . ." and with that the crowd swallowed him up. Shrugging helplessly, Gord stood uncertain as the strains of a strange melody suddenly were struck up, and the place began to become aswirl with dancing couples.

"My lord?" It was the lovely shadow-woman again, smiling up at him uncertainly as she arose from a full curtsey. Gord nodded, and she spoke on. "I am discourteous, but I fear that the king orders me thus.

Rather than dancing, His Gloominess commands your presence in the Vault of Veils. Such an audience during this festive time is unheard of," she added with a hint of awe. "You should be ashamed for misleading a lady so."

Gord could only smile ambiguously at that. Whatever the reason for it being granted, he did desire an audience with the Shadowking. Even though the monarch had anticipated him, the need remained. "Sometimes, sweet lady, necessity demands that we not always appear as we are, or say all that pertains."

The phantom smiled and nodded at his words, a look of relief on her pretty features. "Oh yes, of such I am most aware, Lord . . . Gord?" She made it almost a question and gave a whisper of tinkling laughter at the rhyme. "I should not have felt deceived because you pretended low rank, I know. It was just that I felt drawn by some . . . no matter, craving your indulgence. I chatter so that I am mortified. This is my first festival as Court Duplitrix, and so many notables make me feel inadequate."

"You shall prove quite worthy of the position, I am sure," Gord said, not really having any notion as to what the duties of a duplitrix were — other than carrying messages and gathering up guests and depositing them in other places.

"Here is the entrance to the privy audience, noble Gord. My thanks for being so gracious to me," she said. "If you need further . . . ministration, ask for Lady Sabina."

The dark door before which he stood remained shut. It had no handle, no grill to speak through. Should he knock? Inappropriate. He wished he had asked Sabina about what would be happening, but it was too late for that now. Gord folded his arms and stood waiting in the hall-like alcove off the great ballroom. He could be patient. Both lions sat, likewise awaiting the next move. Minutes passed. No person or thing came their way. Sounds only told Gord that a revel was in progress; save for music and whispery voices, laughter and strange singing, he and the shadow-cats might have been in a world alone. Then the door swung suddenly open to expose its half-foot thickness and the fact that no handle existed on its inner side either.

"Enter." The command was hollow and unhuman.

The Vault of Veils was a double-diamond-shaped room of smallish proportion, although its V-shaped ceiling was twenty feet high. Veils did, in fact, hang everywhere in the place. Gossamer things depending to canopy the room, screen its walls, and divide its eight points. Each cloth was as fine as spiderweb, as sheer as smoke. That such were not to hide anything from view was evident, but Gord felt certain that some purpose for these trappings existed. In the center of the stone chamber was a table that mimicked the room's shape. Fifteen seats there were, set evenly around the oddly shaped surface. One was darker, mistier than the rest. In it was a very tall, thinnish man of aristocratic bearing and arrogant visage.

"You may seat yourself anywhere . . . after you pay homage," the pearly-skinned monarch of shadow said through thin lips as dark as night. His mouth smiled then, but his ashen eyes, the same color as his hair, were as hard as iron.

Gord bent a knee and bowed his head slightly. The gesture was enough to show respect, too little by far to demonstrate humility. This Shadowking set Gord's nerves on edge and made his hackles rise. "My thanks, Gracious Lord of Shadows," he managed to say without any rancor evident. "You are most kind to allow me to see Your Umbrageous Majesty."

That almost made the fellow start, Gord saw. "It was you who destroyed one of my adumbrates!"

Shadowking said accusingly. "How do you explain that?"

From a place opposite the shadowlord, Gord smiled gently, patting the head of Smokemane as the lion rested at the young adventurer's side. "I did not come here to explain, majesty. Suffice to say that the monstrosity dared to attack me after being offensive."

"So, you dare to actually challenge Me in Mine Own Palace! Imprimus said you were meat for the table of the executioner!"

This was all wrong. In a moment the monarch of this plane would be consigning him to whatever passed for dungeons in the realm of shadows, there to await whatever fate was prescribed for criminals in this realm. Based on what he had learned from the folk in Dunswych, this was not the kind of treatment he expected or deserved. There could be only one answer. . . .

Gord rose to his feet and spat out a single word. "Deception!" He meant that he thought the Shadowking was being deceived, but as he jumped erect and spoke, something wavered before his eyes. The tall, pearl-complected monarch had changed to a smutty form, a hunched gloam.

"Ho, ho, ho!" A new figure had entered the room and was behind Gord. The laughter was soft but somehow conveyed heartiness and force at the same time. "You have failed, Imprimus. This one saw through your pose. Be a good sport and toddle off now to plot my overthrow or something equally useless, there's a good gloam!"

Gord turned and saw a replica of the man who had been speaking with him from across the table, only this one didn't strike a wrong note within him, and the smile he now displayed was real. Now Gord made a more humble obeisance, and stood with head inclined until the true Shadowking had ushered the

GORD THE ROGUE

masquerading gloam from the chamber and taken the
seat that Imprimus had usurped. "Your Umbrageous
Majesty," Gord said.

"Gord, wayfarer. I welcome you as a worthy subject of My Realm. Do excuse the silly joke. The gloams
are amusing, but their schemes and pranks can be
tiresome. Now, My time during Twilight is most limited, so I ask you to hand it over, and then you may
have your run of the palace."

The king's request certainly meant only one thing.
"I must wear a blazon upon my cloak announcing
what I bear," Gord thought. Then, speaking firmly, he
addressed the Shadowking. "Your majesty, your kind
acceptance of my unbidden entrance into your realm
is most generous. Know, however, that I came unwill-
ingly as well. I must humbly decline your acceptance
— that of myself as a subject of Shadowrealm — for I
am of Oerth and am vassal to no one."

The Shadowking looked annoyed at Gord's words.
"Oh? By your two pets, there, I assume you have ties
to the Mastercat. Be aware, mortal, that I rule here.
Your present state does not allow you a choice of liege
lords, does it? As your king, I now instruct you to give
to Me what is Mine. This audience is concluded."

Gord rose at that, bowing slightly. The two shadow-lions came to their feet likewise, soft growls
sounding deep within their massive chests. "Do you
claim the scale of the dragon I wear? My sword? What
is it that your majesty asks of me?" Gord asked in
feigned confusion.

"Don't try to play cat-and-mouse with me, whelp
of the Mastercat! Hand over Shadowfire or face my
wrath!"

"The gem is yours, lord . . ." Gord replied smoothly. But as the Shadowking smiled, he added, "as soon
as you restore my memories to my mind and my body
to my own plane."

"You . . . you . . . dare make demands of Me?"

"I crave your pardon, Gloomy Majesty. By no means would I be so foolish as to require anything from so royal a lord as you — unless such generosity and favor were given freely, such as in exchange for some service to your majesty and the realm."

"It is a trifling matter for me to take it from you."

"Undoubtedly so. Your might is fabled, Lord of Shadows."

"Shadowfire. Hold it forth."

"I fear to do so at this moment, majesty. Perhaps when we have discussed the small things which trouble me, we can then view the stone."

Dark forms began to fill the chamber. Terrible things were taking shape, and all were inimical to Gord and the great lions. Gord responded by reaching into his pouch, touching the strange black opal, and willing its power to travel along his arm and into his body. As he did so, Gord's flesh began to radiate an iridescent, opaline paleness that washed outward to make deep shadows penumbral.

In effect he had become the luminary of the chamber, and the beams that he shed had a startling effect. Some of the shadows vanished as the pale beams touched them, dispelling into the nothingness they were in actuality. Those not the stuff of illusion became transparent, as if each were but the ghost of a shadow creature, and, lacking substance any longer, wafted harmlessly through the shadowy material stuff of the place to become helplessly entangled in the veils that festooned the room. Fish caught in nets, once-powerful things of Shadowrealm bleated weakly from their filmy prisons as their overlord watched with a bleak expression.

"So you are conversant with the baser powers conveyed to you by the gem," Shadowking said with a flat tone of resignation in his voice. "Shadowfire bestows such ability because I placed the power within its heart. What I have made, I can unmake." The last statement contained no hint of threat, not a touch of braggadocio. Indeed, the Lord of Shadows seemed rather filled with sadness when he uttered the pronouncement. This moved Gord.

"Be at ease, majesty. I have no desire to usurp your rule, to contest with your might — even to place myself into an adversarial position. With all due respect and deference, I am here by no will of my own, but the circumstances of my situation demand that I protect myself vigorously."

The Lord of Shadows scoffed. "You suggest I regard you as a dear cousin even as your flaunt your lese majesty in My palace! Am I to be blackmailed? Never!"

At that, Gord had to take a firm stand. "Have I made demands of you? It is painfully evident that the situation is quite the opposite. I am without memory of my recent past, a virtual prisoner in this place, this shadowy plane, against my desire, and you seek to strip from me my only means of defending myself here as I seek the means to depart from your realm forever. My cause is just, Shadowking, and my course straight. I have that which you seek — Shadowfire. I know not how I gained it, but never did I take it from you! I will gladly gift the gem to your majesty, but in return I ask your royal word that you will restore my memories and see to it I am carried safely to the material world once again."

"Yet you might be able to usurp the throne, you know."

"Begging your pardon, majesty, I know nothing of the sort, nor do I care to discover if there is truth in your assertion. Once more, I offer the opal to your lordship, asking only the two small favors I require in return."

"You are worthy, Gord," Shadowking laughed, leaning his long spine deeply into the ebon plush of his chair and tilting his pale face back in order to allow the sound to roll forth unhindered. "Without certainty as to strength, potential, or foes, you decide upon a course and walk that line thereafter. Perhaps you do speak truly. . . . I find no guile in your words, nor do the manifold dweomers which cloak this Vault of Veils indicate aught but honesty." The Shadowlord tilted back his massive seat and looked at Gord along his aquiline nose, black eyes deep and unfathomable. "Am I to accept you as both peer and honest petitioner, then?"

"For the nonce, your majesty. . . . Who amongst us can claim equality and forthrightness for longer?"

Again, Shadowking laughed. "I begin to actually like you, master Gord. You rule naught but yourself, and only that betimes, I think. Still, you are clever and amusing and speak openly. I accept that. Now I shall do the same. Many who dwell within My Realm, the Plane of Shadows, are not indigenous. These outlanders come here by choice to continue their chosen ways, and such ones are at odds with me, inimical, as it were. . . ."

"The creatures known as gloams?" Gord asked uncertainly.

"Exactly, young prince, but not restricted to that narrow lot by any means. They are once-humans, you know. The murklings were once gnomes and dwarves; the fuligi, curiously enough, elvish sorts. These migrants, along with evil-natured natives of this plane — shadowkin and others too — have combined to oppose My rule and curry mischief and rebellion. I can no longer trust my adumbrates, for instance, due to the machinations of Imprimus and his ilk. Only the phantoms are basically loyal, and, too, certain other of the lesser creatures of Shadowrealm. This split, the division of my subjects, affects me, of course."

"Disloyalty is always painful, majesty," Gord said to fill the silence, for the lean monarch had fallen into a reverie.

"You misunderstand. It is natural, for you are not one subject to such conditions. When one's realm becomes fractious, then the lord tied thereto suffers accordingly. I, Master Gord, am a dangerous schizophrenic. It is a malady not of my own choosing, nor born of any mental frailty I possess. I am shadow, and as it is torn by factiousness, so too am I. Alternately I am the good, the ill, and the indifferent within the bounds of the plane. Should there develop yet another great division within Shadowrealm, then I fear that I, its monarch, would suffer yet another splintering of my already disjointed personality."

Aghast, Gord leaped to his feet. "Then I must now offer my sword and my service to you, majesty, in order to restore matters to their rightful state or, failing, lose my life."

"Pretty sentiments, no doubt nobly voiced. Why, then, your refusal to give unto Me what is Mine? Restoration of the opal orb will do much to mend my torn psyche."

"What of mine own dilemma, majesty?"

Shadowking looked annoyed. "You are consigned to this plane by means supernatural. Some mighty servant of an evil deity sought your death, or perhaps it was the vile deity personally — no matter! Ere you expired, you sought the power of Shadowfire. It cheated the one who slew you, carrying you here instead of to the kingdom where your slayer sought to consign you. Perhaps even another entity had a hand in that. . . . I can but hazard guesses there."

"Is there aught which will return me to my own place?"

"This place is your own now. Once I might have been able to change the course of things to your benefit. Not now."

"Shadowfire?"

"Restorative, longed for, but insufficient." The lean lord of the shadows slumped gloomily, resigned to his fate.

Gord bowed, placing one knee upon the gray-veined black marble of the chamber's floor. "Majesty," he said softly, drawing his sword and holding its chill blade gingerly in gauntleted hands so as to avoid its enervation, "I offer my self and my sword in your service. Will you accept?"

"Yes, for all it may matter to either of us. I have but scant hope."

"In that event, Lord of Shadows, I gladly give over Shadowfire into your hand," the young adventurer said with firm resolution ringing in his voice. "No vile sect should ever abridge any sovereign lord in his own domain!"

The master of gloom stretched forth his hand, touching the hilt of the sword in token of his acceptance of Gord's pledge. In a twinkling, the young man slipped the blade back into its sheath and brought forth the strange stone so sought after by all who knew of it. As if unbelieving still, Shadowking himself now arose and reached out for the opal. "Long and long have I sought Shadowfire," he murmured.

"It is yours, majesty," Gord said, firmly placing the glowing sphere within the pale palm of the lord of shadows. "May it never be parted from its rightful owner again."

The tall being gazed at the precious orb for long moments, unspeaking, unable to speak. Then the Shadowking smiled slightly. "Arise, Gord," he said in stately tones, "for I now create you a Lord and Knight of Shadowrealm. Stand before me, Count of Twilight,

Knight of Chiaroscuro. I charge you with aiding Me during My times of need, of giving service to the Realm of Shadow, and with faithfulness in all your dealings until such time as you may return once more to the place which is rightfully your own."

These words were sufficient to bring a trickling of recollection back to him. It took a few moments for the surge of memories to emerge, wash over his mind, then sink again into their proper channels. "Dyvers! The black sapphires!"

"That is where you were slain. The gems you seek are here in Shadowrealm."

"But if—"

The Shadowking raised his pearly-palmed hand. "The forces which split this plane now impinge upon Me most sorely. Before long I shall be as malign as the duskdrake. The gloams now work to undo the weal wrought by your gift, Prince Gord. I resist their evil now only through the renewed force granted by the power of Shadowfire. Leave Me now, for I must fight off the attack alone. When there comes an interlude in the assault, I will summon you again, for there is urgent need of your office in this matter. More I cannot say, now, for who can tell what will occur soon?"

With that the lord of the murky plane seated himself with determination stamped on his features. The Shadowking was about to fight a battle, and in it he had to stand alone.

Chapter 21

SNUFFDARK, THE BLACKNESS AFTER TWILIGHT, lay upon Shadowrealm as a lightless mantle of oppression. Even the folk of shadow were subject to the totality. Its strongest were near-blind, weak with the inky darkness that oppressed the plane.

In this grim midnight Gord walked alone over a landscape that moved sluggishly and with convulsive writhings. Snuffdark's black wind howled as a dirge, and even the fearsome beasts of Shadowrealm cowered in their dens, seeking solace in deep lair or high, awaiting the return of dusk to their somber world.

Not so the black-clad young adventurer now named Count of Twilight. He strode through the pitch dark with sureness of step and firm purpose, a short-bladed sword clenched fast in his right hand. Upon the pommel of this weapon was a phosphorescent jewel, a fire opal with a strange, greenish glow in its core. By its power Gord saw, and the magical sight was clear and strong. Shadowking himself had given him the talisman, for the lord of shadows no longer had need of the gem. He had the tenfold might of Shadowfire.

Imprimus. Gloam of greatest evil, vampiric master of a fell coven. Imprimus, lich among gloams. It was this terrible gloam whom Gord sought amidst the storm of Snuffdark. Somewhere within the wilderness

305

of the writhing plane Imprimus lurked in a secret stronghold, awaiting his moment. The foul being would settle for a sundering of the Shadowrealm, a dual direction. He and his evil circle would use their malign powers to force schizophrenia upon Shadowking, a permanent division of mind so as to enable them to govern the plane half of the time. Gord knew that such an occurrence would turn the place toward darker and darker ends. The mind of its monarch would erode, and at some point, as the evil within Shadowrealm grew, make the tortured brain weak and vulnerable. Then would come the final assault, and Imprimus would be Lord of Shadows . . . *le roi est mort, vive le roi noir*!

Gord stood alone between Imprimus and his ultimate desire, but at best the gloam just suspected the fact. Now, during the deepness of Snuffdark, all of Shadowrealm was at its lowest energy level, and Imprimus was weak and mentally blind.

As he moved purposefully across the weird terrain, Gord sought for certain signs that would indicate the presence of the gloam-lich called Imprimus. In this land of darkness, now smothered by so great a gloom as to defy description, the young adventurer looked for a blackness of blacknesses, a greater and more terrible darkness than any that grasped Shadowrealm. Such intensity of black was the key to where the gloam lurked, for Imprimus's own evil gathered the pitchy stuff of Snuffdark to it as a lodestone draws iron.

The green tongue of luminescence within the heart of the fire-opal talisman lent luminosity to Gord's own eyes, and had any been about in the impenetrable murk of Snuffdark, they could have observed this weird for themselves. But no shadow-creature stirred, and so Gord strode through the blackness alone, unobserved. Only the hollow moaning of the life-sapping black wind accompanied him as he sought his foe. Then the monotonous, empty sound changed.

"Hoo, hoo, hoooo . . ." the relentless wind seemed to call. It was a sound somewhere in the lowest audible register, a groaning bellow halfway between a laugh and a lamentation. "Hoo, hoo, ohoooo!" This time the ebon air carried the sound more strongly and with spine-chilling effect. It was no trick of the wind, but the call of some creature abroad in the suffocation of Snuffdark!

When the mournful cry sounded yet a third time, stronger still, Gord blinked and dampened his visual power. Now the young adventurer could see but a bowshot's distance through the swirling eddies of inky blackness, as if he were an arctic wayfarer peering through the swirling snows of a blizzard. Vision opened, then diminished, as Snuffdark's winds drove Shadowrealm into frenzied movement and tenebrous stuff swirled and drifted across the landscape.

A crunching sound came, carried by the black wind. The noise was the sound of something crushing the very substance of the shadow-plane beneath it as it came. Monstrous claws compressing the stuff of the place, crushing and crumbling it to atoms by the sheer mass of its colossal form. "Hoooo, hooooo, oohoooo!" came again now, as loud as if the sound were coming from within Gord himself.

Only one thing could be so huge, one creature sound so fearsome a call. The duskdrake was hunting for Gord, even as Gord hunted for Imprimus. No other monster of shadow could abide the Snuffdark, none but the duskdrake was so large. Knowing that flight was useless, Gord resigned himself to facing the oncoming beast. Better to die fighting than to be caught from behind and devoured as a hound snaps up a hare.

The sooty swirling lessened, revealing a jagged mass of shadowstuff a hundred yards distant. Gord couldn't recall a spire of stone there a minute ago, yet now he clearly saw a great mass of jagged rocks. Then the tall spire crowning the crag split to reveal a cavelike opening, and from this deep hole came a rush of vapors that carried a fell call: "Ohoo, oohooo, ooooah!" The duskdrake had sighted its prey.

Shadow-ground trembled under Gord's feet as the mighty monster trod upon the land, each step covering a dozen yards, flattening whatever it impacted with. "Futter you!" Gord shouted defiantly. The shadows roiled and flattened around the monstrous beast — a reaction to Gord's words? Evidently the duskdrake understood human speech.

Powerful as it was, the duskdrake was not immune to the effects of Snuffdark. The heavy darkness slowed the thing. Its angular neck moved forward and downward, parallel to the ground. It walked ponderously, as if the gigantic beast were moving to the rhythms of a stately gavotte played in courtly half-time. As the hyperdragon moved it issued a ferocious growling, a rumbling that began in its belly and thundered upward, exiting along with a steaming hiss through its massive maw. With the terrible sound came a stream of shadow-fire.

The dim flames issuing from its mouth were not at all similar to the fiery heart of the great black opal. The hissing gout of burning heat was gray and as transparent as a crystal of smoky quartz, although it was shot through with near-black tongues and had tips of diamondlike brilliance. The belching shadow-fire shot across the swarthy stuff of the plane, devouring all in its path, leaving shadow-rock superheated to a smoking dun, washing over the place where Gord had stood defiantly a split-second before. Gord had thought the shadowdragon's breath fearsome, but now he knew the true meaning of the word.

The young thief's lightninglike reflexes weren't enough to save him. Despite the sluggishness enforced upon the duskdrake by the weight of Snuffdark, the monstrous beast was still fast to react. The edge of the spewing shadow-flames caught Gord, and the searing heat burned his exposed flesh with agonizing ferocity. At last Gord knew how terrible was the stuff of shadow-fire, understanding the refinement that resulted in the fabulous fire-ruin that had been used by human mages to devastate an empire.

Even as his nerves sent screaming messages of pain to one part of his mind, he managed to act. The hyperdragon's awful breath had seared him, but in the process the flames had burned and melted so much of the stuff of shadow that a turbidity was created, a thick cloud of cloaking blackness within blackness, through which neither duskdrake nor man could see.

Gord lay at the edge of this concealing mass, and as the monstrous foe stomped and hissed inside the cloud, he ministered to his burns. For whatever reason, the fellow who had first greeted him by name in the Chiaroscuro Palace had later bestowed upon him a small box of salve. Head cocked to one side, birdlike, bright eyes assessing Gord in friendly fashion, this strange man had simply handed the container to him. "Here, Gord. My present to you for your coming quest. You'll need, I fear, much more, but this is all I can offer." When Gord had inquired as to the contents of the box, the man told him it was sovereign for all manner of cuts, bruises, and similarly painful injuries.

The ointment proved efficacious for burns, as he had hoped. Gord smeared it heavily on his burned face, blackened arms, charred hands. The balm brought both surcease from the agony and miraculous healing even as the hyperdragon ground a zig-zag path through the obscuring cloud. "Hissoohh, hissaaahrr!" the duskdrake seemed to pant as it slammed its two massive feet onto the ground, mighty tail lashing, long reptilian neck swiveling and snaking this way and that as it searched the turbid terrain for its minuscule foe.

As Gord's burned flesh healed under the soothing layer of salve, the great beast grew more and more angry at its inability to find and finish the puny human who had abused it. In frustration it lashed forth its neck, jaws distended in fury as the shadow-fire it breathed immolated the land indiscriminately. In his location close to and nearly under the duskdrake's massive tail, Gord was spared a further bath of the incinerating flames.

The tree-trunk-thick appendage rippled and lashed, snaking over Gord's head where he lay in the shelter of a little hollow, then whipping away to sweep the shadow-ground to the far side. When this happened, the young adventurer leaped up and dashed straight toward the sound of the hyperdragon's clawed feet crushing all beneath their burden as the monster marched ahead searching for him.

"Whherre aahhrrr yooo hhhiiiding, sssmaahl hhaarre?" The thing could speak, and it was now calmer too. As Gord approached the gigantic pillars that served to hold its body above the ground as the duskdrake moved about, he saw them flex and strain. The broad belly and chest of the beast was being lowered, and the hyperdragon was stooped so as to allow its smaller forelimbs to scrabble through the rocks and dirt exposed by its scorching breath. It was searching for him, Gord realized, using foot-long fore-talons to toss aside boulders as if they were pebbles.

The murk created by the monster's initial gout of shadow-fire was subsiding around both man and duskdrake, while all round the region before the monster the air was roiling with fresh clouds from the second, more prolonged bath of awful fire it had received from the duskdrake's maw. The huge hyper-dragon was even now turning its tremendous body clockwise, searching with eyes and talons too, its hot belly thundering as its internal organs worked to produce the material for yet another wash of the searing flames that were its most effective weapon.

When Gord had suffered the flaming attack of the beast's fiery breath, the gem set into the pommel of his sword had grown brighter as the licking tongues of gray played over him. The change had not gone unnoticed by the young adventurer, and now, as he stood near the underbelly of the duskdrake, Gord saw that the green within the heart of the fire opal was deeper, brighter, more active than it had been before. If his rapid evasion had been partially responsible for his avoiding the worst of the destruction wreathed by the beast, and the ointment had cured the injury done by the fire, perhaps this dweomered gem, the talisman of Shadowking, had done its part as well. Surely the stone was more vivid now, and the faint silvery sheen of his blade showed long arcs of green playing from pommel to crossguard as he raised the sword to strike.

"Oooohh hhooo!" the duskdrake boomed as its snaking head swiveled and one lambent eye, a flat disc the size of a round shield, caught sight of the glowing stone and flashing electricity it generated. Even as the monster voiced its happy surprise, and one mighty limb jerked up in order that it could stamp downward upon him, Gord struck.

"Ah ha!" he countered, unable to think of anything else to say as the blade sunk between the massive,

angular plates of the hyperdragon's belly armor
These thick scales of sooty black were as spiky and
hard as those of glistening jet that covered the huge
beast's sides and uppermost parts. Here along its un
derside, however, the scales were longer, more plate
like, and the joints between were broader to allow its
underside to flex and curl.

Hot pink played amidst the verdant arcs as Gord
used both arms to drive the sword between two of the
duskdrake's banded scales. Even the skin beneath
these steel-like plates was tough, as thick and hard
as the skin of the largest rhinoceros. It required every
ounce of strength he possessed, the coordination o
legs, back, shoulders, arms, and wrists too, for Gord
to force the keen point home. Legs straightened, back
rippled, arms pistoned, wrists locked as human mus
cle and bone pushed the green-lighted blade of the
sword home, until its full length was buried to the
hilt within the furnace-heat of the beast's gut.

"Ahhrrrooo!" The scream that the duskdrake vent
ed when the bar of metal sunk into its vitals was
deafening. "Haaarrrg!!" it bellowed louder still, as the
green of the fire opal's heart flared and burned, con
suming the gem, shooting up the metal of the sword's
hilt and quillons in a fiery, iridescent display that ate
upward along the length of the weapon, a burning so
fierce that the hide and scales of the hyperdragon
turned translucent beneath the internal glare of it.

Fortunately for him, Gord had been kicked away a
dozen yards by the convulsive movement of the dusk
drake's taloned foot as the beast reacted to the awfu
pain within its body. The horny spikes covering the
thing slashed and tore the young adventurer's flesh
the force of the blow bruised and stunned him. Nev
ertheless, the terrible punishment he suffered also
saved Gord's life, for it drove him away from the mon
ster and its final throes.

The agony of the thrust caused the first great twitching, but then the worse torture of the burning within itself drove the hyperdragon mad with pain. It snapped its jaws and spat tongues of its gray fire skyward as its talons tore solid stone and its body beat the ground so as to turn it into pulverized dust and flying shards of rock. Then, green incandescence met gray flame. The two raged and combined, and the whole of the duskdrake's innards became molten, glowing with an ugly ocher hue as the fires intermixed and consumed the beast.

Gord was up and running, heedless of wounds, enduring the pain of activity. He knew that it was a matter of life and death that he get away as quickly as he could manage. Without the talisman he had no extraordinary visual powers during the total gloom of Snuffdark, but the furnace within the convulsed body of the duskdrake provided ample illumination for the young adventurer.

By the hellish ocher light of the incandescent hyperdragon, Gord sped away, twisting and turning to avoid obstacles as he went. Then he stopped dead. Before him was his own sword stuck point down in the shadow-ground. In its throes, perhaps the duskdrake had plucked the blade out and hurled it, hoping to thus free itself of the fiery green agony. The opal was gone but the short sword unharmed. He picked it up and turned as he heard a roaring sound from behind.

A rubine star shot forth bloody beams, spears of light that thickened and grew more intense instant by instant. Heat washed over his back, and as the wave of radiation struck, Gord dived headfirst to the hard stuff of shadow-ground. There came a deep, sustained booming, a sound like thunder, as the inferno of opaline fire and dragon flame devoured the duskdrake and all that was around the beast. A massive shock wave ran through the land, and then everything was again black.

With great effort Gord climbed to his feet and stood, dazed and shaky but alive. Where the titanic duskdrake had been there was nothing to be seen. Close inspection enabled Gord to discover a great crater. Talisman and hyperdragon both were gone. He now faced the pitch blackness of Snuffdark with no magical aids save his sword and long dirk. Did he still have the means to discover the greater blackness of Imprimus's hiding place? It seemed that the sacrifice of the duskdrake, unintended though it had been, had served the allies of the evil monster well. Gord, their sworn foe, might now be unable to find the lair in which they secluded themselves. Gord slumped in dejection.

Time now to apply more of the salve to heal his new hurts. He needed time too to consider what his next step would be. The grim wind of the Twilight death howled around him, reminding Gord that Snuffdark had by no means run its full course. Yet, even as long as the inky obscurement would persist before the Shadowrealm was again restored to its weird half-light, the interval seemed insufficient to serve. When shadows again slid and swayed across the plane, the power of the gloams would return, and the fate of Shadowking and his realm would be sealed.

Perhaps there was a slender hope left. His sword's enchantment might serve. That, and his ring whose stone had seemingly picked up some of the green fire from the talisman, together might possibly do it. Having nothing to lose from the attempt, Gord shifted his short sword to his left hand and in a minute he stood peering into the blackness. Gord's eyes stared blindly into the pitchy world, unable to penetrate the mantling of Snuffdark.

314

Then, slowly, little by little, his vision began to see variations in the blackness. Here was a darkness the color of coal, there a line of duller shade. Then Gord's vision grew better still, and deep gray and shining ebony were distinguishable with visual ability that saw not but mere feet but outward by yards. Carefully, Gord resumed his hunt, searching for the enemy, Imprimus, in that place where Shadowking had told him was the most probable locale of the malign gloam's lair. There were both time and opportunity after all.

The sudden onslaught of the duskdrake had been more than coincidence, that was certain. The terrible beast's finding Gord in the total gloom of Snuffdark was likewise more than mere chance. The massive hyperdragon had been in the area for some reason, and the most likely one Gord could imagine was to serve as guardian for its ally, Imprimus, during the latter's time of virtual powerlessness. If this theory was correct, then soon his enchanted vision should alert him to that fact. There would be darkness palpable, blackness more intense than any around, for such stuff gathered around the gloam as he lay in torpid repose during the interval of lightlessness.

"Hail, prince!" The coughing roar that conveyed this salutation was familiar. Was there a bit of sarcastic mirth in the greeting? It was hard to tell. Certainly Hotbreath's eyes and bearing showed nothing but respect.

"May your pride always be well-fed," Gord called back in formal response. "How came you here in this vile time?"

"With difficulty, but we too learned from Shadowking where the nest of enemies is likely to be buried. I have come with some of my own pride, and Smokemane too is nearby, accompanied by his females. We are here to serve you once more."

"Because . . .?"

"Because it is the will of our Allking. What other reason could there be?"

"What other reason is needed?" Gord shrugged in retort. At the best of times, big male cats make for uneasy feeling, even in alliance, for whatever reason. "I seek the den of the gloam-lich and his pack now, Hotbreath. Gather your pride members and follow." Without watching to see if the great shadow-lion complied, Gord walked on, intent upon what lay before him.

The deep-chested roar of a male lion came suddenly from ahead. Gord set his body into motion, a bounding run that ate up the intervening distance between him and the location of the roar. There was the bulk of Smokemane, with a handful of large lionesses nearby. The massive male had his head thrown back and was voicing yet a second mighty roar when Gord came springing into the place where the lion stood. "Why do you send forth your challenge?" he demanded.

"I scent the evil reek of gloams," Smokemane answered in deep growls of most ferocious sort. "I announce my intention to seek out such prey to any who would join me in the hunt."

"Now I am come," Gord said to him and his females. "I will lead the way, and you and yours will follow with Hotbreath and his mates. In what comes, Imprimus is mine alone. All others are yours — for any who care to set their fangs and sink their claws. Remember in the stalking and chase that the killing of that one, the gloam-lich, Imprimus, is for none other than me."

"As you order, lord, but let us stop this speaking and seek the prey!"

Feline noses led them to the place where powerful illusions masked the entrance to the gloam's hidden place of safety. The way was barred by a massive slab of shadow-steel. Not even the claws of the huge lions could penetrate such stuff, but Gord's enchanted dagger could. The long-bladed poniard was in the young thief's hand immediately, its magical metal cutting away the hard steel as a whittling knife slivers oak. The flat surface was broken by a rivet-held box that contained the locking mechanism of the portal. It was certain that the door would be barred inside as well, but first he must remove the initial closure. The dagger's edge pared the steel away, sending metallic curls falling furiously, and then the box's face fell away, and the lock was exposed. Next came the thick cylinders of the rivets. They were cut through, driven loose. The lock's inner plate clanged on the floor beyond, and Gord had a square hole he could reach through.

"I have it!" he cried as his groping found a heavy rectangle of metal on the inner side of the portal. Gord pushed upward, and the bar moved, then fell with a louder clanging to join the steel plate already lying on the stone flags beyond. Gord then tried to shove the heavy door inward, but the thing moved not. "Wait," he told the impatient lions. "The gate is held by more than a single bar."

It was difficult, but by straining Gord was able to reach down and locate a second piece of steel securing the door at its bottom. This time he was careful to hold the slab of steel, maneuvering the heavy rectangle so that it leaned upright against the portal it had barred. "Now, one last bit of work, and we should be free to pursue our foe!" The lower bar became a lever for the one Gord had been sure was above. Fortunately, the lockplate had been low on the door and the bars that held it fast were long. The tool served well, and with considerable effort Gord managed to employ it to free the uppermost fastening.

There was a third great clangor, then a fourth as the young thief discarded the bar he had held. When he shoved on the portal this time, the sheet of steel swung smoothly open on well-greased hinges.

"The eclipse of Mool and all the luminaries accompanying it above nears its conclusion, prince," the huge lion named Smokemane growled to Gord as the young adventurer paused before the open entrance. "You must hasten if we are to take these enemies at their ebb!"

At that urging, Gord moved, stalking into the deeper darkness of Imprimus's lair, followed by ten lions and lionesses. The hallway beyond the steel portal was wide and went straight into the low hill, angling downward rather steeply as it went. The man and his company of big cats had proceeded some distance, going mostly by touch and an innate sense that enabled them to move within the total gloom, when the floor beneath them collapsed.

Chapter 22

GREAT CLAWS SCRABBLED as the lions tried to stop their precipitous slide down the polished stone sides of the trap. Gord, as he fell, set his mind, thinking that perhaps the whole thing was some form of illusion.

Neither feline nor human succeeded. The slide continued despite outthrust claws and positive thinking. In seconds all eleven victims were dropped from the steep chute into a circular pit no less than twenty feet deep. The lions landed on their feet, shaken but unhurt. Gord also came through unscathed, for his training as an acrobat enabled him to handle the fall without difficulty and immediately move thereafter to the far wall in order to avoid being crushed by a plummeting lion.

The lightlessness in the circular pit was so extreme that not even the eyes of the shadow-lions could penetrate its murk. Then a pale luminosity issued forth, casting a soft, pale green light all around the small chamber. Some vestige of the talisman's force still lingered within Gord's ring, as he had suspected. The young adventurer had wished idly for light by which to see, and in the next instant a dim radiance began to issue forth from his eyes.

The two great male cats snarled and their hackles rose at the phenomenon. Gord spoke soothingly, and both Smokemane and Hotbreath calmed down, even cuffing their respective females to show the lionesses that all was well and to restore their own lost dignity. That was a very important thing to the big cats.

"This is good . . . perhaps too good to be true!" Gord exclaimed.

"You think a death trap is good?" old Smokemane growled.

Gord could not restrain himself from taking the head of the big lion and roughly stroking it. The gesture was both one of affection and reassurance. "This place was designed to catch intruders and imprison them in its depth until the guardians within the stronghold could come and deal with what they had caught according to need. Now, at Snuffdark, no sentry stands, no warder watches. I will leave this place in a moment, and soon I'll have all of you out too!"

The lions stood still, Smokemane's tail showing jerky twitches of uncertainty. Gord, meanwhile, took his dagger and went to work on the hard and polished stone with which the cylindrical hole was faced. He needed but scant niches for fingertips and toes. The work was simple, and soon indeed he was high above the upturned heads of the lions, legs disappearing over the pit's rim.

He had pretended confidence at his ability to release his companions, but Gord was deeply worried that he would not be able to do so. The males weighed six or seven hundred pounds each, conservatively. The females were only slightly smaller. How could he ever manage to get such massive cats out of a well that was more than twenty feet deep?

A narrow walkway circled the pit. Opposite the place where the victims were precipitated into its depths by the smooth-floored chute, there was an arched opening, a tunnel of about six paces width and somewhat lower than it was wide. Although the radiance cast from his eyes was waning, Gord could still see well enough to manage a rapid exploration of the passage. There were rooms on either side of the tunnel, and behind a heavy grill the young adventurer spied several wooden shapes that could only be ladders.

The lock of the iron grating was easily dealt with, and in no time at all Gord was dragging a thick-timbered ladder back along the way he had just come. He slid the thing over the lip of the well, guided its end to the floor below, and then ran back up the tunnel once again, returning with a second ladder. This he placed beside the first, then slid down it to the bottom of the pit.

"I have placed these two ladders at as gentle an angle as possible," Gord said to Smokemane. "You and your mates must use them to get out of this place, placing half of your weight on each. Go up the incline, and when the uppermost portion of the ladder is reached, it will be necessary to use your forepaws to draw yourselves over the rim. Don't worry — the stone there is rough and cracked." Gord looked into first Smokemane's big eyes, then Hotbreath's. "Can you and the lionesses do that?"

Before either male could growl in reply, a sleek female shot past them, leaped upon the pair of sloped ladders, and clambered up. "Yes," she growled, and then gave a scrabbling leap and was atop the pit's edge, peering down with feline hauteur. While Gord watched, all the remainder of the lionesses then climbed upward and out. The great males followed, with the wood groaning and bending under their weight, but not breaking despite the strain each of them placed upon the timbers. Finally Gord scampered up, doing so as easily as if he were serenely ascending a flight of broad steps.

"It might be beneficial to be a changeling, going

from decent form to that of a hairless ape whenever the need arose," the first lioness to climb free of the pit growled in droll, feline fashion as Gord sprang nimbly atop the well's edge. He made no reply, but thought how nice it would be if he could become a great cat at will!

Soon enough the party of man and lions reached the terminus of the passage. A foul stench warned them of something ahead, and in the square chamber at the end of the passage was the source of the terrible odor — a dozen huge yeth hounds, lying almost dormant.

This place was certainly more than a Snuffdark lair; it must be Imprimus's main headquarters. Its pack of watchdogs, the yeth, were by no means active now, however. Snuffdark had brought all to a languid and torpid state. Under other circumstances, these creatures probably would have been roaming the tunnel, baying their fearsome cries whenever an intruder appeared. At the sight of the lions, though, the hounds were up and snarling. One threw its head back and began a mournful howling, a note that began in the low register and rose quickly beyond human hearing.

The sound made Gord's hair stand on end, and he almost dropped his sword and dagger. At the first baying the lions responded with a chorus of coughing roars. The deep roars reverberated and echoed deafeningly in the enclosed, underground environment. In fact, the lions' challenge to the monstrous yeth was so loud that the canines instantly left off their howling and attacked with bared fangs.

While the big cats were weakened by Snuffdark, they were not so reliant on shadowy light as were the mastifflike yeth. The dogs never had a chance because of this. While Gord fought for his life, fending off a pair of male yeth nearly as high at the shoulder as Gord was tall, the ten lions literally tore up the remainder of the evil pack of night-black monsters.

"I owe you for that," Gord said, panting. Hotbreath had just taken care of the last yeth as the hound had been about to close its massive jaws on the young thief's throat. The short sword and dagger were good blades, but definitely not the best things to use against these huge dogs.

"And you, lord, brought all of us safely from the pit," the big male said, cleaning the dark blood from his paws and jowl. "Ferragh!" the lion growled in disgust. "There is no debt for my service in killing the yeth — you owe me a fat kill so I can get the vile taste of hounds' blood from my mouth."

"Consider it done! I will find some source of light for us, and then we must press on. The hidey-hole of Imprimus must be near." Hotbreath went to the others to pass along the information, and Gord began a search of the large, square chamber. His light-vision was continuing to fade, and soon they would be in utter blackness again unless he could do something.

Three doors led from the kennel chamber. Each was set into the middle of one of the walls, and each of the heavy wooden panels was flanked by a pair of cressets. None were alight, but an examination revealed that there was a residue of oil in each. Using hunks of cloth and old weapon shafts that littered the hounds' kennel, Gord soon had constructed three torches, their rag-topped heads soaked with the fuel taken from the cressets. By plying the tip of his dagger against the stone wall, he created a spark and thus ignited one of the rag-poles.

"Now, friend lions, I shall have to rely upon you entirely for my defense," he said to the cats as he held the flame aloft. "With this torch now our only source of light, there will be little I can do but hold fast to it." The thing cast only a dull illumination. In the realm of shadow, flames normally burned with a pearly, dove-gray radiance. During this season of absolute blackness, the oppression of Snuffdark caused even the hottest of fires to burn a drab and pallid gray. The sooty smoke of the torch rose from flame of dun, and a penumbral circle of light barely made visible objects that were but a dozen feet distant.

"We understand," Smokemane answered for all. "Lead us to the way we're to take, and leave the rest to us. . . ." The huge male's growled reply came loudly in the chamber, the last part trailing off into a snarl that indicated just how the lion contemplated handling his share of the expedition.

"There," Gord responded, pointing to the left of the passage that led to the pit. His keen eyes had seen the dingy hair of the yeth hounds on and around the right-hand portal. That indicated a high probability that behind was nothing more than a storage room, the place the dead hounds' food had been kept in all likelihood, and in any event a way seldom if ever used by the masters of the place. Otherwise, no accumulation of the beasts' shed coats would be there. Similarly, the center door showed minute traces of corrosion on ring and hinges. These, and the fact that it was the only one of the three portals that opened outward, made Gord highly suspicious of it. He was willing to wager that it was a cleverly trapped device to catch and slay unwary intruders. "We go through that way. It is the only portal which sees regular use," he added unnecessarily; lions care little for such reasoning, after all.

The door was pushed open easily enough. Behind it was a short landing and a long, worn flight of steps leading down. As the sputtering torch cast its scant, almost brown illumination, Gord went down the rough-hewn stone stairs, Hotbreath padding before him and the nine other great cats filing after. All were moving quickly, for soon the time of absolute dark would be over. Snuffdark would not recede gradually the way Twilight had waxed. The blackness came instantly at the final waning of the brightness, and it disappeared as quickly. When Snuffdark's grim time was finished, Shadowrealm regained its usual pallor of shadowy silvers, manifold grays, deep blacks, until Mool waxed and the oppression followed again — a year's span, as time was measured on the Plane of Shadow.

When they finally reached the bottom of the long stairway, Gord saw that they had arrived at what must be the very heart of the gloams' stronghold. Above were the places for guards, hounds, and the rest. Down here were the workrooms, laboratories, and libraries of those who sought to usurp the rule of his plane for themselves.

Gord's rapid exploration of the chambers that opened onto the gallery at the bottom of the steps revealed all this. It also provided him and his escort of ions with better light, for in one alchemical study he discovered an oddly fashioned lamp. It was enclosed in a crystal-sided box, making it almost a lantern. The fuel inside it was unidentifiable, but it had what was clearly a wick, and when the nearly exhausted torch was applied to it a healthy flame sprang forth. From this lamp came a misty light of luminous gray. The radiance spread into the hemisphere ahead of the lamp, casting its strange illumination a distance of almost twenty paces. Now the group was far better prepared to see and search.

Although this seemed the nerve center, there were certainly other places that had to be found. During Snuffdark, the gloams would be bolted closed in their personal chambers — unless they were of the same sort as Imprimus. Gord knew that fiend would be entombed in his casket or sarcophagus, awaiting the return of shadows upon the plane, at which time his powers would again be restored and waxing.

When he had attempted to get Shadowfire from Gord, the gloam-lich had been constrained by the power of the approach of Twilight. The brightest and darkest times of Shadowrealm were the only ones when Imprimus's powers were diminished. The brightness of Twilight would certainly slay the vampiric lich if he were not safely hidden from it. The total gloom of Snuffdark made Imprimus very weak and without his full range of powers. It did not harm him physically, as the radiance of Twilight would; Snuffdark made the gloam subject to attack, however, through causing him great weakness. That, Gord hoped, would prove as fatal as the full face of Mool in its single period of glory.

"Gord! I smell bad smells. This way." The rumbling communication came from Hotbreath. His body was in rigid point as he glared toward a dim recess of the subterranean library. With the guidance given by the big male lion, Gord quickly located a secret exit from the place, a door concealed by a shelf of ancient librams and scrolls. Again steps were discovered, and the young adventurer headed down them immediately, bringing a tail of ten lions after him.

There was a charnel reek arising from the narrow stairwell. Even Gord's human hearing could also detect sounds coming from below. Then the light of the lamp shone on the gray pallor of shadow-bones. It was evident that the ghouls and corpse-eaters of the material plane had counterparts dwelling in Shadowrealm, for mingled with the stench of death were the unmistakable odors of those foul creatures who dined upon corpses and delighted in decay.

"What lurks below, friends," Gord said softly, "is such which I can fight but poorly, bearing as I do our light."

"Eaters of dead humans," Smokemane nearly roared in reply. "We have encountered them once or twice, for such things will contest with us over our kills if they have not other flesh to feed on." Gord noted that the cat made no distinction between human folk, such as found on Oerth, and the phantom folk of this plane. The phantoms were, in fact, the parallel of humans, their equivalent in Shadowrealm. But the gloams were something else, something unnatural, as inimical to the phantoms as to all other clean forms of life. The two big males squeezed past Gord and bounded downward. After them went the lionesses, and the battle was on.

Light held high, Gord hastened down the stairs immediately after the last female had shot past him. Snarls and roars were intermingled with the horrible shrieks and yapping of the ghouls and their even worse and more foul cousins, the ghulaz, as they fought to defend themselves from the lions' ferocity. As reflections of the undead of the material plane, these eaters of corpses were severely afflicted by the time of total lightlessness. Although all creatures of Shadowrealm were affected by the gloom of Snuffdark, lions being among the roster of animals, the great cats were by no means as weakened as the ghulaz and ghouls. The slowly moving, lethargic creatures were fighting desperately to save themselves, but their defense was not strong enough either to give serious injury to their attackers or give themselves hope of prevailing. The evil undead quickly understood this fact and sought to retreat.

Unlike the chambers above, where masonry combined with hewn and polished stone to form elaborate spaces, carven pillars, and the stuff of habitation, the place of the undead was stark and foul. The area was certainly a natural cave with only a few marks to indicate that hammer and chisel had worked its

327

stone. Niches in the walls indicated the place might once have been a catacomb — although these recesses might simply have been cut to provide the ghoulish residents of the place a more comfortable and "homelike" atmosphere.

The uneven floor of the cave was a foul mess of bones, partially consumed carcasses, and filth. More bones and rotting cloth were evident in the niches and in odd corners of the large space where ghulaz or ghoul went to feed on some particularly choice morsel of corpse, or to take its ease. The creatures of this charnel cave, however, sought not to hide in niche or cranny. Instead, the smaller ghouls were shambling off toward a dark opening to the left, while the larger, dog-faced ghulaz were seeking refuge behind an upthrust slab of rock at the right rear of the chamber.

Gord ignored the lesser things. "The big ones — ghulaz!" he shouted to his feline comrades. "We must take them. Follow me." With that, the young adventurer headed straight for the place the six dog-featured undead had slunk into. The space the shelter provided was certainly insufficient to hide all six. There had to be some egress there.

As the lamp shed its pale illumination on the place, however, Gord saw nothing but bare stone. No ghulaz, no exit. Nothing.

"I smell the reek of those things," Smokeman growled. "They are near, but I cannot see them."

Obviously, some powerful magic was at work. By utmost effort, Gord marshalled his will and disbelieved as he touched the rock wall of the sheltered spot. The combination worked. A small opening existed here after all — a narrow, low place that a man could squeeze through, but far too small for one of the great shadow-lions to use. "Stay here, my friends," Gord rumbled to the lions. All of them were wounded by now, although most not seriously, but a any rate the big cats could do nothing to assist him in what must be done next. Somehow he had to deal with the ghulaz alone.

"I must take the light and go down this little tunnel," he said quickly to Smokemane. "Use your noses to guard against the return of the death-stinking two-leggers," he ordered, pointing to the place through where the ghouls had vanished. "Wait for me here. If I do not come back in the space of time you take to sleep a short sleep, go the way the stinking ones went. I think there must be a way above in that direction. I cannot offer you more than that."

"We came willingly, lord. It has been a good hunt, and we have killed many. If it comes time, all of us will become prey ourselves without mewling. We will fight and die as lions do, and we will thank you for the honor you gave us," the huge old male said, ending with a coughing that soon became deeper and louder. Hotbreath and the lionesses quickly joined, and in a minute the cave reverberated with the roars of a half-score of mighty cats loudly voicing challenge to the vile inhabitants of this foul, subterranean place.

Gord entered the narrow passage and found, to his mild relief, that the noise made by the angry lions lessened considerably once he was a few feet inside the cylinder. Lamp in his left hand and short sword in his right, he pulled himself through the tunnel opening with his elbows. Once he was past the narrow entrance, the tubelike passage was large enough to allow first crawling on hands and knees, then hunched walking. The way was still difficult, for the tunnel twisted in a generally leftward direction and inclined steeply. Worse, the horrible reek of the ghulaz so filled the little space that Gord had to fight back nausea as he hurried ahead.

In addition to his physical difficulties, Gord had a

mental obstacle to overcome. How would he, alone, with only a sword and a dagger, fight and defeat six of the grisly dog-faced undead? He had to do it somehow, and survive the encounter as well, if he was to attain his ultimate goal of killing the gloam-lich. Failure to find Imprimus soon, very soon, would certainly spell his death anyway; and at the hands of that one, it would be an even more foul end than that of being slain by the ghulaz. If his weapons and his wits failed to see him through, then Gord was resigned to die fighting the hideous undead he pursued.

The stench grew suddenly stronger. Then Gord turned a corner and came face to face with one of the grinning things.

The greater ghoul had certainly meant to be there, waiting to take the young adventurer by surprise. The full glow of the strange light Gord held, though, seemed to affect the dog-visaged creature most adversely. The almost palpable beam of grayish radiance struck the dull, lifeless eyes of the creature, and the ghulaz seemed blinded and confused.

The effect lasted but a brief time, but it was an ample enough interval for Gord. He was already moving to attack at the first sight of the hideous thing. His enchanted blade swept forward in a glittering, upward arc that struck the ghulaz low in its abdomen and continued upward to slice the thing open from groin to ribs. The ghulaz howled, its foul breath gagging Gord as it voiced a scream of pain. Gord struck again with his sword, crossing from left to right along the creature's neck. The keen edge of the weapon nearly sliced all the way through the leathery hide of the ghulaz, and the undead monster toppled backward from the blow, thin neck severed, its head flopping as it fell, attached by only a bit of sinew and hide.

The passage beyond was filled with the comrades

of the thing. Although the tunnel was now high enough for Gord to stand upright, the walls were still only some three or so feet apart — room enough for but a single opponent to engage him. The greater ghoul immediately before him was crouching, beast-like, as if readying itself to spring. Now that the first monster had fallen, the rays of the lamp were now fully in the second one's face. The canine features of the thing contorted, and it turned its head aside to avoid the illumination, freezing into motionlessness. Likewise, the monster immediately behind was affected by the pale light. When the beams fell upon its eyes, the third ghulaz growled foully and tried to back away. In response, Gord thrust the light ahead somewhat and stepped toward the stooped one that had averted its gaze. Neither it nor the one behind could retreat, for the three others behind them were trying to crowd ahead to get at this human who dared to follow them.

Horrible whining sounds came bubbling from the throats of the two ghulaz bothered by the illumination. The first dropped to all fours, now ready to attack. With the strength of desperation, Gord swung his sword down at the near-prone ghulaz's hairless head. The impact jarred him, but the thing's cranium split, exploding in a mess of rotten bone and putrid brains. Without hesitation, the young adventurer stepped upon the foul remains, so as to bring himself closer to the remaining undead monsters.

Now those behind their fellow understood what they were up against and set up a fear-filled yapping and gabbling as they sought to find escape from the terrible foe. It was certainly too late for the foremost of the ghulaz. Gray rays illuminated and short sword flashed, cutting and stabbing to send it to whatever nether plane it belonged upon. The three remaining survivors were now making good their flight, however.

Gord raced ahead, striking hard at the bony back of the hindmost ghulaz. The blow was more than sufficient to sever its spine and send its shrieking spirit into the hellpits along with those of its comrades.

Now but a pair of foul things remained, but both ghulaz were well ahead of Gord. He followed them as quickly as he could, and it was immediately evident that they were not quick enough to make good their flight. The rearmost of the two fell to his ferocious attack as easily as the others had been slain, and the last of the monsters was cowering just ahead, face pressed against a boulder that sealed off the tunnel. It was in a dead end and knew that true death was finally coming for it. Gord gave it a swift, painless end, even though such a thing deserved it not.

As the last of the dog-faced monstrosities fell, Gord noticed glyphs inscribed upon the big boulder it had been standing next to. The shadowy letters and signs squirmed under the light, writhing as do blind slugs exposed to the sun when a rock is overturned. Then the sigils actually began to make a frizzling sound and send up little streamers of oily-looking smoke.

Despite all that activity, the sort that usually presaged the disappearance of such signs, the glyphs remained upon the stone, and Gord feared to touch them. Then he thought of something: The lamp had been found in the gloams' stronghold, so that any wards magically placed here would certainly not be affected by its illumination. Wisely, the young thief suspected that when he saw the strange effects of the radiance upon the glyphs, what showed before his eyes was something to delude any who saw it, to lull an intruder into a false sense of security so that he would think the glyphs had been neutralized and then expose himself to the protective force they still held within.

Although he hated to touch the foul form, Gord lifted the carcass of the last ghulaz he had killed and leaned it against the boulder. Nothing happened, just as he had assumed; not enough force was being applied. Then Gord put his upper back against the slain thing's stinking body and began to push, using the ghulaz as a cushion between himself and the glyphs upon the rock he had to displace.

Now the protective sigils were beginning to do their work. Gord felt bones in the ghulaz's body snapping, muscles and flesh losing their rigidity — the body was actually decomposing, disintegrating, from contact with the magically protected boulder! The stench was so noisome that Gord was actually regurgitating as he continued his exertion.

After a few moments that seemed like an eternity under the conditions, the remains of the ghulaz were almost jellylike, but were still substantial enough for Gord to push against, sickening though it was to do this. He could not stop now, for he had felt the boulder move slightly. Then the big stone shifted abruptly, and the hole it guarded was unblocked.

Breathing through his mouth, Gord tried to clean himself as best he could by wiping hands and torso against the rock wall. Then he stooped and entered the space between wall and boulder, passing with a feeling of hope and dread into what he was sure was the lair of Imprimus.

Chapter 23

"YOU MUST BE EAGER FOR DEATH," a dry voice rustled, seemingly in his very ear, "to have overcome so many obstacles in order to embrace it."

Gord spun quickly, his lamp casting odd, writhing shadows from his motion, his sword ready. Nothing. No one was near. The place was a high-ceilinged grotto, another natural cave of fair proportion. Here the stone was the counterpart of limestone on the material plane, for the grotto had shadowy stalactites hanging from above, thick stalagmites sticking upward from the floor, some of these two sorts of formations conjoined to make columns.

"It is a charming place, isn't it?" The rustling voice spoke the question in a tone laden with mirth, as if it had a secret joke that could hardly be restrained. "Perhaps I'll allow you to remain here as a special guardian," it whispered.

"Imprimus? Where are you, you cringing coward?" Gord shouted his words, making the place come alive with echoes that trailed off, "coward . . . oward . . . ard . . . ard."

"Heh, heh, eh, eh . . . ." The sneering sound of a chuckle whispered throughout the stony space. It had no source, coming from no place and every place at once. "Be patient. I'll greet you soon," the voice rustled sinisterly.

Water dripped somewhere, shadow-water that made a plangent sound as it dropped into a shadow-pool in the underground lair of the vampiric lich. There was a faint hiss from the lamp's burning, and the weird rays it sent out seemed almost to cause a susurration as they washed over the blackness of the grotto. No other sound could be heard. To leave both of his hands free, Gord put the lamp down on top of a thick, flat-topped stalagmite.

"Are you hiding, human?" the dry voice asked. This time, though, it was slightly louder, and there was no smugness in it. "You can't escape; neither is there any place to hide. Wait quietly, and I will make it an easy thing for you."

There was no reply, still no sound other than the hiss and the reverberating plunk of water droplet after water droplet. Gord looked and listened with all the concentration he could muster. Did a darker shadow move within the cloaking gloom? Some shape slide noiselessly through the dimness?

Then he could make out a faint rustling, coming from a place midway up the far wall of the cave, a spot some ten feet above the floor. There followed the whispering of cloth, the creaking of what might have been ancient joints, and a faint hum. Instantly thereafter, four small spheres of dun-hued light winked into existence within the cave. These globes floated at waist height just before the opening that Gord had entered, but their sickly illumination revealed no trace of the young adventurer.

The four split in twain, one pair floating slowly toward the left, the other two moving languidly toward the right. The two sets of dimly glowing spheres circumscribed the grotto's perimeter, making visible for a time anything that they passed near. Stone was all their dun radiance displayed.

A clawlike hand grasped the edge of a sarcophagus made of obsidian. The coffin rested on a ledge ten feet above the cave's floor, and the hand belonged to its inhabitant. A horrible face leered above the taloned hand. The visage was as if a human skull had been distorted and misshapen by some hybridization with a monstrous bat, and then the awful result of the unnatural cross allowed to rot and desiccate in some demon-inspired crypt. It was the face of Imprimus, once human, now gloam, vampire, lich, wrought to true appearance by the weight of Snuffdark upon the Plane of Shadow.

That the skeletal body that bore it could raise this gruesome visage thus, however, indicated that the time of the great dark was waning. In a short span, perhaps mere minutes, the blackness would pass, and then the monster would once again command its full powers. The distended muzzle of the man-bat monstrosity opened to reveal massive fangs.

"So," the dry voice rustled and whispered, "our little man has sought safety in flight after all." Its bat-eared head tipped back to allow a hideous cackling to issue forth, but the sound died before it left the snaky throat. The thing's corpselike eyes fixed upon a great clot of blackness above and suddenly glowed with putrid gray fire.

The snarling form of the young thief sprang down upon the monstrous creature in the sarcophagus. Instinctively, the thing recoiled from the ferocity of the assault. Twisting in mid-air, Gord used his gymnastic skill to direct his fall, and as his feet touched the edge of the casket of black stone, his legs flexed and his body hurtled past the vampiric lich into the alcove behind it.

The hideous face of the demonlike creature contorted in shock and rage at what had occurred. The human was a clever opponent, a foolishly daring one too. He not only dared to make threats, but even now was attempting to make free with that which the monster held most dear.

"Stop!" Imprimus meant the command to boom, but it croaked in dusty tones, for Snuffdark had not yet done with its gloom. Then the monster turned fully and saw what the impudent man was up to, and the glare of rage altered to an expression of concern.

"You are very clever and talented," Imprimus said in its soughing voice. "You have earned my respect and approval. Come and pay me homage, and I shall accept you as one of mine own noble servants."

Gord didn't even bother to turn around. Before him was a heap of treasure, all jumbled and mixed. It was alight with a glow from within, faint but discernible. Somewhere in the mound, he hoped, would be a weapon that would enable him to combat the terrible power of the vampire gloam-lich. Imprimus was presently weakened by the tide of darkness, yet still too formidable a foe for normal means of attack to affect.

Ivory, amber, and jade flew upward and rained down alongside jewelry and great gems, pearl ropes and precious metals, magic amulets, and crystal flasks of dweomered fluid. Some merely spun and rolled, others cracked and splintered or smashed to send their contents mingling with the shards of a ruined ruby or the parchment tube of some ancient scroll of spells. Heedless of the wreckage, Gord went on, burrowing into the vast pile as a badger would dig into the dirt in search of a fat hare.

Bony fingers suddenly grasped his shoulders, long nails sinking toward flesh but foiled by the steel mesh of Gord's hidden shirt of elvish mail. The touch sent a wave of chilling cold through his body nonetheless, and then the searing agony of long fangs puncturing his flesh made the young thief cry out in pain. "Be damned!" he yelled, spinning to dislodge the attacker and striking with his dagger as he turned.

The force of the stab caused the awful creature to release its grip on Gord, hissing in pain as it did so, for the long dagger had sunk deep into Imprimus's right side. The thing stepped back then, glaring hatefully at the frail human who dared to strike it, meanwhile beginning the passes that would conjure up one of the manifold spells the monstrous creature commanded. "Now it is time for you to learn what pain is, manling!" the vampire-lich spat, its batlike face contorted. Then it made the swift passes of conjuration. In desperation, Gord scooped up a handful of the treasure from the mound and hurled it full into the bat-featured face of the Snuffdark-altered gloam.

"Reeeyaaaha!" The enraged shriek that emerged from Imprimus was the most bestial sound Gord could ever recollect, demon and dragon included. The spray of coins and gems had certainly had the desired effect, that was evident. The hail of objects had so disturbed and distracted the horrid creature that the spell was lost in the process. Meanwhile, Gord kept at his work, flinging stuff in the general direction of Imprimus as he sought a suitable weapon. There were, of course, any number of arms in the vast mound. Jewel-encrusted daggers, maces set with glittering gems, ceremonial swords and axes of precious shadow-gold — but all were useless for his purpose and thus ignored.

"Now let us contest more fairly," Gord said just then, springing atop the precious pile as he spoke — just in time. The gloam had again launched itself into an attack, physically attempting to grapple its opponent and sink terrible teeth into human flesh. "No, no! Up here, dungpile!"

The gloom of Snuffdark was nearly gone; that was obvious from the growing lambency of the monster's eyes and the increasing speed of Imprimus's movements. Gord had to madden the thing sufficiently to give him one brief opportunity, a chance to lay the vampiric lich low. His time was running out all too rapidly.

The gloam snarled, glaring at its foe. The human had uncovered and was holding a long, double-edged sword. It was an ancient weapon, one with a leaf-shaped blade and a strange crossguard showing serpents. Why was it there in the trove? Imprimus could not recall, but the old sword-thing appeared to be nothing more than a useless ornament, for it was fashioned entirely out of crystalline material, probably some form of quartz or topaz. . . . No matter. The oppression of darkness that lay upon the plane would soon be lifted, but before Snuffdark fled, Imprimus intended to deal with this arrogant little man who had so painfully reminded the gloam of its weakened condition just now. This one had defied Imprimus's demand for Shadowfire, then actually given it to the petty lordling who claimed the realm as his own. Well, soon the human would be another vampiric servant to Imprimus, and then the gloam would take the mighty black opal from Shadowking — this time to a place far beyond any return. First one, then the other. Imprimus meant to drain the vitality from his foe personally, savoring the rush of power gained thus, as well as reveling in the agony that the upstart man would suffer as his life force ebbed away to be replaced by the cold burning of the negative stuff of unlife!

"Now, you! Come down off the little heap you play king of the mountain on, and I will treat with you," Imprimus said, eyes burning hypnotically into the gray ones of his intended victim. "My generosity will not abide forever. . . ."

Gord shook his head to break the effect of the gaze, the drone of the monster's beguiling speech. Then he kicked another spray of precious stuff into

340

the gloam's face. "Ratshit, batface! You come here and—"

The pelting coins and gems did it. New power born of its rage surged through the gloam-lich. "Too late!" Imprimus roared, and as it did so it launched itself through the air, long-fingered hands clawed, huge mouth opened to enable it to ply its great fangs upon the soft body of the vulgar human who had dared to be defiant. The vampire-lich had such great strength now that its leap carried it up and at the small man as if Imprimus were a spear shot by a ballista. Such speed and power were irresistible. The attack was so sudden and overwhelming that the leap took Imprimus to the impact in the span of a heartbeat, and its iron-hard hands grabbed its foe with viselike power.

"Too late!" The words echoed, but only in a dying mind.

"What becomes of one undead when it becomes dead?" Gord asked this question, but there was no reply. Imprimus's nails tore the young man's flesh as its hands slid slowly down Gord's body. Even in death, if death it was, the terrible thing seemed determined to wreak vengeance.

The hilt of the crystalline sword protruded like a strange tongue from Imprimus's mouth. The point of the sword was buried somewhere deep within the monster's chest. Gord thrust the shriveling remains away with his foot, then watched in fascination as the once-mighty overlord of gloams withered and crumbled into a foul puddle of ooze. Then this too dried and nothing but a shrinking pile of blackish powder was left.

No, not quite all was gone. The crystalline sword remained, no trace of the foul vampire-lich evident upon its transparent blade. Actually, the sword was even brighter than it had been, more phosphorescent by far. "Of all this treasure," Gord murmured, peering around him, "I take only this sword and what I sought when I came here. The rest is befouled by the stuff of Imprimus, but you, good blade, are yet clean!" Then, dagger sheathed and crystal sword in hand, the young thief began his search for the necklace of nine black stones.

Despite his fatigue and his wounds, Gord was determined to sift through Imprimus's treasure hoard, piece by piece if necessary. It stood to reason that the black sapphires would be here; in a land of shadow, gems such as those would be prized above all other sorts, and this was the only treasure trove of any size he knew of in this realm. Not even the Shadowking kept anywhere near as many gems, pieces of jewelry, and other valuable items.

Doing his best to ignore his pain, Gord held the crystal sword in one hand as a light source and meticulously searched the floor, in case the platinum necklace had been among the handfuls of stuff he had flung at Imprimus. It was not to be found among the miscellany scattered around the chamber, so he turned to the remainder of the once-massive pile. Then a thought took shape in his mind.

Of course! If the sapphires in the necklace were as valued here as he supposed them to be, the throat-piece would not be frivolously cast into a pile — it would be in a revered place.

Moving faster than he should have considering his condition, Gord bounded to the sarcophagus where Imprimus had been spending his dormant period. As soon as he thrust the sword inside the coffin, he saw it. The necklace was laid out in a neat circle near the head of the box, as though Imprimus had been using it for a pillow. Even as he thought about the horrible thing that had until recently possessed them, and what else they probably had been through during the last many years, Gord felt a shudder of pleasure and awe as he lifted the necklace and viewed the nine black gems in their settings. Pleasure, awe . . . but not really recognition, and certainly not recollection. They were *his* — somehow he knew that — but he did not know how or why.

Gord gently rolled up the necklace and tucked it into a side pocket of the pouch that hung at his belt. Suppressing his emotions, he told himself that there was time later to ponder what to do with his prize; right now he still had to worry about making his way back out of this awful place.

The outer cave was dark. The strange lamp had burned out during his battle with the greater ghouls and the awful gloam-creature. Gord did not care, because the crystal blade illuminated his path. Each step was painful. The attacks of the vampiric lich had hurt him in both body and in soul. Gord felt tired and weak, and he hurt from the wounds inflicted by talons and teeth. It would be long before Gord recovered from the effects of this battle, and he knew it.

With steps that lagged more and more all the time, he traversed the length of the narrow tunnel and crawled eventually out into the cave where Imprimus had fed his ghoul and ghulaz hounds the leavings from his table — the bloodless corpses of those shadowfolk drained by his insatiable need for blood and lust for stolen life energy.

"Smokemane! Hotbreath!" No lion answered the call. Then Gord saw there were lions in the place, but they were dead. Some combat had occurred here during the time he was confronting Imprimus. The evidence showed that ghouls had returned, and gloams as well, for several of them lay torn and mangled among the half-dozen of the big cats who had died in the fighting with Imprimus's minions. One was the huge old Smokemane, but of the other big lion, or the three missing lionesses there was no trace.

Taking a moment, Gord went to each of the slain cats, touching them tenderly, one by one. "Goodbye, friend and ally. May your journey through the infinite be forever peaceful and serene," he murmured to each in turn. Then, the crystal sword shedding its pale light to show him the way, Gord left the charnel cave and followed the route that the fleeing ghouls had taken when he and his escort had first entered the place.

The stink of rotting flesh was so great that Gord was unable to tell if ghouls or lions or both were nearby. The adit to the small cavern was a natural passage, some fault that bent and jogged in a crazy manner as it wormed its way through the strata of shadow-rock. After what seemed an eternity of plodding progress, the young adventurer finally reached the surface of the Plane of Shadows. It was alight with strange silvers and pearl hues, now that it was not awash with the monochromatic gray-whiteness of Twilight or cloaked by the gloom of Snuffdark. In short, although even at its best this was a world of somber tones, it seemed to the young adventurer that he had just emerged into the bright sun and blue sky of a spring morning on Oerth.

"You live, lord!" The roared greeting came from Hotbreath. The big cat actually bounded to Gord and placed his massive forepaws upon the young man's shoulders, nearly toppling him over in the process.

"You are much too heavy!" Gord managed to gasp, laughing in joy as he shoved the lion off and stood panting. "I am glad you too have survived!" Man and lion spoke together for a moment, Gord relating the struggle against Imprimus, and the dark-maned Hotbreath telling how ghouls and shadowkin had both come to attack him and his comrades when the murk of Snuffdark began to lift.

"That is why we left, Gord," the big male growled.

"We know by instinct and inner feelings too when the gloom of the time is passing. When it was gone and you did not appear, we thought you dead. We are no match for such as that one, the gloam you call Imprimus, so we sought escape, having done all we could to bring harm to the evil ones."

Holding fast to the torn and bloodied mane, Gord said earnestly, "You did so much, friend — you and your pride, Smokemane and his too! — that there is naught I can say to adequately convey my thanks. Shadowking too will know of the sacrifices and service of your kind, and perhaps there will be peace and an end to the animosity between him and the lions of shadow hereafter. Now I must go and seek the lord of this plane, for if I remain here much longer, I know that never again will I be able to return to my own world."

"We too must seek our places. Smokemane's pride must be cared for — some females and cubs remain still, you know. They will now join mine until one of his sons is grown and able to form a new pride to hunt over the territory of his father and those who sired his line. As for Shadowking, what he thinks of our kind is of no import. If he seeks us for sport, we will in turn hunt for him and his. To our liege, though, please do commend us. Speak well of shadow-lions to the Mastercat, and we will always be your friends."

After an exchange of final words, the lions went away, some limping, all bearing signs from the great battle they had fought. Gord also displayed his wounds, as it were, as he slowly wended his way through the weird realm of shadow, again seeking the lord of the plane.

It would be a long, difficult trek, but the young thief meant to locate the Chiaroscuro Palace once again. Even if there was but scant hope that Shadowking would be in residence, it was the only chance he had of escaping to the world he called his own. Glowing brand of crystal upon his shoulder, Gord plodded with measured steps over the shifting surface of Shadowrealm, determined to win through or expire in the trying.

Chapter 24

AT LONG LAST, HE SAW SPIRES rising on the horizon. The palace of the ruler of shadows came into view, drifting toward him as would a ship carried by a slow current.

As it came nearer, Gord stepped toward it, allowing the little island of shadows he had stood upon to slide away from him. By angling in the direction of the huge structure, he was able to arrive at the gate of the great fortress before too much more time had passed.

Even by consciously disbelieving what he saw, Gord could detect no retainers on the battlements, no heralds to alert those within of his approach. The gates of the Chiaroscuro Palace were shut fast. But as Gord came and stood before them, the mouth of a carven face upon one of these valves opened, and a toneless voice asked, "Who stands before the forbidden entrance to the Keep of Shadowking?"

"Only I," the young man said with resignation, fighting off a feeling of boundless despair, "Gord, a wayfarer, come too late . . ."

Another of the wooden visages opened its mouth. "Enter, Gord, and any others who are with you. Our sovereign bids you welcome. Go to the Vault of Veils immediately."

It took him only a little time to go to the place the

magically animated face of wood had instructed him
to seek. As he approached the featureless door to the
chamber, the portal swung open just as the great
gates to the Chiaroscuro Palace had done for him. As
soon as he had stepped all the way into the room, the
door banged shut and Gord was utterly alone in a
space illuminated only by the pale radiance of his
sword of crystal.

Suddenly the place was awash with the hues of
shadow and even faint pastel colors as well. The
transparent form of Shadowking appeared in the
king's seat, and spoke.

"I have left this for you, Prince Gord, against your
return. That you are seeing and hearing this means
you have triumphed, and your victory is mine! I
thank you most sincerely. And I name you Prince of
Shadows, Duke of Shades, and evil ones must now
bend their knee to me and you and all my other noble
vassals. Yet you are no actual vassal; the title is but
meant to honor you.

"When you laid low the duskdrake, the shock of
that malign one's parting was felt throughout all the
realm. Then I grew hopeful, for one able to deal with
that fell creature might indeed find and slay Imprimus before Snuffdark's lifting. Because of this renewed hope, and knowing that your sword's potent
talisman was destroyed in the annihilation of the
duskdrake, I sought out the best prize in my treasury. In the shadows they are greatest, but even in
sun or midnight blackness they are most potent."

As the illusion uttered those words, a flat, metallic
gonging sounded, and a small case appeared before
Gord. He looked inside and found it full of little,
round seeds. "They are shadow seeds, Gord," the
phantasm said. "Use them to create a thicket of umbral sort. Each curtain lasts but an hour, but a pinch
of the stuff suffices."

It was a splendid gift, especially for one who practiced the craft of thievery. Gord smiled slightly as he tucked the parcel carefully into his tunic's inner pocket. The image of Shadowking was still before him, but now the phantasmal voice had paused as though waiting for a response.

Gord did not mean to sound unappreciative of the gift, but there was really only one thing on his mind, and it was that question that he blurted out: "How am I to escape from here?" Then, remembering that he spoke to naught but an illusion, the young man sighed and hung his head in weary dejection.

"By my dweomered sight, noble Gord," the phantasm went on, "I saw you at the end. At the lich-fiend's death, my forces surged, and before my eyes you recovered something which was bestowed to you by your sire when you were but an infant, a babe too young to know. The nine black sapphires in that necklace are your means of returning to your world, prince. This, then, is my . . ."

Gord was dumbfounded. Had the illusion actually heard his plea? He opened his mouth to say something, but the phantasm of the king did not pause to give him a chance.

". . . final gift to you. Free the ebon stars from their prisoning metal. As there are nine dispositions, nine and ninety principal states of existence, so too there are nine gems in your inheritance. Place eight circling one, think of your own place, and there you shall be. Ere you do this, Gord, there is one caution I must give you. As the power of the nine stones grants you leave to pass on to where you will, the sapphires will return to their origin, that place which was the home of your sire, and they will be gone from your ken until you yourself again find them.

"The choice is yours. Keep the stones, stay in Shadowrealm as a prince, my foster son, and in time

349

you will come to the knowledge you seek regarding your origin. Then you will be a great Lord of Shadow, and you will be free to journey to many places, even the realm of your ancestors, but no more will you be human.

"If you use the powers bound up in those dark sapphires, then you lose them for a time at least, perhaps forever. As a mortal man you are subject to the hazards of whatever fate lies in store, but you will be flesh and blood again, in your own world.

"Whichever course you decide upon, you must act quickly, for not even I can halt destiny. If you stay too much longer in Shadowrealm, you will be bound to this place as though you were a native of it. Exactly how much time you have left to decide, no one can know precisely — but I do know that the time for final decision draws nigh. Decide what you will, and may fortune smile upon you either way, Prince Gord!"

The illusion vanished, and the young adventurer was left terribly alone. What was his decision to be? If he stayed, he would be a mighty lord of this place, a walker of planes, and as Shadowking stated, eventually brought to full knowledge of his ancestors. That portended great things.

To counter that, however, was the longing he had for the solid world, the bright sunlight and vivid colors of Oerth. He had no love for Greyhawk, a place of raptors, a city of hawks, but still it was his home. He had few friends, but those he had were cherished and dear to him.

And something else there was to consider too. . . . As he thought about his friend Gellor, the words of the one-eyed man came to mind again. He had said that Gord might be a key figure in a struggle for the world — nay, even more than that! A struggle that pitted the malign against all that was right, a war that would affect not just his world but the many states of the multiverse — Shadowrealm included. Further, the master of all shadows had told him that should fate allow, Gord would someday come to his heritage . . . but perhaps, only perhaps.

The young man set down the crystal blade upon the strangely shaped table in the Vault of Veils. It was a weapon that Shadowking would find good use for against the gloams and other evil ones who forced their way into his land. So much had been granted to Gord by the ruler of this place that it was a small thing to give in return.

"Now I do what I must do," he said, using his dagger point to prize the sapphires from the necklace and casting the metal and diamonds aside. "I am who I am, and will remain a mortal man."

The circle of eight gems began to glow as the ninth was placed in the center of their midst. A second later Gord had vanished from the plane of shadow, and the gems too went to wherever they had come from.

Chapter 25

"HAVE A FLAGON OF ALE with us, mate!"

The invitation was called from a nearby table, a place where a half-dozen brown and hard-bitten soldiers sat. The speaker was a big, burly mercenary with a missing ear and a gap-toothed smile.

Even as he heard the man speaking, Gord swept up the sprinkling of coins before him and stood. "Sorry, comrade. There's a little wench nearby whose heart would be broken if I didn't come as I've promised. . . ." The young thief allowed the double entendre to sink in; then he continued as the warriors vented lusty laughter and began shooting back bawdy jibes at him. "Nay, nay, look for your own ladies, my boys! I thank you for the offer of ale, though, friend," Gord added, speaking to the one who was undoubtedly the captain of this little band of sell-swords. "Another time, perhaps. . . ."

The pale, hard eyes of the burly mercenary crinkled at the corners as he looked up at the young fellow and smiled broadly. His eyes were as empty and distant as ever when he did so. The pale, blue orbs looked into the hard, gray eyes of the small, dark young man and saw kinship there. "Of course. The world is small and the fields too few. Keep your weapon ready until then!"

"As always!" Gord responded. A barmaid was near,

and as he spoke he dropped the handful of coins on the wooden tray she bore. "Here, lass. A round for my comrades there, and the rest is for you!" Then he left the noisy crowd in the tavern, striding out into the night of Greyhawk.

The sounds faded away quickly, but the impact remained. It bothered Gord at the same time it pleased him. The recognition of brave men, the acceptance of him as one of them, was gratifying. Still, Gord wished to think of himself as a young and carefree rogue — and a bit of a dandy and a ladies' man too. He played hard at that, with an outward attitude of derring-do and devils-may-care, but professional soldiers, who knew what to look for, saw him otherwise. Too many times had he faced dragon and demon. Dungeon darkness and the threat of death, or living death in shadow, had placed their marks on Gord.

His face was still young-looking, having developed only a few lines to serve as maps of his past adventures. The giveaway was his eyes. They were old, distant, hard. They had seen war, danger, death. But he didn't have the stony gaze of a killer, or the merciless, empty look of the mercenary who gave no quarter to his foes. Gord's eyes revealed something of his inner troubles, the missing part of his soul. His lost spirit looked out of those eyes, searching for the answer. Who was he? What was he destined to become?

Only a very discerning individual would note the special aspect of Gord's eyes, differentiating it from the look of veteran soldier and sell-sword. Thinking about his internal plight sometimes bothered Gord, but tonight he tried to push those thoughts aside. At least the look in his eyes had advantages, too . . . . He had not lied about tonight. His eyes attracted women; their look was almost an irresistible challenge to many.

"I think perhaps the game wasn't worth the candle," the young man said softly to himself as he strolled down the street. Then he shrugged, squared his shoulders, and went on with a jaunty gait and whistled an almost-merry tune as he walked. Where he was, after all, was much better than the alternative that might have occurred many a time.

Several weeks later he received a message from Gellor that his friend would not be meeting him after all. The missive was not overdue; in fact, it came almost two months to the day from when the two of them had last seen each other. Despite all the time Gord had seemingly spent in the realm of shadow, only a few days had gone by on the calendar of Oerth from when he was stricken outside the temple in Dyvers to when he had abruptly found himself standing in the countryside, within easy sight of the walls of City Greyhawk.

The bit of information from Gellor, whispered to him by an anonymous barkeep, was not very informative at all, but Gord was used to that sort of thing from the one-eyed troubadour. What really made him uneasy was the return of his own discontent and uncertainty here in the city. There was no joy or excitement left in even the most risky of exploits. Gord was alone and felt it very much. All of his old comrades were elsewhere, presumably doing things that were significant, or at least enjoyable and productive for them. Gord was simply drifting, wondering what all life was about, and trying to make his mind up as to what he should do about it.

Then, gradually at first but irrevocably, the whole world changed.

* * *

Far to the west, unbeknownst to the young thief, his friend Gellor and the bald-pated druid-warrior

Curley Greenleaf were given information and instructions that sent them hurrying off. The half-elven Greenleaf was to round up Gord and meet with Gellor in the distant Pomarj. Desperate times had come, with portents of ill, and all were to play a part. The two men said little of it, but both believed that the young man was more important than he could know, or would believe. Neither spoke of it for many reasons, not the least of which was their own uncertainty as to Gord's precise role in the events unfolding.

"Be careful, my rotund druid, and hasten!" The latter charge was hardly necessary, for despite appearances, Greenleaf was as aware of things and as conscientious as the bard was.

"I shall, Gellor, I shall. Much more might rest in our hands than we know. . . ." He allowed the last part to trail off, for nothing further needed to be said. Then he laughed. "I am supposed to be the kind and caring priest, you the hard-bitten troubadour — and you admonish me to hasten and take care as if I were some fledgling about to flutter forth for the first time against the dark foe! Bah!" The expression of disgust was mock, and Curley Greenleaf hugged the one-eyed man even as he said it. "But you too, friend, you too take care! We shall see you soon, and then the test shall commence."

Soon Gellor was off on his own errands, and the warrior-priest too was gone from the secret place where an occult group bent on saving the systems of the multiverse had held conclave. In the chess game that Gellor had spoken of to Gord, those two were perhaps minor pieces, and the young thief a pawn. Yet they were being moved to support the lesser man, as chess terms would have it, and when it was properly protected, the pawn would move.

In the vast, multifaceted contest taking place for supremacy of all, there were many sides and more

pieces than could be counted. Some of the partici-
pants sat idle, however, and most of the playing pieces were unmoving as well — misplaced, powerless,
guarding meaningless squares from nothing in particular. Only two of the many sides in this multiversal
game moved with purpose and understanding. One
was the side championed by Greenleaf, Gellor, and
others of their ilk. The other was hostile, malign, and
very, very evil. How else could it be?

* * *

Evil has many faces, of course. Bestial, leering
demons and grinning devils are at opposite spec-
trums of the vile depths of that force. There is a sink,
a depth greater than the iron-floored pits of the hells,
more profound than the unfathomable depths of the
Abyss of demonkind. The nadir of all wickedness, the
greatest depression of depravity, lies between the two.
Some call that place Hades, others the black void. By
any name, it and its denizens represent the most
wicked of evil, the darkest of the dark. Their hosts
were those in motion on the imaginary playing board,
and they moved against not only the weak and exposed force represented by such as the one-eyed
troubadour and his friends, but also against the gibbering hordes of demons, for those too would not
bend their necks and be ruled.

"Which of the useless turds serves us in this matter?" The daemon who spoke from his dais was Infestix, Overlord of Death, ruler of the deepest darkness.

A decayed creature, some minion of the rotting
lord of Hades, replied humbly in a maggoty voice.
"The ones of scarlet hue, master, move in their thou-
sands to do your bidding. . . ."

"And?"

"The Eight Diseased Ones, master," the thing

choked out, "with all of their servants, daemon and human."

Infestix spat, a wad of horrid, yellowish green that struck the floor of ebon stone at the feet of the rotted servitor. It spread and sank, eating the stone and leaving it riddled as if by worms. "Yet none bring me the quarry I want — not even intelligence of it! I am tired of this dung-headedness. Out of my way, you sweet-smelling blossom," the Overlord of Evil commanded as he rose from the ghastly throne and moved toward the daemon steward.

Virulex, himself a fell and dread lord of the realm, fairly scrambled to make way for his liege. "The matter is far more complex than we thought, master, the possibilities and their permutations impossible to analyze. One nexus after another, all leading to places none can discern. . . ."

"You yammer like a soft-eyed puppy, Virulex. You create excuses for all, but only to cloak yourself. Do you think I am stupid? Be silent and follow, dog! I will personally tear aside the intervening veils and solve this once and for all."

In another smaller but no less hideous chamber in Infestix's loathsome palace, the Eight Diseased Ones and their lieutenants were gathered expectantly. They quickly covered their surprise when the Overlord himself came, each then reporting the results of their seeing and divination. Armies marched, the soldiers of Hades marshalled to contest with the rebellious demons. Spies slunk, assassins lurked, agents served, mages cast their magical nets, while priests of darkness sent forth their own evil meshes. A great hubbub of action and reaction, plots and ploys. Decoys and false trails, sendings and energies to confound and confuse any who sought to pry.

"We are sure to succeed, Master of Death," one of the lesser ones said.

"Your existence rides on that," Infestix said offhandedly as he peered into the misty vapors of a great pool of inky shadows. The massive basin was set into the chamber floor, a scrying pool filled with some undefinable substance. "I thought as much!" The daemon overlord spat that out in his hollow, dead voice as he saw the scenes flashing within the basin.

"Time varies there, master," one of the eight supplied. "Perhaps we can intervene."

"Fool! That would alert every enemy that we have, reveal to them our intentions, destroy whatever secrecy remains!"

Infestix had seen the fall of a massive citadel belonging to the Scarlet Brotherhood. That evil organization worshiped him in the form of his avatar, Nerull, who served the cause. "Besides," the ruler of the lowest thought to himself, "the flow of events is such that even I might misjudge and thereby alter something which would rebound to foil my purpose." Infestix would serve as Tharizdun's viceroy. Better a servant of that greatest one and ruling over an infinite domain than being masterless with naught but the petty plane he had.

"It is the ambitious runt who meddles in our plans, master. If we arrange to have the Prince of Ulek murdered—"

"Silence." Infestix spoke without anger, but the command was quite sufficient to make the whole of the eight still. "Who is that one?"

"It is a slave of the Qabbala, master, one most commonly known as Gellor."

"I thought as much. Watch that one. Wherever he goes we must be before him, ready to thwart his plans."

"I will have him dead, master, within an hour."

Infestix turned and looked at the daemon who had

volunteered that. Then he turned to Virulex. "That one," he said softly, pointing. "Have it removed and destroyed instantly. It is stupid and inferior."

The creature tried to protest, but it had already staked its continued existence on a claim proven false. It mewled and groveled to no avail as the daemon steward dragged it away. The Eight Diseased Ones stood still, silent as statues. Variolaz finally dared to speak. "What, master, makes . . . us . . . need to so respect the feeble Qabbala and its dogs?"

"They have The Rede," Infestix explained as if to a child. "That relic which is the codex to the multiverse. With it they could manipulate any dimension, space, probability. It is small comfort that they do not fully understand its usages yet. . . . A pair of their lackeys won it from a demon guardian — rot those idiotic lords of the abyssal planes! Had they but given it to me. . . ."

"Cannot we eliminate those vassals of theirs, then? By destroying their tools we will curtail their power. Then we Eight can move to recover the relic for you, master."

"A most pleasant suggestion, and well put. The very thing, were it not for the rest who oppose us. No, better to allow those dogs to run and follow their yapping than to try to intervene and be discovered. It is the one-eye we must be most careful of, I think. The rest are nothings. Look. That one shows no aura at all, and has no cord!"

"He was one of the two who stole The Rede," said the chief of the Eight Diseased Ones.

"That one will die soon," Infestix said with a plea-sure-laden tone. "I will watch a while yet."

The overlord of all daemonkind and his eight were viewing the scenes in the scrying basin when Virulex returned from his executionary duties. He too joined them as they watched tiny figures go through their meaningless little actions on the material plane, on the world known as Oerth. At times the scenes faded, masked by intervening mists. Infestix tried to clear those vapors, rend the veils, but even his powers were insufficient. Still they stood and watched what they could, and the overlord of them all never allowed a hint of his frustration and uncertainty to show.

The citadel fell; armies marched and fought; men, dwarves, and humanoids died. Here a little band went off to seek one thing or another. The demons came then, and the daemons snarled as their own servants failed because of the intervention of the Abyss. "We must do something!" The chief of the eight was infuriated. Infestix remained calm.

"The unruly brawlers bring attention to themselves — see! Now all forms of antagonists gather to contest for their prize. That is the middle Theorpart, the Arouser. My servants have the Initiator, and it calls to its own. Neither human mage nor demonling shall have it!"

Yet even the master of daemons was proved wrong by the events that followed. Mighty armies clashed over the relic, that which would awaken the sleeping one of greatest evil, that king to whom even Infestix would bow, for he was Tharizdun. Tharizdun, greatest of Evil, he who would restore all the multiverse to the malign powers. Locked away in nothingness, comatose, chained now. But the means to pierce the nothingness, dispel the unconsciousness, free the bonds, had been unearthed at last.

Soon, despite all hopes to the contrary, Infestix knew that the tripartite relic would be conjoined, the dweomers destroyed, and Tharizdun freed. It could never be otherwise. Evil was stronger than Balance, more powerful than Good. It held no interfering ethical beliefs, suffered no qualms. In the end it must prevail.

"It goes to the demons, master!"

Infestix turned and exited the chamber in silence.

"Are we beaten?" The leader of the Eight asked that quietly, unbelievingly.

Virulex stared at the group with unwavering gaze, his dead-black eyes unwinking. "Never! Watch on, but interfere not — especially as to any foreseeing with respect to the relic or those who serve the Balance. Our master warned us well, I know. Believe! There can be but one final result." With that, Infestix's steward too left the scrying room.

The Eight Diseased Ones, the nobles of Hades, remained at their post, watching and waiting. So many sides contesting, so many forces arrayed, so many players and pieces. Even the super-powerful intellects of those mighty ones of daemonkind had difficulty seeing all, and assessing what they viewed. Still, they knew and believed.

"A pawn has just been taken," one of the eight observed tonelessly.

Another nodded. "It was the auraless one, the one the master said would die."

"I cannot find a trace of him," the first speaker observed. "To what end did he go?"

"To annihilation," the other said unemotionally. "Where else? Otherwise there would be a trace, the shadow of the cord."

"Of course," the first said. Being the least of the Eight, it was his duty to observe the least important of events. The assurance from one of greater status was sufficient. Besides, he had commented on the occurrence, and it had been noted. The explanation of it supplied by Pneumonias set the burden squarely on that one's decayed head. That was doubly satisfying. "The martinets of the hells do have their uses," he finally commented to the seven others. "If we can't intervene directly, at least the devils can serve."

"Of course. Infestix has commanded it," the greatest of the Eight said. Then they returned full attention to the scrying, and silence reigned in the purple-washed hall.

* * *

At various other places, on other planes and in secluded places, men and more-than-men observed events in much the same fashion. So many watchers, so many energies flowing, such cross purposes were involved that there was a swirling vortex soon. It seemed to come naturally enough, and was so slowly and gently formed that it went all but unnoticed.

The surge of magical currents was not disruptive; rather, the energy vortex that was generated grew as more and more attention was focused on the material plane and distorted perspectives there. It did so in so subtle a fashion as to be virtually undetectable. What demons, daemons, and devils saw was different from the observances of the denizens of the planes of light, those powers that sought for good, weal, and justice.

So too was different the view of the ones who believed in all as part of a whole, those who understood that without evil no good could be known, that without darkness light was not truly comprehensible, was not true. Perhaps this was more real than the other views, or perhaps the great ones of Balance saw more because they had fewer preconceptions, no sacrosanctities that had to remain inflexible as judgment points upon which information must founder if not in agreement. In any case, those beings were suddenly aware of what had occurred.

"How is the vortex come?" asked a demiurge.

"The flow and surge, the fluxes . . .?"

"The energies form the vortex," the being observed to the ancient human archimage who had replied to his query, "but I am not certain that they formed in and of themselves. Observe how there are ghosts and distortions present. What is actually occurring, what has happened, and what will happen are unreadable in the force of the swirl."

The arch-wizard pondered that for a long period. "There are two unknowns then, lord. The first is the cause of the distortion; the second, the actualities masked by it."

"Exactly, my old companion. Succinctly put. I fear we may only guess at either."

Other members of the Balance, hierophant priests and other humans as well as beings similar to the demiurge, then proposed a number of possibilities and posed certain questions as well. The great worker for wholeness finally spoke after each, in turn, had stated the conditions as perceived individually. "We all concur, then, that some force unknown is a likely cause of the shaping of energies, although coincidence can be ruled out. We must, therefore, continue to act as if coincidence was indeed the sole cause of the vortex."

"We will continue to play off demons against the combined Evils?"

"That is correct. Moreover, our agents on Oerth will continue to work toward the foiling of the plots of Hades with respect to all matters save one."

"What is that one exception, lord?" the venerable archimage asked.

"We can no longer accept events as they seem. It has been our belief that a final struggle is occurring. Perhaps that is so, but I now see that it is but true in part. We must resist the evil ones, for if they combine and succeed in their aims, then light will be no more. With its loss, so too must we all perish."

"Speak on, please."

"It seems possible that we are less than we imagined. Beyond us, beyond the lord of Evil and powers of Good, unbeknownst to the masters of Order and the forces of Chaos, a greater one might be laboring."

"For or against us, lord?"

"Who can say? Neither? That seems a reasonable suggestion. That power does as it does toward an end which is yet hidden from us. It is logical to continue as we have been, but to observe carefully as well. There is a strong probability that what will occur is far beyond the scope we have previously considered."

"I believe you are on to something there, lord," said the arch-wizard suddenly. His vigor and animation were those of a schoolboy as he went on. "There is no Balance if things are as we perceive them to be. Consider, sirs, the misshaping of things if all save the benighted must forever strive to prevent one of their number to ascend over the multiverse! Is there such a one in the ranks of the upper beings? Do we have such a champion? Those answers are self-evident, and if the question is put with respect to chaos, to law, the answer is the same. None exists save in the depths of Evil."

A hierophant seemed unsure. "Could this anomaly not exist in a multiversal probability?"

"Probability is not as intense an infinity as that," the demiurge said. "What of Balance were it so? There would be none, and we would be false."

"Unless something above, something greater, existed," the archimage filled in. "Then a singular force of lesser nature might indeed exist. If the greater was its counterpoise, but one perhaps more attuned to wholeness, then we would be the instrumentality it would employ."

"It is certain that those of light are not marshalled in unity," the chief of the hierophants noted in concurrence. "But if what you say is so, there are inescapable conclusions as to the greater one. It is no more potent than the darkest evil, and it moves blindly. We are not directed!"

"Fie!" The great worker was adamant. "Probability might allow a complete unbalancing, and the unknown power might have to struggle against unintelligent energies as well as the rest. Who can say? However, what makes you, any of you, believe that we are not directed? Perhaps this direction is not evident to us, but we cannot, therefore, presume that it does not exist. We must each continue on as we purpose, but with an attitude of acceptance of new information as valid until disproven. We will work our own plans, seek the end we desire, until such time as inescapable evidence directs us otherwise. This will be done, though, with the everpresent knowledge that what we suppose, what darkness strives for, what ancient powers are being unearthed at this time, and the results of the struggle which is foreordained might well be but facets of some greater whole which we do not yet perceive."

When the demiurge finished, the other chief ones of Balance spoke. With agreement and understanding reached, the many members of the group returned to their own places. There was always much to do, perpetual ministrations that would be eternal . . . or so they hoped.

* * *

While high and low scried and schemed, while those of Balance pondered, Gord rode away from his foster city in company with the druid-warrior Greenleaf. These pieces in the game being played moved at the direction of the Balance, but of course with free will and chance playing their own roles in the game. There were combats and battles, journeys and discoveries, elven friends and humanoid foes.

In the end those neutral to the ethoi of Good and
Evil, of chaos and order, missed their goals, failed in
their missions. The gibbering hordes of demonkind
won the prize, and Gord lost his own life. Infestix
himself came upon Oerth in his Death form, great demons too took material form and interfered with human activities. But in the end it seemed that demons
prevailed over all other forces. Evil was torn in twain,
and Good and all the rest benefited thereby — all
save those who were quick no longer and benefited
naught from anything mortal.

Again Gord died, and was revivified. Only magic
allowed both this saving and his first one to occur.
His ring, he learned, was powerfully dweomered to
save him from death up to nine times, so that seven
reincarnations remained. For that he was grateful.
Concurrently, Gord knew his part in the game, understood the play, and thus moved from least pawn
to something greater.

If each soldierlike piece in the imaginary game was
assigned a promotion value, the least would be that
pawn that represented all pawns, and the greatest
soldier would be that pawn representing the kinglike
piece of a given side. Through his victories over those
evil ones who had fought him, Gord had moved successively from one sort of pawn to another, becoming
more potentially powerful, more centrally placed on
the playing field, each time he so triumphed. At last
he reached the end of his long trek across the check-
ered grounds of the struggle.

In the likening of the various forces' agents to
chess pieces — pieces and pawns in a vaster game
than conventional chess — Gord had reached the last
rank and become a piece of some considerable power.
He could be considered to have the abilities of a
knight combined with the so-called hopping bishop,
the ship of Earth's ancient Chatranj or Chatturanga

chess. He controlled not a single space immediately
around him, and his range was most limited considering the size of the vast board of the contest. Yet of
the sixteen squares that were each one removed from
his actual position, he could command fully twelve
and vault over any man who intervened. Gord was a
powerful minor piece now. He comprehended not only
his role but the game at large as well, so he was
doubly dangerous to his adversaries.

Chapter 26

"AND THUS THE EVENTS of the past few years have
been spun out," Rexfelis, Lord of All Cats, said, looking squarely at Gord.

"You played no part in these?" the young man
asked doubtfully.

The Catlord shrugged. "Some, but not directly.
The rings I made and dweomered so long ago have
certainly had some effect on the course of things, I
suppose. . . ."

"Mine and the eight others, you mean? I know how
my own ring can change me from man to leopard, allows me to see and perceive as a cat does, and has
spared me from death and worse twice now. Yet I do
not understand why it works as it does for me, and I
do not appreciate the part of the other rings, nor for
that matter the reason for you making them."

"That is a matter for another time. I may be super-
human, Gord; by standards of men, I am a powerful
being. Still, I have limitations and am subject to
many shortcomings. I have need to learn much before
I am prepared to discuss the rings. Some I know
already, and more I will learn soon, I think. The time
is not far off, my young protégé, when you and I will
again speak of the rings — and I think of the matter
of your heritage, too."

"You know of that?" Gord shot up, as if propelled

from a catapult, from the couch on which he had been reclining. "Tell me!"

The long, sinewy fingers of the Catlord squeezed the young man's shoulders reassuringly as his hands pressed Gord back upon the seat. "Be at ease. I have nothing but suspicions at this time. When we speak of rings, then we will also discuss the mysteries which surround you, Gord. As I said, I have no divine knowledge to impart. Just as you, I too must seek and find, study and learn, gather intelligence and analyze information.

"I have suspicions, suppositions based on you, but that is all they are. Your weird is masked, Gord. We have spoken of that before. Some facts I have discovered, but most of these are already known to you as well. You are more than you were, would you not say so?"

Gord nodded at that and would have replied, but Rexfelis was not finished.

"I am not much concerned," the Lord of Cats continued, "with affairs of men or the powers dwelling on other planes. I am disinterested more than uninterested. Those who seek equilibrium are similar to me, but they also actively meddle in things when one side or another seems to be tipping the balance toward itself. You have served the Balance and will do so in the future. In fact, you might just be the very fulcrum of things to come."

"You speak in riddles as always, Lord Rexfelis. What must I do to get straight answers from you?" Gord asked crossly. He was still agitated, and this was plainly shown by his expression, voice, and tense body. In fact, the young man resembled an angry cat confronting another one, ready to spring at the least provocation.

"You must not presume upon my friendship," the Lord of Cats remarked, turning his back upon his

370

guest. He walked over to where a sideboard held a tall ewer of kumis and poured himself a goblet of the fermented milk. He turned, drank, and then spoke to Gord again.

"I am fond of you personally, and you have a role which is important. But I am not sure if I like what you might do, nor do I believe that I will be pleased much by what is to come. Do not again speak to me so, Gord the Unknown, Gord the Rogue — not unless you are prepared to accept my enmity and accept a challenge from me."

That was unthinkable. The young man knew very well that although he could best any of those minions of the Catlord that surrounded him, Gord was certainly no match for Rexfelis in any respect — save perhaps at swordplay, and even that was doubtful. Furthermore, Gord had no desire to quarrel with this being, a lord who had most certainly given him more than any other personage, human or otherwise.

"I beg your forgiveness, Lord of Cats," Gord said with humility. "I allowed my heart to rule my head, and my frustration to wag my tongue. I ask your pardon, and I shall not so offend again."

Rexfelis smiled, a cat's unfathomable smile. "You have it, even though I am quite positive you will offend me in the future."

"Future, lord? You speak of that most often, yet you also say that you are not able to have my rede. You see my point?"

"Yes. Of course. In that I am somewhat remiss. I meant to speak to you as to exactly what I am certain of. Please have some refreshment, relax, and I will do so now."

Gord complied with difficulty. For some time now, the young adventurer had suspected that something lay behind Rexfelis's unexpected appearances and seemingly casual interest in his affairs. This meeting

371

confirmed Gord's suspicions. As the Catlord began speaking, the young adventurer composed himself as well as he could so as to absorb every word. Rexfelis told him that the interaction between himself and Gord had occurred with seeming coincidence, but the Catlord was himself uneasy about that, for seldom did he relate to humans as had happened with Gord. Therefore, Rexfelis had begun some investigation of things.

"You are entangled with me, Gord, with the Balance, with demons, and even with the foul Infestix. It was no accident, I think, that he himself came to slay you in his avatar of Nerull. It was foreordained, just as your coming here was written. Because of the tangling, and the interference, I can see but little more of your skein, my young friend. Be comforted, though, for if I cannot, it is most improbable that any other can either, including your greatest enemies, demon, daemon, or devil.

"Think on it. The hells sent a great minion of theirs to slay you, the bestial pig-thing which you slew and which in turn seemingly did for you. They could not foresee the result!"

"Nerull failed for the same reason, then?"

"Correct, Gord. None but yourself can see what is written for you — perhaps even you can't pierce the veils, but possibly you will. You must try, if you can."

"Of dweomers and scrying I know nothing," the young man commented. "But if it seems possible, I will try. . . . Can you tell me nothing more than that?"

Rexfelis sighed, nodding slowly. "You must know all, mustn't you? Curiosity, Gord, killed the cat!" Both laughed at that, and then the Catlord resumed speaking. "A bad joke, really. I have seen that you will have more trials, perilous journeys, tests, and duels to the death — hardly unusual stuff for an adventurer such as you, young fellow! And first you will have to face those of my own folk who mean to test you. I fear that you are not uniformly liked here. . . ."

"That's no surprise," Gord interjected. "Some of your cat-folk here are haughty and overbearing to the point of annoyance. I have brought one or two of them down a peg."

"Yes," the Catlord observed dryly, "that you have. Thereafter, Gord, you will be tested mentally and physically by those of Evil, as well as by nature itself. If you somehow survive that, and I mean the survival of mind and ethics as well as pure physical survival, it seems that you must return to the City of Grey-hawk one last time."

That puzzled the young thief. "Must return? One last time? What I do is my own will, and Greyhawk is my only home. I shall go there or not as I choose, and it will be more than once, I trow!"

"Do you now? You are no more free to do as you would than am I — less so, in fact. Let that be. Per-haps it is a changeable condition. Whatever you think, I did foresee that you would return to Grey-hawk but once more, and that only to repay some past debt. The debt I cannot get the rede of, but it seemed to be one not directly connected to you. I mention that," the Lord of Cats added, "because there was an inkling in the foreseeing."

"Of what?" Gord asked quietly.

"Of a vendetta. That settling of old scores was tied to your past, your family, I think. There was some-thing stranger still. So unsettling that I hesitate to mention it."

Gord was again tense and filled with the unease of foreboding. "I do not mean to press you, lord, but I request with all respect that you convey the remain-der of your knowledge on this subject to me."

"Of course," Rexfelis said. "Having gone this far, I could not very well do otherwise. The matter of vengeance seemed to go beyond Greyhawk, well beyond. It came here, back to me somehow, but I am not sure how. I am not concerned, but I am. It is puzzling, disconcerting to me, I admit!"

"Then that is it?"

"No, Gord, not quite. Your quest, for want of a better word, might go beyond that. There were breaks, other paths, but it seemed there was one line which was stronger than all but one other. It led to the lowest depths, to the realms of darkest Evil, to Nerull and beyond."

That made the young man pale. "What of the other, stronger line, lord?" he inquired uncertainly.

"That led to indecision, inactivity, and a horrible death."

"Then I am doomed no matter what, it seems. . . . I have no hope!"

"Wrong, most misguided and wrong! There is always hope, young fool! Didn't I just tell you that I am not perfect? What I saw was only a series of possibilities. Granted, the most probable courses were very plain, but there might be other branches. Again, my seeing is possibly faulty. That we both understand. You alone will be able to decide the exact course you follow. Although some destinies you cannot shun, there are places where you have total freedom of decision. Perhaps, in the end, you are foredoomed, but of that neither you nor I have certain knowledge. Yet there is one certainty. If you deem yourself as good as finished, then you are!"

It was heartening, that last statement, and Gord managed to throw off his depression because of the encouragement. "Thank you, Lord Rexfelis. Although what you have related to me is troublesome — nay, worse than that, even — I appreciate your frankness. Now I will set about things with a different view. Prepare myself mentally and physically too. Whatever comes to me will find me as ready as I can be, and I shall remain alert, watchful. The best course might be very difficult to seek, to follow."

"You are growing wiser already, my human friend. The words you speak are true always, even when life itself does not hang in the balance. Enough of this now! Here," the Catlord said with an air of congenial sort, "allow me to serve you more of this excellent kumis. We will drink together as peers, you and I, until both of us are in a merry mood and ready for frisking and frolic!"

"As long as I don't have to sing much . . . or listen to very much of the noise which passes for music hereabouts!"

"My feelings are hurt! Welladay," Rexfelis went on with a mock sigh and forlorn expression, "I shall take no offense and make sure that whatever entertainment eventually follows is to your taste, for I am your host, and a guest must be humored," he concluded, pouring liquor into Gord's flagon until the milky stuff overflowed. Without another word, the Catlord quaffed his own beaker of kumis, and Gord needed no encouragement other than that, tossing his own down with equal relish.

Some time later, much later in fact, and after a soulful duet in which Gord actually took the lead in singing, Rexfelis ended the wassail with a grin and a wink.

"Off you go now, Gord. I have things to do, and you need more exciting company too. See that little kitten, Tirrip!" Gord was more than content with that, and so the evening ended.

Chapter 27

TIRRIP WAS A LOVELY GIRL. No, she was a beautiful
tiger who could take the form of a gorgeous woman.
Well, perhaps she was something else, an intelligent
being from another plane whose actual form was unknown, but which could be either that of tigress or
woman when she was on the plane of the Catlord.

At any rate, Tirrip and Gord were intimate friends,
and that had been the cause of some difficulty for the
young adventurer. Her cousin, Raug, and several others of his group resented the relationship and dis-
liked him. With effort, Gord had put the matter aside
in his mind after several confrontations and contests
with Raug and his friends. After all, Tirrip liked them
well enough, so Gord set aside his mislike and ignored them studiously.

He was doing just this the day after his audience
and drinking bout with Rexfelis, during a stroll with
Tirrip. He and the pretty tiger-were walked slowly,
hardly noticing or caring where they were, as she listened to the young man recount the matters he and
the Catlord had spoken of, until they were suddenly
interrupted.

"Hoy! It's Tirrip! Come with us, cousin! We're going
on a hunt!"

Gord saw Raug and a half-dozen or so others at a
little distance. The big fellow had pointedly ignored

Gord's presence, so as Tirrip called and waved a re
turn greeting, the young thief looked away from th
group as if they didn't exist.

"Come on, Gord!" Tirrip said excitedly. "You ca
take leopard form and come along! Let's join them!"

"I think not," Gord replied slowly. "I wouldn't fin
the company even slightly amusing. I'm surprise
you would. . . ."

"Oh, don't be a silly dog," she said, her voice sti
filled with enthusiasm. "Raug and the others are a
right — honestly! I haven't been out in the wild
hunting in ever so long, Gord. Please, let's go. I
would mean a lot to me, dearest."

"You run along and join them," Gord said with
detached tone. "They're your kith and kin, after al
not mine," he added with ice in his tone and a dis
dainful expression. "I'll manage to amuse myse
while you're gone. . . . Lady Cheeba has asked me t
call upon her several times."

At that Tirrip spun to face him, her face angry
She brought her hand around and slapped him o
the face so quickly that Gord could not avoid the a
tack. "You are an insufferable cur!" Tirrip spa
"You're jealous of my friends and sensitive about you
size just because they jape because they're all muc
bigger than you!"

Gord stepped back and looked at Tirrip in ston
silence. He thought of several retorts, but somethin
made him hold his tongue and remain silent still.

"Very well, Master Nobody!" Tirrip went on. "I sha
join them and have fun as I like. I'm sick and tired
having to mope around with you all the time an
bored with your talk of quests and heritage and des
tiny — bored to tears! Who cares about that anyway
The lineage and future of an orphan human luck
enough to have curried a little favor with Lord Rexfe
is is fitting for a brief entertainment at a dull part

378

ut it grows wearisome at other times. You are a boor
. . a churl . . . a . . . a nobody!"

"Now, dear lady Tirrip, that was well and nobly
aid!"

Gord jerked his head around to see who had spo-
en. While he and Tirrip had been exchanging heated
vords — while she was berating him, rather, and he
ad been giving it back to her through chilling stares
- Raug and his comrades had approached. Certainly
he group had been drawn by the slap and the loudly
poken rebukes she had delivered. The male who had
ongratulated Tirrip was called Lurajal.

"Abuse is never laudable," Gord said in an even
one, looking squarely at the fellow.

Although Lurajal was smaller than Raug and the
thers, he was still taller than Gord and somewhat
tockier. His brown skin was smooth and rippled
vith muscles when he moved, and he prided himself
n his speed and power. Lurajal scowled at Gord's
vords, staring at the young adventurer with hatred in
is yellow-brown eyes, "Dogs, even wolfish ones, are
ut mutts and curs fit only for abuse. To strike or
corn them is a laudable act, dog!"

Tirrip froze at those words, but Raug and the oth-
rs laughed and slapped one another. Gord didn't
other looking at them, however, for his gaze was fas-
ened on Lurajal. "Well, bragging is quite natural for
knave and coward quite unable to do anything but
abber so. You see before you the one you called cur,
raggart! Strike — lest you are afraid, of course."

He was a relative newcomer, so Lurajal had no
lea as to the true merit of his antagonist. He had
een told stories, of course, but they centered on
ord's trickery and unexpected moves. He had tested
imself against Raug and the rest of his group, and
urajal had found himself but little weaker and far
aore agile and swift.

379

Lurajal knew that the little dog who dared t
speak to him so, dared him to strike, would be n
match at all compared to Raug and the rest. Bette
still, there would be no aid for him this time, eithe
the Catlord himself or some of the humans who ha
previously been around to assist Gord out of trouble
Lurajal had heard plenty about how Rexfelis o
Gord's human friends had rescued him before, or els
Raug or his cousins or fierce friends would have fin
ished the dark little upstart once and for all. It woul
be Lurajal's pleasure to accomplish that. With suc
thoughts flashing through his mind, the golden-eye
Lurajal leaped upon Gord.

The man's body hit Gord with full force. Those wit
nessing the attack were certain that Lurajal's sprin
had effectively taken his foe by surprise, overborn
him, and that soon Gord would be fully at the merc
of the fierce yellow-eyed attacker — but would ge
precious little mercy from that one!

It did seem that way, but only for a moment. A
Gord's back hit the ground, his arms had come up s
that his hands could lightly grip his antagonist's rib
cage. As he fell, he had pulled his knees up to hi
chest. Then in the next instant, before Lurajal ha
fallen full upon him, Gord's legs pistoned upward an
out, thudded into Lurajal's groin, then hooked to cu:
over his head, carrying Lurajal's body along in tha
direction as Gord's hands released their hold. Luraj
screamed in pain as the kick struck him, fle
through the air, landed with a heavy thud on hi
back, and writhed on the ground, gasping, trying t
regain his senses.

Gord finished his backward roll, used hands an
feet to spring upright, then did a back flip high in th
air. He was filled with pent-up rage, a white-burnin
fury that would not be quenched easily, but an ange
that did not flame unchecked. Gord knew exactl

what he was doing, how it should be done, and when to do it.

As he reached the apogee of his arcing back-spring, Gord tightened every muscle, made himself into a tight ball, and plummeted downward. Lurajal was directly beneath him. He aimed as he straightened his legs, so that both heels were together and thrusting spearlike for the prone man's throat. Trachea and jugular were exposed. It would be over in an instant. Then the young acrobat altered his course slightly, perhaps through some innate reflex, and his feet struck Lurajal's chest instead of the prone man's neck. Ribs broke, but the blow wasn't fatal as would have been the case had the thrusting heels struck the throat.

By throwing himself to the side and doing a shoulder roll, Gord completed his routine. A split-second afterward he was standing at his opponent's head, looking down into the pain-wracked eyes of the groaning Lurajal.

"Not a dog's work, is it, braggart? Never forget what brought this upon you — and never say it again, or next time I won't spare you!" The fellow couldn't speak, and there was blood coming from his mouth as he gasped for breath. Gord felt suddenly sorry, ashamed that he had handled the bullyish fellow so. In truth, Lurajal was blameless by no means, but he had been encouraged by Raug and the rest of his comrades. Gord turned his sorrow for Lurajal into anger at how the episode had begun in the first place.

"Now that you've gotten your dupe injured fighting your battle for you, Raug," he said, staring hard at that one as he spoke, "perhaps you'll be bold enough to step up and see if you can't do better yourself." Raug's neck muscles bulged, and he was about to accept the challenge when Tirrip intervened.

"Leave be, cousin! That little killer is dangerous

381

and an unfair fighter. Do not soil your hands on the
likes of him — Lord Rexfelis will deal with him soon.
He has just harmed one of our lordly peers, a relation
of ours — and our liege lord's as well, of course." She
turned to glare at Gord over her lovely, smooth shoulder. "You are a nothing! I hope Lord Rexfelis has you
tied and flogged for what you just did!" Then she went
off, tugging at Raug so that he had little choice but to
follow. The others in the party glared, scowled, and
muttered at Gord but then traipsed off after Tirrip
and her cousin, leaving Gord to minister to the fallen
Lurajal.

"Shit," Gord said softly and without feeling behind
it. Then he looked at his fallen opponent again. The
fellow was nearly unconscious from pain, having tried
to sit up and fallen back to groan helplessly on the
trampled and blood-spattered sward.

"Lie still, man! Don't try to move around on pain of
life," Gord said more gently. "You're badly hurt, but it
isn't mortal unless you make it so. Here," he said as
much to himself as to Lurajal as he dug into his gir-
dle, "I have a little bit of salve which will soothe the
pain and perhaps even heal you somewhat."

Lurajal tried to snarl, fight off the ministrations
but he was too weak. "But that doublet must come off
first," Gord went on, ignoring the attempted rejection.
In a moment his long dagger was out and doing its
work. Gord was very careful not to allow the magically keen blade to slice flesh, and he was gentle as he
cut the garment away to expose the man's chest.
Where his heels had struck the skin was discolored,
swollen, and there were abrasions too.

"Hold very still now. I shall be as quick and careful
as possible — I don't relish this any more than you
do — but you need seeing to here and now. Later
some priest or other will heal you, never fear."

"Why are you doing this?" Lurajal was unable to

understand this foe. First Gord could have killed him, but he had simply broken his ribs and incapacitated him, and then he had decided to aid him. It made no sense to the golden-eyed man, none at all. "I attacked you. I would have shown you no mercy, given no quarter. . . ."

"What you did was no true fault of your own, Lurajal. Your fault was one many have — you listened to the wrong counsel and took it to be truth."

"I don't understand."

"I am not surprised," Gord said, carefully spreading the ointment. He got the stuff onto his fingertips and then smeared it gently upon the worst-looking places on Lurajal's chest. As he worked, Lurajal's breathing became easy, unlabored.

"What is that stuff?"

"A dweomered salve," Gord replied, glancing a bit ruefully at the empty container. "I received it from a strange chap in Sha— a place I was forced to visit not long ago. What a shame it is all gone now," Gord lamented again.

Lurajal could raise his head now, and his voice was stronger too. "You are a nonesuch," he said with a small shake of his head as he watched Gord tuck the empty box away. "I have heard of magical ointments of that sort, but none with such efficacy!"

"Hmmm," the young thief said to acknowledge Lurajal's comment. "I think it was gifted to me by the one who made the original, the very namesake for all lesser ones made after its fashion. That would explain much, including its potency, wouldn't it?" His eyes met the golden brown of Lurajal's.

"I do not apprehend of what you speak, Gord, but I do appreciate that you used some special gift to assure that I would live. Don't you know that as one of the royal line I have no fear of injury or death?"

Now it was Gord's turn to be puzzled. He helped

Lurajal sit upright, then assisted the man to his feet a moment later when he indicated he was ready to stand. "Now," Gord said, "what is this about not fearing injury or death?"

Managing a painful chuckle, Lurajal accepted Gord's shoulder as a prop as the two walked slowly back toward the Catlord's home. "I thought all denizens of this place were aware of the special prerogatives held by the descendants of Lord Rexfelis."

"Well, I for one am not aware, although I am by no means a denizen of the Catlord's realm."

"Nor I, actually, although someday that may be otherwise. At the death of my own sire some few months back, I was called here by our liege so as to become acquainted with the place and its nobles and such."

"And that gives you immortality?"

Lurajal made another series of chucklings and gaspings. Between the pain of laughing and the attempts to suppress it to avoid the pain and so as to not offend Gord with it either, he had a difficult time of it for a while, so the two had traveled a fair distance farther before the golden-eyed fellow was able to explain again.

"I am not immortal, not at all. But I can heal rapidly enough — even without your help I'd have been able to drag myself back here by nightfall and be well in a day. And if I should meet death I am revived and made quick again—"

"Because of your cat's-eye ring?"

It was again Lurajal's turn for astonishment. "How do you know of mine own royal ring?" He stared at Gord for a second, then at his own unadorned fingers, then spotted the ring Gord wore. "It is remarkably similar to what you wear," he said slowly, "only its jewel is of a different, finer sort."

"Oh . . ."

"How came you to know of the ring?" Lurajal was not going to let that question pass.

"I think Tirrip might have mentioned it," Gord suggested, not wishing to lie directly.

"That is a possibility. She too has one, of course, being of royal lineage also." He seemed satisfied, and went on. "As to having new life bestowed, no, it is not the ring. The benison, as well as the gift of healing, is bestowed directly by Lord Rexfelis when he accepts one as one of his heirs. Tirrip, myself, Lowen, and the rest all have such a gift. It is a wonder that she didn't mention that fact to you," Lurajal concluded.

"About the rings . . ." Gord said suggestively, hoping that the fellow would be willing to discuss them further. However, before Lurajal could say more, a hail came from the buildings ahead. Lord Lowen, the seneschal, came hurrying out to meet them with four stout retainers, men who resembled the blond-maned castellan but were of less noble bearing and of slightly smaller stature as well.

"See that Lord Lurajal is comfortable in his own chambers," the seneschal commanded after a cursory appraisal of the two. "Then report back to me." The four bustled about to assist Lurajal, then off all five went as ordered. That ended Gord's hopes of learning more about Rexfelis's special rings.

"Now, Master — Sir Gord, I suppose — it wouldn't do to have princelings brawling with common folk, would it?" the big man harrumphed. "I think you need to have some rest and time alone to reflect yourself. Please go to your quarters, and I will have some refreshments brought there directly."

"Of course, Lord Lowen."

"Splendid. I will speak with my liege of the matter. When that is done I will come and tell you what sentence you might expect, or what judgment is to be handed down."

Gord was anxiously awaiting the second interview, as it were, with the seneschal, when he heard a sharp rapping at the huge slab of rosewood that closed his antechamber from the hall without. Gord jumped up, took a step, then stood still and composed himself. "Enter, please," he said loudly.

The thick door with its gleaming panels of fine-grained wood swung inward, and through the portal stepped not Lord Lowen but Rexfelis himself. His face was graven, his eyes unsmiling. "You assaulted one of my own blood," he said heavily.

"That is correct," Gord replied.

"Have you any excuse?"

"None, Lord Rexfelis."

"Do you plead for mercy?"

"No, Lord, that I will not stoop to. I have made my peace with Lord Lurajal, and I have settled my own thoughts as well. I am ready to accept your judgment squarely."

"It is this," the Lord of Cats said slowly. "You accepted a challenge from one who unjustly interfered in an affair not his own, you fought all too well, and then spared the instigator and his lot too, if I am a judge of such matters. Your conduct was correct, noble, and above reproach. Nonetheless, you did bodily harm to one of my blood, so I must mete out a fair punishment," the Master of Cats said as he fixed his gaze upon the young adventurer.

Gord managed to return the look without wavering. "Which is?"

"You will offer apologies to all concerned — Lurajal, Raug, even Lady Tirrip. They will accept them, I will see to that. Then all of you will accompany me to my audience hall. There I will hold the ceremony necessary to make you an officer of my lands, a knight more or less, to put it into human terms."

Gord was thunderstruck. "I . . . I . . . It is a most

undeserved honor, Lord Rexfelis," he managed to stammer. "But . . . but why?"

"Lord Lowen pointed out that as long as you are here, you are likely to be at odds with Lord Raug and his lot — silly stuff, but typical of immature toms, I know. He suggested the honor, and I could not deny the sense in it. After all, there is no insult or injury when a peer accepts a challenge from another — even if that other be of royal lineage."

Gord dropped to one knee, speaking his thanks freely. "It is a most royal and generous favor—"

"Up, up. Enough of that! Think you that I am unaware of your honors elsewhere? Your actions in Greyhawk have been of mixed sort, often dubious, but are you not also an honored member of that city now?"

"Well, yes, I suppose . . ."

"No supposing about it, sir, none at all. Think you not that we lords speak not with each other? Those of Balance commend you. He of All Shadows more than that! Well, now you have noble status on fully three planes, my fine young sir thief! Material, Shadow, and Catsreach all — you have justly deserved respect on all three. I am not to be outdone!"

In fact, Rexfelis was not to be outdone. When the apologies were finished, he personally led the train into the chamber where a ceremony full of pomp and ritual was duly conducted by various officials and presided over by Rexfelis. From his own hand he bestowed the honor upon Gord, making the young man a Leopard Guardian, Lone Chevalier Sentinel, Duke of Catsreach, Protector of All Felines, and so on and so forth.

When it was all finished, however, Tirrip and Raug and their coterie left with scarcely a word. With them went several others with whom Gord was virtually unacquainted, although he had seen them around and spoken briefly and formally with one or another on occasion. He shook his head, wondering what the outcome of all this would be.

Lurajal stood close by. He placed his hand on the young thief's shoulder in comradely fashion. "Congratulations, Lord Gord," he said with hearty warmth. "I bear no grudge, you know; I would call myself your friend, if you would take no offense."

"Offense? Why, no, quite the contrary," Gord said with a smile, and he extended his hand.

Lurajal shook it vigorously. "Then friends we are! You'll need all you can get now, I think," the fellow added. "Both tigers — long-toothed and short — are ranged against you, so too the ancient ones of liondom and the lions of the mountains. Old Lowen will take no such stance, but his sprat will certainly troupe with those others. Lynxkind is not in attendance, nor is the Royal House of Leopards — save that you hold honorary grant to a position therein. That will probably mean their support, should their number ever come to this court again. Thus fully five are certainly ranged against you, Gord."

"Five what?"

"Five of the nine Royal Houses. There are three noble ones as well — Domesticus, Ocelotus, and Jaguarundis, my distant kin. The primordial demesnes belong to House Smilodon and Paleoleo. The ancestral fiefs are Tiger, Lion, Jaguar, and Catamount. Last, but not least, are the estates of Leopard, Cheetah, and Lynx. Each is ruled by a royal scion of our liege, Catlord Rexfelis."

"I see . . ."

"And so much for lessons, my friend," Lurajal said under his breath. "Here comes Lord Sergetta and his lady. Welcome them warmly, for he is the Prince of Cheetahs — you need all the support you can get." So it went. In the end, the only ones who showed their friendship were Lord Lurajal and the lords of the cheetahs. Those of the house of Lynxkind arrived late and did stay at the festivities, but made no formal introduction of themselves.

It was like a game to Lurajal. The Lord of Jaguars was strong, honest, and sincere. He loved the intrigue; this was evident and plain to see. In short, Gord thought, his friend was a staunch ally but no sage, to put it kindly. Plain to see, it was Lurajal and Gord alone against the faction of Raug and Tirrip. The noble Sergettas were friendly, but not directly aligned. Lord Lowen was neutral, as were the nobles of the last of the nine houses. Some faction! Some intrigue!

"I would see my own land again," Gord finally said aloud one day.

"What, Oerth? That place is a pesthole!"

"True enough, at least in part," Gord admitted to his friend, "but it is a broad and many-faceted place. If the factions of one place are bothersome to you, you need simply ride somewhere else in the Flanaess or even beyond."

Lurajal was unconvinced. "There is virtually no end to this plane of our liege lord's — my plane, and yours now too, Gord!"

The young man smiled at Lurajal and then tilted his head slightly. "It is not home."

Lurajal didn't have a reply for that. Eventually he met Rexfelis at an opportune moment and mentioned to the Catlord the difficulties he and Gord were having. "Yes, prince," he said in reply to the golden-eyed noble's statements. "I am all too aware of the growing unease in my court which the hotheads are creating with their petty squabbles and grudges. It is time for you to return to your personal fief — only a short interlude, Lurajal, rest assured."

"What of Gord, sire?"

Rexfelis gave the Prince of Jaguars his best smile. "You are so stout and true a one. Put you on a track and you will not swerve, will you?"

"Never, my liege!"

"Just so. Gord too is like that, in his own fashion. That is why you two are boon companions. Well, as to him, I have spoken with . . . old associates of mine, shall we say. They have some interest in him and his employment."

"Is he to be bound over as if he were some serf or apprentice?"

"No, not at all," Rexfelis laughed, reassuring the honest-faced fellow as he expressed his mirth. "Think of it as a sort of noble service for a just and worthy cause. After all, Gord does grow bored and restless here. He himself fans the flames of the antagonism between my kin because it gives him something to keep his interest. It is an unconscious thing, I am sure, but effective nonetheless."

"Well . . ."

"Yes. It is well. You shall be off to attend to your domain for a time, and I shall personally accompany your friend, Gord, on the first portion of the journey that lies in store for him."

"It is not an exile, then? Only a brave and bold service?"

The Catlord was grave. "That, dear Lurajal, is it exactly."

As the young lord left, Rexfelis added under his breath, "No exile at all — unless Death has his way."

Chapter 28

WHILE DEMONS SCHEMED in the Abyss and the masters of the pits of Hades machinated with their diabolical allies, the fates worked as they would. First one side moved in the cosmic chess game, then another; sometimes many sides moved multiple pieces simultaneously. The vast board was complex, confusing, unenlightening.

What had seemed an unassailable position for one force crumbled under a flanking attack. The attackers were demoniacal, the losing force responsible to Infestix. The only problem for the Abyss was that in usual circumstances each of its pieces, every pawn, worked as it alone saw fit. It was highly unusual, but effective, that on this occasion many of the pieces of demonkind worked in concert — and it was also singular that Hades failed to note this compromise.

Perhaps even the massive intellects of beings such as the daemonlords and the dukes of the Nine Hells were incapable of grasping the whole of play, intent as they were upon clearing the way for their most powerful piece, a man which might be likened to a combined king, queen, knight, and giraffe* of Great Chess. No other side had such a figure, so such a failure was somewhat understandable. If freed to

---

* See Author's Note following this chapter.

move, this piece would command so many spaces that nothing would stand before its power, no opposing man would be able to approach with impunity.

Even as their position crumbled, however, the great intellects of Evil worked, and the way became less congested. It could not be long now before the violet-hued forces of Hades, with their blood-red allies from the hells, successfully fought off the others — black, white, gray, blue, golden yellow, tawny. Only the green pieces and pawns, those affiliated with the Balance, were positioned correctly . . . and there were but a few of those men left on the field.

Green, in its exposed and surrounded central position, seemed the weakest. In truth, it had suffered many losses. But the men of paler shades of vert — chartreuse, aqua green, light emerald — as well as those of olive hue, bottle green, and the other deeper shades of that middle color, were now free to move to confront their foes. With no threat from elsewhere, the whole of their forces could be used against the dark hordes. The bright, verdant men of Balance were being supported by shadowy green and emerald, by greenish citrine legions and dusky olive.

"We are being outmaneuvered!" The cry of rage came from one of the Eight Diseased Ones. The other seven bent closer to the scrying basin, peering with their lifeless eyes to observe what their associate had seen. "Inform the Master," the chief of the Eight commanded one of his fellows. "I will see that this brashness does not go unpunished."

Another of the Diseased Ones tried to object. "Lord Infestix ordered us not to interfere . . ."

He was silenced by a glare and a rejoinder from the leader. "If I do not act immediately, we will lose a major piece and our foremost position!" In fact, the hordes of Death did hold their own for a time, but then the deep ebon forces of the demon princes moved, and all was undone. Hades' right flank was *en prise*, and the Abyss struck to assure its capture.

"What is this?" Infestix saw what had happened and was appalled. The greatest of the eight servitors was made least, and he who had dared to object was elevated to chief. The overlord of daemons would have done worse to the offender, but the situation was too critical, and Infestix knew that he needed all of his lieutenants if he was to triumph.

"Errors, unforgivable misjudgments, stupid blunders have been made. Yet we have by no means lost this contest. Be reassured. Work diligently. Spare no one, least of all yourselves," he told the Eight. "The opening game has ended, but the middle portion is just beginning. We will move cleverly now, take our positions, marshal our forces, and lay our traps. When the ending phase comes, I will suddenly open to reveal our true strength, and then only the deepest purple will remain in play."

"Traps, Master of Death?"

"Yes, traps. Traps, and a sacrificed place or two, I think. Ask no more questions!" The grim overlord of the pits left them pondering his words. He alone knew exactly what moves he would make.

The major ones of demonkind fought and squabbled, sending their pawns of dull black, darkest sepia, or glistening jet here and there. The minor ones of their host imitated their masters' methodology, doing as they themselves willed, and the position of the demons was fraught with chaos. Their power and numbers were such, though, that the inky hordes of the Abyss spread like a stain over much of the field, and the demoniacal lords rejoiced.

Iuz the dreaded cambion exulted, for he had obtained the citadel position and had two great queens to strengthen his safehold. Graz'zt rallied disparate men and brought demon pawns by the legion to the field. Others of his ilk quarreled with one another or contested with men of other stamp — gold or blue, white or gray, orange or hellish red. It was the battle and the killing that mattered. The emerald army was not worth bothering with, not when there were so many others of greater size and fiercer powers to attack. Black was moving, its advance unstoppable, and the pleasures of mopping up would wait. The violet ones, the pompous men of purplish hue, were already pulling back, entrenching, shivering in dread anticipation of the end of this marvelous, slaughter-filled game.

* * *

Far away from the contested squares, on the material plane, the world called Oerth, in the city of hawks, only one inhabitant had the slightest inkling of the struggle being fought. He was a savant and demonurgist. Nobody knew his real name. Perhaps even he himself no longer remembered it, for it was as deadly to reveal one's true name as to not properly bind a demodand or dreggal brought by sorcerous conjuration.

Children in his neighborhood called him Master Beanpole. He laughed at that and made horrible faces at them. That caused the urchins to shriek in mock terror and run away. The adults observed that and smiled. To them he was Norund the Gemner, a half-dotty old coot who occasionally gave away a chip of emerald or amethyst for some simple favor such as a pot of stew brought over as a kindness.

The lord mayor and oligarchs of Greyhawk knew far more of the man. To them he was a mystical seer, one steeped in wizardry and priestcraft too. Although old, tired, and short of gold and silver, Rundon Tallman was a valuable informant for them as to the happenings roundabout and in the whole of the Flanaess. That the old fool was a tool who was much used and underpaid was common knowledge to all of the officials who benefited from his efforts. Even great dweomercraefters and high clerics were amazed at his skills, and the fees for their services were ten times greater than those paid to Rundon. But the lean fellow was content, for he neared dotage and dwelled in austerity. That was good, the lord mayor and oligarchs told themselves. If he were content, then so were those who paid him so little and gained so much. These ones would gladly accept his due and live in high style indeed.

Of course the demonurgist knew very well what others believed, but it was his aim never to let on that he knew this. Only one of the council of the city of hawks was aware that he was something other than a doddering gemner or a failing seer. The master of assassins of Greyhawk knew him as Undron Nalvistor, low priest of Nerull and sorcerer extraordinaire. His guises were many, and his efforts on behalf of darkness neverending.

The guildmaster regarded Undron Nalvistor as his chief agent, a figure more important to him than any save his first assistant, another spell-binder who was now skilled in the arts of assassination. Thanks to Undron Nalvistor, he had worked his way to headship of the guild and recently taken a chief position among the oligarchs. This tall and thin old man was a keen edge to be used with delicacy and skill, and the guildmaster paid him well. What the man did with the vast sums he received was his business.

It was expected that Undron would maintain his disguises and remain as he was. One day, perhaps, he would outlive his usefulness. Then one bright morning the old man would be found dead in his bed, and it would be said that he passed on quietly in his sleep. Smothering with a pillow left that impression. It would never do to have a doddering, senile old man stumbling around telling tales with a wagging tongue, of course.

Norund-Rundon-Undron knew all of that and was content. He truly served only one, and that one was the superior one — himself. To further that end, he was an agent of Infestix, worker for Nerull, servant of the pits, seeker of lowest Evil. His true master, Death, called him Gravestone, both as a remark on his ability to place his human foes into their last earthly home and to remind the savant that he was but a mortal man. In truth, the Master of Hades was slightly uneasy in this one's presence. And Gravestone-Norund-Rundon-Undron minded that not the least. Nerull would never allow him to die as long as he was useful, and he would always and always be that, for he had knowledge and powers unknown even to Death.

The demonurgist had bound to him two great demons, Pazuzeus and Shabriri. Although even those of the Abyss thought of the two as their own, neither Pazuzeus nor Shabriri was actually a demon. Both were spawn of the depths, of course, and they dwelled in the dark reaches of those evil realms. Yet the two were of different, older origination. They sprang from a race of older beings that had originated in the nadir of darkness, the home of Infestix.

Pazuzeus and Shabriri were his own agents, forced perhaps, but perhaps not, to labor on his behalf. When the great darkness came over all, then those two would be freed by the demonurgist. That was his promise, and he would keep it — if the Lord of Unrelenting Evil commanded he do so. The demonurgist doubted that would occur . . . ever. His service was too useful. It was not unthinkable that a man, one no longer mortal, might become chief under Tharizdun.

With three hounds on a leash — Shabriri, Pazuzeus, Infestix — he would be a fine satrap indeed. There was a small problem just now, though, and the savant-demonurgist was concerned.

He understood the full span of the field, the nature of the game, the forces engaged, the pieces and pawns in play. Currently he stood near the purple king, a vizier, a weak but important piece for guarding against unexpected assault. Not even his own lord knew that the demonurgist commanded two of the minor pieces of the black array. At his command, those two would change from ebon to amethyst, join with him, and change his status to that of a major figure. Far-ranging, powerful, a fit eliminator of adversaries, he would be an optimum choice for crowning as a new king . . . only there was one obstacle in the path of that goal.

Long ago in terms of man, he had worked to assure that the rise of absolute darkness occur unhindered. He had been the spider who had spun webs, the puppeteer who had pulled silken cords. His plan had succeeded, his plot come to fruition perfectly — almost. One insignificant victim had somehow slipped away. That one was now a pawn in one of the many enemy armies which dared to oppose purple. Many times the demonurgist had moved his own pawns to threaten that one, but each time the escapee managed to capture or avoid. Nerull himself knew naught of the initial failure on the demonurgist's part, nor was he aware of the successive miscalculations either. The savant worked doubly hard to keep all such information arcane. Now the enemy was moving again, and his own position was being slightly compromised. He summoned his vassals.

"Pazuzeus, speed to the manifold planes of the Abyss and make certain that the boorish princes there send forth their most fell champions to elimi-

nate the green!" The winged seeming-demon was gone
in a flash and a thunderclap to obey.

Shabriri watched with burning eyes, all four of
them fixed on the demonurgist. The man noted and
thought he saw doubt. "Never doubt, little demonling!
Else you shall suffer for it. . . ." Shabriri dropped his
burning eyes in mock servility, and the demonurgist
seemed not to notice the sham. "Go you to those who
work here upon the material planes. Insinuate the
same instructions which Pazuzeus gives forthright to
his peers. Succeed, 'Briri, and you will assume the
righthand position; fail, and we shall see how you
enjoy further foreshortening of your appellation. . . ."

Wincing at the threat, Shabriri likewise departed
in flame and thunderous noise to fulfill the command. Still, he was not convinced that the great dweomercraefter was doing right. He was but a mortal,
after all, and mistakes were made most often by
such. But the thought of gaining freedom from his
bondage, of taking the unnamed quarry in his strong,
many-handed embrace, made the demonlike being
exult inside.

Alone, the demonurgist pondered the developing
moves of the middle game and was satisfied. Even
now black and red pieces moved to check the green.
He was unknown, safe, and in command. Soon that
rule would grow. With a contentment he had not felt
for a long time now, the lean man relaxed and
watched. . . .

Author's Note

Readers not familiar with variant chess forms and types of the game played by other nationalities might well wonder what is meant by a *giraffe*. Great Chess, and its later expansion, Complete (or Timur's Complete) Chess, are played on a board measuring ten squares top to bottom and eleven squares side to side, with an extra, or *citadel*, square added at the far right of each of the two players' second ranks. At the start, the board is arrayed with three rows of pieces: pawns closest to the enemy, then lesser pieces on the second ranks, and lesser and greater pieces mixed on the first ranks. Once the board is somewhat cleared of other men, one of the most powerful and devastating pieces is the giraffe.

Compare: A knight moves one square laterally and, essentially, one diagonally. The camel, another variant/national piece, moves two squares horizontally or vertically and then one diagonally. Thus, the knight always changes from a square of one color to a square of the other color when it moves, but the camel stays on squares of the same color (and is a slightly weaker piece for this reason).

The giraffe has a more complicated move, and may end up on a square of either color at the completion of any move. In the first stage of its move, it must travel *three* spaces in a straight line before it moves one diagonally. There the resemblance between it and the knight and the camel ends. The giraffe, while not able to vault opposing or friendly men as the knight and camel can do, has a much greater range and more dangerous movement capability than either of the two lesser pieces.

Once the giraffe has completed its diagonal movement, it can stay on the square it has reached or can continue along the rank or file it occupies, in the direction of the linear move it made prior to its diagonal move. Thus, a giraffe stationed in or near the center of the playing board has a tremendous range and commands a significant number of squares. The accompanying diagram is included for the edification of the truly inquisitive reader. — G.G.

If it has a clear line of travel through all of the squares marked with bullets (•), the giraffe (G) can capture on or move to any of the squares marked with an X.

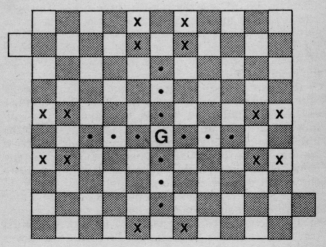